WHAT READERS ARE SAYI

*Double Shot of Sc*

Hamilton St. James may not be able to 'leap tall buildings in a single bound' or be 'faster than a speeding bullet', but he knows at good drink when he tastes one and a bunch of BS when he hears it. Peter Cleveland, with his background in forensic accounting, brings to print an attention-getting murder mystery that couples together all the things that will want you to read page after page. From board rooms to dingy bars, St. James looks at all the angles. He takes a bullet for his trouble but breaks a mind-bending cyber code, which begins to unravel many unanswered questions. This novel brings a whole new meaning to the expression "pulling an all-nighter."

*Brian Brooks, retired commercial banker*

At the end of a high-stress week, my best escape is delving into a good mystery. Michael Connolly's Harry Bosch has been my go-to. Now I'm pleased to add Peter Cleveland's Hamilton St. James to the list! Like Bosch, St. James untangles an intriguing web of deadly mischief. For someone like me, who loves numbers, Cleveland's vast knowledge of the business world provides the perfect landscape in which his hero St. James operates. I wholeheartedly recommend *Double Shot of Scotch*.

*Bill Knight, corporate director*

Who knew a Chartered Professional Accountant could live such an exciting life! Hamilton St. James and his team of unique sidekicks solve crimes that I didn't even know existed. I have consumed many thrillers in my day and the car chase through Ottawa was as wild as any I have read. The author even made taking inventory interesting. Looking forward to more of the same.

*Jennie Enman, Retired Public Servant*

As someone who has been reading mysteries and thrillers since childhood, I thought I had discovered all the genres I could enjoy. But, after reading Peter

Cleveland's *Double Shot of Scotch*, I've added business mysteries to the books and authors I would follow. Especially if they featured a central character as fascinating as Hamilton St. James and are as well researched and written as this thoroughly enjoyable book. I'm already looking forward to the next in the series.

*Stephen McGill, President, McGill Buckley*

As a retired banker I found Peter Cleveland's book *Double Shot Of Scotch* well thought out, kept me wanting to know more, and kept me focused. The characters were as unique as the roles they played in their respective companies. The book is very engaging and we all know people who have some of same characteristics. The book keeps you engaged 'til the last page.

*Steve Cannon, retired Senior Vice-President Commercial Banking*

I have always been a fan of murder mysteries, with well-developed characters and plots, and a love story for good measure. *Double Shot of Scotch* stands out in every category. Hamilton St. James, a financial sleuth, is a delightful character who holds you in suspense throughout the book. The plot is well developed, and keeps you focused as it unfolds. I look forward to the next in the series – Hamilton and his crew have much more to do, chasing the bad guys."

*Stephen Gallagher, retired Chartered Professional Accountant*

# Double Shot of Scotch

## A Hamilton St. James Mystery

### PETER CLEVELAND

IGUANA

Copyright @ 2020 Peter Cleveland
Published by Iguana Books
720 Bathurst Street, Suite 303
Toronto, ON  M5S 2R4

Publisher: Meghan Behse
Editors: Heather Bury and Toby Keymer
Front cover design: Meghan Behse
Author photo by Lindsey Gibeau

ISBN 978-1-77180-441-7 (paperback)
ISBN 978-1-77180-442-4 (epub)
ISBN 978-1-77180-443-1 (Kindle)

This is an original print edition of *Double Shot of Scotch.*

*To my wife, Judy, who has given me the undying support that has allowed me the many hours to create this work.*

*And to my family — sons Matthew and Adam, and daughter-in-law Chelsea — all of whom I adore.*

# Chapter 1

Everyone was still, the vast lecture theatre quiet except for the hum of an air conditioner and the voice of the man down front.

Fifty-two students were scattered around the room, all eyes glued to the tall man giving the lecture. Twenty or so from Beijing, Moscow, and Mumbai, the remainder from across Europe and America. Vastly different backgrounds, vastly different cultures; some wealthy enough to be there without a worry, others struggling under the weight of student loans.

The university year was young, barely two weeks old. Yet the man below had already captivated the students with the principles of business ethics, and the rights and wrongs of organizational behaviour.

He spoke of fraud schemes created by fast-talking confidence men, polished, dressed as if straight from Wall Street. He described how schemes worked and why people fell for them. He talked of shares in non-existent companies sold with the promise of above-average returns — returns that never come.

The man down front said, "If it seems too good to be true, it probably is too good to be true."

Hamilton St. James's lanky frame dominated the stained-oak lectern he stood behind. Wearing a light-brown herringbone jacket and grey slacks, the six-foot-three private investigator projected unquestionable authority over the subject he taught.

As he was about to finish the lecture, a hand rose in the first row.

"Professor St. James," the student said.

St. James didn't mind students asking questions. It meant they were paying attention, at least enough to ask something, intelligent or not. But when he was about to make a critical point, he found such interruptions quite annoying.

"Yes, Miss Stone," he said without a trace of irritation.

Wearing a white Escada pantsuit, the short, attractive Christina Stone said, "Business wrongdoing is steadily on the rise. While certainly not accepted, it seems expected by a cynical public. The trend is troublesome for those of us striving to become next-generation leaders. How can we truly understand the mindset of a commercial criminal?"

St. James looked up at the large black wall clock and said, "A huge question, Miss Stone. One that I'm afraid demands more time than we have left today."

St. James scanned the room. "How many share Miss Stone's concerns? Hands?"

Fifteen or so hands shot up.

"Very well. Lectures for the next two Fridays are already prepared; the one three weeks from now will be on what molds the criminal mind. That's it for today. Don't forget Monday's quiz, and just to remind you, it's worth ten per cent of your total semester mark. And remember, next Friday's lecture is at 8:30, not 3:30. Have a great weekend."

The room suddenly erupted into noisy chatter: groans over Monday's quiz, sounds of textbooks slamming shut, and chirps from computers shutting down, followed by the usual boisterous exodus up the stairs to the theatre exit.

As St. James packed papers and his laptop into a black leather case, he decided on the Dirty Duck for a pint of Bass. He slipped on the lightweight black leather jacket he had draped over a chair before class, rode the elevator from the fourth floor, and stepped out onto Laurier Avenue to be greeted by a warm September breeze and the smell of fresh-cut flowers from a nearby vendor cart.

It was the beginning of fall. The air was fresh and crisp, but an overcast sky loomed in the distance. Boats of all shapes and sizes crept along the Rideau Canal while restaurant patios continued to thrive at near capacity.

A string of passing cyclists weaved in and out to avoid potholes and opening car doors on Laurier. Students crowded around a nearby transit stop while a cycle cop busied herself ticketing windshields on time-expired vehicles.

St. James's usual route took him down Waller to Rideau, across Dalhousie, and on to Clarence, and the Dirty Duck.

Turning onto Rideau he felt a drop in temperature and dark clouds began to roll in over the city.

*Storm comin'.*

For a moment his thoughts turned to his current investigation.

*Did Thomas Stevens steal the $23 million or was he kidnapped by the thief? Conflicting theories. Conflicting evidence. Needs more work. Have to step up my game if I'm to get anywhere with this.*

Just as St. James entered the pub a sharp crack of lightning shot across the sky, and rain began to pelt down.

Twenty or so patrons were sprinkled among dark wooden tables. Servers shuttled pitchers of beer to each and empties back to the kitchen.

Anna Strauss stopped long enough to kiss St. James on the cheek, her smile huge as they hugged.

St. James settled at his usual table in a window alcove and signalled Sidney Gunther, a gruff, portly bartender, for a pint of Bass, which Sid put down in front of him without a word minutes later. An out-of-shape loner, Gunther preferred his own company to that of others. A full head of salt and pepper hair, square jaw, and thick bushy eyebrows made him a dead ringer for Leonid Brezhnev.

Anna smiled at St. James as she darted among tables.

Customers continued to wander in, the Friday afternoon din increasing proportionately. Smells of fast food permeated the room as servers placed plates down on tables.

St. James's thoughts drifted to the lecture on the workings of a criminal mind he had promised the class. He'd written a number of articles on the topic so was quite comfortable with it; preparation was not an issue.

"Sid, another Bass please," he shouted.

"Anna, bring St. James a Bass," Sid barked.

Anna was a soft-spoken, slender lady in her late thirties, attractive with long blond hair, smooth radiant skin, and high cheekbones. Her brilliant brown eyes and warm personality captivated everyone in her wake.

St. James and Anna had met at a bluesfest several months before, introduced by a mutual friend. St. James thought nothing of it at the time. Then, one afternoon after solving a long and difficult case, he strolled into the Duck and Anna was serving. Warmth between them grew, and St. James found himself drawn to the Duck more often at the thought of seeing her. It wasn't long before they began dating.

Anna pulled her hair back into a tight ponytail, applied a black hair elastic, and glided behind the bar to oblige St. James with a second pint. She gently pulled the Bass lever and delivered St. James's drink minutes later.

"There you go, Hamilton," she whispered, kissing him lightly on the cheek once again.

Sid forced a clearing of the throat.

Loud laughter erupted from the next table.

"Thanks Anna," St. James said.

She smiled.

"Have you eaten since lunch?"

"No."

"Hungry?"

St. James returned the smile. "Funny you should ask. Two beers do wonders for a man's appetite."

"Probably something in my refrigerator if you're interested. Won't be anything fancy, haven't had time for groceries yet this week."

St. James sipped his beer and grinned. "Whatever's there will be great, I'm sure."

"My shift is over in half an hour. I can be ready right after," she assured him.

St. James nodded. "Great."

Anna rushed off toward the kitchen.

Sid placed both palms on the bar and mumbled something St. James couldn't hear.

St. James drank the second beer more slowly than the first to soak up the last half hour of Anna's shift.

A scruffy-looking unshaven stranger wearing dirty construction clothes and work boots covered in mud staggered up to St. James.

"You that detective fella?" he managed to blurt out, weaving back and forth, hands moving uncontrollably like Jack Sparrow's, beer spilling with each weave.

"I am," St. James replied, waiting for an introduction.

"Good," the stranger gasped as he straightened. St. James watched with amusement as the man dropped to the floor, the thud shocking the room into sudden quiet. For a moment everyone stared at the body, only to lose interest seconds later when laughter filled the room once again.

It didn't seem like a half hour had passed when Anna emerged from a backroom wearing a long black leather coat and carrying a matching purse and umbrella.

"What happened?" she asked staring down at the stranger.

"Can't hold his beer, poor fellow," St. James said with a grin.

Sid looked on, shaking his head in disgust. "Hey!" he yelled, pointing to others at the stranger's table. "Get him out of here."

Three men shuffled to their feet, picked the man from the floor, and dragged him toward the door like a heavy sack.

Sid yelled again, "Hey! You didn't pay."

The tallest of the three dropped his end of the body, staggered up to the bar, handed several bills to an angry Sid, and gave him a mock salute.

Sid scowled as they left. "Assholes."

Anna shrugged as if to say, *what-a-ya-gonna-do?*

"See you tomorrow Sid," she said cheerfully.

Sid said nothing.

It was early evening when Anna and St. James strolled leisurely along Clarence toward Anna's apartment.

The thunder and lightning had passed but not before leaving puddles to dodge. The air felt fresh and clean, but a stubborn light mist continued to plague those without umbrellas. St. James was grateful Anna kept one at the pub.

Anna threaded her arm through his.

"So happy you came to see me."

He squeezed her arm and smiled. "Couldn't stay away. Thirsty, you know. Needed a pint," he said with a wink.

Anna looked at him lightheartedly. "Don't want to guess which was more important, me or the beer."

St. James just laughed, wise enough to say nothing.

Anna's apartment was on the second floor of a small two-story grey clapboard building on Guigues Street, just off King Edward. The exterior was recently painted, iron bars bolted over ground floor windows new.

Climbing the inside stairs St. James banged his head on the low ceiling. "Ouch!"

"Mind your head. Ceiling's low," Anna said with a giggle.

"No kidding," St. James said.

"You did the same thing last time. Guess it didn't knock any sense into you." Anna giggled a second time.

Anna's apartment was modest but tastefully decorated. While she put coffee on and kept busy in the kitchen, St. James made himself comfortable in an orange rocker in the sitting room.

"Feel like steak and kidney pie?" she asked, moving items around in the refrigerator.

"Perfect."

"Great."

Turning on the oven to pre-heat Anna tore the pie's tinfoil, checking for freezer burn. Satisfied, she placed it on a metal cookie sheet, slid it into the oven, then poured two coffees and moved to the sitting room.

"There you go," she said, handing St. James a cup and then kissing him.

"Thanks."

Anna turned the stereo to a soft music station and settled down on the chesterfield, letting her coffee cool before attempting to drink it.

*Dean Martin singing "Remember Me."*

St. James stood and peered into the street. Like Anna he found the coffee too hot and placed it on a nearby table to cool.

"So how's the Stevens case coming?" she said, picking up her mug. "Must be difficult. You seem quite distracted lately."

"Difficult for sure!"

\*\*\*

Thomas Stevens, a senior partner in the Washington accounting firm Stevens, Gables & Strong, had disappeared a few days before his client Malachi Jensen's $23 million was discovered missing. Jensen's holding company invested in construction and land development. Stevens personally managed the man's business affairs.

When Jensen discovered that the money was missing, he accused Stevens of theft and demanded Stevens, Gables & Strong reimburse him for his loss. When the reimbursement wasn't paid within thirty days after Jensen Holdings demanded it, Jensen Holdings filed a $23-million lawsuit against the accounting firm, in turn forcing the firm to file an insurance claim with Global Insurance.

When Global analyzed the claim, they found it ambiguous and inconsistent. Was Stevens accused of stealing or malpractice, two entirely different issues? Theft was theft: intentional harm. Malpractice was merely negligence or incompetence: unintentional harm. The ambiguity raised a red flag in Global's New York office, prompting Vice-President Mary DeSilva to call Hamilton St. James to investigate.

\*\*\*

Anna's serious look suggested interest in St. James's investigation.

"Twenty-three million, right?"

"Yeah."

"Thought that's what you said. Lot of money by anyone's standard," she mused. "I forget the name of the insurance company."

St. James turned from the window.

"Global, out of New York."

Anna drank coffee. "Stevens a typical case?"

St. James smiled. "No such thing as a typical case. Every one has its own wrinkles, twists, and turns."

Anna nodded. "Police found him yet?"

"No. He's still in the wind."

St. James returned to the orange rocking chair to drink his coffee.

Anna looked surprised. "Not having the primary person of interest would make everything much more difficult."

*Dean Martin's low voice crooning "Detour."*

St. James winced. "Damned near impossible. Without someone to question, all I have is theories with no way to prove or disprove any one of them. No idea what happened to him or the money. FBI thinks Stevens was kidnapped. Local police believe he stole the money."

Anna tucked her legs under herself in search of a more comfortable position.

"What do you think?"

St. James shook his head. "Lot of conflicting circumstances muddying the water."

"For instance?"

"Wasn't a single fingerprint in Stevens's office, other than his own, that is. Place was clean ... *too* clean. Clients in and out all day, not to mention his executive assistant. Should have been a ton of prints."

Anna pulled the elastic from her ponytail, letting her hair fall naturally and curling out-of-place strands behind each ear.

"Wouldn't police think the same thing?"

St. James shrugged.

"Maintenance people completed a major clean that day. Apparently, these *sanitation cleans*, as they're called by the firm, are conducted quarterly. They are more commonly known as deep cleans. Everything's wiped down. Police think that's why there were no prints. Junior staff saw Stevens wandering about his office after the cleaners left, which pretty much accounts for his prints being there."

Anna studied St. James for a long moment. "Doesn't seem like you believe the cleaning works."

St. James frowned. "Do you think cleaning staff are that thorough ... that there wouldn't be at least one print, even a smudged one?"

"You have a point there," Anna conceded. "But why does it matter? Money wouldn't be kept there anyway, would it?"

He nodded. "No. Money moves electronically. But fingerprints could match those of a suspect that police identify later."

Anna shot him a look. "Your face tells me there's more to it than that."

St. James ignored the poke.

"Well, there *are* other things bothering me."

"Like what?"

"For starters the guy's character. Well-respected leader. Tireless fundraiser for public causes. Great career. Well off. No IRS or financial trouble, that anyone's aware of anyway. No logical reason to steal. Not the profile of a thief."

Anna smiled. "Maybe he's so brilliant he's bored. Wanted a little excitement. Maybe he snapped. Decided to live on the edge a little.

Steal a little money. Take off to the tropics … another woman, perhaps. Doesn't seem much of a mystery to me. Money's gone. He's gone."

St. James countered. "Not quite that simple. His laptop was left in his office."

Anna looked baffled, "And that's odd?"

"Quite. He and his computer were inseparable. Never apart."

"Then the police must question that too?"

"Believe it or not, no. They found nothing when the laptop was scanned. They concluded it wasn't relevant. Can you imagine a high-profile professional with a blank computer?"

Anna placed her empty mug on the table. "Could've been covering his tracks."

St. James shrugged but said nothing.

"Would you like more coffee?" she asked.

He smiled faintly. "Half cup would be grand."

Anna took the two mugs into the kitchen, poured a small amount in each, and returned to the sitting room.

*"You're Nobody till Somebody Loves You" quietly in the background.*

The stove buzzed just as Anna sat down, signalling the steak and kidney pie was ready to serve. They moved to the tiny kitchen, where St. James struggled to find room for his long legs under the small wooden table while Anna apportioned most of the pie to him, a smaller amount to herself.

"What's the next step?" she said as she placed a plate in front of him.

St. James gathered a forkful of pie. "Well, Louis's trying to make some sense of the code he found on Stevens's computer. So far, he hasn't found much. But codes can take time depending on length, number of characters, complexity, that sort of thing. Right now, that's the primary focus."

Anna nodded. "Will you have to go back to Washington?"

"Probably, but not until I think something good could come of it."

St. James ate pie.

Anna was quiet for a moment then changed the subject. "You never told me how you hooked up with the university."

"After I solved a number of large cases the university asked me to teach a course on commercial crime investigation. Guess they thought I'd attract more students, bring something other universities didn't offer, maybe even donations." St. James smiled. "Sounds arrogant but that's what they said, in so many words."

Anna smiled at his modesty.

"At first I declined. Cases are very unpredictable. No way to know when they arise or how long they'll take to solve, if they can be solved at all."

"Yet, you're there, teaching. How did you make the leap?"

St. James wiped bits of crust from a shirt sleeve.

"The university was determined to have me on faculty, no matter what. So, when I said no the third time, the Dean offered a strong PhD student to cover for me when I'm away on cases. I reluctantly agreed."

Anna smiled. "Nice to be popular."

St. James shook his head. "Not always a good thing, I assure you."

Anna smiled and changed the subject once again. "You haven't introduced me to your sister yet."

"Well, it's like I said before, when her husband died suddenly it left her bitter. She has a grudge against the world. I've avoided introducing you mostly because she has a way of bringing everyone around her down. Didn't want to expose you to that."

"I understand." Anna said slowly, touching his hand as a gesture of sympathy. St. James turned slowly, pulled Anna closer, and they kissed for a long moment.

Walking home St. James noticed a white 1987 Cadillac pull away from the curb just as he turned onto York. His instincts were activated immediately. Past cases taught him threats can come fast and furious any time from any direction; caution was now second nature.

He walked another block, entered a pub, and sat at a window table facing the street. He ordered a beer and watched the old Cadillac park across the street. Streetlights made limited vision possible. The Cadillac didn't move. St. James finished his beer, walked another block, then entered a coffee shop and grabbed a coffee, again sitting by a window to observe. The Cadillac advanced and parked across the street, confirming he was under surveillance by someone, for some reason. The coffee shop manager allowed him to exit through the back door, and St. James gave the Cadillac the slip.

# Chapter 2

St. James spent most of Saturday morning sorting through files and preparing next week's business. By mid-afternoon he'd caught up and called Anna about dinner at The Fish Market Restaurant on William, his favourite Market restaurant.

"Seven okay?" she said.

"Perfect."

It was 2:30 p.m.

St. James hadn't walked in four days. He was afraid if he put it off much longer he'd drift out of the habit altogether, and that would be very bad. It was the only really good habit he had.

He slipped on a pair of Nikes and headed for the exit stairs. Taking two steps at a time he popped out 700 Sussex's fire door minutes later.

The sky was slightly overcast, and strong cool winds rustled trees along the Rideau Canal. Sussex traffic was heavy for a Saturday.

St. James's walking route stretched down Colonel By to Bronson, across the bridge, and back home by way of Queen Elizabeth Drive, a beautiful eleven-kilometre walk, about three hours at his regular pace.

Under the Bank Street Bridge two men fished, the taller reeling in a bass just as St. James passed, a good size, about two pounds.

Four brightly coloured shells dominated the middle of the canal, eight scullers to a shell, coxswains yelling pace through traditional cox boxes, each team determined to outpace the other.

Cyclists wearing bright red spandex whizzed past, yelling "on your left" as they approached St. James from behind.

St. James smiled at a thin, odd-looking fellow power walking, looking rigid and rickety at the same time, reminding him of the Star Wars character Jar Jar Binks.

As St. James climbed onto the Bronson Bridge he felt the humidity rise.

*Rain coming.*

Feeling the first few drops before Queen Elizabeth Drive.

His cell vibrated as he stepped onto Queen Elizabeth.

"Hamilton, it's Louis."

"Louis, how are you? Good to hear from you, my man," St. James said enthusiastically.

A short, balding, off-the-wall eccentric computer genius in his late thirties, Louis Smythe was a younger Don Knotts who worked with St. James on cases that hinged on technology. He was completely unaware his bad comb-over drew more attention than the baldness it attempted to conceal.

Smythe's eccentricity manifested itself in clashing plaid clothes. Friends nicknamed him *Two-Plaid-Louis*, mockery he lightheartedly brushed off.

"Fine," Smythe answered. "But I've made no progress with Stevens's code. Still breaking down permutations and combinations."

"It'll come. I have faith in you," St. James said, more to encourage Louis than to express his own confidence.

Smythe said nothing.

St. James said, "By the way, where are you?"

"Just leaving the Canal Ritz. Dropped in for a quick sandwich."

"Great timing. I'm walking up Queen Elizabeth close to Bronson, soaked. Can you pick me up?"

"On my way."

\*\*\*

Not long after commencing the investigation into the missing $23 million, St. James had brought Smythe in because Stevens's computer had been wiped clean and the police were getting nowhere. Smythe spent days with Stevens, Gables & Strong's IT officer, and finally, with the help of advanced software, discovered a code partitioned deep in Stevens's hard drive.

*(g,cnbtkyk1,j), (ABA#021000089-36148883-012-67141-co-na-csprite1), (Virgo23+7+8+4+6+3), (G, F, D, C, F), (1104-419, 1130-1930, 700-1106, 145, 905), (U3743-5847, A3570-B0112, D4883-1916, A194, A3657) (A21+11)*

The code meant nothing to anyone: not the accountants in Stevens's firm, not his family, nor anyone else St. James or the police interviewed.

While Smythe worked on the code, St. James interviewed the firm's chairman, Nathan Strong, and a number of partners, as well as the plaintiff, Malachi Jensen, and Stevens's wife, Beth.

He asked detailed questions concerning Stevens's character, behaviour, spending habits, and financial status. No one saw any changes in the man before both he and the $23 million disappeared.

St. James usually began investigations with a suspect's lifestyle. Excess living often drove people to theft when their lifestyle cost exceeded their ability to pay with honest money. When one had it all, one wanted to keep it all, affordable or not, theft always an option when honest means were exhausted. A way to maintain the wealth charade, avoid the embarrassment of falling to a lower station in life.

St. James waded through Stevens's bank records and telephone bills looking for transaction patterns or names, a lead of some sort. Boring but necessary. Nothing even resembled a lead. That would have to come from the code itself, whatever it meant, when Smythe deciphered it, if he could. The combination of letters, numbers, and characters would have to tell a story of some kind.

Jensen was red-faced and grossly overweight with military styled reddish-brown hair and an unprepossessing face covered in pockmarks that resembled tiny craters. Rings the size of miniature rodents rounded out a mob boss look.

Jensen wore a blue pinstriped suit to every meeting with St. James. St. James wondered if it was the same suit or if he had several identical ones. Either way, the large man was attempting to make some sort of fashion statement, as much as a man his size could.

St. James's first interview with Jensen was long and tedious. Difficult to get straight answers from a crude man with all the characteristics of a bully. But St. James persisted. He owed it to both Global Insurance and Jensen to conduct a fair and complete investigation, to understand the claim as best he could, how it arose and why Jensen felt the Stevens firm was responsible.

As Jensen described it, he had instructed Stevens to purchase shares in companies he wanted Jensen Holdings to own. As far as St. James could tell, Stevens more or less followed those instructions. Money went to investees' lawyers and share ownership transferred back to Jensen Holdings in exchange for that money. Simple enough. Cash for shares. Like buying a car, except it was a piece of a company. St. James got the impression that Stevens did the job well.

What happened to the money after that was, at best, murky. Jensen said it flowed from investee companies to construction companies for the purpose of building retirement homes around the country, money to fund progress payments as construction phases were completed. But Jensen Holdings's $23 million never made it to the construction company as intended. It disappeared before it could reach its intended destination, according to Jensen anyway.

St. James said to him, "If Stevens transferred money to companies you directed him to, and funds were moved after that by different people, how can you possibly have a legitimate claim against Stevens's accounting firm?"

A flushed Jensen replied, "Before I purchased shares, Stevens had to assure me he had investigated the company and the people involved, that they were legitimate and my investment would be safe.

I relied on Stevens's word that companies were bona fide, well managed, and honorable when it came to meeting their obligations."

St. James drilled further. "Then why didn't your claim against the firm specifically state that rather than accuse Stevens of stealing?"

Jensen had difficulty answering but eventually waved his meaty hands to emphasize a point. "Wasn't easy to tell at first whether it was bad advice or theft. I had to make sure the claim covered all the bases."

St. James had trouble with this. "If Stevens took money, it couldn't have been passed to investee and construction companies," he said forcefully, "unless Stevens had signing authority in the investee company itself. And that would be a conflict of interest. He couldn't have honestly represented you and companies you invested in at the same time."

Jensen just shrugged.

The point was pivotal to St. James's investigation, and he was determined to push Jensen for logical, if not believable, answers. He framed questions carefully and fired them rapidly, keeping up the pressure on Jensen so as to minimize the time he had to manufacture answers.

"Did Stevens have signing authority in any company you invested in?" St. James barked.

Jensen's voice raised angrily. "No! Absolutely not."

"Did you have any direct ownership in the construction companies themselves?"

"No idea," Jensen responded gruffly. "And furthermore, I don't care. I relied on Stevens's investigation to make investment decisions. If Stevens said the investment was good and my money would be safe, I invested. Otherwise I didn't. And that was that."

Determined to get a clearer answer, St. James pushed even harder. "Just to make sure I have it right: In your opinion, did Stevens actually steal the money or was he professionally negligent?"

"I really don't give a damn. Whichever way you look at it, the loss was caused by Stevens."

That was three weeks ago. Smythe continued to work the code while St. James golfed in the Carolinas, downtime he thought would clear his head. A chance for case-reset. It didn't happen. He just played bad golf.

*** 

It was now raining harder and St. James was drenched. But it wasn't long before Smythe's red Miata convertible came flying down Queen Elizabeth. Smythe pulled over and St. James jumped in.

"Glad I got here before you drowned," Smythe said, grinning.

St. James wiped his face and neck dry with tissues from the Miata's supply.

"You got here none too soon, Louis. Head for my condo, I need to shower and change."

"Condo it shall be," Smythe said, lightly tapping his pointed nose.

For a long moment St. James eyed Smythe's purple shirt, yellow and red sport coat, and green pants.

"Glad I don't have a hangover, Louis."

Smythe didn't catch the insincerity in St. James's voice. "What do you mean?"

"Even in the rain I'd need sunglasses to look at you. Head would hurt too much."

Smythe glanced scornfully at St. James and flipped him the finger.

By the time Smythe wheeled the Miata into the underground at 700 Sussex, the rain had eased. He parked the tiny sports car in a corner space designed for smaller vehicles, and they crawled out and rode the elevator to St. James's fifth-floor condo.

St. James's condominium had a well-appointed entrance area and a bar-style kitchen. The dining area led to a cozy living room populated with black leather furniture and mahogany tables. A five-foot high black projection screen dominated one wall, brightly coloured paintings of Italy's Tuscany, France's Bordeaux, and Corfu another.

The smaller bedroom served as St. James's study. A mahogany desk and large green leather captain chair dominated the space.

Standing in front of an entrance mirror, Smythe repositioned long strands of sparse hair, then went into the kitchen, pulled a beer from the fridge, and settled on an island stool while St. James showered and changed. When St. James emerged from the bathroom pulling a fresh golf shirt over his head, he found Smythe surfing the internet.

"What are you doing?" St. James said.

Smythe was in the advanced stages of frustration and threw his hands in the air.

"This thing is driving me crazy! Trying to match different parts of the code with various databases is time-consuming as hell. Deep searches of criminal databases, professional registries, and various other sources have yielded nothing! Not even a sniff."

St. James leaned over the island to view the computer screen more clearly.

"Perhaps you're looking in the wrong place for the wrong thing," St. James suggested cautiously. "Maybe it's a set of steps leading to something."

Smythe continued to stare at the computer screen. "Could be."

St. James admired Smythe's disciplined, methodical approach to breaking codes, eliminating every possible source one by one in a sequence known only to him, leaving nothing to chance.

Two minutes to six.

"Have to go soon Louis. Meeting Anna for dinner at seven. You're welcome to stay. In any case, let's talk first thing Monday morning when I'm due to give Global a progress report."

Smythe nodded. "I'm going too. Meeting the boys for a beer. I'll call at nine on Monday."

Smythe left for an evening with friends at 6:15, St. James at around 6:30 to meet Anna at The Fish Market Restaurant.

As he crossed Sussex to York, St. James wondered if the Stevens code would be the first one to stump Smythe. He couldn't imagine what that would do to his ego.

# Chapter 3

Weeks earlier...

Thomas Stevens sat slumped over his desk, staring blankly down at the grey carpet, his disheveled appearance exaggerated by a wrinkled grey suit, a stained blue silk tie and a white shirt unevenly open at the neck.

Two years ago, this was not Stevens. Then, he was at the top of his game and on every party list along with the who's who of Washington, everyday dress two-thousand-dollar Armani suits, five-hundred-dollar French cuffs, and eight-hundred-dollar Italian shoes.

It wasn't enough for Stevens just to be successful: he had to *look* successful. Expensive clothes, Rolex watches, and fast import cars were necessities of life for anyone competing to be *Washington's most successful professional.* Known at all high-end restaurants, Stevens's counsel was sought by most well-respected Washington entrepreneurs.

Stevens played the professional game well; anything less than well was mediocre performance. And for a man like Stevens who measured everything by gain, mediocrity wasn't an option.

But in recent months the game began to wear, take its toll, making keeping up appearances more difficult to endure. Tired more often than not, his life was a treadmill with no end in sight.

A feeling of hopelessness had crept over him. Dark and sad sunken eyes and chalky skin contributed to a face belonging to a man much older than forty-five years. Once thick black hair was now thinning, more salt than pepper. Twenty pounds had disappeared from an otherwise healthy body, weight he could ill afford to lose. Thoughts of suicide came and went.

Stevens occupied a large corner office on the fourth floor of an eight-story grey brick building. Plush dark-grey carpet covered an oak floor, and matching handmade drapes enveloped sliding doors that opened to a spacious balcony overlooking downtown Washington. In the distance, the White House.

Stevens's thoughts suddenly became erratic, a constant stream of consciousness. Professional life. Marriage. Children. Professional life. A jumbled mixture of emotions flickering in and out of focus like a 1920s movie.

He visualized his rise to partner at twenty-eight, a reward for building a profitable practice. The many wonderful client relationships he'd developed, some lifelong friends. Long work hours. Fiery partner meetings. All passing at machine gun speed.

*To what end? Where did it get me?*

He thought of the $50 million he helped raise for a new hospital wing, $5 million for a homeless shelter, and $6 million for a halfway house for convicts to have a fresh start, each demanding hundreds of personal hours.

*Too much for me.*

For what? Recognition? A sense of fulfillment? Whatever, it no longer mattered. Now he looked at life through a more balanced lens, having realized he'd missed the most important thing in life: family.

Two daughters now on their own, Emily in university, Sandra working for a large investment house in New York City. Both beautiful, smart young women.

Business had always come between him and the girls. No time to celebrate achievements or console about failures. Could have made time. But didn't. An exaggerated sense of professional duty somehow diminished the priority of home. Now he realized how shortsighted that was.

Sandra a high school basketball star and a straight-A student. Stevens missed most of her games and, because of a client merger, her high school graduation. Sandra was devastated.

*How could I have been so stupid?*

Beth covered for him every time, went to everything Sandra was involved in, never missed a basketball game or class variety show, or the three plays in which Sandra starred as leading lady.

He apologized each time; he'd be there the next time. But the next time never came. Something always came up, a meeting, a work deadline. After a while Sandra didn't hear his apologies. She resented the benign neglect.

*My God! If I could do it all over, how different it would be!*

Not wanting to feel her sister's hurt, Emily counted on her father for nothing. Dad was just someone who shared the house, someone who came and went, like a tenant.

At eight Emily took flute lessons, an escape from a dysfunctional family. With time, her passion for the instrument grew to more than the escape it was once meant to be. She was driven to master the instrument, to be the best, and the best she became. At nineteen she was invited to join an orchestra, a brilliant accomplishment for anyone at any age.

*And where was I?*

His thoughts turned to Beth. Now living separate lives in the same house, their only discussions were major household decisions and matters related to the girls. Education, Emily's first car, major legal commitments demanding both signatures.

There was never any arguing, yelling, or unpleasantness. Just cold co-existence.

They used to be so happy, did everything together, travelled the world, shared likes and dislikes, goals and desires.

*Where did it go wrong?*

With time, focus on firm business had grown. Not intentional. It just grew. It was about success, for the family. To have a better life. But somehow the means became the end. An obsession. So consumed with generating wealth he neglected everything and everyone around him.

*Somewhere I lost my way, my soul.*

Not the first to fall into this trap and certainly not the last. He hated himself for letting it happen. Hate grew into self-loathing, and self-loathing grew into depression. Professional help made little difference; the power work had over him became all-consuming. Medication and therapy were no match for out-of-control, obsessive behaviour.

*Should have been there for you, Beth.*

Most nights he came home late, tired and irritable. Only natural for Beth to drift away. Choosing work over family cost him his family. A huge price. One he now regretted paying.

*So sorry Beth...*

He weighed all this against feelings of sadness, trying to make some sense of it. But there wasn't any sense to be made. It was life, the hand he'd been dealt. Intellectually he knew this; emotionally it was unbearable.

*I saw nothing else.*

He wiped away a tear and then shook his head like a dog destroying a stuffed toy, as if that would make the pain go away.

For a moment he looked around the office, wondering if he would ever see it again. His desk was bare except for the laptop. He hated cluttered desks.

Eyeing the room he noticed the cleaners hadn't placed the furniture back where it belonged. Never did. Annoying. He rose and re-positioned the black leather sofa and chairs to their rightful places, smiling faintly at his own compulsiveness. Even depressed, obsession for neatness dominated.

Through beveled glass he could see junior accountants working late, milling about, anxious to finish, to be with their families. For a moment he hoped their marriages would not end like his, that they'd be more aware of life's purpose.

He ignored a vibrating cell in his pocket, not bothering to see who was calling.

7:45. He felt hungry yet dreaded the thought of eating alone like every other night.

For a moment he thought of the options he had considered and hoped everyone would somehow understand the choice he'd made.

# Chapter 4

Saturday night traffic in ByWard Market was extraordinarily heavy, people heading to favourite bars and restaurants, or the movies, or a play at the newly renovated National Arts Centre.

A chill had crept into the damp air since St. James's rainy afternoon walk. Skies, though still cloudy, had cleared some but not enough to eliminate the possibility of another shower. This time St. James remembered an umbrella.

The Fish Market Restaurant had two dining rooms. One on the main floor, another upstairs. Downstairs was full to capacity with no sign of Anna, so St. James made his way to the upper level where he found her sitting in an alcove sipping Pinot Grigio.

They embraced and St. James sat in the chair opposite her. A heavy-set round-faced waiter wearing a black suit that was too small appeared instantly to drop menus at the table.

"I'll have a Barolo, please," St. James said without looking at the wine list. The waiter nodded and smiled as he wandered off to another table.

Anna reached out and took St. James's hand in hers, holding it tightly as she stared into his dark-blue eyes.

"You look fabulous tonight, Anna."

"Thank you," she replied graciously with a nod, "you're very handsome as well. One nice compliment deserves another."

St. James was about to say something but changed his mind. Anna picked up on the body language.

"What?" she said cautiously.

He squirmed slightly. "We've been dating for a while now, and I thought it might be time to talk ... you know ... about where we're going."

Anna tensed.

"You didn't invite me here to break up, did you?" she said, abruptly pulling her hand back in fear of what may be coming.

"No! No!" he blurted, attempting to reassure her. "Not at all! My investigations usually involve travel." St. James looked pale. "What I am trying to say is my feelings for you have grown. I want more of us ... together. I don't know how you feel ... or what you think. Do you want more, or am I just making a big fool of myself?"

Anna was silent, her expression moving from rejection to relief to a smile almost instantaneously.

The portly waiter reappeared with St. James's Barolo and asked for food selections. St. James gestured Anna to go first.

It took a moment for Anna to shift from her emotional ride to food. "Red snapper, please," she said finally, "and another Pinot."

"Certainly Miss, and for you, sir?"

St. James's focus slowly shifted from Anna's eyes to the waiter. "I'll have the citrus-glazed salmon."

"Excellent choices, both of them," the waiter said as he gathered menus and rushed off toward the kitchen.

St. James never quite understood how a woman's emotions could travel from one extreme to another at such lightning speed.

For a moment they quietly drank wine.

Anna tucked strands of rogue hair behind each ear. "For a time I've wondered how you felt. It's wonderful you ask."

St. James could think of nothing to say.

Anna reached across the table and took his hand in hers once again.

"I feel the same way. I would very much like more of you too."

St. James let out a long, slow sigh.

Anna's face brightened. "Hamilton, you're as white as a sheet. You're uncomfortable talking about feelings?" she said with a broad smile. "The man who's frightened of nothing has a soft underbelly."

"You noticed," he said sheepishly.

Anna suddenly became animated. "What does all this have to do with travel?"

"I hate travelling alone. Most of my travel has been work related. Lonely. Never been anyone to share experiences with. Hoping you would come on one or two trips with me."

"Couldn't think of anything more wonderful," she said warmly, slowly shaking her head, "but I don't think Sid would approve. He doesn't like employees dating customers, let alone running off with them. Then there's my rent. I have to work to live."

"You let me worry about Sid and your rent. I'll deal with him," he said emphatically.

Anna looked doubtful.

"Very generous, but don't be so sure. He's a difficult one."

"What's with him anyway? He has trouble just being civil."

Anna took another sip of Pinot Grigio.

"Peculiar man. Angry most of the time. I don't know what goes on in his head, how it works. Lately, he's been asking about you."

St. James grinned.

"Maybe he likes me."

"Not a chance in hell," Anna said laughing. "Sid doesn't like anybody. I don't even think he likes himself."

Minutes later the waiter arrived with the snapper, Anna's second Pinot Grigio, and St. James's salmon.

"Will there be anything else for the moment?" he asked, gently placing the plates in front of them.

"I'll have another Barolo," St. James said. "Then I think we'll be fine."

The waiter nodded and moved to another table.

A noisy group of six seated themselves at the next table, and it became obvious St. James and Anna were about to lose their privacy.

"Hamilton, tonight has made me so happy," Anna said quietly, tears of happiness forming.

St. James couldn't seem to find the right words, and even if he could, he doubted they'd come out in any coherent way.

After a few moments eating in silence St. James said, "You know, Anna, I was thinking, you're way overqualified to be a server. You're bright and smart, capable of doing more challenging things with your life."

Anna was surprised by the out-of-the-blue observation.

"Like what?" Her voice reflecting her curiosity.

"For one thing you're great with computers. You'd be an excellent researcher. And … you're wonderful with people. You'd make a terrific manager in hospitality."

Anna was amused by the thought of herself in those roles.

"Most people hold back, consumed by self-doubt. Thinking only of reasons dreams can't be realized instead of relentlessly pursuing them. They see obstacles everywhere. Nothing but mountains they can't climb. Anna, you could do anything you put your mind to."

Anna smiled. "You're beginning to sound like my father."

St. James suddenly covered his face with both hands.

The waiter waddled over with St. James's second Barolo, looking amused by their exchange.

"Oh my God! I don't want to sound like your father. That's not what I meant by a closer relationship."

They both laughed.

Anna was quiet for a beat.

"I have a confession to make," she said cautiously.

"What's that?" he said, cutting the salmon.

Anna's eyes looked larger than normal. "I'm not a server."

St. James's forehead furrowed. "I don't understand."

"Part of my job with a company in Germany when I was in my twenties was research. Mostly corporate research: potential new products, possible new hires, senior management travel arrangements, intel on competitors, that sort of thing. Trained by a very thorough, disciplined woman boss, military style. Brutal, but effective training one never forgets."

St. James was stunned.

Anna smiled. "You think of me as a waitress because that's all you've ever seen. But I'm not. My profession is corporate research."

"Then why are you working as a server?" St. James finally managed to say.

"There was nothing available in my field when I moved to Ottawa. Only government research, which doesn't interest me in the slightest. I needed money to live, and this is how it turned out. I'd have to move to Toronto or the United States to find a job in my profession. But I like it here and have no desire to move."

St. James nodded, still surprised by Anna's confession. "Good to know. I may need some help from time to time."

A moment later he said, "How's the snapper?"

"Excellent. The salmon?"

"Done to perfection."

Having consumed sufficient wine, the table of six was now louder, making it difficult for St. James and Anna to hear one another speak. So, they finished quickly, and St. James signalled the waiter and paid the bill.

As they rose from the table Anna said, "Let's go to my place."

St. James nodded and off they went toward Guigues Street.

When they arrived Anna threw her arms around him before he could even remove his coat and led him down the hall to the bedroom.

# Chapter 5

Monday was the beginning of the fourth week of September. It was fifteen degrees, and the sun was streaming through a cluster of cirrus clouds, creating a mystical array of light across the Ottawa skyline. Traffic on Sussex was already building, cars and pedestrians scrambling to face another week of work.

St. James's phone rang at 8:47.

"Louis here."

"Right on time, Louis. Good man. What do we tell Global about Stevens?"

"I can say with complete confidence each grouping of the code's letters and numbers represents something completely different from the rest. Patterns are such that all groupings taken together can't possibly be for any one thing. The code most likely represents a series of steps or actions. I eliminated every other possibility."

"What makes you so sure?"

"I put this thing through every process known to man. It doesn't behave like a single code. By about midnight last night I was ninety-nine per cent sure the code was a plan of some sort."

"Hmm. A plan ... A plan for what?" St. James mused.

"Don't know. Whatever it is we have to look at it differently. A friend of mine lent me the latest probability software. I'll run each section through that, see what the probable meaning of each could be. One combination could represent a license number, leading to motor vehicle registries, and another could be a street address. I don't know. These are just illustrations. But it does offer hope. And after days of cyber-groping I'll settle for hope. It doesn't seem like a breakthrough, but it's something.

"Okay. Keep going. I'll call Global and let them know where we are."

Global Insurance was the dominant professional liability insurer for most companies selling advice of some sort or another around the world. It was St. James's largest client, and he reported to Vice-President Mary DeSilva in New York whenever he was investigating an active case for them.

Mary was one of the smartest people, if not *the* smartest person, St. James knew, able to analyze complicated problems without a single scrap of paper. A member of Mensa. St. James figured her IQ north of 180.

Mary insisted that St. James update her weekly on the Global cases he was investigating for her. Information could drive claims up or down depending upon evidence he uncovered. Evidence refuting claims reduced Global's liability; money it didn't have to pay out, at least not in full. Evidence validating claims increased Global's liability. Total legitimate claims were continually recalculated as evidence came to light, to forecast the quantum and timing of substantiated claim payouts. For this reason Mary adjusted worldwide claims weekly.

Global paid St. James ten per cent of claims it did not have to pay as a result of his investigations, real cash savings. Document errors, fraud, or recovered assets all reduced Global's liabilities, usually by millions, which translated into substantial success fees for St. James.

Mary was happy with St. James's progress. But he was not. It was taking too long to make a breakthrough in the Stevens case.

# Chapter 6

Past Threats

St. James frequently checked in with an old friend, RCMP inspector Pierre DuPont, to determine the status of criminals they had brought to justice together, who was in prison and who was not. Those who remained inside, DuPont and St. James were relatively safe from, "relatively" being the important word. Those incarcerated could still control the streets from inside and issue orders anytime through coded messages anyone else would consider gibberish. Convicts back on the streets usually carried out threats personally, no proxy necessary.

A Miss Barnes answered when St. James tapped Pierre's number into his Samsung cell.

"Inspector DuPont has a very busy schedule," Miss Barnes said authoritatively. "He does not wish to be disturbed."

St. James wasn't in the mood for attitude, nor gratuitous gatekeeping. So, he pushed back, gently at first, and when that didn't work, harder. Realizing he wasn't taking no for an answer, she buzzed the inspector.

Back on the line in seconds Barnes said, "Inspector DuPont will see you for forty-five minutes at 2:15," obviously displeased her authority had been overridden.

*Thinks Pierre's authority extends to her.*

At 2:00 sharp St. James stepped out of a taxi at 1200 Vanier Parkway and asked the driver to wait. For a long moment he eyed the complex where he and DuPont had spent many late nights working cases.

DuPont and St. James had met years before when chasing the same cyber-gang, but for different reasons: DuPont to solve a case of identity theft, St. James to prove an insurance claim fraudulent. They teamed up and solved the two cases more quickly than they would have on their own.

In the years to follow they became good friends. Mutual trust grew. Now when one was stuck on a case, they called the other for counsel, to determine if something important had been overlooked; perhaps a fact not adequately thought through, or a crook's motivation not properly considered.

Their investigative styles were vastly different. St. James's flowed from general concepts to specific facts. A theory first, then an exploration for facts to prove or disprove the theory. When disproved, St. James moved to a new theory. Process of elimination. Pierre's approach was the reverse. Specific facts came first, mixed and matched until permutations and combinations morphed the facts into a provable theory.

St. James walked down the second-floor corridor and knocked on a door bearing Inspector DuPont's name.

"Mr. St. James, you are early," said Miss Barnes as if he had committed a wrong.

St. James restrained himself. "Yes, I am. Would you kindly tell Pierre I'm here, please?" he said in a stern voice.

The short, stout Miss Barnes became abrupt. "He left strict instructions not to be disturbed until 2:15."

*Wouldn't last fifteen minutes with me.*

An inner door swung open and Pierre's tall, slim frame emerged, his face lighting up when he saw St. James.

In his late forties, DuPont was broad shouldered, muscular, and fit. Thick wavy brown hair and a carefully trimmed moustache emphasized a notable presence. He rose through RCMP ranks quickly by solving cases others could not and due to high praise from the Paris police chief for helping to capture an identity theft ring while on secondment in France.

"Good to see you, *mon ami*," he said in his usual gregarious tone. They shook hands enthusiastically.

"Good to see you too. How are Hélène and the girls?"

"Great. She's planning a trip to the south of France this fall. Girls are off to college next year."

"Wow. Seems like only months ago I held the twins on my knee," St. James mused, shaking his head. "Where does the time go?"

DuPont nodded, beaming with pride.

"I'm a little pressed for time, but come in and let's catch up," he said with a sweeping hand motion toward his private office.

Miss Barnes looked miffed.

St. James settled in a grey leather chair in front of Pierre's large oak desk. Pierre sat in the matching chair behind. He leaned forward and took an unlit pipe from a spotless ashtray and placed it firmly between his teeth.

"Still smoking that thing?" St. James said, smiling.

DuPont grinned. "I quit. Turns out it's easy. I've done it many times."

St. James laughed.

Pierre's jocularity gave way to serious business.

"Remind me again what case you're working."

"I just call it the Stevens case. Getting back into it now. Took a week off to play golf. Kept running into brick walls in my head. You know how it is."

DuPont nodded as he carefully placed the pipe back in the ashtray.

"Happens to me almost every case now," he said with a smile.

St. James told DuPont about the old white Cadillac following him.

"Get the plate number?" DuPont said anxiously.

"Too dark. Have you checked force databases lately to see if any of our boys are back on the streets?"

"Not lately, no. Why, something bothering you?"

"Just a hunch."

Pierre's face scrunched. "Ouch! Your hunches make me nervous. They start out hunches and end up expensive. Or worse still, life threatening. Like that car chase in Paris. Remember? You wrote off four cars and a sidewalk bistro helping me catch those cyber-crooks." Pierre's laugh shook his entire upper body. "Paperwork was brutal."

Colourful memories resurrected in St. James's head and he chuckled. "Every once in a while I think of that bistro owner screaming and yelling, chasing me down the Champs-Élysées with a meat cleaver in his hand, threatening to chop my head off. I was more scared of him than the cyber-gang. If it wasn't for Detective Roux de-cleavering the guy, I might not be sitting here."

DuPont was still laughing as he summoned Miss Barnes.

"Miss Barnes, pull status reports for inmates in Canada, United Kingdom, and United States apprehended by St. James or me or Kingston or Slate."

"Kingston and Slate, sir?"

"David Kingston is Scotland Yard. Slate's FBI."

She noted the names and waddled out as quickly as she came in.

"New?" St. James asked, pointing to the door closing behind her. DuPont just rolled his eyes.

"What about Stevens himself?" he said.

"Police still haven't found him. No sign of the money either."

"How much did you say?"

"Twenty-three million."

DuPont whistled.

"Did Louis figure out that thing he was working on?"

"The code? No, not yet."

"The code," DuPont echoed thoughtfully, running hands through his hair. "What does it look like?"

St. James pulled a crumpled piece of paper from his pocket and handed it to Pierre.

"Just what you would expect. Letters and numbers."

*(g,cnbtkyk1,j), (ABA#021000089-36148883-012-67141-co-na-csprite1), (Virgo23+7+8+4+6+3), (G, F, D, C, F), (1104-419, 1130-1930, 700-1106, 145, 905), (U3743-5847, A3570-B0112, D4883-1916, A194, A3657) (A21+11)*

DuPont mumbled something under his breath. "Formula of some sort. What do you make of it?"

"Not much yet. Louis is still grinding away."

DuPont started at the code for a few more minutes. "Sections are bracketed which suggests separate messages within each. Commas reinforce that. I suppose Louis tried everything on the Internet?"

"Couple of times."

"Criminal databases?"

"Yep."

"Maybe it's not related to anything like that? Could be something completely different?"

"That's Louis's thinking now he's exhausted all the usual sites.

DuPont peaked over half-glasses. "It could be a code for directions, or an event, or a location of some sort. Something leading to the money or Stevens himself."

"Or both," St. James added, nodding. "That's what Louis said this morning."

About ten minutes into the conversation Miss Barnes returned looking quite pleased.

"What did you find?" DuPont asked.

"Four men were released within the past several months, cases worked by some combination of the four of you," Barnes replied triumphantly.

"Who?" DuPont asked.

"Roger Nells."

"Nells," St. James echoed softly, "a mean one."

DuPont nodded, "No match for Slate though."

Barnes continued. "Nells got out in the States four months ago. Spance was released two years early for good behaviour, and poor health."

"How long was the original sentence?" DuPont said.

Before she could answer, St. James said, "Eight years ... Sales fraud."

"Why so long?"

"Remember? He drained that elderly couple of everything. Left them homeless, penniless, without means even for food. Judge took particular offence. Threw everything at him."

"Yes, yes, now I remember. Too many cases in between, I'm afraid. Sometimes they all seem to run together," DuPont said, arms folded, peering thoughtfully at the ceiling.

Miss Barnes interrupted. "Jeremy Stern. Released in Toronto after a couple of years. And Clifford Dunning, forty-five days ago in London, England."

"Thank you, Miss Barnes. That will do," DuPont said dismissively. "Notify Slate and Kingston. They may want to take precautions."

She nodded and left the room.

St. James slouched in his chair and remained silent for a moment.

Finally he said, "Nells, Spance, Stern, Dunning? Looks like you and I have to be careful for the next little while, Pierre. They threatened to kill us both, remember?"

"Yeah, I know," DuPont said, nodding solemnly. "Goes with the job, I'm afraid. You think these guys may have followed you in the Cadillac?"

"That's what I'm thinking."

"Be careful, for God's sake."

St. James shrugged. "I will."

Pierre sighed and looked at his watch. "I have a meeting momentarily. Let me know if you think I can help."

The taxi was waiting when St. James emerged from RCMP headquarters. On the way home he felt a bit better about the Stevens affair. Smythe seemed to think he'd made a breakthrough of some sort. And had expressed similar hunches. That told St. James they were headed in a logical direction, if not the right one. Mary DeSilva was happy, at least for the moment. A fool's paradise, perhaps, but nevertheless St. James was feeling better.

# Chapter 7

Just as St. James had finished the following Friday's lecture and the last student had disappeared up the theatre steps, a shuffling sound emanated from above. St. James looked up to see a short, portly, and stoic-looking middle-aged man with snow-white hair, wearing a dark blue suit and horn-rimmed glasses. St. James's attention was immediately drawn to the one wider eyebrow.

*Spencer Tracy,* St. James thought.

The man descended the steps with an air of aristocracy, approached the lectern and extended a hand for St. James to shake.

"My name is Nelson Graves," he announced with a strong British accent. "Hamilton St. James, I assume?"

"I am," said St. James enthusiastically as he shook the man's meaty hand.

"Dean Ramsey said I would find you here. I wonder if we might have a word, in private."

St. James nodded. "My office is only one floor up."

"That would be acceptable," Graves said haughtily.

When St. James had finished shoving things into a leather case, Graves followed him up to the theatre entrance, down a noisy pale-yellow corridor filled with students rushing in every direction, and up concrete stairs to St. James's fifth-floor office, where they exchanged business cards. St. James motioned Graves to a guest chair while he settled in his.

Graves surveyed the soft green room, appearing somewhat uncomfortable. It occurred to St. James that his visitor might have no idea how simplistic a professor's office could be.

*Broom closet in his world.*

When St. James noticed Graves's eyes shifting from plain green walls to plastic floor plants, he guessed what the man must be thinking.

"Universities are terminally poor," St. James offered with a faint smile. "Never any money for decorating."

Graves nodded without smiling, as if to indicate an understanding, if not an acceptance, of St. James's circumstances.

"Well, Mr. Graves, what brings you here?" St. James asked.

"Please, call me Nelson."

This surprised St. James. Graves's highbrow manner suggested he'd demand a more formal address.

St. James reciprocated. "Call me Hamilton. What brings you here?" he repeated.

Graves leaned his sizeable girth forward and whispered as if someone was near enough to overhear. "I'm told you are very discreet and can be trusted to handle delicate corporate matters."

St. James smiled inwardly at the man's overstated drama. "What kind of matters?"

Graves raised a plump hand to protest St. James's interruption. "Please … let me finish."

St. James shrugged.

"I'm the Chairman of the Board of Directors for Canadian International Seafoods Inc. CISI we call it."

St. James moved papers to one side to make room for note-taking.

"I've heard of it," St. James said, pulling a fresh writing pad from the desk's bottom left-hand drawer and a gold monogrammed pen from an inside coat pocket.

Graves's wide eyebrow twitched. "Most people have. The company is public, you know. One hundred and twenty-five years old. Operates twenty fish-processing plants around the world. Revenues last year were nineteen billion, net income after taxes ninety-four million."

Now it was St. James's turn to raise a hand. Graves stopped midway through his description of the CISI's business.

"Details of the company I can get later. I'd like to understand what you want, and if I can accommodate. First, who referred me?"

Graves pulled a handkerchief from his suitcoat pocket, removed his glasses, and began cleaning the lenses.

"One of my fellow board members, Al Dunlop, gave you a strong endorsement."

St. James leaned back in his chair. "Al's an excellent man. You're lucky to have him."

Graves ignored St. James's assessment, taking a moment to replace his glasses and wipe his leathery brow before returning the handkerchief to its pocket.

"My board feels something's not quite right. Naturally they're concerned about director liability. Directors carry enormous responsibility nowadays, you know."

"What makes you think something's wrong?"

"We don't really know if anything *is* wrong. It's a feeling more than anything ... a feeling that the chief executive officer, shall we say, is not telling us everything."

Surprised by this, St. James said, "Unusual. Is the company financially stable?"

"Very strong. Very profitable. Revenues growing faster than the industry average."

St. James shrugged. "Then what's the problem?"

Graves's wider eyebrow twitched once again.

"Things are too good ... too good to be true, to put it bluntly. It's incumbent upon us to find what may be lurking in the shadows, or at least confirm there's nothing to be concerned about."

Graves pointed to St. James. "That's where you come in. We'd like you to review the management team, investigate if there are, or could be, irregularities."

St. James cocked his square head sideways. The absurdity of what Graves had just said caught him off guard. He stared out the window for a long moment, noting heavy Friday afternoon traffic on Laurier.

Graves's forehead furrowed. "What's wrong?"

"Management usually does the engaging. Most unusual for a board to engage someone like me. For one thing, what do you tell management? That you think they're hiding something? So you're hiring an outsider to find out what! You won't get much cooperation that way."

"We thought of that. Cameron has been asked to engage you to review cost efficiencies. Your findings and recommendations are to be reported directly to him. Anything by way of unusual management behaviour you will report only to non-executive board members. Reviewing cost efficiencies should get you close enough to behaviour to fulfill both mandates. Of course, Cameron has no knowledge of the second mandate. He's accepted your appointment to keep the board happy. He feels pressure from us and sees engaging you as a reasonable compromise."

Graves's stare suggested him trying to decide whether to take a chance on St. James.

"Cameron is the CEO, I take it?"

Graves nodded. "Yes. Cameron Anderson. Bit of a salesman, as you will see. Overconfident. Puts a spin on everything."

"Do all board members know you're here?"

"Yes."

"Are they fully supportive of this 'review,' as you call it?"

Graves shrugged. "All but one."

St. James's body stiffened.

Graves brushed lint from his suitcoat. "There are nine directors, including the chief executive officer. One director, David Blakie, a friend of Cameron's, believes this is a witch hunt on my part. Complete waste of time and money."

"Is it?"

"Is it what?"

"A witch hunt."

"Certainly not!" Graves replied as if St. James meant to insult.

*Sensitive.* St. James managed not to smile.

Graves said, "You will likely interview the board as part of your mandate. You can ask their perception of my motives then. All but Blakie's will be positive, I'm sure."

St. James scribbled notes. Graves noticed St. James was left-handed. "Very well. When does this have to be done?"

"We want you to start as soon as you are interviewed by the board."

St. James looked slightly startled for a second time.

Graves broke into a broad grin, his first since the meeting began.

"I see you are not used to being scrutinized, Hamilton," he said.

St. James smiled. "On the contrary, Nelson, it happens every time I am engaged … but usually before, not after."

Graves's face clouded and he cleared his throat. "What about cost? How expensive is this likely to be?"

"I have a standard contract, which I'll prepare and email to you. The fee is $5,000 US per day, plus out-of-pocket expenses, billed on the last day of each month, payable on the fifteenth of the following."

Graves's face tightened. "Your fee could be quite substantial at those rates. Can we not agree on a fixed fee?"

St. James grimaced. "Absolutely not! I don't know how long the assignment will take, nor what I might find, or what cooperation I may receive. I will not rush my work to shoehorn it into an arbitrary fee," he said forcefully.

Graves's forehead rose, and his face reddened. "I'm not used to such open-ended arrangements. Why, it's like writing a blank cheque."

St. James frowned and rested both elbows on the desk. "Yes, it *is* like writing a blank cheque," he said sternly, staring straight into Graves's eyes. "But you're the one with the problem. You want special expertise, not a commodity. Yet, you expect commodity rates." St. James leaned back in his chair. "In any case, I am not in the habit of compromising on my fees."

Graves looked pained.

St. James ignored the expression and said, "I am well known for what I do, Nelson, otherwise you wouldn't be here. If Cameron hasn't heard of me, he'll google my name. Then he's not going to believe the management review is legitimate. Simple as that."

Graves frowned. His tone was authoritative: "You're very sure of yourself, Hamilton. I hope you're as good as Dunlop says you are. I hope I won't be sorry I trusted you with this delicate matter."

St. James leaned forward again. "I assure you you'll not be sorry, Nelson. Even if there are no issues, you'll at least have the benefit of knowing one way or the other."

Graves shrugged as if he had no choice. And he didn't. St. James knew it. And Graves knew it. Graves's board would expect him to negotiate fees. But St. James was having no part of it.

Graves cleared his throat again. "Do you actually have time to do this? That is, do you have other cases that would interfere with this project?"

"I have one other case on the go right now, an investigation into a possible fraud in Washington. It takes priority for the next couple of weeks. Then I'll be free to devote time to CISI."

Graves's grin was feeble. "I should think there would be many fraud cases in Washington."

St. James ignored the attempt at humour.

Graves abruptly stood, signalling an end to the meeting.

"My executive assistant will send you possible dates for the board meeting. I suggest you be well prepared."

St. James nodded and the two shook hands.

As Graves left, St. James leaned against the doorjamb watching the short figure walk the brightly lit white hall toward a bank of elevators at the far end. He imagined Graves thinking he shouldn't have come to Ottawa to engage a man he couldn't control. For a moment St. James wondered if he really wanted this mandate. Something felt off.

After Graves left his office St. James walked his usual route to the Duck for a Bass fix. Anna was not on duty. Grabbing a table close to the bar he yelled to Gunther for a pint. Beer in hand, he opened his laptop, double-clicked on a file labelled "Standard Engagement Letter," then fished Graves's card from a pocket and typed CISI's information in the appropriate spaces.

For a long moment he watched traffic build on Clarence. Cars backed up, waiting to climb a deteriorating multi-floor parking garage, prevented other vehicles from passing through to Sussex.

St. James leaned back in the chair, running fingers through his hair, contemplating a ten per cent success fee for CISI. Smiling faintly as he rejected the idea.

*$5,000 a day was frightening enough for poor old Nelson.*

After guzzling the last of the Bass, he placed the empty glass on the time-worn table and carefully proofed the CISI engagement agreement. Once satisfied he slid the cursor over *send* and the contract headed off into cyberspace.

# Chapter 8

Ten o'clock Saturday morning St. James's cell vibrated, Smythe's number on the call display.

"Hamilton, it's Louis," he said, sounding quite pleased.

"What's up, Louis?" St. James said cheerfully.

"Entering the whole first section of the code in the new probability software draws a complete blank," Smythe said.

St. James's cheerfulness quickly evaporated. "So, what do we do now?"

"Well, after I put the first section through every search option with no result, I considered sections within the section."

"I don't follow."

"Do you have the code with you?"

St. James pulled the code from a pocket and smoothed it out on the coffee table.

"Got it."

"You see the first letter is '*g*' followed by a comma and the last letter is '*j*' with a comma preceding it."

"Yes, I see that," St. James said, running a finger across the paper.

"In between are seven letters plus the number 1 with no punctuation. I considered the middle part may mean something on its own, without the first and last letters."

"Go on," said St. James slowly.

"So I carved out the seven-letter middle section plus the 1 and ran that through search engines and databases."

"And ..."

"It comes up as the transfer code for the Cayman National Bank."

"How do you know?"

"It matches the bank's SWIFT code."

"What the hell's a SWIFT code?"

Smythe lowered his voice to emphasize an incoming jab. "And you call yourself a knowledgeable investigator."

St. James ignored the poke.

Smythe let it go. "SWIFT stands for Society for Worldwide Interbank Financial Telecommunication. It's an organization that provides registration codes for country-to-country, bank-to-bank wire transactions.

"SWIFT codes consist of letters and numbers to identify where money is going. If you breakdown '*cnbtkyk1*', the first four letters represent the bank; '*cnbt*' is the symbol for the Cayman National Bank Ltd. The next two letters, '*ky*', represent the country code, which of course, in this case, is Cayman. The next two, '*k1*', is the bank location code within the country. Usually there's an additional three digits on the end to identify which branch receives the transfer. That was left out for some reason. It's possible this section is the first part of a wire transfer to Cayman."

"Hmm, could make sense, but with legislated bank reporting how can money be transferred without a trace?"

"Don't know the answer to that, man."

"So, what could '*g*' and '*j*' mean?" St. James said.

"Don't know that either. All I know is when you include those two letters and search the total section as one piece, it doesn't mention a SWIFT code for Cayman. That tells me the letters '*g*' and '*j*' have nothing to do with the bank itself."

"Hmm. Good work, Louis," St. James said encouragingly. "Keep at it."

He spent the morning in the study filing and tidying papers. He went into the kitchen, made a ham sandwich, pulled a club soda from the fridge, and settled on an island stool to have lunch. At two he went for a stroll in the Market. It was 3:00 when he returned to the condo, just in time for a second call from Smythe.

Smythe launched into his work without so much as a "Hello."

"Since section one identifies the Cayman National Bank, I thought section two might reflect some sort of bank transaction. Maybe a transfer initiated by the crooks. Maybe where the $23 million ended up," Smythe said in an upbeat tone.

"So I called the Bank to ask how the transfer process worked. Explained we worked for Global, chasing stolen funds. I spoke with a lady named Antoinette who schooled me on privacy rules. Painful, but I made it through. I wasn't allowed to ask questions about particular accounts or real customers. She used fictitious information to explain how things worked. Made-up names, account numbers, and events to walk me through the system.

She said each transaction from one bank to another had its own identification number. That's how they track funds."

"Are they made up of a certain number of characters?"

"Antoinette says typically three letters followed by nine digits. The first three letters identify the country banking system originating the transaction. Second part is a nine-digit number identifying the transaction itself.

"To find out whether Stevens's code contained a transaction ID, I slowly read out each section and asked her to see if any part was an ID. When I got to the end of the second section she interrupted. That's a transaction ID right there, she said. Which part, I asked. She said, ABA#021000089. Three letters followed by nine digits."

"So what does that give us?" St. James said anxiously.

"ABA stands for American Bankers Association. It's a transfer of funds from a United States bank to the Cayman National Bank."

"Do we know whose account?"

"No. Confidential. Antoinette wouldn't budge on that."

"Do we know if the transaction actually took place?"

"No. All we know is the code contemplated one taking place. Not that it actually did."

St. James was silent for a long moment. "Well, where do we go from here?"

"I saved the best for last." St. James heard a smile in Smythe's voice.

"Well?"

"Antoinette confirmed the numbers following the transaction ID are an actual account number! 012-67141 is eight digits."

St. James's spirits suddenly picked up. "Now we're getting somewhere! So what does the last part of section two mean? The '*co-na-csprite1*'."

"Haven't a bloody clue."

# Chapter 9

Monday morning St. James considered spending Wednesday and Thursday in Washington reviewing police files a second time.

Before making arrangements he emailed Jason Williamson, the detective in charge of the Stevens case, asking if files could be made available tomorrow. He copied in FBI Inspector Slate, who'd be in charge if Stevens was kidnapped. FBI jurisdiction. Jason would be in charge if it was theft. And Jason *was* operating on the assumption Stevens did steal the money. In the meantime Slate remained on standby, prepared to move at a moment's notice.

Slate replied, inviting St. James to dinner the next evening if meetings with Williamson were confirmed. Jason responded a half hour later, saying files would be available as well as an office to use while St. James was in Washington. Jason would be in meetings most of Wednesday but would have time for St. James on Thursday morning.

Satisfied the timing would work St. James fired up his laptop and booked a flight to Washington. Satisfactory arrangements made, he confirmed dinner with Slate.

Wednesday morning's flight was twenty minutes late, with low fog blanketing the Ottawa airport. But St. James still made it to First District Division on M Street shortly after 10:00.

The inside of the rectangular three-story brick building reminded St. James of RCMP headquarters, with officers busily chasing down leads, searching databases, and running GPS traces on persons of interest.

He was escorted to an office designated for visiting police by a short bald overweight office manager chewing tobacco and wearing clothes St. James thought could have been made in the 1950s.

The Stevens files were packed in three boxes stacked one atop the other on the floor of the office. He helped himself to coffee from a machine down the hall and settled into a space slightly smaller than his university office.

St. James pulled the top box down, flipped open the lid and found a small white plastic box containing pictures of Stevens's office and computer. He looked closely at each one, trying to spot anything he might have missed the first time around, noting the neatness of Stevens's desk and office surroundings, but not much else.

Next St. James studied interview notes Jason and his partner had made, reading each page carefully, once again looking for information he may have overlooked during his first trip to Washington.

Approximately fifteen people had been interviewed, including the firm's chairman, Nathan Strong. Detailed interview notes for cleaning staff and accountants came next. Then Stevens's wife, Beth, and their two daughters, Sandra and Emily. Normal procedure. Standard questions. Nothing of interest, except that the notes for Beth Stevens had a line scribbled in the margin in Jason's handwriting: *marriage in serious trouble.*

Memories of his interview with Beth flashed before St. James's eyes. He thought the woman had to be bipolar. One minute she was morose, pleasant the next, angry the one after that. A very awkward and difficult interview. But Beth did manage to confirm all Stevens's clothes were accounted for. No suitcases were missing, and his passport was still in the basement safe.

No one interviewed noticed a change in Stevens prior to his disappearance. No clues in his desk. No strange pattern of travel leading up to the crime date. No unusual charges on credit cards or suspicious telephone calls.

"Just as I remembered," St. James said aloud.

Rummaging to the bottom of the box, he found the registration for a Mercedes Benz S550 4matic he hadn't seen the first time. He compared the license plate and serial number to the code, but no combination or permutation of numbers or letters matched.

Then he pulled a file labelled "Bank Statements." Jason's people would have traced every bank transaction for a year prior to the crime date, looking for unusual transfers between Stevens and third parties. But St. James had to see for himself. He ran a finger down each page. Nothing suspicious or unusual jumped out. Not even one small transaction with the Cayman National Bank. No notes concerning SWIFT codes, transaction IDs, or account numbers. Everything seemed to be what would be considered normal business.

He pulled a file labelled "Miscellaneous." Police often filed unidentifiable or seemingly irrelevant documents under miscellaneous, with no other logical place for them at the time. St. James paid close attention because documents discovered later could render those in Miscellaneous very relevant, helping to support or refute a theory.

The first thing he came across was a shareholder agreement between a company called LTC Holdings Inc. and Jensen Holdings Inc. Behind the document was an email from Jensen, dated a week before the shareholder agreement was signed, instructing Stevens to transfer $50,000 to LTC Holdings's lawyer. Since Jensen was in the business of investing in real estate St. James considered this to be normal activity. In other words, not suspicious, on the face of it, anyway.

The next file was labelled "Investments"; it consisted of ten to twenty emails written to Stevens by Jensen instructing him to make similar transfers to various privately held companies in exchange for common shares. Amounts varied, but most related to nursing and retirement homes. Also familiar from St. James's first visit.

"Nothing new here," he grumbled.

The next file contained Jensen's investment plan, outlining demographics and the shortage of retirement homes to accommodate the elderly baby boomers. There was money to be made building new homes.

*Makes sense with aging baby boomers.*

Three hours behind an undersized desk in the small office was causing cramping in St. James's long legs and a feeling of claustrophobia. He decided to walk to the hotel for fresh air, to clear his head, and to check in.

He grabbed the oversized duffle he had brought that morning and headed out. The day had grown cold and quite windy since he'd landed at Dulles International. The skies were overcast, yet a sliver of sun struggled to poke through east of the city.

Traffic crawled, making it difficult for drivers to make time. Sidewalks were crammed, people rushing to do whatever they needed to do that day.

Minutes later St. James arrived at the hotel on 1$^{st}$ where he had reserved a room. He checked in and made his way to his fourth-floor room to freshen up.

Smythe was taking a long time to break the Stevens code and St. James was feeling the weight. He needed to know what the jumbled letters and numbers meant in order to make further progress. So far he'd found no evidence Stevens had ever been to Cayman. No airline, hotel, or restaurant credit card charges, not even a single phone call to the island nation.

But Smythe's progress was not the only impediment to solving the case. St. James could no longer avoid meeting with another potential source of information. He had to interview Beth Stevens a second time.

When Beth answered the phone she was decidedly cool.

*Complicated woman.*

Instinctively St. James knew she had little feeling left for Stevens. But he *was* still her husband, and he *had* disappeared. Surely she'd have some anxiety, want to know what happened, volunteer whatever she could to help find him.

He'd have to tread softly if he was to get anywhere. Her personality shifted so many times in the first interview that he couldn't get a good read.

"Beth, I'm in Washington reviewing police progress with your husband's case and would appreciate an opportunity to ask additional questions," St. James said in a low, monotone voice.

"Thought you asked everything you needed to weeks ago," Beth replied coolly.

"New information has come to light. I would like the opportunity to share it with you."

"What new information?" she said anxiously.

"I'd prefer to speak in person."

"Too busy. Appointments all day," she said abruptly.

"How about coffee tomorrow morning?"

Momentary silence. "Very well. My place. 9:00."

Beth disconnected without another word.

St. James shook his head.

# Chapter 10

When St. James finished talking with Beth Stevens he caught the latest news on television, and then headed back to First District.

So focused on documents all morning, he had given little thought to lunch. Now reminded by a growling stomach, he popped into a small crowded deli on Half Street that reminded him of a '50s diner. Grabbing the only vacant stool, he ordered roast beef on whole-wheat and a bottled water.

It was 2:45 by the time he entered his tiny temporary office. And for the next hour and a half he waded through the second box, which contained mostly police progress reports that after a dozen or so all sounded the same. There were many more investment directives from Jensen. The third box contained less important documentation.

At 4:15 St. James called Slate to see about dinner arrangements. Slate would pick him up in front of the hotel at 5:30.

*Perfect.*

He packed the few notes he had made, files, and laptop and headed back to the hotel. There he stood under a hot shower for fifteen minutes before toweling down and dressing for dinner.

At 5:25 he exited the white concrete and glass building just as an ad-plastered airport shuttle rolled in front. When the shuttle doors flew open, passengers piled out seemingly all at once, forcing St. James to quickly step back.

He eyed a park bench and positioned himself there to wait for Slate. At 5:40 Slate pulled up driving a new four-door white Lexus sedan. St. James jumped in and they exchanged pleasantries.

"I seem to remember you needling me for not buying American cars," St. James said with a grin. "We should be loyal to our jobs instead of letting them disappear offshore, you said."

"I was waiting for that," Slate said with a smile, "but I was hoping to get another block or two before hearing it. I *was* loyal up until *my* government used *my* tax dollars to bail out American manufacturers making cars nobody wanted to buy."

St. James laughed.

Slate was fifty-something with thinning red hair and an expanded girth from an abundance of fast food and little exercise. Twenty years with the Bureau had molded him into a tough agent, which sometimes got him into trouble. St. James thought superiors gave him considerable leeway because he solved the most difficult cases.

Slate and St. James met a few years back during the Texas Airport Authority case, Slate chasing a conspiracy theory, St. James investigating financial losses. After a few shots were fired they successfully brought the crooks to justice.

"Where are we going for dinner?" St. James said.

"Picked a restaurant near Dupont Circle called Luigi's. Best Italian in D.C."

Slate maneuvered the Lexus through a number of side streets to avoid traffic, arriving at Luigi's on P Street minutes later, after circling the block twice to find a parking spot.

"It's a townhouse?" St. James said when they were standing in front.

Slate smiled. "Yes. Quite small. That's why I made reservations for six, when it opens. Never get in after seven. Hope you're hungry. The usual is five courses."

A short dark-haired maître d' greeted them at the door and immediately seated them at a table in a far corner of the dimly lit dining room. A wiry little waiter with bulging eyes wearing a thin mustache and a cheap toupée hurried over to ask about drinks.

"I'll have Forty Creek on the rocks," St. James said jovially.

"Sam Adams for me," said Bill.

While the waiter fetched drinks, they studied the menu, made selections, and rhymed off their choices when bulging-eyes returned.

The dining room was every bit Italian, a perfect replica of an old country restaurant. They could be anywhere in Italy. The walls were faux yellow and brown, plaster cracks painted here and there to create the centuries-old look. Wall sconces evenly spaced cast soft light over period paintings of Florence, Rome, and Venice occupying spaces in between. Wine bottles plugged with lit candles acted as centrepieces for the tables. Checkered tablecloths completed the authentic look.

St. James said, "How are Joan and the grandkids?"

Helen, Slate's wife, had passed away three years before from an aggressive form of breast cancer discovered too late to be treated. They had only one child, a daughter, Joan, who married a surgeon; they had two boys, Bobby and Josh.

"They're great. They've been my life since Helen died. I take Bobby and Josh to ball games and movies. Joan and Fred have me over for dinner regularly. If I didn't have them, I'd go out of my mind."

"They sound wonderful."

Bulging-eyes arrived with small plates of antipasto.

"Say," Slate said as he draped a linen napkin across his lap, "did you hear Nells was out?"

"Pierre told me. Guess we'll have to watch our backs now."

"Mostly me," Slate said, fiddling with his silverware. "I'm the one he hates."

"We all helped put him away, Bill. I think he'll look for all of us sooner or later."

They discussed the Syrian crisis and how the United States was so divided on just about every major political issue.

Slate said, "Everyone's angry over one thing or another. Sluggish economy, immigration policies, but most of all the inability of politicians to fix any of it. Don't know how we got into such a mess."

St. James shook his head. "Seems like we sled downhill an inch at a time, Bill. More out of benign neglect than anything else."

The odd-looking waiter reappeared to deliver bowls of Italian wedding soup and whisk away empty plates.

He returned to ask about wine.

"Sure," St. James said without hesitation.

"You choose," said Bill. "What I know about wines you could put on the head of a pin."

"Okay. Special occasion, special wine."

Running a finger down the list, St. James settled on a bottle of Brunello di Montalcino.

"Sounds expensive," Slate said.

"My treat."

"Thank God. Probably couldn't afford it anyway on a government salary."

"Have anyone watching Nells?" St. James asked.

"Nope. Short staffed. Politicians are insisting on huge manpower reductions. Unfortunately, criminals don't have the same budget constraints. They're still out in full force."

"Do we at least know what he's doing?" St. James said, finishing the last of his soup.

"Nothing confirmed, but we think he's working for a legitimate company."

St. James skepticism was obvious. "Uh huh. Don't happen to have a name?"

Slate pushed his empty soup bowl aside. "Not off hand. I can check tomorrow if you like. Will you still be in Jason's office?"

"I will."

"Let me see what I can find out."

The waiter placed Caesar salads in front and took away the soup bowls.

"Anything new at the Bureau?" St. James asked.

"Everyone my vintage seems to be retiring naturally or taking one of the new packages."

They began eating salad.

"New packages?" St. James said, forking lettuce.

"Yeah. Part of the war on budgets is early retirement packages. Reduce headcount by shifting costs from an anorexic operating budget to an obese pension fund."

"Interest you?"

Slate looked solemn. "Might have, if Helen were still alive. Now the job's the only thing that gets me out of the house. Not sure what would happen if I just played golf and moped around."

St. James felt Bill's pain and changed the subject.

"Any interesting cases on the go?"

"Been assigned to a series of drive-by shootings we believe are related somehow, but can't find the connection, not so far, anyway. No business connections. No drugs, no mafia, no gang wars we're aware of. They seem to be random, without purpose."

"They're the hardest ones to catch a break on," St. James said, shaking his head.

"Like unraveling a rope with no ends," Slate said, waving a fork jammed with salad.

"If they're just shootings, why is the Bureau involved? Wouldn't that be local police or state trooper jurisdiction?"

"Normally yes. But they cross four state lines."

"I see," St. James said and ate more salad.

They spent time talking about holidays. Next spring Slate was taking Bobby and Josh fishing on his favourite lake up in Vermont.

"They've never fished before, so grandpa is going to teach them how to catch trout," Slate said beaming, as excited as St. James imagined the boys to be.

St. James told Slate about Anna.

"If she is a great lady, which she would have to be for you to be interested, don't lose her. Life goes by fast. It's no fun being alone," Slate said, pointing an empty fork in St. James's direction. "Trust me."

Halfway through the bottle of Brunello di Montalcino, bulging-eyes delivered two generous portions of chicken Alfredo, which St. James and Slate quickly waded through. Later he tempted them with dessert, but both declined.

St. James paid the bill, and Slate dropped him in front of the hotel exactly where he had gathered him just hours before.

"Thanks, Hamilton. I can't tell you how wonderful it is to have a friend like you. Someone with the patience to listen to me vent," Slate said sadly. He raised the driver window and slowly rolled the Lexus onto 1st Street. St. James stared at the Lexus taillights until the car was out of sight, feeling a huge heaviness for his friend.

*"Live every day to its fullest" is not just a cliché.*

Riding the elevator, St. James felt a wave of disappointment wash over him. Nothing useful had come from the trip so far.

He mumbled to himself, "Should have been some indication of the man's intentions, where he was going, a fear or threat of some sort, something out of the ordinary."

But there wasn't. Everything now seemed to depend on the code. It would have to lead somewhere, if Smythe could ever solve the rest of it.

As soon as he entered the room he checked emails and made a number of online bank transactions. His Visa bill was past due by four days, and the power and cell bills had arrived two days before. One by one he cleared each to zero.

He expected a progress report from Smythe, but he found nothing in Outlook.

He called Anna. She had had a down day and was looking to St. James to cheer her up. Sid was being more rude than usual. Most of the time she could brush it off, but now she was feeling the buildup of several weeks of his uncivil behaviour. St. James did what he could to lift her spirits, but with little success.

"Have you found anything to help the case?" she asked in a low voice.

"No. But I am meeting Jason in the morning. We'll see what that brings."

They talked a few more minutes, exchanged loving thoughts, then said goodnight.

St. James moved to the room's small desk to scribble additional thoughts. What could be the Cayman connection? Is that where Stevens went after he disappeared? But there was no evidence to support that. Nothing on his credit card, his passport still in the home safe. He could have travelled under an assumed name, but that would require false papers, a different passport. Difficult to acquire, but not impossible if you know the right people. Or maybe he was taken to Cayman under duress? That would require a private plane or boat.

The only thing he was sure of at this point was that Stevens didn't steal the $23 million. The interview with Jensen as much as told him that. The fact money passed from the investee company at the hand of others after Stevens initiated the investment supported that conclusion. Yet Jensen's lawsuit claimed Stevens stole the money *and* was negligent at the same time, which just couldn't be. If Stevens *was* guilty, it could only be for one thing, theft or negligence, not both. That's what had given rise to Global's suspicion in the first place, why Mary DeSilva had called him.

Nothing seemed to bring him closer to a breakthrough.

# Chapter 11

Beth Stevens lived in Washington's trendy Georgetown area on a street off Prospect, in a two-story Georgian house not far from the Francis Scott Key Bridge.

Before leaving for Beth's, St. James checked out of his room and placed his duffle in storage with the concierge. The concierge had arranged an Enterprise rental to be delivered to the hotel at 7:30 that morning, a new dark-blue Lincoln.

The meeting with Beth wasn't until nine, but St. James left the hotel at twenty past eight to allow time for the unexpected, like getting lost. But he encountered no problems and eased the Lincoln to a slow stop in front of Beth's house at 8:45. And there he sat, checking and responding to emails for the remaining fifteen minutes.

For a long moment he eyed Beth's well-constructed red brick house with its high white gabled windows and traditional arched oak door. The lawn was perfectly manicured, and mower tracks were ramrod straight.

At 9:00 sharp he pressed a buzzer that looked like it had been painted over several times. Seconds later the door swung open, and he was warmly greeted by a smiling Beth Stevens.

"Come in, Hamilton. I have coffee made for us."

*Wow! The nice Beth.*

Regardless of her emotional state Beth Stevens was an attractive woman, with black shoulder-length hair and fiery dark-blue eyes that looked as if they could burn holes through just about anything.

"Thank you for making time for me, Beth. I know this is very stressful for you and the girls, and my presence is a huge reminder of what you've been going through."

Beth's long, slow sigh suggested she had resigned herself to the situation.

"Well ... you have a job to do, don't you."

"Thanks for understanding."

She showed St. James into a living room filled with expensive antiques and period paintings.

Beth motioned him to a maroon antique chair that St. James thought hailed from circa 1920.

"Cream and sugar?" Beth asked.

"Just black, thanks."

She disappeared into the kitchen, returning minutes later with a large glass tray supporting two mugs of coffee and a plate of homemade peanut butter cookies, which she placed on a perfectly preserved mahogany table in front of St. James.

"How did you know peanut butter was my favourite?" St. James said with a smile, hoping to break the ice with a light comment.

A stone-faced Beth drank coffee. "Lucky guess. Now, what is this new information that's 'come to light,' as you put it?"

St. James bit into a cookie, drank coffee, then placed the mug on the tray.

"Did Tom ever mention a bank account in the Cayman Islands?"

Beth momentarily stared into her mug. "I can't recall him ever mentioning Cayman at all, bank account or no bank account," she said slowly.

"Would he ever have reason to go there? Client business or personal?"

"Not that I am aware of, but then again communication between us hasn't been the best lately. The only way I'd know he left the country would be if his passport was missing from the basement safe, and if suitcases and some clothes were gone."

"Do you check the safe?"

"Frequently." Beth placed her coffee on an end table and tucked hair behind each ear, which reminded St. James of Anna. "But only when he doesn't come home for days at a time. If the passport's there, he's probably somewhere in the country. But, if the passport's not there, it doesn't necessarily mean he's out of the country. He could require formal identification to sign legal documents at an attorney's office."

"I see," St. James said thoughtfully. "Were there times during the past year you discovered the passport missing?"

"No."

"Are you absolutely sure?"

"I would remember. It rarely happens. So rare that I make note of it. Don't know why I do that, but I do."

That surprised St. James. "You keep a log?"

"I do."

Beth stood and went into an adjacent room, returning minutes later with a black leather booklet. Flipping through a dozen pages or so, she came to one headed *Safe check* and handed it to St. James. He noted three columns. The left one listed dates she checked the safe. Middle said *yes* if the passport was there, *no* if it was missing. The third was blank.

He quickly ran a finger down the page, noting the passport missing only on two occasions in the past twenty-four months, both over a year ago, long before the crime he was investigating occurred.

"Thanks, Beth. Could I have a photocopy?"

Without a word Beth went into the same room and returned with a photocopy of the log, which St. James shoved into his attaché case.

"May I see the passport itself?" he asked.

"Sure," she said. "Follow me."

Beth led St. James down a dark, narrow, beige corridor, through a large bright yellow kitchen to a green door that opened to stairs that led to the basement.

The basement wasn't finished. Shelving along one wall bore neatly stacked boxes, Christmas decorations, garden tools, a carpenter's toolbox, and a number of used paint cans, all positioned with order and purpose.

*Stevens was certainly neat,* St. James thought as he passed by.

In the far-left corner sat a single large movers' box. To the naked eye it looked heavy, but Beth pushed it aside with relative ease, exposing a combination safe embedded in the floor.

"Full of old stuff from a previous move," she said pointing to the box. "No one would ever suspect it concealed a safe."

St. James nodded.

Beth bent down and quickly spun the dial twice to the right and once to the left, each time making sure St. James couldn't see where it landed.

The safe contained a number of official-looking documents. Probably a deed to the house. Maybe investment certificates, or bonds, or wills, or contracts of some sort.

Beth moved a number of papers around before pulling Thomas's passport out and handing it to St. James. The first thing he noted was the document would expire in six months. Not long enough for some international travel.

He noted the most recent trips. "He went to Mexico during April last year," he said. "Do you know what for?"

Beth shrugged. "I assume work."

He looked at Beth. "Before that, Honduras?"

"Not a clue."

St. James carefully studied passport stamps to satisfy himself there were none for Cayman, or any other location that might trigger a clue. None. He handed the passport back to Beth, and she placed the document back in the safe, closed the lid, and spun the dial to neutralize the combination.

They made their way back upstairs to the living room, to the same chairs they occupied several minutes before.

St. James made some notes and then continued. "Did Tom ever mention the word 'csprite1'?"

"What's that?"

St. James unfolded the now crumpled paper bearing the code from Stevens's hard drive and placed it on a table in front of Beth.

Taking a moment to smooth the well-worn document he said, "I showed this to you when we first met. You had no idea what it meant. But then you were understandably distraught, and perhaps not of a mind to focus."

Beth studied the paper. "Yes, I remember this." Looking down she rubbed her forehead with both hands. "I was in such a state then. You're right. I couldn't focus," she said thoughtfully.

"Understandable," St. James said, giving Beth a moment to eye the letters and numbers.

"I see the word 'csprite1' in the second part, but I have no idea what it means."

"My tech guy believes it's connected somehow with the transaction ID for transferring money to the Cayman National Bank. The one at the beginning of the parenthesis." St. James pointed to the transaction ID *ABA#021000089.*

Beth's face strained as if that would bring recollection. "Means nothing to me. Nor had I seen it before you showed me last time."

"Okay. What about the set of digits following the transaction ID?" St. James pointed to *012-67141.* "Does that ring a bell?"

Once again Beth's face strained. "Nothing. I'm sorry."

"That's okay, Beth. No need to be sorry."

St. James briefly explained SWIFT codes and how the one in the code identified a Cayman bank.

"Oh my ... And this was on Tom's computer?" she said softly, slowly shaking her head.

"Yes ma'am."

"Why was it the only thing on there?"

St. James sat back.

"Not exactly sure. We think it was something Tom actually wanted us to find. Maybe trying to tell us something."

"But what and why?" she said, trying to make sense of everything.

St. James shrugged. "We don't know. Cracking the code will tell us, maybe, or provide a lead of some kind, maybe. That's what we hope anyway. We'll see."

St. James studied Beth as she stared down once again at the code. There were no distinguishable facial expressions. Nothing to indicate a familiarity with any section of the code. Nothing suggesting she might be holding something back.

"What does your man think the rest of it means?" she said finally.

"Numbers following the transaction ID have been confirmed as an account number by the bank. As I said we have no idea what the last part, 'co-na-csprite1,' means. The remaining sections have yet to be worked out. That's why I wanted to meet in person. I thought the Cayman connection and the passage of time might trigger a memory of some sort."

Beth pointed to the other sections. "Mixture of numbers and letters doesn't trigger anything. I'm afraid I'm no help, Hamilton. Would you like more coffee?"

"Please. And I'll take another cookie if I may," St. James said, smiling.

"Help yourself," she said, picking up both mugs and heading back to the kitchen.

When Beth returned St. James said, "You remember Tom's client Malachi Jensen?"

Beth's expression instantly went from sweet to vicious. She reddened, and her fists clinched tightly. "That bastard ... son of a bitch."

St. James pulled back, startled by the sudden change. He shouldn't have been. The transformation was similar to the first meeting. Yet the volatility was still off-putting, the speed of change frightening.

Beth didn't notice the effect she had had on St. James.

"Tom worked his heart out for that tyrant, and in return was treated like dirt. Made the bastard a lot of money too. So Tom makes one bad decision after making the thug millions, and he gets hung out to dry. Ungrateful piece of shit."

Beth suddenly realized her state and went quiet for a beat.

"Now," she said calmly. "Where were we?"

St. James struggled to get back on script.

Finally he said, "Did you and Tom ever have clients for dinner?"

"Yes," she said with a smile. "Many clients many times."

"Anyone stand out as having odd, unusual conversations, strange behaviour, that sort of thing?"

Beth squinted. "To me they were all strange. I had nothing in common with any of them."

St. James hesitated for a moment, trying to pick an approach that wouldn't set her off again, yet would still lead to something worthwhile. A difficult line to walk. "Let's see if we can break it down into degrees of strange, starting with the worst."

Beth stared at a crack in the plaster ceiling, trying to gather her thoughts.

"There was one couple. Can't remember their names. He was in imports … booze, clothing, and decorative things from around the world, to sell in America. She was nice enough. But he was a buffoon. Got very drunk. She was so embarrassed. I felt sorry for her."

"Remember anything about him?"

"I seem to recall him being a heavy man, always bragging about his business success. A total bore."

St. James made a note, then thought for a moment. "Remember anything about the conversation?"

"No. It was the darkest time of our relationship."

"Relationship between you and Tom, you mean?"

"Yes. He insisted I put on that dinner and I reluctantly agreed to keep my peace. For the sake of the girls, you know."

St. James nodded.

"But my heart wasn't in it. Not like it used to be, anyway. You know, back when Tom was a new partner and we were happier together."

"I understand. Were there other dinners that stand out in your mind?"

Again Beth took a minute to reflect. "There was a fellow in from out of town one time. A very strange man. He had a kind of scary look ... you know?" Beth nervously played with a coffee spoon.

"What do you mean by scary?"

"Don't know really ... Almost like he would do or say anything to get what he wanted."

"What made you think that?" St. James said carefully, trying to maintain her even temper.

"Ah ... it was a look that made me feel very uncomfortable. Dangerous look. Can't point to anything specific ... woman's intuition, I suppose. Natural instinct to protect myself."

"Was it a sexual predator's look?"

"No. That I can handle," she said with a faint smile.

"What then?"

"He seemed like a man ... a man who could, and would, kill.

"Do you remember his name?"

"No. Seems to me his first name began with S ... Sam, maybe? Or Seth? Perhaps Stan? I don't remember."

St. James nodded and noted down her answer.

"Remember anything about his features, a description of some kind?"

Beth's face scrunched.

"I seem to remember him as a man on the smaller side, homely, scrawny-like. Best I can do, Hamilton."

"That's great, Beth." St. James noted the description.

Next he took Beth through descriptions of people and companies connected with both Stevens and Jensen, allowing her time to digest each, at the same time being careful not to say Jensen's name.

Nothing clicked.

"Never met any of them at business functions or parties," she said finally.

St. James reached over and placed a hand on hers. "It's okay, Beth. You can only remember what you can remember," he said softly.

She smiled warmly. "Thank you for your help, Hamilton."

He looked at his watch. "I have to meet Detective Williamson at the station at eleven. Better get going. Thanks for the coffee and cookies."

"Anytime."

St. James grabbed his attaché case, rose and made his way to the front door, Beth close behind. Leaning against the door, she watched him stroll down the walkway.

Partway down he looked back. "Things will get better, Beth. I promise."

"They have to, Hamilton. They can't get much worse."

# Chapter 12

It was a fabulous clear autumn day, a crisp sixty-two degrees with the fall sun beating down, seemingly brighter than usual for the time of year.

St. James sat in the Lincoln in front of Beth's house, trying to piece together the conversation they had had in her antique-furnished living room. He was certain she knew nothing about a Cayman bank account just by the way she answered. Body language. The eyes.

And the intensity with which she had put Jensen down meant she still had some respect, if not love, for Stevens, otherwise she wouldn't care whether Jensen had treated Stevens poorly or not. Then there's this fellow with the killer look, the man who came to dinner, the one who made her uneasy, a small homely man; possibly a Stan, a Seth or a Sam. Perhaps a lead if St. James could determine the name with certainty.

St. James slipped the Lincoln into drive, turned in Beth's drive, and edged the vehicle toward downtown.

When he arrived at the hotel, he handed the rental keys to the concierge, grabbed his duffle, and piled into a cab that took him to First District.

Jason greeted him with a smile and an apology for being unavailable the day before.

"Not an issue, Jason," St. James reassured. "I needed a day alone with the files, regardless."

Jason Williamson was in his mid-thirties, young to be a full detective; a six-foot-four blond athletic American who had won a basketball scholarship to the University of Maryland, College Park, where he came first in his year in criminal justice and law enforcement. Washington Police snapped him up the very day he graduated. He systematically passed every departmental exam as fast as the chief would let him write them. St. James was sure he'd be chief one day.

They settled in Jason's dark-blue leather chairs and St. James took a moment to survey the room. "Bit nicer than the office you put me in," he said with a grin.

Jason laughed. "I have news for you, my friend, you weren't in an office. We're so short of space around here we hijacked a storage room just for you."

"Thought that might be the case," St. James said in a light-hearted, sarcastic tone.

St. James filled Jason in on his meeting with Beth Stevens and the conclusions he'd drawn. Jason made notes, paying particular attention to the Stevenses' dinner guest with the killer look.

Jason said, "Thoughts? Questions?"

"I'm intrigued by how Stevens operated. In Canada accountants don't manage client money, although the profession's talking about it. They don't have signing authority over bank accounts or authority to commit transactions. Insurance premiums would shoot through the roof. Insurers would have great difficulty insuring professional work like Stevens does. Countless $23 million-like claims would haunt them. Then there's the independence issue. Accountants can't audit their own transactions and still claim to be independent."

"It's not all that common here either. Stevens's practice was unique. He developed relationships with estate lawyers who referred clients. Mostly wealthy families who, for one reason or another, wanted a third party to manage investments. Maybe a status thing. As far as we could tell that's how it all began. Of course, wealthy families hang around other wealthy families, so word got around Stevens was a trusted manager."

"Up until $23 million disappeared, anyway," St. James said.

Jason nodded without smiling.

"Lot of money going into retirement homes down here. System's not equipped to handle the tsunami of aging baby boomers."

St. James agreed. "Same up north."

"Jensen was in the habit of preparing annual plans to support what he wanted Stevens to do. There's one in one of those boxes."

"Yeah, I read it. Remembered it from my first visit." St. James hesitated. "Have your men traced funds after they were invested?"

Jason looked pained. "No. Couldn't justify the time. With signed directives from Jensen carried out to the letter by Stevens, the chief wouldn't authorize the extra manpower. Not enough evidence to warrant the cost."

St. James was incredulous. "But $23 million has been fully accounted for with transfers Stevens made. Something has to have happened after that. Doesn't that fly in the face of the theory Stevens stole the money?"

"On the surface, yes, but we're checking who benefitted from Jensen's investments. If Stevens held shares in companies Jensen invested in, it could be motive enough to take the investigation further. If that was the case, the chief would likely allocate additional resources."

"How did you persuade him to check shareholders?"

"Didn't," Jason replied with a grin.

St. James's forehead furrowed. "You're running skunk works on the chief?"

"Not exactly. My first cousin's in third-year law. He's doing it because I help with his tuition."

St. James laughed. "You're resourceful, my friend, I'll give you that. Mind sharing what you find?"

"Of course not. If it's insurance fraud, you're entitled to it anyway."

"Must be more directives than stored here," St. James mused.

"Hundreds dating back several years are in storage at SG&S, all in the same format, only amounts and names differ. If I brought everything down here, we'd be paying a lot more for storage. Wouldn't go over very well in this budget climate."

St. James nodded. "Smart. How long do you think it will take your cousin to get through every company?"

"He's about two-thirds through now. Give him another ten days or so and I'll email the report to you."

St. James said, "Have you spent more time grilling Jensen?"

"Interviewed him a couple of times since you were here. Didn't get much more out of him. Rough diamond. Don't trust him one bit. Could have taken the *Godfather* role away from Brando."

"I agree," said St. James, rubbing his neck. "Is he still saying that he put all his reliance on Stevens vetting his investments?"

"Doesn't budge an inch."

St. James spent the next hour or so asking a number of questions about Jason's investigation procedures and steps.

*Thorough. No holes.*

"Thanks, Jason. Is the storage room I used yesterday still available? I'd like to make a call."

"As long as it's local," he said with a grin. "At the rate budgets are being cut around here, one long-distance call could put me in front of Internal Affairs."

"Yeah? Bill's complaining about FBI cuts too. Seems to be running through every police authority. The new reality."

"How's Louis doing with the code? By the way, I am very grateful you took on that job. By rights we should be doing it as part of the investigation, but our guy is up to his neck. Almost every case now has at least some computer component to it. Louis is the better man anyway."

"He's made some progress, but I'm not confident enough yet to share. When I am, you'll have everything."

"Great."

St. James made his way back to the tiny office he occupied the previous day. There, he punched in the telephone number for Stevens, Gables & Strong.

"May I speak with Nathan Strong please?" he said to the receptionist.

"I'll put you through to his assistant."

"Mr. Strong's office, this is Catherine."

"Hi Catherine, Hamilton St. James. We met a few weeks ago, if you remember."

"Yes, of course," she said in a gravelly voice.

"I'm in Washington reviewing police progress with the case and would like a follow-up with Nathan, if I could. Wonder if he could spare a few minutes?"

"I'll see, Mr. St. James. Just one moment."

Back in seconds, Catherine said, "He has about fifteen minutes at two. Do you wish to see him or talk by phone?"

St. James checked his watch. 1:45.

"I'm not far away. I'll see him in person. Thank you, Catherine."

When St. James disconnected, the phone rang.

First District operator.

"Mr. St. James. I have a call for you from Inspector Slate of the FBI. When I hang up, he'll be on the line."

"Thank you."

"Morning, Bill."

"Good morning. I made a few enquiries about Nells this morning. Sources tell me he works for The Carstairs Group."

"Know the company?" St. James said.

"Never heard of them. Apparently they're headquartered in Chicago."

"What business is it in?"

"Something to do with retirement homes. Construction or managing properties, that sort of thing."

St. James went quiet.

# Chapter 13

Stevens, Gables & Strong's 12-partner, 125-staff office had built a healthy stable of profitable clients, mostly family-owned businesses focused on niche markets larger firms passed over, a focus that made SG&S very profitable.

The firm branded itself an extension of client management, a strategy St. James thought brilliant because it created a certain dependence on SG&S, making it difficult for clients to move to another firm.

When he stepped off the elevator, St. James was met by a middle-aged receptionist, who immediately buzzed Strong's assistant. Catherine appeared seconds later.

Late-forties, of average build, and completely bald, Nathan Strong was round-shouldered, his demeanor all business. St. James didn't believe Strong had much of a sense of humor and had no intention of finding out.

"I went through police files yesterday and met with Beth Stevens first thing this morning, Detective Williamson after that," St. James reported.

He recounted his meeting with Beth; her behaviour was no surprise to Nathan.

"Sometimes she forgets to take her meds," he said solemnly. "I feel sorry for her. The stress of all this would have magnified her mental health issues for sure."

St. James nodded. "I was very disappointed with the police files yesterday. Nothing of interest came to light. I know Williamson kept only a few of Jensen's; I'm hoping to have better luck with your files."

"There's a lot of them. Over 130 companies," Nathan said, lightly scratching his furrowed brow. "You're welcome to them."

The list of companies hadn't been compiled when St. James had interviewed Nathan weeks ago.

"Do you have the final list now?"

"We do."

Nathan buzzed Catherine for a copy for St. James.

"Police already have the list and are in the process of identifying all the shareholders." Nathan hesitated a beat, then said, "They want to see if Tom is a shareholder in any. They're convinced Tom siphoned the funds somehow, directly or indirectly."

For the time being St. James wanted to keep his opinions to himself. He wasn't prepared to tell Nathan he didn't think Stevens stole the money, not yet anyway.

"But as you said during our first meeting, you don't believe he's capable of that."

Nathan's brow furrowed once again. "I've known Tom Stevens for over twenty-five years. We not only practiced together, we took family vacations together. I know him as well as you can know anyone. I don't believe for a moment he could bring himself to do this kind of thing.

"Hope you find him … and soon. As you can appreciate, we're anxious to clear up this mess. It's hurt the firm's reputation immeasurably."

St. James nodded. "I can imagine how the partners must feel."

Catherine entered and handed two copies of the list of companies to Nathan, who immediately passed one to St. James. St. James quickly ran a finger down the names but didn't recognize a single one.

Pointing the document in Nathan's direction St. James said, "And this is what you gave Williamson?"

"The very same."

St. James folded the paper and stuffed it in a coat pocket, then said, "Williamson said his people would have the list of shareholders for each company sometime within the next ten days," St. James said. "I'll email it to you to check, to see if your partners know anyone."

Strong made a wide sweeping gesture, his tenseness visibly off the charts. "Anything you want, Hamilton," he blurted. "We want this behind us as soon as possible. The partners are upset, anxious about the bad publicity and worried how much insurance premiums will increase next year. It's all I can do to keep them focused on clients. Times like this, client service is even more important than usual, if that's possible. Clients need reassurance the firm hasn't lost its values, that it remains worthy of their respect, confidence, and business."

Nathan returned to calm. "By the way, did that odd-looking little fellow working on Tom's computer figure out what the letters and numbers meant?"

"You mean Louis," St. James said, smiling faintly. "He has some clues, but nothing we can talk about yet. It's long and tedious work I'm afraid."

Nathan nodded. "I understand."

"Do you mind if I have a look at the files here? Don't have much time, flight leaves at seven."

"Not at all."

Nathan led St. James down a cream-coloured hallway, peppered with what St. James considered horrible abstract art, to a locked, windowless office where Stevens's files were kept.

Nathan looked at his watch and shrugged apologetically. "Sorry, I have to go. If there is anything you need, just ask Catherine. I'll be in meetings until the end of the day, I'm afraid. Good luck, Hamilton, and let me know if I can be of further help." Nathan turned to leave, but before he passed through the tiny room's doorjamb, St. James said, "One last question."

Nathan stopped and turned. "Of course."

"Have you ever heard of The Carstairs Group?"

Nathan thought for a long moment then said, "No. Why do you ask?"

"Just curious."

Nathan nodded and left.

At most St. James had a little over two hours before he had to leave for Dulles Airport.

Jason was right. There were 139 companies, all with files containing directives, correspondence, and legal documents, each in the same order with the same labels. Stevens was a very neat and organized man indeed. It certainly explained the order in the Stevenses' basement.

He didn't have time to go through every document for every company. And even if he did, he doubted it would yield much more than diminishing returns. It would be more efficient to concentrate on larger investments that could total the missing $23 million. No sense wasting time on anything less.

He selected the five companies with the most transactions with Jensen Holdings. The first, GLZ Investments, carried the signature of a Samuel Franklin. Second, Saltwater Investments, owned by an Adam Derringer; third, Cook Enterprises, owned by a Bertram Cook; fourth, Fletcher Family Holdings, owned by an Amanda Fletcher; and fifth, Macadamia Investments, owned by a Stan Gyberson.

The names meant nothing, but he made note of them anyway. The tone and choice of words in correspondence among the five suggested they were more than just business acquaintances.

One by one he eyed amounts transferred from Jensen Holdings to each of the five companies. The first four received investments totaling $18 million, not the $23 million St. James was looking for, so not worth pursuing on their own.

He turned his attention to the fifth company, Macadamia Investments. There was correspondence back and forth between Stevens and Gyberson.

"First name beginning with 'S.' Wonder if he's the man with the 'killer look'," St. James mused. "Possible." He made an additional note.

Jensen Holdings made a number of investments in Macadamia totaling something in excess of $23 million. The lead he'd been looking for, or just a coincidence? St. James would have to dig deeper.

It took an hour and a half to get through all the files, and by the time he'd finished with Macadamia it was time to leave. Staying longer meant missing the flight home.

He took a moment to phone Anna.

"Can you research everything on The Carstairs Group?"

"Who are they?"

"Hoping you could tell me."

"Smartass."

"I believe they're located in Chicago, not sure."

"Okay, on it."

St. James left SG&S's office at 4:15, made his way to the lobby, and turned the corner to a taxi stand. The ride to the airport was exceptionally slow, late-day traffic quite heavy. But Air Canada made up for some of the delay with a faster check-in, and by 6:05 he was sitting on an airport bar stool with a double Glenfiddich in hand.

It was close to 11:00 p.m. when St. James unlocked the door to his condominium. Immediately he jumped in the shower, and after a good five minutes under forceful hot water, toweled down and put on the most comfortable thing he owned — baggy sweatpants and an oversized T-shirt. He went into the kitchen, opened a bottle of Gabbiano Chianti, and poured a healthy glass.

Rooting through the fridge he found enough sliced chicken to make a sandwich. With Chianti and sandwich in hand he turned on the news channel.

He should have called Anna to say he was home safe, but it was late and, for some reason, he needed time to think, to reflect on where things were going with Stevens.

When he had his fill of sandwich and news, he turned off the television, refilled his wine glass, and stared out onto Sussex, thinking about Washington. What he had found, or rather what he hadn't found.

*Hopefully the shareholder list would bear some fruit. Surely Strong and his partners would know someone on it. Then there was the $20 plus million invested in Macadamia Investments by Jensen Holdings. Is that the missing money? Or is it a different investment altogether? And this Gyberson fellow, the 100% shareholder of Macadamia, was he the dinner guest who made Beth Stevens so uncomfortable? Lot of moving parts. Many pieces would have to fit together before the story could unfold and the theory be proven ... or not.*

# Chapter 14

Sitting in the darkened living room in his fifth-floor condo at midnight, St. James's mind drifted to The Carstairs Group and Nells. Was it a coincidence Carstairs was in the same industry as Jensen's investments? Not likely. St. James was not a believer in coincidences. He would have to continue the investigation assuming the coincidence was genuine, until proven otherwise, that is.

Once shareholders of the 139 companies were identified, he'd have to interview Jensen again; essential to determine if Jensen had a relationship with any of them.

*We'll see what that brings.*

With that, St. James went to bed.

Next morning the phone rang at 9:00.

Smythe.

"Ninety per cent certain," he said without even saying hello, "that *'Virgo23'* refers to astrology."

"Zodiac signs?" St. James said in disbelief.

Smythe was emphatic. "Yes, zodiac signs!"

"Whatever in God's name brings you to that conclusion?"

"It's the number 23 that boosts the probability. Virgo runs from August 23 to September 22 so *'Virgo23'* is the first day of the zodiac sign. Software gives it the best chance of being statistically correct."

"Hmm. What could that mean?"

"Could be referring to a birthday, or a personality description. I looked it up. Virgo people are supposed to be analytical, observant, helpful, reliable, and precise. Fits the description of an accountant, don't you think?"

"Not too helpful if he steals $23 million," St. James said. "Don't think that's the avenue we want. What about the date itself? Maybe it's the day something was to happen."

"Have no idea. Money disappeared on the twenty-third but wasn't reported missing until the thirtieth, the only events we know for sure."

"But look at the next part of the code, Louis: '+7'; 23 plus 7 is the thirtieth of August, the date the funds were reported gone."

"Is that too simple?" Smythe said anxiously. "If that's it, what would +8, +4, +6, and + 3 mean? If you follow the same logic all the way through it gives you September 7, 11, 17, and 20. September 11 is a significant date only because of the Twin Towers. Not aware of anything else that has or is about to happen during the rest of September."

"Beats the hell out of me. Maybe the dates don't mean anything public. Maybe they're private actions. Not dates at all."

"Maybe. Still think I'm right. Everything related to Virgo in the code is captured in parentheses. That tells me '(Virgo23+7+8+4+6+3)' is meant to be a complete thought on its own. It's a command, or a confirmation of actions, or dates for things to happen."

"Maybe, Louis … maybe."

# Chapter 15

Graves phoned St. James after class the following Friday morning.

"Next week is the third week since our meeting in Ottawa. Are you far enough along with the Washington case to begin work with us? The board is anxious to begin the project," he said with his strong British accent.

St. James paused, then said, "I'm not finished that case yet, but I am far enough along to at least meet your board ... next week if that's convenient."

"My executive assistant polled the board members yesterday to determine availability. She managed to speak with everyone and the earliest they can meet is next Tuesday at 2 p.m. here at Toronto HQ. Will that work for you, Hamilton?"

"That's fine, Nelson," St. James said without referring to his phone calendar.

"Excellent. You have the address."

St. James clicked off.

Late in the afternoon St. James and Anna met for dinner at Restaurant E18 on York and then went to Anna's for the night.

Next morning St. James woke to the sound of rain dancing on the windowsill. Eyes closed, he reached for Anna only to discover an empty pillow.

The smell of freshly brewed coffee drifted in, enticing him to rise, dress, and make his way to the tiny kitchen where he found Anna diligently preparing breakfast. Hair pulled back in a neat ponytail, she wore a grey track suit and blue running shoes.

"Good morning," he said, putting his arms around her from behind and gently kissing her neck. "You were wonderful last night."

"Weren't so bad yourself," she said, turning in his arms for them to kiss. "Bacon and eggs?"

"Works for me."

St. James sat at the small table, drinking coffee while Anna finished breakfast preparations.

"What are you doing today?" she asked.

"I have a new case starting in a couple of weeks and have some time this weekend to do preliminary research."

"Oh. What's the case?" Anna said quizzically.

"Company called Canadian International Seafoods Incorporated, CISI, a large fish-processing company headquartered in Toronto. The chairman called me yesterday to confirm a meeting with directors next Tuesday. They want a management review, which sounds a bit odd to me. That's all I know at the moment. But I want to learn as much about the company as I can before that meeting. What are you doing today?"

"First I'll tidy up here. I have mending to do and a book I want to start. That's about it. Not very exciting, is it?"

St. James smiled. "In addition to the research I asked you to do on The Carstairs Group I could use some help with this new client."

Anna shifted a fry pan to another burner.

"What do you want me to research?" she said after a few minutes' silence.

"I'd like you to find everything you can on a Nelson Graves."

"And he is who?"

"The chairman of CISI."

"And what am I looking for?"

"Anything and everything. Nothing's too trivial. Something you see now, no matter how insignificant it may seem at the time, could be of great importance later as the story unfolds."

"I think I can handle that," she said, smiling.

"Meanwhile I'll see what I can learn about CISI itself."

Walking through the ByWard Market, St. James wondered what CISI's chief executive officer could possibly keep from the board. And why? What could be significant enough to motivate withholding information? A major asset write-off maybe, lurking somewhere in financial records? One Anderson might want to cover up, perhaps? Or was he siphoning funds? Or was there a contingent liability about to rear its ugly head? Perhaps a potential lawsuit or government fine for bad fish?

Once again St. James asked himself why he had accepted the mandate. Wasn't a crime, although there could be when all was said and done. A block later he concluded intrigue motivated his acceptance of Graves's mandate. A board unable to extract information from its CEO intrigued him. CEOs are accountable to boards, not the other way around. And Graves didn't strike St. James as one who tolerated resistance.

# Chapter 16

It was almost an hour after leaving Anna's before St. James slid the key into his condo door. He went into the study, settled at the mahogany desk, opened his laptop, grabbed a notepad from the bottom right-hand drawer, and began gathering director biographies from CISI's website.

Leaving Graves to Anna, he excluded Al Dunlop, who he knew well: no research required. And for the time being he put Anderson aside as well. St. James would research Anderson later when he had a handle on the others.

Blakie was chairman of his own human resource firm. Of the remaining five external directors, John Coughlin had thirty years' experience in marketing with a major consulting firm. In-house counsel Andre Fox had practiced twenty-five years with a prominent Toronto law firm. Nancy Slitter served thirty-three years in Canada's civil service, the last five as Deputy Minister of Fisheries and Oceans. Harold Tewkesbury was a forty-year veteran of Canada's largest bank. And Cheryl Tomkins was the former United States Ambassador to Portugal.

*Excellent credentials.*

As Graves said, the company owned twenty plants around the world. St. James noted five in the United States, three in Canada, two in Great Britain, two in Spain, and one each in Portugal, Russia, Israel, Turkey, Japan, South Korea, Barbados, and Brazil. The worldwide market for seafood and related industry sectors approximated $300 billion US, fast approaching $400.

Anderson appeared on the third website page, announcing a $30 million overhaul of the Brazilian plant and the construction of a third plant in Spain. An exaggerated smile showcased perfectly straight, white teeth. Jet black hair greying at the temples made him look the part of a distinguished CEO. St. James guessed him to be about six feet and forty-five years old.

CISI employed approximately ten thousand people worldwide. Five hundred at head office, the balance spread among plant locations roughly in proportion to size and production volume.

High-value shellfish products, mostly crab, shrimp, and lobster, accounted for sales of $2.2 billion; remaining revenues were spread almost evenly over twenty or so groundfish species such as haddock, halibut, cod, basa, tilapia, and perch. Fish guts and waste, called offal, was converted into fish meal, while products such as eels, sardines, and other delicacies found their own specialty markets.

At $19 billion the company was tracking a little over 6% of the world market, which St. James thought amazing, huge by any standard.

The United States accounted for 18% of sales, Canada 4%, the Far East 28%, the balance spread throughout Europe, South America, and the Middle East.

Google searches revealed three major competitors: the German Grunn Rolf Fisheries, the Swedish Emano AB, and the South Korean Nao Tungsau. All public companies, which meant financial information was readily available on websites. St. James printed documents from each site and spent an hour or so calculating comparative performance statistics.

CISI's gross margin was higher than its competitors by three full percentage points.

*Impressive.*

Shareholder equity among all four was comparable, within 2% of one another. CISI inventory was slightly higher.

*Perhaps different species mix.*

Without realizing it St. James began to mumble. "Anderson won't believe cost efficiency as the reason for hiring me, especially if he does the same analysis I just did. He's not dumb! There's no motivation to analyze cost efficiencies when you're already number one in the industry."

*More to this than meets the eye.*

12:15. Time to call Janice McPherson.

Janice was St. James's assistant at the university, the one proposed by the dean so St. James would accept a professorship. Pursuing a Harvard doctorate in business forced Janice to hold down three part-time jobs just to make ends meet. Being St. James's assistant was one of them. Aside from marking student assignments, Janice presided over exams and handled classes whenever St. James was away working cases.

"I'll have the papers marked and on your desk within a couple of weeks," she assured.

"Great Janice. Would you mind emailing the class to say when they can expect them?"

"Consider it done," she replied warmly.

As soon as he clicked off Janice, the phone rang, and Anna's number popped up on call display.

"Hi sweetheart," he answered.

She had found three Nelson Graveses. One was Nelson H., living in Toronto; the second, Nelson A. in London, England; and the third, Nelson G. in Los Angeles.

"I immediately dropped the LA Nelson but kept the London one because you said he was British. Later I discovered Nelson H. was the one appointed chairman of CISI's board, so I dropped Nelson A."

"Excellent," St. James said, obviously quite pleased. "What did you find on Nelson H.?"

"Born in Fowey, Cornwall, England sixty-eight years ago. Educated at Oxford. Five years in the military, rising quickly to colonel. He joined

IBM in London right after military service. Thirty years with them; fifteen in England, five in New York, and the last ten in Toronto, managing Canadian operations. When he retired, CISI snapped him up. He sits on three other boards, Craven Chemicals Ltd., Dusten Pharmaceuticals, and Craig Automotive Inc."

"Is he chairman of those?"

"No, just a director. Although he does chair the audit committee for Craven Chemicals. It doesn't say here anywhere, Hamilton, but from all I've read the man seems like a real no-nonsense guy."

"My take too. Any firings?"

"No. Stellar career."

"Anything unusual?"

"The only thing I found that seemed out of step with his career was he fell into financial difficulty in the late 1970s, forced to declare bankruptcy in England."

St. James perked up. "Interesting. Did it say who the trustee was?"

"Yes, but I didn't make a note of it. I should have. I'm sorry. You said to note everything, no matter how trivial."

"Don't worry about it. It's your first day. Find the name again, if you can. Google to see if the company still exists. If it does, call. Say you're conducting a credit check on Graves and would like to know if he handled himself properly during the bankruptcy process."

"What do you mean?"

"Was he honest with the trustee."

"On it."

Anna was about to hang up when St. James said, "Oh, Anna. You did such a great job on Graves, would you do the same for Cameron Anderson?"

"He is …?"

"The chief executive officer."

"Okay."

"And Anna, good work."

"Thanks."

St. James could hear the excitement in her voice.

*Could be a big asset; smart and anticipatory.*

St. James spent the next couple of hours researching more about the fishing industry.

By early evening he had had enough and went into the kitchen, poured a glass of J. Lohr, and checked out three-day-old refrigerated Chinese food that he promptly deemed unfit for human consumption. Into the garbage it went. And into the living room he went. With the lights off he flipped on the radio and sat down on the love seat, content with just wine and the Eagles singing "Take It Easy."

He thought about CISI's financial performance. He found nothing to be concerned about. Quite the contrary. Like Graves said, the company was growing faster than the industry average. If there were efficiency issues, they certainly weren't significantly affecting financial results. Definitely the strongest company in the industry.

So, why was the board so concerned? "Why am I here?" he said to an empty room. Was Anderson really keeping something from them, or was this board paranoia gone wild? By all rights they should be lauding Anderson for his success. Maybe Graves really was on a witch hunt.

# Chapter 17

Mid-morning the following Tuesday the CISI Directors gathered in the head office boardroom where Graves's superiority complex was out in full force.

"Okay, let's begin. Please take your seats," he said authoritatively, sounding more like the colonel he once was than chairman of a large public company. Everyone finished their coffees and quickly found a place around the boardroom table.

"As previously agreed we're engaging an independent expert to review cost efficiencies, and, where appropriate, make recommendations to Cameron. You're aware Al recommended a gentleman by the name of Hamilton St. James to be that independent expert. I interviewed him in Ottawa several days ago and am satisfied with his credentials. You'll meet him at two this afternoon. Experienced in managerial reviews. Harvard graduate. CPA. I checked with a number of lawyers and bankers. All seemed to hold him in high regard."

St. James's profile made its way around the table.

Graves continued.

"Cameron agreed to have operations reviewed and assess recommendations that may be forthcoming. Right, Cameron?"

All eyes turned to Anderson.

"Correct," Anderson said in a reluctant voice.

The short, portly Cheryl Tomkins, wearing a conservative brown suit and no makeup, immediately picked up on Cameron's lack of enthusiasm.

"Cameron, the board needs to know you're one hundred per cent behind this initiative," she said in an uncompromising but respectful tone.

"I assure you I'm fully behind it. If you sense reluctance it's because our people are extremely busy, and this takes time away from demanding duties. Then there is the cost of this fellow. He isn't cheap, and we have a budget to meet."

Blakie, a slight man with greying hair, dark complexion, and wire-thin lips was determined to challenge the need for all this. "I checked around; my sources say he's quite arrogant. Do we want someone like that working directly with our people?"

"David, half our people are arrogant," Dunlop said sharply. "If we picked people based on personality rather than merit we wouldn't be nearly as successful."

Coughlin nodded. "I agree."

"I called my old firm to see if the partners had ever worked with him," offered Andre Fox, a man of average build. "I found two who had. They said he accomplished wonders with firm clients about to blow up over ethics."

"What was their experience with the man?" asked Harold Tewkesbury in a low, almost inaudible voice.

"In one case a chief technology officer for Zanics Technologies didn't test software to the extent advertised. After several hundred products had been sold, design flaws began to bring down customer systems, every company's nightmare.

"When complaints poured in, Zanics engaged St. James to manage the crisis. In two days he uncovered how reliability had been misrepresented and immediately advised Zanics to blow the whistle on itself. Go public before the media gets a hold of it, he said. But management thought the advice tantamount to brand suicide and vigorously argued against it. They insisted on dealing with the problem quietly, behind the scenes, away from the public eye.

"There was a huge debate between St. James, management and the board, at times quite heated, I'm told. St. James argued the issue was public confidence, not faulty software. Employees didn't do their job. Why should customers ever trust Zanics again, was his point. The company had to show public trust was far more important than the cost of fixing software. In the end, Zanics reluctantly agreed.

"Publicly, Zanics apologized for the software disaster. Testing employees were immediately terminated for cause on the grounds of misleading customers and senior management.

"Zanics replaced all the defective software with the next generation, at no cost. And customers were assigned free onsite technical support until all problems were identified and resolved. Zanics was determined no customers were to lose business because of the software failure. That was the promise it made to the public."

"Cost must've been shockingly out of sight," Blakie concluded, shaking his head.

Harold chimed in, "It would break the company."

Fox's grin broadened. "On the contrary, gentlemen. Zanics was voted company of the year for honesty. Didn't lose more than five customers, and apparently those were chronic complainers, even in good times. Sales rose 13% the following year. Publicity from the honesty award generated more than enough new business to cover the cost of the software fiasco.

"Zanics publicly held itself accountable when St. James forced the issue. Refusing to hide behind lawyers, it admitted the wrong and made it right, at no cost to the customer. Trust in Zanics actually rose. Customers felt safer with Zanics than any of its competitors."

Al nodded agreement. "Natural tendency is to fix things quietly. Avoid negative press. Try to sneak solutions by before the public finds out. But, if the press catches wind before the problem is announced, allegations of cover-up explode in every form of media — journalism, radio, and television. Social media now the deadliest of all.

"Media thrive on cover-ups. They stop at nothing until every morsel of the story is ripped from the soul of an organization. Like piranhas, feeding on corporate flesh. Whipping the problem into multiple stories, each one more damning than the last. All to convince the world that if the company covers up one thing, what else might it be hiding? That, my friends, *is* brand suicide.

"It takes years and thousands of dollars, maybe millions, to crawl back from a publicity disaster like that."

Graves's meaty hand adjusted his horn-rimmed glasses as he interrupted. "Okay, let's get back to St. James. John, what do you think?"

"I'd like to know the effectiveness of marketing expenses. How much revenue is created by every marketing dollar spent? Which initiatives work, and which do not?" said Coughlin.

Anderson bristled. "You know, John, we analyze marketing expenses in detail twice a year. We're constantly weeding out programs that don't generate sufficient revenue to pay for themselves."

"Yes, I know, Cameron," John replied sympathetically, "but it would be comforting to have an independent view to show shareholders we're cautious with their money."

"That's a two-edged sword, John," Blakie said curtly. "We'll be lucky if St. James doesn't cost more than $250,000. If no value is added, we *have* wasted money."

Graves's wider eyebrow twitched as he held up a hand to re-establish order.

"Ladies and gentlemen, may I remind you we've made the decision to hire someone, presumably St. James unless you have some violent objection this afternoon. That's final. This argument is pointless."

The room went quiet.

Cheryl Tomkins was first to speak.

"I would like to know about inventory. I've never clearly understood how it's calculated. The adjustment after last year's physical count was huge. Too large. As directors we must have a better understanding of this. Next to plant and equipment, inventory is our largest asset."

Nancy Slitter chimed in. "I agree with Cheryl. I have the same issue."

"Yes, it would be good to have a greater understanding," Al said, nodding.

Graves looked pained, obviously unhappy Cheryl had raised the question. "What specifically would you want to know?"

Anderson looked to be about to speak, then changed his mind.

"I'd like to know about counts and pricing. And what percentage of inventory goes bad? What percentage of inventory's sold on the verge of going bad?" said Cheryl.

"Auditors check all that," Blakie argued with a look of irritation.

A frustrated Cheryl snapped, "I know that, David. I'm concerned with product liability. Auditors make sure inventory is fairly stated on financial statements. They insist on allowances for aged products or freezer burn. But they don't know if fish is about to *become* bad before it actually *is* bad. I worry about people becoming sick. I don't need to remind everyone of the Maple Leaf Foods story. Tainted food costs a lot in public trust. Not to mention liability claims."

Nancy, John, and Harold all nodded agreement at the same time.

Graves drummed the table. "Very well. So we have marketing efficiency and inventory as agenda items this afternoon. Anything else?"

"When I was in banking," said the crusty Tewkesbury in a monotone voice, "I pushed clients to justify overhead expenses on an annual basis. It would be good if this St. James fellow would have a look at those for us."

Graves eyed faces around the table. "Good. Anything else?" he said again, anxious for closure.

The room went quiet once again.

"Okay, let's break for lunch. Please be back by 1:45," Graves commanded.

Everyone stood and placed documents in file folders, away from wandering eyes, then went their separate ways to lunch.

It was 1:50 when St. James entered CISI headquarters on Front Street and announced himself to the receptionist. She noted his name, directed him to a chair in the waiting area, then announced his arrival to Graves's executive assistant.

St. James watched a number of people he knew to be directors from website pictures parade into the boardroom. Then Graves came out, shook St. James's hand, and asked if he would mind waiting just five more minutes until they had dealt with a small recurring agenda item. St. James had no objection.

# Chapter 18

Graves was true to his word. Exactly five minutes later he reappeared to escort St. James into the boardroom where he made his way around the table shaking hands.

When he got to Al, they hugged.

"Great to see you, Hamilton."

St. James smiled broadly. "You too, let's grab lunch or a drink soon."

"Why not both," said Al, smiling in return.

Handshakes complete, everyone sat.

It was a traditionally styled boardroom: solid mahogany walls, richly painted oils, and a long dark oak table elaborately trimmed, hand-carved in exquisite detail. An oversized nineteenth-century chandelier centred the room; its light too dim, an array of pot lights was necessary to compensate.

Graves sat at the head of the table, as St. James expected. Looking somewhat puffier, he wore the same suit and tie he had in Ottawa just days before. St. James wondered if he and Jensen had the same image consultant.

Graves called the meeting to order.

"Hamilton, this morning the board discussed what it would like you to investigate. There are three distinct themes. First, the effectiveness of marketing expenses. Second, inventory compilation and quality. And finally, the level of overhead expenses. Do I have the themes correct?" Graves eyed each director around the table one by one.

Everyone nodded in sequence, like children agreeing with a teacher, whether they did or not.

St. James made notes while Graves continued.

"Hamilton, what I have called the three themes is certainly not enough detail for you to fulfill the mandate. Cameron will provide you with specifics later."

St. James nodded as he scribbled.

"You'll report directly to Cameron. Of course you'll require more to conduct the assignment. I suspect interviews will have to be arranged, documents and correspondence made available and the like. My assistant, Juanita Mendoza, will see to your needs. I leave that to the two of you to organize.

"Now, I throw the meeting open to questions and discussion."

Graves looked around the table.

Cheryl Tomkins raised her hand.

Graves nodded for her to proceed.

"How many cases have you successfully completed?" she asked cautiously.

"I can't be certain of the exact number. I'd say in the neighbourhood of fifty," St. James offered.

"Thank you," she said with a smile. "I don't expect you to be exact. Which would you say was the most difficult?"

St. James thought for a moment.

"I would have to say the Texas Airport Authority case."

"Could you tell us a little about that, just the highlights I mean?"

St. James smiled. "Sure. The Authority engaged me to investigate why it was losing money when airside traffic was up 20% from five years earlier, a time when it was making substantial profit. Street-side business was up 50% over the same period. The Authority was aggressively following a strategy to reduce economic dependence on airline fees. It couldn't understand why there were losses amid such growth. And management failed to ease their concerns.

"Six months later, after considerable investigation, a number of dead ends, FBI involvement, and four attempts on my life, we arrested an employee ring who were using an elaborate computer scheme to siphon cash."

"Someone actually tried to kill you?" Nancy Slitter said, shaking her head in disbelief.

"Yes ma'am, they did," St. James said nonchalantly.

"Does this happen often?" Harold asked.

"More than I would like," St. James said casually with a smile.

A number of directors stirred, looking astonished.

"Do you carry a weapon, Mr. St. James?" Blakie asked.

"Not often. Carrying handguns is illegal in Canada. But there have been times when RCMP, FBI, or Interpol have granted me temporary permits to carry, usually when we're closing in on dangerous suspects."

"I certainly hope that doesn't happen here," Andre Fox said.

"Me too," St. James said, continuing to smile.

Anderson leaned forward. "I spent time researching you, Mr. St. James, and it seems you're known mostly for corporate ethics investigations, not management reviews. How do you account for that?"

"I don't," St. James replied bluntly. "In many cases I'm asked to conduct a management review that evolves into ethical problems, and vice versa."

"Have you been asked to investigate wrongdoing here?" Anderson persisted.

St. James skirted the question. "I never begin by suspecting anything. Investigations usually happen because management feels uncomfortable about something. Chips fall where they may."

"I assume," Anderson continued, eyeing St. James closely, "when you discover wrongdoing, you are discreet. You bring the information only to the person who engages you, so the matter may be handled properly. You speak to no one else."

"Absolutely, except —"

"Except what?" Anderson interrupted.

"Except when the wrongdoing is done by the one who has engaged me."

Anderson squinted, his body language suggesting disapproval of St. James's flippant response. He sat back and said nothing further.

"Hamilton, why don't you tell the board a little about your methods so they have some idea what to expect over the coming days?" Dunlop said, hoping to get the meeting back on positive ground.

St. James spent three-quarters of an hour outlining approaches; different places investigations could take the investigator. Then he answered a number of questions before the meeting adjourned at a quarter to four, when everyone but St. James and Anderson hustled from the room.

Anderson signed St. James's engagement letter and outlined management's expectation of the mandate in greater detail.

"Any issues whatsoever, you bring them to me and no one else, you understand?" he said tersely as he handed St. James the letter.

St. James studied the man for a brief moment, considering his seemingly adversarial approach. "I understand," he said finally, in an equally stern tone.

Not a good start.

"We expect you to start Monday," Anderson said as he half-heartedly shook St. James's hand, and then left the boardroom.

*Charming fellow.*

He took the train to Lester B. Pearson Airport, checked in, and made his way through security. He had half an hour to spare before boarding the flight, time he happily dedicated to Cabernet Sauvignon in the Air Canada lounge.

He made a note about Anderson's aggressive behaviour. So vastly different from Graves's description! Graves said Anderson was a salesman who put a spin on everything. He made notes of Cheryl Tomkins's gravitas and Blakie's concern that he carried a weapon.

Nancy Slitter was focused only on business results. Harold Tewkesbury didn't add much value. Andre Fox behaved like the lawyer he was. John Coughlin had said nothing. And Graves allowed the exchange without interruption, which on the surface seemed out of character.

The flight back to Ottawa was uneventful. St. James arrived in the condo around 7:45 and, before doing anything else, he phoned Anna. She would be anxious to hear all about the CISI meeting. He brought her up to speed on everything, including Cameron Anderson's aggressive behaviour.

Anna was appalled. "Why would someone at that professional level speak to another professional that way? Especially someone he didn't know, and in front of all the others."

"Don't know, dear. Most likely it's because I wasn't hand-picked by him and he saw me as a threat. Or maybe there's an undercurrent among board members and I'm to be collateral damage. I'm sure it will come out as the project moves along."

# Chapter 19

Wednesday morning St. James discovered two voice messages on the home phone: Janice McPherson saying she'd soon be finished marking the test, and Anna asking him to call as soon as possible. He tapped her number on his cell.

"Just heading out to start my shift. Sid's been phoning every ten minutes demanding I come in early. More customers than usual, and the new girl's having trouble coping."

"I see. Why were you calling?"

"Oh yes! Cameron Anderson. He's forty-seven … Been in three major prior jobs, all vice-president of sales positions, no chief executive roles."

"That ties in with Graves's account. Unusual to pick someone with no previous CEO experience to head a large public company. Small private one, maybe. But it's a big leap from vice-president of a private company to CEO of a public one the size of CISI," St. James mused.

"I don't know about that," Anna said matter-of-factly. "I'm just giving you the search results."

"Okay." St. James smiled at her officious response.

"Interesting, he left each VP role quite suddenly, but was praised for his contribution to each company; accolades for growing sales by double digits each year. Seems CISI was interested in him for that reason. Newspaper articles said CISI sales were flat for five years prior to Anderson joining."

"Great work, Anna."

"Thanks. Oh, by the way, I found Graves's bankruptcy trustee."

St. James felt that twinge of excitement investigators experience when they stumble on a potential lead. Graves's bankruptcy was now decades old and the chances of finding anything meaningful were, at best, remote.

"Did you get any information?" he asked anxiously.

"I spoke to a lady named Patricia Havelock in London, England. She said Graves's files were in storage, and she'd require £1,500 to retrieve and review them. I wouldn't commit without your approval."

"Tell her we'll cover the cost. It's billable to CISI."

"What am I supposed to ask?"

"Ask —"

"Just a minute. Wait till I get a pen and paper."

Back seconds later Anna said, "Okay, go ahead."

"First, were all Nelson's assets accounted for to the satisfaction of the trustee? Second, did the trustee have to take legal action to recover fraudulent preferences or conveyances?"

"What's that?"

"Doesn't matter right now. If he did something wrong, I'll talk to her directly. Additional questions will hinge on the circumstances."

"Okay. Anything else?"

"That's it."

"Okay, sweetie, I'm on the case," she said enthusiastically.

*Enjoying her role*, St. James thought as he disconnected.

St. James was feeling cooped up, anxious, and in need of a walk.

Although the day had begun with a promise of sun, the sky clouded by late afternoon, and fog began rolling in over the city.

*Not pleasant for walking.*

Nevertheless, St. James completed the three-hour jaunt. Traffic along Colonel By was steady but not the worst he'd ever experienced. The usual barrage of cyclist, joggers, and power-walkers crowded paths on both sides. No sign of Jar Jar Binks.

St. James landed back home at 5:45 and immediately poured a glass of Gabbiano Chianti and checked the phone. No voicemails.

He went into the study and gathered the rough notes he'd prepared for this coming Friday's lecture, then moved to the living room.

The lecture plan called for morality, pillars of beliefs, and universal values to show what good people strive to do, what they applied to their own behaviour to avoid wrongdoing. St. James considered the *Meditations* of Marcus Aurelius for a long moment and concluded it a good fit.

*Aurelius believed in five universal values: the pursuit of Truth, Justice, Courage, Moderation, and Wisdom. Solid foundations for proper business behaviour.*

*Wrongdoing originates in lies. But not all lies are equal when it comes to the damage they cause others. Wisdom is necessary to decide which lies cause the greatest harm, which must be challenged, and which should be let go.*

*Concealing truthful information or manipulating financial statements are examples of lies resulting in wrongdoing to business stakeholders. If others permit such wrongdoing to occur, they do not have the courage to reveal the injustice, which is in itself an injustice, albeit passive.*

He made a number of changes until he was satisfied he'd built the foundation for good and bad business behaviour. Linking ancient philosophies to modern day business seemed to work well. But why does man deviate from truth, and why are businessmen motivated to grey the difference between right and wrong?

*Businessmen spend considerable time setting both personal and corporate goals. There's potential for great conflict between the two. Personal goals often centre around wealth creation and career advancement, which tend to place greater emphasis on short-term financial success, for the individual to earn career and financial rewards. Corporate goals such as growing revenue by 12% per year and increasing profit by 5% or acquiring a new business often involve longer-term investment strategies at the expense of short-term profits. Choosing between personal and corporate goals often creates conflict with business leaders. A lot of wrongdoing originates there.*

He expanded the theme using three different business scandals to demonstrate the relevance of his points, then gathered the notes and placed them in a file labelled "Lectures."

He poured a second glass of Chianti and settled on the couch to watch the news.

An hour later the phone rang again. Anna.

"Hi, you," she said in an upbeat voice. "It was quiet here, so I called Patricia Havelock about Nelson. She'd anticipated we'd guarantee her costs, perhaps it was my enthusiasm when we spoke, and had arranged for Nelson's files to be delivered from storage. According to her, your Mr. Graves transferred a piece of real estate located in the English countryside worth approximately £400,000 to a brother-in-law for no consideration a year prior to his bankruptcy. Graves thought he was in the clear because a year had passed, that he and his brother-in-law would benefit personally from the asset rather than his creditors. So he didn't declare the property on his sworn statement of affairs. The trustee learned about this by accident from a solicitor friend and subsequently threatened Nelson with legal action if he didn't return the property to the estate."

"Hmm. Keep going."

"Not much more to add. Graves returned the property to avoid criminal charges and a lawsuit he probably wouldn't win. By the way, what does something that happened so many years ago have to do with CISI?"

"Everything and nothing," St. James said lightheartedly.

Anna became impatient. "What do you mean, 'everything and nothing'?"

"Tells me everything about Nelson, and nothing about CISI. Everything and nothing."

They disconnected.

St. James wondered where his relationship with Anna Strauss was going. He knew he cared for her deeply. That was not the issue. Bringing a girlfriend into the business was a potentially dangerous move. Any number of things could go wrong. If they had known about it, his friends would call it strategically stupid. He wasn't worried she'd fail at research: she'd already proven her value there. A relationship gone sour would mean losing professional help and companionship all at the same time. That would be too much. Time would tell whether this was his biggest mistake or the smartest thing he had ever done.

# Chapter 20

Friday morning came soon enough.

St. James rose at seven, shaved, showered, then had toast and peanut butter for breakfast.

Before running off to 8:30 class he emailed the golf club to secure a Saturday morning tee time for him and Pierre and then confirmed the time with the inspector.

At 7:40 he locked the condo door and hoofed it down Elgin and across the Laurier Bridge and entered the classroom shortly after 8:15. There he set up a PowerPoint presentation and organized lecture notes before students piled in to take their seats.

St. James led the class through Marcus Aurelius's concept of universal values and delivered a complete explanation of truth, justice, courage, moderation, and wisdom, including live examples relevant to business ethics. He emphasized Winston Churchill's belief that passive injustice was just as wrong as active injustice, meaning if employees stood by while wrong was committed, they were just as guilty as those committing it. All just as he had outlined in the notes prepared the previous weekend.

Twenty minutes in St. James paused, drank water, and asked if there were questions. A hand went up in the third row.

"Yes, Mr. Shaw?"

"Companies generally don't put their universal values on websites. How do we know if they have values they actually practice?" Ben Shaw asked.

"I have a list of key characteristics stakeholders look for when assessing companies holding themselves accountable. I believe this will answer your question, Ben."

St. James scanned his computer desktop and double-clicked on a file marked "What Investors Look For," and the contents popped up on the overhead screen.

"This is what stakeholders use when evaluating culture and corporate governance. It's an excellent checklist, one I've used many times.

"I'm emailing the slide to you all as we speak."

"Thank you, Professor St. James," Ben said.

St. James looked around the room. "Other questions?"

Jane Stewart's hand rose.

"Yes, Jane?"

"What *really* influences us to be accountable? I get the historical significance of thought leaders like Aurelius, but when it comes down to the modern-day person, what influences accountability is murky to me."

St. James took a moment to gather his thoughts.

"There are many influences on our ability to be accountable. It begins in childhood. Were we taught right from wrong by parents, teachers, those we admired, and organizations that touched us? And was that teaching consistent enough to stick, to be engrained in our character? Were we taught to believe in good over evil? Or were we allowed to misdirect blame?

"Young years are the most important years. They form us. Years we remember the most, for the rest of our lives.

"How many of you did wrong by accident when you were young and then blamed someone else?"

Four hands went up.

"The rest of you are not being truthful," St. James said, smiling. "By not raising your hand you're telling me you learned nothing about right and wrong. I personally learned the hard way.

"I threw a ball to my friend Randy when I was eight. It went wide, smashing Mr. Bishop's window, our next-door neighbour at the time.

I blamed Randy when I told my parents, but Mr. Bishop saw it was me who threw the ball and told my father what really happened. My father was furious. Not that I broke the window, but that I lied about it. He made me pay for a new window from my allowance, apologize to Mr. Bishop face-to-face while he stood over me, plus I couldn't sit down for an hour or two."

St. James ignored the giggles.

"My father said, if you had knocked on Mr. Bishop's door, said it was you who threw the ball not Randy, said it was an accident, you were sorry, and you would replace the window, that would have been the end of it. Blaming Randy made things a lot worse than the consequences of just breaking the window. That was my first and greatest lesson on truth, justice, moderation, courage, and wisdom, all in one huge blow, and all at the age of eight.

"It touched me in so many ways. That's what made the lesson stick. Financial pain, paying for the window. Personal pain, the embarrassment of apologizing to Mr. Bishop. All reinforcing the greatest lesson for getting through life: accountability!

"For some strange reason what my father did made its way into my DNA. It formed part of my character. I was with him many years later when he died and thanked him for the lesson. He smiled but couldn't speak. It was his final moment.

"Exposed to bad people long enough, good people eventually do wrong. Small things at first, maybe. But like any addiction small wrongs have a way of growing, turning into larger ones over time. You steal a loonie. You don't get caught. You steal ten dollars. You don't get caught. You age. Now you manage a company, in a position of trust. You have the opportunity to manipulate thousands, maybe even millions, of dollars to benefit yourself. Stakes rise, risks rise, especially if not checked by consequences along the way.

"No good person wakes up one morning saying, 'I think I'll pilfer a million dollars from my company today.' Patterns of smaller wrongdoings grow into larger ones. Little wrongdoings give insight into character, about larger wrongdoings to come.

"The first rule when assessing corporate ethics is — character is everything.

"If someone doesn't work hard enough or fails to achieve committed goals and there are no consequences, strong employees say, 'Why should I follow the rules, these people didn't, and nothing happened to them!' No penalty for underperformance, financial or otherwise. No consequences.

"The second rule when assessing corporate ethics is — consequences are everything.

"Punishment from my father was pain that manifested itself into wisdom that has served me well ever since, made me a stronger and better person, and, I believe, contributed to whatever success I have enjoyed.

"In an organizational environment, collective employee behaviour together with rules, policies, and procedures form the culture. If that culture permits poor accountability, eventually good people do wrong.

"The third rule when assessing corporate ethics is — culture is everything."

St. James took a moment to clear his throat and drink water.

"In the end, we all decide who we want to be. That is, our own personal truth. And we must have the courage to ward off negative influences that eat away at that truth.

"Character is everything. Consequences are everything. Culture is everything.

"If a weak character works in a weak culture with no consequences for wrongdoing, the probability that person will do wrong is extraordinarily high. There's no culture of consequences to encourage them to be accountable.

"If a strong character works in a weak culture with no consequences for wrongdoing, that person slowly erodes into apathy. Eventually they don't care, because no one else cares.

"If a strong character works in a strong culture with consequences for wrongdoing, that person has every opportunity to experience truth, justice, courage, and wisdom. Why? Because they live in an ecosystem that supports accountability."

There St. James stopped and looked first at the clock, then around a still and silent room.

"I see I have kept you ten minutes longer than usual. I'm sorry for that. Janice will give you back your quiz marks in a few days. Have a great weekend everyone."

Christina Stone stood. Everyone else remained seated. A sense of awe had blanketed the room. Christina hesitated a moment, looking around at her fellow classmates.

She turned back to St. James.

St. James didn't know what was coming.

"Professor St. James," she said. "I can't speak for everyone, but for me you've given a very powerful insight into the practical influences on good and bad commercial behaviour. Any behaviour for that matter. I've not read a more complete explanation of how we are molded than the one I heard today. Thank you for a splendid lecture. I am moved by the experience you had with your father. I … I envy you."

The rest of the class stood and, seemingly in one single move, began to clap.

St. James found himself blushing.

"Thank you for those kind words, Christina. Thank you, everyone," he managed to get out.

The usual noisy mass exodus followed as students rushed up the stairs to their next class.

St. James felt overwhelmed by the recognition. Part of him just wanted to sit and take in the moment. But he had personal things to do. He hadn't restocked food in ten days, he was in bad need of a haircut, and, most important of all, his wine stock was severely depleted. All necessities for life to continue as it should.

# Chapter 21

St. James called Anna later that morning to tell her about the class response and to suggest a special evening at the Casino in Gatineau.

"Hamilton, I'm so proud of you. I wish I'd been there to cheer you on."

St. James devoted the afternoon to satisfying his domestic needs. First a haircut and a barber shave, which he treated himself to once a month. Much smoother than his own shaves, which usually resulted in bloody nicks here and there. Next, he purchased various bottles of favourite wines — mostly reds, a couple of Chianti Rufina, Primitivo, Carnivor, and Conquista Mendoza. A few whites thrown in too. Finally, a trip to the grocery store to fill a long list. By 4:00 he was set for the week.

A little before 6:30 he picked Anna up in front of her apartment. She was stunning, dressed in an all-black pantsuit and white blouse with a matching pearl necklace and earrings. Her hair was down and flowing freely as she glided toward the BMW.

"You look handsome tonight, Hamilton. Nice haircut!" she said climbing into the passenger seat.

"Thank you. But I am outclassed by you," he said, sounding corny but meaning every word.

St. James pulled the BMW 750 up to the Casino entrance and passed the keys over to a young valet. A second valet opened the passenger door for Anna, and minutes later they strolled through the main doors of Casino du Lac-Leamy, a first-class gambling establishment housing multiple bars and restaurants.

Le Baccara was St. James's favourite. Its open kitchen enabled guests to view wonderful dishes being prepared by fabulous chefs. The wine cellar was something to behold, with 500 different wines in a 13,000-bottle collection.

Inside, an instant panoramic kaleidoscope of flashing slot machines, cherry wood panelling, plush carpets, bars, and people; hundreds of people, some wealthy enough to be there, others not so much.

*Paycheques will be lost tonight*, St. James thought.

They walked straight to the back of the large room, past bars and noisy machines, blackjack and craps tables, into a glass elevator that took them to the third floor where Le Baccara's maître d' eagerly greeted them.

"*Bonsoir madame et monsieur. Bienvenue au Baccara.*"

"*Bonsoir,*" St. James said, his poor pronunciation a dead giveaway. The polite maître d' switched to English immediately to prevent St. James suffering further embarrassment.

"Do you have a reservation, sir?"

"Yes. The name is St. James."

He nodded and ran a finger down the reservation list.

"*Bon*, please follow me."

He led St. James and Anna to the back of the restaurant, to the very last table on the right, by a window. Privacy always being important to St. James, the table was as secluded as he could have hoped for. The maître d' placed menus in front and announced Jean-Paul would be their server for the evening. Minutes later a short thin dark-haired man with a narrow face, pointed nose, and round metal-rimmed glasses appeared at the table.

*Couldn't possibly weigh more than a hundred pounds*, St. James thought.

Jean-Paul introduced himself and asked if they would like drinks. St. James looked at Anna.

"I feel like red wine tonight," she said casually.

"Me too. How about Châteauneuf-du-Pape?"

"Perfect."

St. James looked at Jean-Paul. "Châteauneuf-du-Pape it is. A bottle, please."

Jean-Paul noted the request. "*Bon.*"

St. James and Anna turned to each other.

"Did you hear from Louis today?" she asked.

"No. We talked yesterday. He'll call on the weekend. He knows I have to speak with Mary DeSilva Monday."

"So what's on for the weekend?" Anna asked, hoping to be included.

"Golf with Pierre in the morning. CISI planning on Sunday. And as much of you as I can get." St. James smiled.

Anna looked disappointed. "Sounds like you won't have much time for me."

"Not so. We'll finish golf about 2:00. The rest of the day is for you. Would be nice if you could stay over and spend Sunday with me."

"I think I may be able to arrange that," she said teasingly.

Minutes later Jean-Paul reappeared with an uncorked bottle of Châteauneuf and two crystal glasses. He poured the customary dribble for tasting, and St. James gladly obliged. With their glasses full, Jean-Paul asked if they would like appetizers; they took a moment to peruse the menu.

Anna went first.

"I'll have the shellfish bisque. Sounds wonderful."

"Excellent choice, *mademoiselle*," Jean-Paul said, turning to St. James. "*Monsieur?*"

"I'll have the seared duck."

"Also excellent."

Jean-Paul noted the choices and rushed off toward the kitchen.

"We should look at main course selections before he returns," St. James suggested.

He ran a finger down the entrée section. "I don't think we can go wrong with poached lobster."

Anna did the same. "I'm torn between that and the roast Québec lamb. The dish descriptions are very creative. Listen to this — salted herbs, vegetables, and lamb neck cannelloni, creamy polenta with watercress, melted rebellion blue cheese from La Fromagerie Montebello, lamb jus. Sounds almost melodious, don't you think? Makes my mouth water."

"I think that's the idea of it all," St. James poked.

When main courses were decided, they folded menus and raised wine glasses to toast the future.

"Wonderful choice, Hamilton. Full bodied. Very nice."

"Always one of my favourites, rich in flavour but not too expensive. Except here. Here everything's expensive."

They both smiled.

"Have you ever played the slots or tables?" he said.

"Not the tables but once I lost ten dollars playing the slots in Niagara Falls. I felt guilty about wasting the money."

"We'll play a little after dinner. You can waste my money."

"Afraid that won't make a difference," Anna said, shaking her head. "Doesn't matter whose money it is, I still see it as a waste."

"Do you mind if I play a little blackjack later?"

Anna brushed hair behind each ear. "Not at all. If you enjoy it, you should."

"Fair enough."

Minutes later Jean-Paul appeared with the appetizers.

"Wow," Anna said. "The shellfish bisque looks fabulous."

"The duck too."

"*Bon appétit,*" Jean-Paul said as he slipped away to the next table. They took time to savour each mouthful.

A few minutes later Jean-Paul returned from taking drink orders at another table.

"For the main course, *mademoiselle et monsieur?*"

"I'll have the lamb," said Anna. "A little pink in the centre, please."

Jean-Paul nodded and smiled. "But of course, *mademoiselle. Monsieur?*"

"Poached lobster."

"Very good," he said, scribbling on a small pad.

He topped up their wine glasses and rushed off once again.

For a moment they watched Jean-Paul dart among neighbouring tables, asking if everything was satisfactory.

St. James grinned. "I see why he's so skinny. The man never stops."

"I updated my resumé," Anna said, ignoring Hamilton's assessment. "Dropped it off to managers at the Green Turtle Grill, The Lazy Politician, and Yesterday's News. Can't take it anymore. Sid's become too difficult. He's getting worse. Yesterday he yelled at Jim for not leaving a tip."

"No! Old Jim? Why, he must be eighty-five," St. James mused, staring out at the dusk. "Been a Duck regular for years. He can barely afford a pint on his meagre pension. Doesn't deserve to be treated like that."

"No, he doesn't. He's the most respectful customer I serve. Dare say we won't see him back again. Few of his friends either. I've never seen so many angry people."

St. James nodded, then changed the subject. "You enjoying the research?"

Anna smiled. "Yes, it's fun. More challenging than my regular job. Boss is more civilized too."

St. James smiled. "Good to hear. But you're comparing your research boss to a very low standard."

She shrugged playfully as if to say she wasn't sure.

"What do you like about it?"

"In some respects it makes me feel part of something … a team. You make me feel useful. Appreciated. Guess that's the bottom line. Hard to feel appreciated as a waitress. Even harder when your boss is a tyrant."

"It really helps you were research-trained in Germany. Kiel's loss, my gain." St. James winked.

Jean-Paul stopped to pour water.

Anna said, "Speaking of research, I found information on The Carstairs Group."

"Oh?" he said expectantly.

"The company's in the construction business, located in Chicago, just as you thought. Just a couple of projects on the go. Commercial ones of some sort. No residential. Nursing and retirement homes, that sort of thing. Hundred per cent owned by a company called Macadamia Investments, which as far I can tell is owned by a fellow by the name of Stan Gyberson."

St. James felt his brow furrow. "Recognize the name from the Washington files. But there was no mention of The Carstairs Group there. I only became aware of it recently, from Slate."

"Slate?"

"Close friend. FBI agent."

"Oh. Carstairs ran out of money in the middle of constructing a retirement home just outside Chicago. Newspaper said the project was abandoned suddenly without warning."

"Did you see the name Nells anywhere?"

"No. No Nells."

"Hmm."

They chatted about places they'd like to visit. Anna told St. James her parents had been Americans living in Germany when she was born. She attended an English–German high school there, became perfectly bilingual, and lost her German accent by eighteen. Her family took European vacations, but she was too young to remember much.

The main course arrived, and they continued discussing travel as they ate.

When they declined dessert St. James looked at his watch. 8:30.

"Let's go downstairs," he said, excitement in his voice.

He handed a credit card to Jean-Paul who darted to the front of the restaurant only to return minutes later with a portable bank machine. St. James added a generous tip and signed off.

They rode the same glass elevator down to the main level and were hit once again with a barrage of flashing lights and ear-piercing noise.

St. James purchased five hundred dollars in chips. Anna gasped as he peeled off hundred-dollar bills.

Gaming tables were lined in neat, even rows like cars in a dealer's lot. Strolling up and down aisles, St. James eventually found an empty seat at a blackjack table in the third row.

The dealer shuffled cards and asked St. James to randomly insert a cut card into the deck, presumably to show no sleight-of-hand had occurred to improve the house's odds.

St. James placed a $25 bet. The dealer dealt him the ace of hearts, a card to each of the four other players at the table, and the king of hearts to himself.

St. James signalled for a second card. Three of hearts. He paused, then tapped the table for another. Three of clubs.

"Seventeen," the dealer said.

Against all odds St. James tapped once again, and the dealer flipped over the four of diamonds.

"Twenty-one," he said without inflection.

The dealer dealt himself the three of diamonds, then the ten of diamonds.

"Twenty-three." And in one sweeping motion he slid two chips in front of St. James. $50.

St. James put down $100 in chips. Anna gasped again.

"Looks like you may have a gambling problem," she said cautiously.

Again the dealer dealt a card to each player and one to himself. Ace of clubs to St. James. Ace of diamonds to himself.

"I have a certain penchant for throwing caution to the wind," St. James replied.

Anna shook her head.

St. James tapped for a second card. King of hearts. Blackjack.

Dealer took a second card for himself. Three of diamonds. Four or fourteen. Then a third card. Seven of spades. Twenty-one.

The dealer was expressionless.

St. James turned to Anna and smiled. "A very satisfying win."

Her forehead furrowed, and her eyes rolled with disapproval.

"Blackjack beats an ordinary twenty-one," the dealer said, then slid $200 in chips St. James's way.

St. James turned to Anna.

"How much is your rent?"

"$1,000."

He passed her chips. "Here's $175 of it."

St. James played the next game and lost $25. Anna frowned.

The next game was much more exciting. St. James's first two cards were aces, which meant he could split them and play two hands at once; make two bets. He placed a $200 bet on the first ace. Splitting the cards meant he could bet another $200 on the twin hand for a total of $400. He thought Anna would faint.

The dealer dealt himself a seven, the jack of clubs to St. James. Blackjack.

His twin hand drew the queen of spades. Again blackjack. Now, St. James thought he would faint. He didn't know the odds of two blackjack hands on a split, but it had to be a fraction of one per cent.

The dealer — twenty-two.

"Let's get out of here, Anna," St. James said with excitement, "it can only go downhill from here."

St. James cashed his chips and gave Anna the balance of her rent.

"You are out of your mind, Hamilton St. James. I think you need help," she said as they walked out of the casino.

"Fine thing to say to a gentleman who just won rent money for you. Not very appreciative, I'd say.

# Chapter 22

They stepped out of the casino to a cool, damp evening. A light mist glittered beneath the soft street lighting lining the boulevard up to Autoroute 5.

A valet pulled the BMW around front and St. James opened the passenger door for Anna to slide in. He tipped the attendant, crawled into the driver's seat, pulled the vehicle into drive, and rolled the car up Boulevard du Casino to merge onto Autoroute 5 toward Ottawa.

At the bottom of the down ramp St. James glanced in the rearview mirror and spotted an older Mercedes approximately four car-lengths behind. Suddenly the Mercedes accelerated, rapidly closing the distance between the two vehicles. Seconds later it rammed the BMW with enough force to catapult St. James and Anna forward almost at once. The airbags didn't inflate and the seatbelts didn't grab. St. James winced when thrust into the steering wheel, his chest bearing the brunt of the impact. Anna screamed as her head slammed into the dash.

The Mercedes continued its attack, ploughing the BMW sideways until it ricocheted off the guardrails.

"What's happening?" Anna cried.

"Rammed us on purpose," St. James yelled.

The BMW fishtailed back and forth as it broke free from the Mercedes. Instinctively St. James jammed the accelerator to the floor, pulling the car straight as its speed increased.

Anna sobbed, holding her head in both hands, her blond hair sprinkled with blood.

St. James was tense, his focus alternating rapidly between the road ahead and the Mercedes behind. The Mercedes kept charging, closing the gap yet again. Darkness prevented him seeing the driver with any clarity.

The second ramming was even harder than the first, causing Anna's neck to whiplash more violently and the BMW's rear bumper to break loose enough to drag on the pavement, sparks streaming behind it.

Again St. James accelerated to widen the gap, again the Mercedes closed in. Gap widened. Gap narrowed. More sparks. St. James was quiet; he was tense and totally focused. Suddenly the BMW's bumper let go completely, the Mercedes nearly losing control as it swerved to avoid the flying chrome.

Racing across the Macdonald-Cartier Bridge into Ontario and onto Sussex, the vehicles fifty, maybe a hundred feet apart, whipping passed the National Art Gallery in tandem.

"Why are they doing this?" Anna cried, blood streaming down her forehead.

With one hand on the steering wheel and the other holding his throbbing chest, St. James dredged up what little remained of his sense of humour. "It's just a guess, mind you, but I think they're trying to kill us. Hold on. This isn't going to end well, Anna."

Both cars rounded the National Peacekeeping Monument at speeds much greater than the city limits, tires squealing as they wheeled onto Murray.

The situation was now more perilous. There were many people crossing ByWard Market streets without a care in the world, not expecting a high-speed chase to be roaring their way.

St. James ran a red light at Parent and Murray. The Mercedes slowed to avoid four pedestrians crossing Murray, allowing St. James precious seconds to widen the gap. Both vehicles shot right onto Dalhousie and again onto George.

ByWard's bright lights revealed a second man sitting in the Mercedes's passenger seat.

St. James wheeled onto Sussex through a red light at York, narrowly missing an elderly man crossing the street with the aid of a cane. Just past the American Embassy he swerved to avoid t-boning a red Jaguar emerging from St. Patrick.

A third crash sent the BMW into a violent three-sixty spin. St. James rapidly spun the wheel in the opposite direction, hit the brakes hard, then jammed the accelerator to the floor, creating enough speed for the vehicle to right itself. Now doing 140 the BMW once again increased the distance between the two vehicles.

Police sirens could be heard coming from the south.

On a split-second impulse St. James eased the accelerator, gently tapped the brakes three times, and then pulled the steering wheel a hard right. A high risk move that could have easily flipped the car if not executed just right, yet necessary to avoid another ramming.

Rounding the corner onto Cathcart on two wheels, the BMW slewed back and forth on wet pavement, St. James struggling to maintain control as he narrowly avoided a flatbed trailer.

Anna sobbing uncontrollably, her blouse was now more red than white.

As he regained control St. James spotted a single-story two-bay brick garage on the right, just behind the hospital, to the left of the garage, a laneway he guessed to be the hospital service entrance. Once again he yanked the steering wheel and raced into the service laneway coming to a screeching halt just behind the brick garage.

They jumped from the car and ran to the side of the garage to peer out onto Cathcart.

The police sirens were now much louder, maybe a block away.

In two, maybe three seconds the Mercedes roared onto Cathcart. Fishtailing out of control on wet pavement, the vehicle skidded toward the low-level flatbed attached to a Freightliner tractor on the left side of Cathcart. Both loading ramps were down, resting on the pavement. The vehicle's driver-side wheels caught the flatbed's right ramp, propelling it up onto the flatbed floor and leaving only the passenger-side wheels running on the pavement below. Momentum drove the vehicle the length of the flatbed until it crashed into a steel header with enough force to flip it onto its roof and make it skid thirty feet before coming to a complete halt. Its two occupants hung limp upside down, held in place only by seatbelts.

For a few moments St. James and Anna just stared at the smoking wreckage, stunned. Liquid dripped from the rear, sparkling in the wake of streetlights, like a calm lake under a full moon. But it wasn't a lake. It was gasoline. A small fire broke out around the buckled engine hood, and two minutes later the entire front end was engulfed in flames. Seconds after that an explosion completely destroyed the vehicle, lighting up half of Cathcart Street.

# Chapter 23

It was 2:00 when the firemen, police, and paramedics finally finished with the crash scene.

Three police cars arrived seconds after the explosion, paramedics and firemen shortly thereafter. Two firemen sprayed the wreckage and surrounding properties, containing the fire until it burned itself out approximately fifteen minutes later. Smells of smoke and burnt rubber filled the air, and water spewing from a pumper truck flooded the west end of Cathcart.

Looking very much the loser in a demolition derby, the Mercedes was unrecognizable, almost every surface dented, its roof pushed in touching the dash, paint burnt from most of its body. One wheel, blown clear, had rolled forty feet down the street; the remaining three were completely melted, rims still bolted to the charred vehicle.

Onlookers came from houses along Cathcart, some in nightclothes, obviously awakened by the explosion, others from Sussex, most likely from a night at the pub.

Two policemen cordoned off the area with yellow tape and identified evidence to be logged, marked, photographed, and then placed into sterilized containers for the lab to examine. Potential evidence for criminal charges, or lawsuits, or insurance claims, whatever followed.

A paramedic gently guided Anna to a green-and-white fully equipped emergency unit where she sat in back on a gurney while he bandaged her head, administered a sedative, and monitored her blood pressure. A second paramedic asked to check St. James, but he refused.

When the Mercedes had sufficiently cooled, firemen and police used the jaws-of-life to remove the two severely burnt bodies and carried them away in body bags.

The detective-in-charge was a plainclothes officer named Mark Spencer, a man in his early forties, of light complexion with thick blond hair and a scar over his left eye. Muscular. Thorough. St. James thought him good at what he did.

Spencer grilled St. James on the incident, taking detailed notes as St. James recounted every moment of the evening as best he could.

"Do you have any idea who might have wanted to do this?" Spencer asked, scratching his head with a pen.

"That would be a very long list," St. James replied nonchalantly, brushing dirt from his sports jacket.

Spencer didn't care for the flippant answer to his serious question. St. James caught the irritated look and quickly explained. It turned out Spencer had heard of him from police chief Carl Howowitz, whom St. James had met at Pierre's barbecue the previous summer.

Spencer relaxed as he listened to St. James's explanation. "I see why it would be a very long list," he said with a smile. "Man in your line of work would have more than his share of enemies."

St. James nodded. "Unfortunately. Goes with the territory."

"Once I type up your statement," Spencer said, "I'll need you to come by the station to verify and sign it. Meantime, if you can think of anything else, here's my card."

Spencer paused and looked toward the paramedic truck where Anna was being treated.

"A miracle no innocent people were killed tonight," he mused and turned to St. James.

"You should get your lady friend home soon. She'll be traumatized, for sure. I'll have someone drive you. We'll flatbed your car to the compound. Our technical people will want to look it over for evidence."

St. James nodded. "That'll be fine, detective. Thank you. I'm sure we'll be speaking."

They shook hands.

The pain from St. James's ribs was excruciating. Holding his side tightly, he walked gingerly toward the paramedic truck where he found Anna hooked up to a blood pressure machine, the paramedics checking one last time. 139/82 came up on the screen as St. James approached the rear of the vehicle.

"She's out of danger. Blood pressure was out of sight first reading. She can go now," the paramedic said. "I gave her a sedative. She'll sleep for a good twelve to fourteen hours, maybe longer. Her head will be badly bruised tomorrow. Here's the name of the sedative."

He handed over a piece of paper, which St. James shoved into his pocket without looking.

"Her doctor will want to know what it was. She should be seen tomorrow to get a prescription, most likely a lighter one, not as strong as the one we just administered. The trauma will have dwindled some by tomorrow, but she'll have trouble sleeping for a few days. Give her Tylenol Extra Strength for the whiplash. You should have your chest X-rayed too: I suspect you have a cracked rib."

St. James nodded and thanked him.

Anna mumbled something, sounding more drunk than sedated.

A police car pulled alongside, and St. James helped Anna into the backseat. 700 Sussex was just minutes away.

When they arrived at the condo building St. James asked the night concierge to fetch a wheelchair, and it wasn't long before he returned wheeling a collapsible one. He helped St. James transfer Anna to the chair from the car.

St. James thanked both the policeman and the concierge, then wheeled Anna onto the elevator, up to the fifth floor, and into the condo where he slipped off her clothes and slid her into bed as gently as he could. She mumbled several words. Only his name was audible.

It was 2:45 a.m.

With Anna resting comfortably St. James went into the kitchen, opened the liquor cabinet, and poured a double Macallan Sienna single malt. It was a special bottle, not for sharing, and only dipped into after unsuccessful attempts were made on his life. It was a ritual, a celebration, his way of thanking God for survival. And he did thank God he had had the same bottle for five years.

St. James would never admit it, but attempts did rattle him — a lot. For several minutes he shook, sitting in the living room partially lit by streetlights and passing automobile headlights streaming in from Sussex.

*Would be a very long list,* he had said to Spencer. *Could have been anyone.*

"Who?" he wondered aloud. "Nells? Dunning? Or maybe Stern? What about the Stevens case? Could it be someone from that? Don't think so. Haven't pissed anyone off, yet. CISI? No, just beginning. Maybe someone further in the past. Someone harbouring a grudge. God knows I gave a lot of people good reason."

St. James smiled inwardly when he realized he was talking out loud.

Now there were things to do. Things he didn't have to do yesterday. For one thing he had to call the insurance company to report the accident. No accident, but still, it had to be reported. He had the police report number; that would be the first thing they'd ask for. And, he had to get the car appraised for the cost to restore it to pristine condition.

His side continued to throb. He went into the bathroom, retrieved a bottle of extra-strength Tylenol from the medicine cabinet, and popped three, swallowing them with the aid of a drop of Scotch.

He finished the double hit of expensive Scotch and considered a second. But his ritual was only one double per close call. That's how he knew how many close calls there had been. Seven hundred fifty millilitres translated into just under twenty-six ounces on the old scale, still his way of thinking. An estimated four ounces left after tonight meant twenty-two consumed. Assuming a double was approximately three ounces that roughly translated into seven attempts on his life, maybe eight, not sure, he didn't use a jigger. He reckoned that was about right. On that thought, he went to bed.

# Chapter 24

Saturday morning St. James woke at noon. It hit him as soon as his eye met the large red numbers on the bedside clock. *Pierre.* He had arranged a 9:30 tee-off for them the previous day. He was now two and a half hours late. DuPont would have been on time; he was always on time.

St. James tried to get out of bed without disturbing Anna, but the chest pain caused him to flop backwards on the pillow. Anna didn't stir. He persisted, succeeding only on the third try. He scuffed into the living room holding his side, grabbed the phone, and punched in Pierre's cell.

"I heard you're having barbecue thugs for breakfast," he said with a chuckle. "*Pardonnez-moi* if I skip the invitation."

"You know?" St. James blurted.

"Superintendent phoned early this morning and told me what happened."

"So you weren't waiting for me at the golf club?"

DuPont heard the stress in St. James's voice.

"No. *Mon ami*, don't worry," he said quickly. "When I heard I knew you wouldn't be there. But I'm still pissed."

St. James was incredulous with Pierre's response. "Why?"

"Because now I have to help my wife garden all day instead of enjoying a game of golf with you," DuPont said, again with a chuckle. "You owe me two golf games now."

St. James sighed.

"Okay, Pierre. Thanks."

With that St. James disconnected.

He winced with pain once again.

He punched in his insurance broker's number. They weren't open on Saturdays, but he figured he'd leave a message anyway; they'd have it first thing Monday morning, one less thing for him to worry about.

Favouring his side meant basic hygiene took longer than usual, and it was 1:30 by the time he managed to shower, shave, and poach an egg.

He checked on Anna. She was still sleeping. Now he was conflicted. Paramedics wanted her to see a doctor today, but St. James had no idea who her doctor was. At the same time she needed to sleep as long as possible, essential for the healing process. In the end he concluded the doctor was more important. She could sleep later.

Doctors didn't keep weekend hours, but some medical clinics did. St. James found one online in the Bank Street area. He tapped the clinic number and spoke with a lady named Peggy who heard about the crash driving to work.

St. James described Anna's state and Peggy strongly urged him to bring her to the clinic as soon as possible. "She could have a concussion, which can be quite serious."

"Okay. We'll be there as soon as we can," St. James said and disconnected.

Throbbing ribs made it difficult to breathe, but St. James thought he could stand it long enough to have Anna looked after. He was about to take three more extra-strength Tylenol when the phone rang. Smythe.

"Hey man, I just heard the news. You okay? How's Anna?"

"We're okay. Anna's still sleeping. She's quite traumatized and has a nasty gash and bruise on her forehead. Paramedics gave her a sedative around two this morning. Been sleeping ever since."

"What about you?"

"Ribs hurt like hell, other than that I'm fine."

"Good. Man, you had me worried."

"Had myself worried. Have to go by the police station to sign a statement and get Anna to a clinic when she wakes up. Not a good day."

"Do they know who the two roasted guys were?"

"Too badly burnt, no identification. The detective said DNA and dental records would be necessary in this case."

"Doesn't matter anyway," Smythe said matter-of-factly. "Hired guns. Probably nobodies from the United States. We want the guys who hired them."

"Agreed. But that's for another day."

They disconnected.

St. James heard Anna stir.

"Wait for my help," he shouted, "you'll be too wobbly on your own."

He rushed down the hall as quickly as he could and found Anna sitting on the edge of the bed.

"Tell me it was all just a bad dream, St. James," she mumbled, her words barely audible.

St. James's voice was soft as he took her hand. "Afraid not, darling."

He sat on the edge of the bed and wrapped his arms around her. She buried her head in his chest, whimpering. He held her for a long time without speaking.

Finally he said softly, "I've made arrangements to have you seen at a clinic this afternoon, so we have to get you dressed and arrange a taxi. Are you able to shower on your own?"

"Think so."

"I'll follow you to the bathroom just in case."

St. James helped her stand. She grabbed the doorjamb to steady herself and slowly moved toward the bathroom. St. James thought her stable enough as he eyed her walk.

"I'll get clean clothes from your suitcase. You stand in the shower for a while. Hot water will loosen the muscles, help you relax. Don't let the hot spray hit the wound. Could sting, maybe start the bleeding again."

"Okay," she whispered.

Anna was in the shower for a good twenty minutes, and each time St. James checked, she was okay. Thirty minutes passed before she emerged fully dressed and looking very pale.

"While you were showering, I called a taxi. Should be down there now."

He helped with her coat, grabbed his own, locked the condo, and pushed the elevator button for ground. Helping Anna into the taxi, St. James recited the address to the driver, and they pulled into the clinic parking lot ten minutes later.

At first St. James asked the driver to wait, but then changed his mind. It could be a while, especially if the waiting room was crowded. So he gave him a twenty for coffee and donuts and asked him to be back in half an hour. The driver nodded with a smile when the twenty caught his eye.

Turns out there were only two people in the waiting room, and the counter card said two doctors were on duty, both facts that greatly improved Anna's chances of being seen quickly.

Peggy remembered St. James's call and talked as if they were celebrities. Main news of the day. She handed him a form to fill in Anna's medical history and medications. Anna struggled to focus. St. James completed the form and returned it to Peggy.

Five minutes later Anna was called in to see Dr. Singh and she shuffled into the examining room, where she remained for twenty minutes. When she emerged, a fresh bandage had replaced the one paramedics had applied the night before. Dr. Singh followed close behind.

"Are you the gentleman who brought Miss Strauss?" she asked in a soft pleasant Indian accent.

"I am."

"She told me what happened. Are you all right?"

"I have a couple of sore ribs. That's about it."

Dr. Singh stepped closer and lifted St. James's golf shirt to gently touch the side he favoured. He flinched with pain. "Let me give you an X-ray requisition. There're a few places you can go. Addresses are on the bottom of the form. You should go as soon as possible. If ribs are broken, you may need to be strapped."

St. James nodded but said nothing.

"Here is a prescription for Miss Strauss," she said. "Two pills at bedtime. She needs a week's bed rest and shouldn't be left alone. She may experience flashbacks. Someone should be close by to keep an eye on her."

She handed St. James the X-ray requisition and Anna's prescription. They thanked Dr. Singh and said goodbye to Peggy as they left the clinic.

The taxi was faithfully waiting for them. On the way home they stopped at Shoppers Drug Mart long enough for Anna's prescription to be filled and to purchase a supply of replacement bandages; then it was straight back to the condo.

This time Anna didn't need a wheelchair.

When they entered the condo she said in a weak voice, "I'm going to bed, Hamilton."

"Okay, dear. Do you want something to eat first? You've had nothing since dinner last night."

"No thanks. Not hungry."

St. James remembered he had promised to sign a formal statement for Spencer today. He called the police station and learned Spencer was off. The duty sergeant said it would be okay to leave it for a day or two. He would leave a message for Spencer that St. James had called.

Now St. James needed to think about Monday, Anderson, and the CISI director interviews. Anna couldn't be left alone. He couldn't ask his sister, Betty, to stay with her, they'd never met. Both would be uncomfortable under the circumstances, and Betty was scary at the best of times.

Once again St. James was conflicted: begin the CISI assignment in Toronto Monday or cancel the trip altogether to look after Anna? If he went, his mind would be on Anna, not the interviews. He wouldn't concentrate, ask the right questions, interpret the answers, nuances and body language of interviewees. If he stayed home, he could do the interviews by Skype while keeping an eye on Anna.

He decided cancelling the trip was the right thing to do. So, he emailed Juanita Mendoza to ask for phone numbers and Skype addresses for each director he was to interview. He would stick to the Monday schedule, but by Skype rather than in person. Some body language would be lost, but the job would proceed without risk to Anna. That's the way it was going to be, whether Anderson liked it or not.

# Chapter 25

The condo phone rang, and St. James answered.

Smythe said, "Did you get Anna to a doctor?"

"Just back. She's gone to bed."

"What are you doing now?"

St. James winced. "Sitting here holding my ribs, what do you think?"

Smythe ignored the sarcasm. "I have a few things on Stevens I'd like to go over with you. Are you up for that or do you want me to wait a couple days?"

St. James thought for a long moment. He wasn't feeling up to preparing for CISI. He'd done all he could for Anna; sleep was now her most important ally. And Dr. Singh said she shouldn't be left alone, so he wasn't about to leave for X-rays. It was down to Smythe or the television, and he decided Smythe would be the more entertaining of the two.

"Come over, Louis, and we'll chat for a bit. I'll just take more Tylenol."

"Okay man. Be there as soon as I can."

St. James cradled the phone and decided to lie on the couch until Smythe arrived.

It was twenty minutes before the buzzer sounded, and Smythe barged in with a laptop under one arm and a mountain of files under the other. He parked himself at the dining table and spread everything out so it could all be viewed at once. There was the code he had written on pink paper, several sheets of notes, website references, and photocopies of sites themselves. And, for the next thirty minutes, Smythe spieled off everything he had done, the logic he had used, and dead ends he had encountered as he tried to decipher each section of the code. The whole enchilada. Then he focused on the code itself.

*(g,cnbtkyk1,j), (ABA#021000089-36148883-012-67141-co-na-csprite1), (Virgo23+7+8+4+6+3), (G, F, D, C, F), (1104-419, 1130-1930, 700-1106, 145, 905), (U3743-5847, A3570-B0112, D4883-1916, A194, A3657) (A21+11)*

"As I explained before, the centre part, '*cnbtkyk1*', of the first section, '*g,cnbtkyk1,j*', is the SWIFT code for the Cayman National Bank. Antoinette said it's the main branch. I don't know what the '*g*' before or the '*j*' after mean.

"Whoever used the confidential transaction ID '*ABA#021000089*', which is the beginning of the second section, used it at the main branch. I don't know for sure but the middle number, '*36148883*', I think is some sort of temporary receiving account that accepts all transfers before they're allocated to designated client accounts. So, we have location, confidential ID, and a set of digits, '*012-67141*', confirmed by the bank to be an account number. We just don't know whose account it is. We have no clue what the last part of section two is, '*co-na-csprite1*'. It has to tie into the transaction ID and account number somehow: it's within the same parentheses."

"I see your logic but I'm not so sure."

Smythe paused to gather his thoughts.

"Go on," St. James said anxiously.

"The part you don't believe is the next section, the third section. You don't like the idea of Virgo referring to the astrological sign."

Wincing once again, St. James said, "Convince me."

"Virgo begins on August 23. Because the whole section is bracketed I believe it's meant to be read as one unit, the same as section two."

"And what would that be?"

"Just as I said when we talked by phone, I am now certain they are dates."

"Dates?"

"Yes, dates. The August 23 plus 7 is August 30, the day the crime was discovered. August 30 plus 8 is September 7. September 7 plus 4 is September 11, 9/11 as we now know it. But I'm certain this has nothing to do with 9/11. It's just a date, a coincidence. September 11 plus the next digit, which is 6, brings us to September 17. And finally, September 17 plus 3 is September 20. Incremental dates for events, or commands to be enacted. Five dates."

Smythe pointed to the pink paper.

"Now look at the next section, section four. '(G, F, D, C, F)', five letters separated by commas.

"Now look at the fifth section, '(1104-419, 1130-1930, 700-1106, 145, 905).' Five sets of numbers also separated by commas.

"Look at section six, '(U3743-5847, A3570-B0112, D4883-1916, A194, A3657).' Five sets of letters and numbers again separated by commas. Whatever's taking place is taking place in fives. Each successive section most likely builds on the previous, in some way or another. If we solve one, the rest should come, maybe not easy, but easier."

"Maybe," St. James said. "What about the last section, section seven? '(A21+11).' It breaks the rhythm of fives."

"That's tough," Smythe said, scratching his head. "Haven't gotten that far yet."

"Okay. Let's stay with your theory of fives for the moment. What would make sense? Five commands?"

"Or five actions?" Smythe offered.

"Or five actions for five people?" St. James countered. "One of which would be a transfer of money to that account number with the confidential ID 'ABA#021000089'."

Anna crept down the hall and stood behind Smythe and St. James.

"I was wondering who you were talking to out here," she said to Hamilton in a weak voice.

Smythe and St. James both jumped at the same time.

"Anna!" Smythe said, lunging to hug her. "You've had a rough time."

"A bit," she said. "I'm feeling better now. Now that I've slept some."

Smiling faintly at Smythe as she touched his three-day-old stubble. "I appreciate your concern."

Anna turned to St. James.

"I'm feeling a little hungry now. I think I could eat something. Maybe a sandwich."

"There's sliced chicken and roast beef in the refrigerator. I'll make you one."

"No, I'm okay to do it. I need something to do. You guys are in the middle of something anyway. I'll make it."

"Sure?"

"Sure."

Smythe and St. James went back to discussing Stevens but kept a close eye on Anna.

When Anna had made a roast beef sandwich and poured a glass of water, she sat at the table opposite Smythe. She had removed the bandage to clean the wound. It wasn't as bad as St. James thought it would be. More of a bruise, large and purple with a long half-moon cut in the centre.

Anna ate slowly, chewing every bite several times as though her mouth was sore and the sandwich was rubber. St. James looked for signs of instability.

Anna spotted Smythe's pink paper.

"Is this the famous code you keep talking about, Hamilton?"

"It is," he said.

She slid the paper closer to her plate and studied it while she ate. Smythe and St. James went over a number of possibilities.

Suddenly Anna said, "I know what this is."

"What?" Smythe and St. James blurted at the same time.

She held the paper up so they could see and pointed to what Smythe and St. James were calling section six.

"What do you mean you know what it is?" Smythe asked incredulously.

St. James sensed Smythe's fear a waitress might decipher a code in minutes that he couldn't in weeks. Her being a professional researcher didn't necessarily extend to breaking codes.

"These are airline flights. Look." She pointed to '*U3743-5847*.' "Those are United Airlines Flights 3743 and 5847. Two numbers separated by a dash with a letter in front of the first number only and not the second means a connecting flight with the same airline. If that had been U3743-A5847, a passenger would leave on United Airlines Flight 3743 and connect with American Airlines Flight 5847."

"What makes you so sure?" St. James asked cautiously.

"Remember I told you I worked for a company in Germany doing research and arranging executive travel? This is how we recorded flight information for senior executives."

Smythe's mouth was now wide open, eyes big as saucers, head rapidly whipping back and forth between Anna and St. James, like Don Knotts's character Barney Fife whenever he'd been duped.

St. James started to laugh.

"Louis," he gasped. "Stop that. Laughing hurts ... my ribs." Smythe stopped, but only after three more whips.

Anna ignored them both and continued to explain.

"'*A3570-B0112*' is American Airlines Flight 3570 connecting with British Airways Flight 0112. '*D4883-1916*' is two connecting Delta flights. '*A194*' and '*A3657*' are two separate American flights, separate bookings, maybe a day apart. They're separated by a comma not a dash."

St. James thought Smythe's eyes would pop out of his head.

St. James said, "Honey, can you show us? I believe you but there's a lot at stake here. We have to be absolutely certain."

"No problem. Louis, can I borrow your laptop?" she mumbled.

A stunned Smythe turned the computer around so the screen faced Anna. She punched in each airline's website and then the flights listed in the code, carefully noting details as she went. When she had worked her way through all the flights, she showed Smythe and St. James.

The first flight, U3743, was United's from Atlanta to Chicago, connecting to Fargo on U5847. The second flight was American Flight 3570 from Pittsburgh to JFK, connecting to Heathrow on British Airways Flight 0112. D4883, a Delta flight from Columbia, South Carolina, to Atlanta, connecting with Delta 1916 to Denver. A194, an American flight from Miami to Baltimore. A3657, American from Baltimore to Toronto.

"Well," St. James said, shaking his head. "That's wonderful, Anna. You're wonderful. Isn't she wonderful, Louis?" he said with a huge grin.

"She's wonderful," Smythe said slowly, sounding robotic. "But what does it tell us?"

St. James felt the damage to Smythe's pride. It would heal in time, he hoped.

"Now we have to figure what sections four and five are," St. James said, trying to refocus Smythe.

Smythe regained his composure, at least enough to come around the table and look over Anna's shoulder at section five.

"If your theory of dashes and commas holds true for every section, what does that tell us about section five?" he asked Anna.

"Not sure."

Smythe's eyes moved back and forth between the pink paper and Anna's scribbled flight notes a number of times.

Showing renewed excitement, Smythe blurted, "Section five shows the flight times for section six.

"Look: if you add colons and remove the dashes, each number matches the fight times you noted. 1104-419 becomes 11:04 and 4:19, flight times for U3743 and U5847; Atlanta to Chicago and Chicago to Fargo!"

# Chapter 26

Arthur Spance's 275-pound frame more than covered the bar stool in Earle's Bar & Grill, a fixture of one of Boston's seediest districts. His dirty grey overalls, long, matted red hair, and scruffy beard made him look more like a beggar than a man just released from prison. Short of breath and wheezing, he was drinking a pint of Coors.

A thin, six-foot man with close-cropped grey hair and missing two front teeth sat on the stool next to Spance. Eyes sunken, wild and dark. Face badly scarred, probably from defending himself in prison. The few teeth he did have were brown from years of smoking and lack of care.

Spance wheezed, "When did you get out?"

"Four months ago," the thin man said, scratching week-old stubble with one hand, holding a pint of Guinness with the other.

"Heard you had it rough in the joint. Ganged up on pretty bad," Spance said, sounding in need of oxygen.

"Nothing I couldn't handle," the thin man replied gruffly.

Located in the slums of Boston, Earle's Bar & Grill's rundown building had an unsavoury history dating back to the 1940s, probably the last time it was painted. Bar stools, badly worn and wobbly, were completely devoid of varnish. Booths were covered in initials of disrespectful patrons. The floors were filthy. Smells of stale beer and urine hit anyone who dared darken the door. The place catered to ex-cons, thugs, and gangs. Only the tough ventured inside, that is, if they weren't beaten and robbed before they got there.

"Where's Nells?" Spance said, straining to control his wheezing. The thin man drank Guinness. "Ain't comin'."

"Ain't comin'! What do you mean ain't comin'?"

The thin man turned and looked wild-eyed at Spance.

"Just what I said. Ain't comin'!" he barked, wiping beer froth on a dirty sleeve.

"Why? He hates Slate just as much as the rest of us."

"I know. He's got something else going. Another job, I think."

"Why aren't we in on it, then?" Spance asked in a dejected tone.

"Think he wants to break away from us, Arthur. Try something new."

"Shit. I thought we were a good team."

"Getting caught doesn't make a good team, Arthur," the thin man mused with a forced grin. He downed more Guinness. "Up to this point we've been caught every single time."

After a few minutes Spance asked, "Do you know where he's living?"

The thin man cleared his throat and drank more beer. "Someone said Chicago, working construction, but I haven't talked to him since I got out."

Spance nodded. "Where are Cliff and Jeremy?"

"They'll be along shortly, I suspect."

"Good. We've got planning to do. I want to get on with it."

"Just cool your jets. We're going to take our time with this one," the thin man barked sharply.

"What about St. James?" Spance wheezed.

"I have a man watching him."

# Chapter 27

Smythe left shortly after the section five and six breakthrough and headed to a party at a friend's house. St. James figured that was a good thing. Being shown up by a waitress would set off a certain amount of brooding in a guy as proud as Smythe. A couple of cold ones and a few laughs would be just the ticket for his busted ego.

Anna wanted nothing more to eat after her sandwich, so St. James made a soothing cup of herbal tea for her and a small chicken stir fry for himself.

She wasn't content to stay in bed as Dr. Singh had ordered. Instead she lay on the couch while St. James waited on her with tea, water, and juice. No wine, not with the medication she was taking. He, on the other hand, had received no such medical advice, nor was he on any prescribed medication. But he *was* in pain. And as far as he was concerned, that was a license to self-medicate. So, he took great liberties with Chianti while they watched an action movie on the large projection screen.

They awoke on Sunday morning to a gorgeous fall day. St. James opened the living room doors and eyed two fluffy white lines ripping across the eastern sky.

*People flying somewhere,* he thought.

The fall sun sat high over Ottawa's cloudless sky, keeping watch over orange and yellow leaves floating aimlessly in the warm, gentle breeze, a sea of unmanageable stringless kites.

Sounds of church bells drifted in from the cathedral down Sussex; sidewalks were filling with people, some scurrying to mass, some piling into the bookstore across the street, others most likely looking for a satisfying Sunday brunch.

After he and Anna had toast and coffee he said, "Since you're feeling better, do you mind if I slip out to the police station to review my statement?"

"Only if I come too," she said with a bit more spark than Saturday.

"But … you know what Dr. Singh said."

"I feel fine now," she argued. "Anyway, I should review the statement too. After all, we were both witnesses. What if I don't agree with what you say? Wouldn't police want both versions?"

"Aw hell, get your coat. Don't blame me if you pass out in the police station."

Fifteen minutes later the taxi pulled in front of the police station on Elgin. The duty sergeant for the day handed St. James a brown envelope containing two copies of the statement left by Detective Spencer. They sat on a bench in the foyer, each reviewing a copy.

"Were we rammed two or three times, Hamilton?"

"Three. Twice in Gatineau and once on Sussex."

"That's right. I was confused for a moment."

"Pretty hard to argue facts when you're confused," he quipped.

Anna's smile suggested her usual playfulness was slowly making a comeback. "Oh, shut up."

"Is that how you win an argument, by telling your opponent to shut up?"

"Don't know if I should arrest you two for disturbing my Sunday or get you a room," the duty sergeant said in a grumpy voice.

"Could go either way, officer," St. James said, grinning.

Spencer's chronology of events was well written and factual as far as they could see, so they signed off on it and gave one copy to the sergeant, keeping the second for their own records.

Outside the station Anna grabbed St. James's arm, turned to face him, and flashed a determined look. Her hair was flaring, unmanageable in the breeze, dark-brown eyes unwavering as she glared into his.

"Now it's your turn to be stubborn," she said.

"What do you mean?"

Feigning crossness, Anna said, "Since we were hit by that Mercedes, you've done everything for me and nothing for yourself. You've been holding on to your ribs since you woke up yesterday. I insist you get an X-ray right now! Tell me you're not going to argue."

"Absolutely not," he said calmly. "That would make me just as stubborn as you."

Her pretend crossness turned into frustration. "Ooooh ... you're incorrigible, Hamilton St. James!"

The only clinic he could think of that X-rayed on Sunday was the Heron Medical Group, a storefront on Bank. He hailed a taxi one block north of the police station, then googled the clinic's address and gave it to the driver.

The clinic wasn't all that busy, so St. James found himself on the X-ray table within five minutes. A lady named Amira with light-olive skin, dark eyes, and short black hair was the technician-on-duty. Her demeanor was cool; definitely not the friendly type. Amira didn't talk much. She just mumbled short commands.

"Lie on your back."

St. James did.

"Lie on your right side."

St. James did.

"Lie on your left side."

St. James did.

"Roll over on your stomach."

St. James did.

Finally Amira gave him permission to roll off the X-ray table and put his shirt back on.

Back in reception Amira said, "Results will be available to Dr. Singh in a couple of days."

St. James thanked her and off they went back to 700 Sussex.

When St. James unlocked the condo door, Anna immediately headed down the hall to pour a bath while he got started on the CISI case.

Before preparing tomorrow's interviews he decided to call Al Dunlop. Al was a friend, a straight shooter who wouldn't hold back whatever he thought, regardless of what was going on at CISI. St. James had once said, you ask Al his opinion, you'll get it, pure and simple.

St. James popped a couple more Tylenol, headed for the study, fired up the computer, and discovered an email from Juanita Mendoza listing director phone numbers. Attached was a note she had sent to everyone describing St. James and Anna's unfortunate Friday night. There were emails back from most directors expressing concern for their health and safety. St. James noted no such email from Graves or Blakie.

He tapped Dunlop's name into the database and a number popped up. He looked at his watch. Ten past three.

*Might be on the golf course.*

Dunlop picked up on the third ring.

"Do you have time to talk, Al?"

"I have about a half hour," he replied. "Are you and Anna all right?"

"We're fine. Anna is shaken with a bruised forehead, and I have a couple of sore ribs, that's all."

"That's enough," Dunlop said sympathetically.

St. James went straight to business.

"Al, I want your take on CISI before I start."

"Are you sure you want my biases?"

St. James pictured Dunlop grinning.

"I'll chance it. What's your view of Anderson?"

"He's a salesman. A bit of a control freak. Doesn't really trust his people. Double-checks everything they tell him with others."

"Isn't that smart?"

"To a point, but Cameron takes it to the minutiae, to things CEOs don't usually bother with."

"Like what?"

"Phoning plant managers to see if preventative maintenance was done on equipment the previous week, or if they're sure all inventory has been counted; normally the concern of the COO, not the CEO."

"I see. What about Blakie?"

"Cut from the same cloth. That's why they get along so well."

"What do you think Anderson might be keeping from the board?"

"Don't know if there *is* anything. That's why I recommended you."

"Let me put it another way: why is the board uneasy?"

"All through last year we were far from meeting the profit target. Then, in the last three months, profit suddenly jumped, and the company exceeded the budget at year-end by one per cent. We pressed Cameron for reasons for the dramatic turnaround. He chalked it up to expense trimming as well as year-end inventory adjustments. The auditors stated financial statements were presented fairly, but external board members remain unsettled. Timing and size of the adjustment was troublesome. There had never been an adjustment that size in company history."

"When Cameron was hired were his past positions thoroughly checked?"

"Glowing references," Dunlop said.

"You mean for his performance as vice-president of sales?"

"Yes. CISI sales were flat at the time, and it was his ability to drive revenue growth in previous positions that made him an attractive candidate."

"Did reference checks cover character?"

"I was on the search committee at the time and I don't recall anything negative."

St. James persisted. "But did anyone *actually* ask previous employers about his character?"

"The committee was assured by the firm that headhunted Anderson."

"Hmm. Okay. How is he compensated?"

"If I remember correctly, his salary is $800,000, plus stock options and a bonus. Typical compensation for public companies of this size."

"When was the last time his compensation was reviewed?"

"Last year. By an independent firm."

"Was there a written report?"

"Yes. Juanita can send you a copy, if you wish."

St. James spent the next fifteen minutes asking Al his perceptions of other board members and the overall management of the company. Dunlop felt the external directors were relatively strong and generally asked the right questions. The company was well managed and consistently profitable, though he thought the board could benefit from an independent review of its performance.

When the call ended, St. James wrote Juanita requesting the corporate strategic plan, the current year's business plan, and the report on Anderson's compensation, as well as all correspondence with the auditors. It was a start. As time went on he'd want more. There was always more.

Anna walked into the study. St. James noticed some colour had returned to her face: she looked more relaxed after the hot bath.

"How's it going?" she asked softly.

"Good. I made a start on CISI. Requested documents from the company and conducted one interview."

"You've been busy," she said with a faint grin.

"Indeed I have, my dear," he said smiling.

"Think I'll read for a while. I'm at a good place in my book. I'll be in the living room if you need me."

"I have a couple hours work. Then we'll have supper, either here or out, whichever you like."

Anna said, "I also want to check my apartment. I need fresh clothes if I am going to stay longer."

St. James spent the next two hours preparing Monday's interviews. External board members would be first; Cameron last. He wanted eight opinions of Cameron before he interviewed him. Cheryl Tomkins first, then work his way up to Graves. No particular reason. Just seemed a good place to begin.

At 4:30 they took a taxi to Anna's apartment, where St. James checked if anything had been disturbed while Anna packed things for the week. He didn't tell Anna that whoever had tried to run them off the road might also attempt to kidnap her to lure him into a trap. She wouldn't take that well. And the more he thought about it, the more additional protection seemed necessary. He'd never forgive himself if something happened to her because he didn't take the proper precautions.

Anna turned the heat down when she had finished gathering what she needed, and they descended stairs and jumped into a waiting taxi.

Time for more Tylenol.

Before dinner Anna phoned the Dirty Duck to say she wouldn't be at work the coming week. She explained the crash, head wound, and trauma she'd suffered. The doctor had ordered bed rest. Sid acknowledged it all with a grunt.

When she disconnected, Anna just shook her head.

At six they walked next door to the Château Laurier for a quiet dinner at Wilfrid's, eating mostly in silence. Anna didn't feel like talking, and St. James had CISI on his mind. They were home in a little over an hour.

At 2:00 in the morning St. James awoke to Anna sobbing: the flashback Dr. Singh had warned about. He held her for twenty minutes or so until the fear faded, and she drifted back to sleep. He wondered if this would be the first of many.

First thing Monday morning, St. James booted his computer to an email from Jason Williamson listing shareholders for the 139 companies Jensen had invested in. Jason's nephew had completed the searches sooner than expected. St. James printed the document, and one by one focused on each name. Some names were familiar, people who had signed documents he had found in the boxes in Nathan Strong's office. Stevens's name didn't appear anywhere.

*Dead end for Jason.*

St. James forwarded the list to Nathan for his partners to check, then did the same for Slate, DuPont, and David Kingston at Scotland Yard, and, finally, Mary DeSilva. Any one of the names could appear in multiple databases.

# Chapter 28

St. James's first interview was at 9:00 with Cheryl Tomkins. He called her on Skype, so he'd have a visual. Not as good as face to face, but much better than just on the phone. He'd guessed Cheryl to be about fifty-five. Not the most feminine of ladies. Brown hair cut short, parted on the right, no makeup and dressed in what looked like a man's grey suit, white shirt, black Alaskan cufflinks, and wide black tie. She looked like a model from an old haberdashery magazine.

As former US ambassador to Portugal she had helped negotiate fishing treaties between the two countries, gaining significant industry knowledge along the way to make her an attractive CISI board candidate.

Cheryl was a talker. St. James expected this to a certain extent, ambassadors being politicians in disguise. Unfortunately, great talkers also tend to hijack meetings, which is exactly what happened to St. James.

The first fifteen minutes saw Cheryl boasting of her many diplomatic accomplishments. Meetings with the president of the United States, the prime minister of Portugal, and various other heads of states. What she didn't know was that St. James knew the last agreement between Portugal and the United States didn't go well, ending with the president quietly replacing her as ambassador. It was amusing as he listened to her speak as if still in Washington's good graces.

He tried numerous times to wrest control of the meeting from her. Finally, after several attempts, he shoehorned in a question.

"What are your impressions of Cameron?"

"Very capable CEO. Strong public face for the company. Very engaging. Has a tendency to get too far down in the weeds though, if you know what I mean."

St. James nodded.

"He rejuvenated the sales group. Developed a strategic plan that was unanimously accepted by the board and is vigorously pushing through its implementation."

"What, if anything, makes you uneasy?"

"Well, we exceeded budget last year, which seems a miracle to me. Profit was behind after nine months. Then, all of a sudden, we exceeded for the year. He's given logical explanations but keeps selling us on reasons, as if we don't believe him. The irony is we believed him at first, but after repeating himself in different ways we began to have doubts. Does that make sense?"

"Perfect sense. Like a friend of mine, a judge, who once said that when a witness begins an answer with 'to tell you the truth,' I expect the next words out of his mouth to be a lie."

"Yes! Good analogy," she said, sounding pleased he got her point.

"Is there anything else?" St. James asked.

"Nothing I can think of at the moment, related to Cameron, that is."

"Related to anyone else?" he pressed.

"While I respect all my board colleagues, I think Blakie's too close to Cameron. Sometimes I wonder about his objectivity. He refuses to challenge Cameron on anything. And becomes annoyed if the rest of us do. I find that odd considering it's a director's responsibility to challenge management performance."

St. James continued. "What about the chairman?"

"Consults as he should. Stickler for detail."

"Isn't that a good quality for a chairman?"

"Maybe stickler is the wrong word. Maybe some mixture of 'officious' and 'pretentious' stirs up a more accurate picture. Or maybe ... maybe he's just British."

Just as St. James smiled the Skype connection flickered, creating a wavy return smile from Cheryl.

Over the next half hour or so he asked a number of questions concerning typical board meetings, who participated the most, who was constructive, who was not, then thanked Cheryl for her time and disconnected.

He went into the kitchen and found Anna sitting on an island stool still in her housecoat, coffee in hand, and reading a book.

*Even in the raw she's attractive.*

"Hi there," she said, her robust smile showing signs of recovery. "Heard you on the phone. I gather you've started your interviews."

"First one of the day now behind me."

"Appreciated you comforting me last night," she said softly. "Maybe I'm not as ready to go home as I thought."

St. James smiled. "Never thought you were. Was just waiting for you to realize it yourself."

She threw him a look that only Anna could, a cross between a smirk and a scrunched face, with a slight tilt of the head. St. James was afraid to ask what it meant. It couldn't be good.

He poured a coffee, kissed her gently, and returned to the study to Skype the next director. An email from Juanita with documents he had requested attached popped up on the laptop screen.

*Tomorrow's reading.*

The next three interviews went much faster than the first. For one thing, no one hijacked them like Cheryl Tomkins; big time-saver right there. And St. James seemed to develop an efficient rhythm with successive interviews on the same subject. The first was always the longest. The trailblazer. Successive ones were more focused, deeper dives into information learned from the first.

Nothing new was learned from Nancy Slitter, John Coughlin, or Harold Tewksbury. Next was Blakie. Because of his close relationship with Anderson, St. James left out questions around Anderson's competence and character. He treaded softly, wanting Blakie to accept him rather than obstruct the investigation.

St. James said, "I know from the website you own an HR consulting practice. Have you been practicing long?"

"About thirty years, I guess," Blakie replied in a brisk tone.

"Does your firm specialize in any particular area of HR?"

Blakie's tone sharpened. "Look, Hamilton, I'm a busy man, pressed for time. Is this call about my firm or CISI?" he snapped.

"Okay, David," St. James said sternly. "What do you think my focus should be?"

"I don't know why we're even doing this," he said abruptly. "Cameron's doing a great job. Revenues are up. Profit is up. Expenses are under constant review and kept to a minimum. The bank is happy. Shareholders are happy. What's the point of all this?"

"So, there's no room for improvement?" St. James interjected.

"I didn't say that," Blakie said defensively. "There's always something to improve on."

"Okay … So if you had to pick three areas Cameron could improve on, what would you say?"

"There might be one, but certainly not three."

St. James tried not to show his annoyance.

"And what would that be?"

"Communication," Blakie replied authoritatively.

St. James went no further. Communication was the answer everyone gave when they didn't have an answer. A general answer to a specific question amounts to no answer at all.

Andre Fox was more helpful. He led St. James through Anderson's employment contract, page by page. The independent compensation review recommended greater weight on Anderson's contribution to corporate profit, which Andre said had been unanimously accepted by the board.

St. James considered the potential impact.

*Definitely motivation to improve profit, but was it enough to make him manipulate the bottom line?*

An avenue to pursue.

St. James surprised himself by finishing all the interviews by 4:15; he thought for sure some would spill over into Tuesday. But common threads emerged more quickly than anticipated: concerns with the sharp profit turnaround during the last quarter of the fiscal year, and the close relationship between Anderson and Blakie.

Clearly, no one understood the year-end inventory adjustment. Even though adjustments were made every year, this was the largest in company history. $95 million additional inventory included in net profit. Prior years' adjustments had never exceeded $18 million. Huge discrepancy.

On Tuesday morning St. James called Marcel Lapointe, CISI's independent auditor, to explain his mandate. Marcel required CISI's permission to speak with him, which he obtained by email from the CFO while on the phone with St. James.

St. James purposely didn't tell Marcel he was a Certified Public Accountant: Marcel would have assumed him financially literate and concluded there was no need to explain accounting details to a fully trained professional, details where relevant clues could be buried.

That's exactly what St. James didn't want. He wanted inventory calculations explained step by step as if he were an untrained person off the street. Only then could he identify weak financial controls or places where manipulation might be hiding undetected.

St. James wanted to know the local times that trawlers tied up at processing plants around the world on count day, and what made Marcel confident that the inventory counts were accurate, priced correctly, and totaled to the amounts reflected on CISI's audited balance sheet.

Marcel pulled CISI audit files and walked St. James through the inventory adjustment over the phone. 175 million pounds of various species sitting on trawlers around the world, waiting to be unloaded on count day.

"Trawlers are counted late in the day," Marcel explained. "If you calculate the full cost to process a pound of ground fish, for example, you start with landed cost per pound of whole fish, 'round fish' it's called in the industry. Fish is cleaned, and waste, called offal, is converted into fish meal. What's left is pure fish meat, fillets you buy in stores ... 'yield,' it's called."

Marcel took St. James through last year's audit, taking care to explain inventory costing in detail, from raw fish landed to fillets delivered to grocery stores. He had found no errors in CISI calculations.

Marcel continued. "175 million pounds on trawlers and boats consisted of multiple species, ranging from monkfish to lobster, low to high value. Yield cost per pound was applied to processed pounds, labour and overhead added bringing the total adjustment to $95 million."

"Do you ever insist on an adjustment at CISI?"

"No, they adjust on their own. Model clients. Very conscientious about the quality of financial information. Wish all my clients were like them."

"Hmm."

St. James asked a few more technical questions, thanked Marcel for his time, and clicked off the call.

The message light flashed: a voicemail from Dr. Singh saying his ribs were badly bruised but not broken. They would take a month to heal completely.

St. James spent the rest of the day reading CISI's strategic plan, Anderson's employment contract and the independent remuneration study. The strategic plan was impressive.

*Aggressive, but achievable.*

He made notes of things to consider as he went. The plan called for revenue to double in seven years. But not all growth could be organic if CISI was to achieve that goal. The company would have to make acquisitions along the way. It would have to buy revenue in order to double in seven years.

*Only so many fish in the sea.*

St. James checked his watch.

He hadn't reported to Mary DeSilva as usual but had emailed to say more time was needed to study the Stevens code. Mary wouldn't be happy with just that. She'd expect more.

He tapped her number on his Samsung. First three tries, busy. She answered on the fourth. He explained in detail how sections of the code had been solved: transactions to an unknown person's bank account in Grand Cayman, airline flights and times, and that everything seemed to be happening in fives. Much to St. James's surprise, Mary was delighted.

"Do you have a sense Stevens was part of a scheme, Hamilton?" she said anxiously.

"Not at this point."

As with every other case the client hoped St. James would find the claim fraudulent or unsubstantiated, flawed in some way, enough to let Global off the hook for a $23-million payout. But there was no evidence to date one way or the other.

Before they clicked off, Mary said, "By the way, Hamilton, we don't know anyone on the list of shareholders for the 139 companies."

*Another avenue closed.*

Around 3:30 Anna wandered into the study.

"Hamilton, I'm feeling anxious. I don't think I can stay much longer just reading. I think I'll go home. Maybe do a short shift at the pub tomorrow."

St. James knew better than to argue.

"Tomorrow's Wednesday," he said. "Stay tonight. If you don't have a flashback, I'll take you home tomorrow. No argument. One more day's rest would make it five, about what I'd hoped for."

"Agreed," she said with a smile.

St. James found himself once again thinking that someone could kidnap Anna, use her for bait to flush him out. He concluded that now was the time to prepare for that eventuality.

"There's something I need to talk to you about," he said in a more serious tone.

Anna's smile disappeared.

# Chapter 29

St. James and Anna went into the living room and sat side by side on the black leather couch. Anna's tension meter was off the chart, anticipating the worst. So St. James wanted this over with, and quickly.

He took her hand. "The attempt to kill us last Friday night will not be the last."

"But those two guys are dead," she said anxiously.

St. James shook his head. "Just hired thugs, Anna. Dime a dozen. Whoever hired them will hire others."

A tear formed in each eye. "You're scaring the hell out of me, Hamilton."

"I know, that's why I waited until you felt better, until I thought you could handle it."

Anna became more distraught.

"I don't think I can handle this any time, feeling better or not."

"It's something we have to discuss. I need to know you're okay with engaging protection. It would give us peace of mind."

Anna wiped away tears.

"What protection?" she asked after a few seconds of sniffling.

"I have a friend, Erasmus White is his name, but he goes by the nickname Bulldozer. I just call him Dozer."

Anna's eyes lit up, a look somewhere between curious and amused. Still sniffling, she said, "You're joking, right?"

St. James didn't smile. "Not something to joke about. I met Dozer five years ago when I was working the Texas case. There were a number of threats against me. Bill Slate recommended him as the best to watch my back. So I hired him. We clicked, and I've used him a few times since … with great results."

"I'm scared to ask how he got his nickname."

"University years. The star of Toronto's football team. He made more touchdowns than anyone three years in a row. Bulldozed everyone in his way. His teammates nicknamed him Bulldozer for that reason. The name stuck. He's six-five, 275 pounds, with a black belt in karate. Shaved head. Gentle as a lamb, but scary as hell to look at. LL Cool J 3 point 0. He's the only one I would trust with someone as precious as you."

Anna made a slight attempt to smile. "You're a helluva salesman."

"You okay with this?"

"I'm okay. If you trust this guy that much, I guess I do too." She suddenly began to laugh.

"Why are you laughing?"

"Listening to your description of Dozer I just had a visual of him and Louis standing together, side by side."

St. James smiled and shook his head.

"Certainly a sight to behold, I can tell you that."

Erasmus "Bulldozer" White owned a mid-size detective, surveillance, and protection agency in Toronto. In fifteen years he'd built an operation from a one-man show to seventeen well-trained, highly effective operatives. Outstanding success branded it *the* firm for ethics and modern investigation and protection techniques. It focused mostly on commercial crime, leaving peephole business to lesser agencies.

Dozer handpicked new recruits and put them through advanced psychological testing to determine if they had the right temperament to make rapid lifesaving decisions under pressure. No panic allowed: panic costs lives, and that was never good for business.

If candidates survived the psychological testing, they went through an intense physical boot camp designed for Dozer by a friend in the US Marine Corps. Dozer demanded a sharp mind and a disciplined physical regime at all times. Those who didn't follow the program consistently were severed immediately. White Investigations Inc.'s brand was not to be compromised, not even for a minute. That was Dozer's promise to his clients, and himself. And a very firm promise it was. He constantly hammered it into his people: *Strong brands take years to build and minutes to lose.*

Physically, Bulldozer looked like someone who'd start a fight with anyone, anywhere, anytime. But nothing was further from the truth. A Big Brothers volunteer, Dozer was a strong role model for wayward boys who could have chosen a much different path. But not on Dozer's watch: he would see to that.

St. James remembered Dozer chasing a guy who stole a beggar's cash container in downtown Toronto. Chased the crook five blocks before tackling him, like the quarterback he once was. He wrestled the container back from the thug and returned it to the beggar, money intact, and including an extra fifty. The beggar didn't know if the fifty was Dozer's or a donation from the thief. St. James had no doubt it was the thief's money. Penance for wrongdoing. It was Dozer's way.

Anna was becoming more relaxed with the idea of protection, so St. James called Dozer to check his availability. Turned out he'd just finished a huge case in Vancouver and had some time to spare. St. James explained the situation and his concern for Anna's safety.

"Okay, man," Dozer said. "I'll fly to Ottawa tomorrow morning. Should be at your place shortly after eleven. You'll have the coffee pot on if you know what's good for you."

"Great. Do you want me to arrange accommodation?"

"No need. I have a brother living there. I'll bunk with him."

"I didn't know that," St. James said curiously.

"Thought I told you."

St. James wanted to work the CISI case on Thursday, so Dozer's timing was perfect. He sent an email to Anderson asking for a meeting Thursday morning. Anderson was available at ten for an hour. St. James confirmed.

He turned his attention back to Anna.

"Since you're anxious hanging around here, why don't we do dinner and a movie?"

Her face lit up.

"Oh, Hamilton, can we? That would be wonderful."

Anna was silent for a minute, then said, "On one condition."

"What's that?"

"That I pay. Lately you've been paying for everything. It's making me feel bad, like a kept woman."

St. James smiled. "Done."

He tapped "answer" on his vibrating cell.

Detective Spencer.

"Hamilton, just to let you know, we identified the two guys in the Mercedes."

"And?" St. James said anxiously.

"The driver was a Martin Clayton from Indiana. Passenger, Clint Wagner from South Dakota. Both small-time crooks. Obviously hired by a bigger gun."

"Any idea who?"

"No. Car was too far gone for the lab boys to find anything useful."

"Thanks for letting me know, Mark."

"One more thing before you go," Spencer said. "Your airbags and seatbelts were manually disconnected. These guys are serious."

# Chapter 30

Anna and St. James settled on Mel's Steak House and the latest James Bond movie for their evening out. St. James thought the diversion might boost Anna's spirits, or at least take her mind off her fears, if only for a couple of hours.

They talked about Dozer as they savoured Caesar salad, grilled striploin, and a bottle of Conquista Mendoza. What Anna should expect, how Dozer would interact with her.

"He'll shadow you wherever you go. Sometimes you'll see him, other times he'll just blend in with his surroundings, and you won't. Periodically he'll approach to make sure you're all right, to see if you've received any threatening texts, or phone messages, or emails. He watches for recurring faces in crowds, suspicious behaviour, that sort of thing. If he sees someone questionable, he'll track them. He may or may not confront them, depending on his assessment of the risk."

"What am I to do?" Anna asked.

"Nothing. Just go about your business as you always do. Forget Dozer is there."

Anna's face clouded. "Easier said than done, Hamilton. I'm scared. I'll show it. My face is an open book."

"Just do your best to act normal. Janice will teach Friday's class, so I can be in Toronto Thursday and Friday. Dozer will text me how you're doing. I don't know, but I could be back in Washington next week. Possibly Cayman too. If I do, I'll take you with me."

"That would be nice. What do I tell Sid?"

"Tell him the truth. You're in protection. He'll certainly wonder who Dozer is when he shows up at the pub. Should be good for a laugh when you see the look on Sid's face."

"Suppose you're right. Truth is always the best."

"Always works for me. Don't need a good memory to tell the truth," he said. "If Sid gives you trouble, I'll have a word with him."

"He might fire me."

"We'll cross that bridge if we come to it. Right now I just want to be sure you're safe."

Anna kissed him on the cheek.

"I'll have more research work for you. You'll be paid for that. So, for the moment you're not to worry about money. Okay?"

"Okay."

The movie was typical Bond, packed with action, beautiful women, and corny lines, and for two hours they forgot all about threats. It was 10:45 when St. James unlocked the condo door.

Feeling all the better from an excellent meal and an entertaining movie they sipped a small triple sec each and then turned in for the night.

On Wednesday morning St. James went into the study to make calls. The first three were to Cameron's previous employers with contact information Juanita had provided. He told the CEO of each reference company that he was auditing CISI's service providers and wanted to know if the search firm who recommended Anderson had asked about his character. Each confirmed that they had and that Anderson's character was above reproach.

Then he called the CEOs of Craven Chemicals, Craig Automotive, and Dusten Pharmaceuticals, all companies on whose boards Graves currently served. What kind of board member was he? Did he attend all the meetings? What did they think of his participation? His advice?

St. James lied, saying Graves was shortlisted for another board, and he wanted to check his performance with the boards he currently served on. All the responses were positive: no concerns.

St. James looked at his watch and quickly calculated the time difference: 4:00 p.m. in London. Good time to call Patricia Havelock. She answered right away, and they spoke for twenty minutes concerning the property worth £400,000 that Graves had tried to hide in the 1970s. His bankruptcy was long before Patricia's time, but she had obviously read the files thoroughly and was able to provide satisfactory answers to all St. James's questions.

Just as he disconnected from Patricia, the door buzzed.

"It's me," said a deep, baritone voice.

"Dozer?"

"Hey man, you were expecting maybe Flip Wilson?"

"Naw, he's dead."

St. James opened the door and Dozer appeared, larger than life, the very moment Anna came down the hall.

Anna froze instantly at the sight of Dozer.

"Oh my God, Hamilton! You weren't kidding!"

"This beautiful lady must be Anna," Dozer said, brushing past St. James to Anna. "Hamilton, you didn't tell me she was gorgeous."

St. James smiled. "I wanted you to help because of our friendship, not because you'd be protecting a beautiful woman."

Dozer's wide grin displayed brilliant white teeth. "Yes, but this is a bonus."

Anna's face lit up. "H-e-l-l-o you two, I'm standing right here. Stop talking as if I'm not."

"Forgive me," Dozer said softly as he gently took Anna's hand. "That was rude."

"Anna, did I mention he can charm a woman off her feet?"

"Must have slipped your mind," she said, smiling at Dozer. "But I'm liking it."

Dozer's touch was tender as he hugged her.

Anna made coffee while St. James and Dozer settled at the dining table. St. James took Dozer through every detail of the Stevens and

CISI cases, the police reports, and the names of the two guys burned in the Mercedes. Dozer would have to know everything. He'd likely be needed for more than just Anna's protection. Every case had its surprises, most of them unpleasant. And when they happened, St. James wanted Dozer by his side.

Dozer rubbed his shiny bald head. "Doesn't have to be someone from a current case, you know, Hamilton. Could be anybody you helped put away."

"Could be, I suppose. As a matter of fact, Inspector DuPont and I were talking recently about vengeful ex-cons who may have it in for us. Something to watch for."

Dozer nodded. "I'll get details on them later. Right now I'm interested in the two current cases."

"I just started on CISI. Not close to anything there yet. Odds favour the Stevens case. I'm a ways along there and have learned things that could make some people nervous."

"If you play the odds," Dozer said casually. "Let's spend a few days, see if any cockroaches crawl out of the woodwork. What I'll do now is check out this place. Then we'll go to Anna's. Examine windows and doors for vulnerability in both places. Who has a key to this place?"

"Just me, Louis, and Anna. Oh, and the cleaning lady, Mrs. Hendricks."

"How long she been your cleaning lady?"

"About two years."

"Hmm. Okay. I'd be more concerned if you had just hired her. Greater chance her being a plant for someone with ill intentions. If she was a plant two years ago something would have happened long before this."

Dozer slowly worked his way through the condo, room by room, thoroughly examining each as he went. Opening and closing windows and doors, checking wall thickness, assessing vulnerabilities from rooftops across the street.

"The area is well lit at night and there's a lot of day traffic," Dozer concluded. "It's not likely anyone would try something here. Too easy to be seen, get caught."

He turned to Anna. "Let's look at your place."

They taxied to Anna's apartment, and Dozer repeated the same examination he had conducted on St. James's condo while Anna and St. James waited in the sitting room. When Dozer finished, they all went outside where St. James and Anna waited by the curb while Dozer walked the perimeter of the building. Dozer returned minutes later shaking his head.

"I don't like it, Hamilton. I don't like it at all, not one bit," he said, continuing to shake his head. He pointed to the upper floor. "It's old and only two stories, easy to get into by the fire escape. Locks are cheesy and could be opened by any amateur. Windows are the old wooden-framed type, with rotting sills and puttied glass. I could put my fist through the wood anywhere. It's impossible to protect Anna here. An igloo would be harder to break into with a hot knife."

Anna frowned.

"Well, what do you suggest?" St. James asked.

"Two things."

"What?"

"First, Anna gets whatever she needs right now and moves in with you until this thing is over. I'll ask the concierge to watch people coming and going. Note unrecognizable characters and unusual behaviour. Only Spiderman could climb the outside of your building. The likelihood of anyone trying something there is remote. More than likely they'll wait until she's out of the building. Then, I'll be with her."

"What's the second thing?"

Dozer pointed to Anna's apartment. "Make the place look like Anna's still here. Three or four times a week I'll bring her over to enter the front door. That will give the impression she's coming home as usual. So, it has to be at her normal time. She'll go straight out the back. The yard is small and secluded: no one will see her there. I'll be waiting. There's an alleyway from the yard to the next street over where my car will be waiting to take her back to your place. When it snows her footprints will reinforce normal living patterns.

"I brought some new equipment with me, Hamilton. Left it with your concierge. Rotating timers for lights, television, and radio. Not the ones that come on the same time every day. Crooks know right away no one's home. No one turns on the lights at exactly the same time every day. Guy who invented them was terminally stupid." Anna's brow furrowed. "My timers activate randomly. As unpredictable as humans themselves. More believable.

"I also have special traps to put under windows, the most likely entry points. Least difficult to jimmy."

Anna was silent, digesting it all, evaluating what was happening to her world.

"These traps, are they legal?" St. James asked suspiciously.

"I can use them if I get written consent in advance from the guys they trap," Dozer said sarcastically. "Of course they're not legal."

Anna's brow furrowed again.

St. James smiled. "Thought so."

Dozer grinned. "Have a new electronic toy I'm anxious to try. Series of listening devices. Runs off cell phone applications. Someone enters a room and an alarm goes off here." Dozer tapped the cell screen. "Starts recording right away. If I just touch the screen again, I can actually listen to what's said, real time."

"Wow! Neat," St. James said enthusiastically.

"Say there's a window break-in. The intruder steps in. Trap snaps a leg," Dozer said as he acted out the steps. "If he's not alone, he yells for help, panics. Evidence is recorded. If he escapes, there's blood for DNA testing. And he'll need medical attention right away, otherwise he'll bleed out. Traps are forceful, enough to take down a large bear. The teeth are an unusual shape. On a man, it goes through to the bone and leaves a permanent identifiable scar, shaped like a leaf. Evidence that lasts. Police have the wound description to distribute to hospitals and clinics, so the perpetrator has a difficult time hiding for any length of time."

"But the traps are illegal," St. James protested.

"I didn't say they were illegal. I said they weren't legal. Illegal means they're against the law. Not legal means they're not approved by the law. Big difference."

St. James shrugged and turned to Anna.

"You've been quiet through all this, Anna."

"I'm just absorbing it all," she said slowly, looking more puzzled than scared. "You're very thorough, Dozer. I can see why Hamilton has such confidence in you."

"Thank you for that, Anna," Dozer said with a huge smile.

St. James said to Anna, "How about you go up and gather what you need? Then give your key to Dozer so he can set things up. I'll come up in a few minutes to help with bags."

She nodded and made her way up to the apartment.

Dozer pointed to the side of the building. "Hamilton, you watch the alley around back. I'll watch out here. We don't want her seen leaving with bags. Defeats the plan."

"Okay," St. James said obediently and then walked through the alley around back.

Neither Dozer nor St. James saw eyes on the place.

Dozer called a cab on his cell, giving the address of a house on St. Andrew, the street immediately behind Anna's.

When several minutes had passed, St. James went upstairs. Anna finished packing and they descended the back stairs to the small backyard, following a narrow footpath between two houses through to St. Andrew. Dozer was waiting there, standing beside a cab. He helped load Anna's luggage into the trunk and she handed him her keys to the apartment. Then Anna and St. James piled into the taxi; they were gone in three minutes flat.

Dozer watched the taxi turn off St. Andrew, then made his way back to Anna's. He stopped to make a long, slow scan around Guigues and Anna's building. Satisfied there was nothing to be concerned about, he locked Anna's apartment and headed to 700 Sussex.

When he arrived, he retrieved the equipment from the concierge and asked him to diligently watch comings and goings, noting descriptions of people he didn't know and the times they entered and left. He should walk the building a couple times a day. Any unusual behavior was to be reported to Dozer immediately. Dozer gave him his cell number and $500 for his trouble, then left for Anna's with equipment slung over his shoulder.

The first thing St. James eyed when he entered the condo was the flashing message light. He punched in the password and listened to the insurance adjuster estimate the repair cost for the BMW at $21,630. St. James called them back and said he'd like it repaired at the Hunt Club dealer. The adjuster confirmed and reminded St. James his policy covered the full cost of a rental while his own car was being repaired.

That made St. James's next call an easy choice: Enterprise Car Rental. A lady at the Bank Street franchise promised a car that very afternoon. They'd require Anna's license information if she was to be an occasional driver, and St. James gave it over the phone.

Anna moved to the study and began researching Gyberson and Nells. It wouldn't take away her heightened anxiety, but it was a welcomed distraction.

St. James realized he needed a strategy for tomorrow's meeting with Anderson to deal with the offensive way the CEO had spoken to him in Toronto.

He sat at the dining table and debated different approaches. Anderson had behaved as if St. James was the reason the board didn't trust him. If St. James ignored that, he'd effectively be giving Anderson power over him. And that didn't sit well. On the other hand, if he verbally hit Anderson too hard it could blow up the whole project. He didn't want that either. Weighing everything, he concluded a stern conversation was in order. It might trigger a rough start, but the air had to be cleared.

# Chapter 31

Thursday morning St. James arrived at CISI's headquarters at 9:50 and was escorted into Anderson's opulent office at 10:00.

Anderson stood to greet him and shake hands.

*Friendlier than last week.*

Cameron Anderson was every inch the consummate executive. Five-ten, of average build, with perfectly coiffed sandy hair, a thin face, and a perfectly formed nose. A huge smile showcased even, white teeth, just as St. James remembered from the website pictures. He was too young for the statesman look, but professional in every other way. His Armani suit, calm demeanour, and an air of confidence accentuated the look.

Anderson's office was a mini version of the Charles Dickens boardroom down the hall, with dark mahogany wall panelling, heavy, plush, handmade area rugs, and multiple recessed lighting pods to compensate for the room's darkness. A gas fireplace occupied one corner.

Anderson came from behind a large walnut desk and gestured St. James toward a sitting area furnished with a grey leather chesterfield, two matching armchairs, and a glass coffee table between. He offered St. James the chesterfield and then sat in an armchair facing him, crossed his legs and steepled his hands.

"How would you like to proceed?" he asked quietly.

"In a clear and transparent way," St. James replied, voice stern but polite.

Anderson's eyebrows rose. "What do you mean?"

"I work hard for my clients, but when a relationship begins with rude behaviour, the air has to be cleared. If it can't be, it's no place for me. So, if you plan to continue your aggressive behaviour of last week, I will resign now and provide clear reasons to the board."

Still and expressionless, Anderson said, "Perhaps we got off to a bad start. I'm very frustrated with the board's lack of appreciation for the company's success. Rather than praising management for outstanding financial results, the directors remain suspicious. I apologize for my behaviour last week. Let's see if we can start over."

St. James leaned forward.

"Okay, but let's be clear: the board asked me to get involved here because they think you're keeping something from them. We could spend a lot of time dancing, or you could help me get to the bottom of whatever is going on, if anything is at all. Then I'll be out of your life all the faster. My time will be less. My fees will be less. And you'll be closer to meeting budget."

Anderson said nothing.

St. James continued with a less aggressive tone.

"A cost-efficiency review is bullshit … it's a game, you know that. No good ever comes from corporate games. Everyone looks bad."

"Did you tell Nelson that?" he asked calmly.

"No, I did not."

"Why not?"

"I was intrigued by a board that allegedly couldn't get information from its CEO. My reading of Nelson was I had to fall in behind or I'd never find out why. So I let the game go on."

Anderson stared at the ceiling for a few seconds.

"I see," he said thoughtfully, "and … now that you're in you want to shut the game down, so to speak?"

St. James didn't hesitate for a second. "That's right. Now I'm part of an investigation. My brand is tied to it. That makes the difference. Means there'll be no games."

Anderson smiled.

"Perhaps I underestimated you, Hamilton."

St. James pulled a notebook from his attaché case.

"So, let's get down to it," he said, his tone returning to normal. "Your annual bonus is tied to, among other things, corporate profitability. Greater emphasis has been placed on that as a result of the independent compensation review last year. Your contract says there are two tests before you're bonused. If CISI's profit is less than $90 million, you receive no bonus. That's the floor, the threshold, so to speak. Right?"

"Right. I see they've given you a copy of my contract," he said with a slight smile.

St. James didn't respond.

"Surpassing the $90 million minimum profit is the first test. Last year, before the inventory adjustment, profit was $85 million, $5 million less than the $90 million minimum for your $500,000 bonus to be granted."

St. James knew the answer to the next question but asked it anyway. Anderson would not have received a bonus without the huge write-up of inventory. His bonus was without question a motive to manipulate profit.

"How much was the inventory adjustment again?"

"$95 million," Anderson replied coolly.

"So, $85 million net income plus the $95 million adjustment brings net income to $180 million, $90 million past the first threshold test. Correct?"

"Correct," Anderson said without a flinch.

St. James continued. "After all bonuses are paid and expensed, profit cannot drop below $90 million. The second test. So, you can't have a $90 million profit trigger a $500,000 bonus, reducing profit to $89.5 million. The second test wouldn't be met.

"Bonuses paid last year totaled $2.5 million, including your $500,000, right?"

"Correct."

"So, net income after the $95 million inventory adjustment minus total bonuses of $2.5 million means you were way ahead on the second test too, right?"

"Right."

"So, we can agree you had motive to manipulate inventory?"

"Absolutely," Anderson said without hesitation. "However, you're assuming I'm the only one with that motive. There are twenty-eight people in the senior management profit pool, each allotted different bonus amounts. The other twenty-seven also have that motive. That is, if there actually *was* manipulation. And I'm not aware there was. So this discussion is purely theoretical."

Anderson folded his arms.

St. James challenged Anderson. "A number of the twenty-seven employees would not receive a bonus great enough to motivate inflating inventory, to take the risk of being fired. And most of them would not get close enough to inventory numbers, either financially or physically, to pull off such a caper."

"I am in the worst position of all to manipulate anything financial," Anderson countered, his voice calm and sincere. "I'm further away from plant operations and inventory control than anyone in the pool. If I wanted to manipulate profit, I'd have to control the three layers of management between me and inventory around the world. There'd have to be a hell of a lot of collusion among a lot of people for me to pull something like that off."

"Same could be said for many others in the pool," St. James argued.

St. James didn't admit it, but Anderson had a point. He eyed the man closely for a long moment.

Uncomfortable silence.

"What's wrong?" Anderson finally asked.

"You! Despite my direct approach you didn't outright deny the plausibility of inventory manipulation, by anyone."

"Perhaps we've underestimated each other," Anderson said, raising an eyebrow.

"Let me come at it a different way," St. James suggested. "Are you concerned in any way some wrongdoing in the company may have occurred?"

Anderson stared at the ceiling a second time, taking a long moment to reflect.

"It's a distinct possibility," he said finally.

St. James thought this must have been very difficult for him to admit, and probably the first time he had expressed it to anyone, maybe even to himself.

"Who has opportunity as well as motive?" St. James pressed.

Anderson paused once more, wanting to choose his words carefully.

"Apart from me? I would say my chief financial officer, Karen Van Hoyt, would have opportunity by virtue of her position. However, I have the utmost confidence in her integrity."

"How long has she been with CISI?"

"About eight years."

"Happy with her performance?"

Anderson nodded. "*Very* happy. Stellar work ethic. The auditors love her. She makes their job so easy and is always ready when they arrive. They sail through on time and on budget.

"Karen is also strategic. She adds value around the management table. Not just with numbers, ideas too. She'd be extremely difficult to replace."

"Could she manipulate profits on her own?"

"I suppose she could," he offered, scratching his head, "but it would have to be through something like a general journal entry. Something she could pull off with no one else's help. Everything else is touched by multiple hands. She'd need partners to collude."

"If she manipulated inventory with a general journal entry, she would only need your approval to do so, to protect herself. She would only need to collude with you, not several others. No one is going to challenge the two strongest executive members," St. James retorted.

"Perhaps you're right, Hamilton," Anderson said calmly. "But I didn't, and I think your investigation will prove that. I reviewed the year-end inventory adjustment and all its supporting documentation because of the size. Everything supported the adjustment down to the last penny."

St. James nodded. "How much is Karen's bonus?"

"$100,000."

St. James stroked his chin. "Significant enough for a CFO pay grade."

"CISI is generous to high performers," Anderson said proudly.

"For inventory to be physically inflated, who would have to be involved?"

"Well, count teams number two to four in an average plant, three to six counters to a team. Two teams are assigned to freezers and the plant, and two to trawlers if more than two are tied up on count day; one team if there's two or less."

"Could a trawler captain manipulate a count?"

"No. They're not involved after the trawlers tie up."

"Are count teams bonused on profits?"

"No. Plant managers are the lowest level to receive profit bonuses. Below them there's no point. Employees can't significantly influence results."

"Hmm. But employees might conspire with the plant manager if they were promised something," St. James suggested.

Anderson nodded.

"Count teams deal only with pound quantities, right? Or would they price and extend costs too?" St. James asked.

"Just quantities. In-plant accountants use Excel to price, extend, and total plant inventory. Then the plant manager reviews everything. When he's happy it's accurate, he signs off and emails documentation to Karen's group here at HQ."

St. James wanted to be clear on this.

"So, the plant manager is always the last to see paperwork before it's sent to Karen?"

"That's right."

St. James nodded. "Does Karen know I am here?"

"Yes, she does. I spoke with her this morning. She said you didn't ask to see her but that she'd make herself available if you needed anything. Her office is two doors down on the left."

"Great."

St. James changed course.

"I'm told you objected to me being here before last week's meeting. Said your people were too busy and I was too expensive. Is that true?"

"That's exactly what I said, yes," he replied, again without hesitation.

"Was that the real reason?"

"Actually, that *was* the reason. I know the board members think I'm stonewalling but you'll find head count around here tight. Very little slack in anyone's schedule. Taking time for an efficiency review is difficult at the best of times. And the budget is very tight, tighter than last year's. It'll be a squeaker to achieve even without your cost. It'd be different if we didn't review expenses on our own. But we do, a couple times a year. But now that you're on board you have my full and unconditional support. The silver lining is maybe putting my own mind at ease."

Once again St. James changed direction.

"You explained to the board that the company exceeded profit by cutting expenses and landing extra inventory on the last day."

"That's correct."

"They also said you kept repeating that explanation. Is that true?"

"That is also correct."

"Care to explain why?"

"Board members have varying degrees of understanding when it comes to operations, inventory, and finance. I find myself explaining things more than once, in different ways, to reach everyone at their own level. Most are not financially literate. Then there's the size of the adjustment. That added further communication challenges."

St. James nodded and returned to his original line of questioning. "Okay. What's the bonus expectation of a plant manager?"

Anderson rubbed the back of his neck. "It ranges based on size of plant, as you would imagine. Can be anywhere from $30,000 to $50,000."

"What is a manager's base salary before bonus?"

"Again, it depends on plant size, but also on seniority and the individual's scorecard assessment. Between $75,000 for small plants and $125,000 for larger ones."

"So bonuses approximate forty per cent of normal salary? Is that the same for all plants, regardless of size?"

"That's right."

"Isn't that counter-intuitive? Don't larger plants have greater influence over profit?"

"Ah, yes they do," said Anderson, "but smaller ones have more aggressive targets. We expect them to catch up to larger plants as soon as possible."

"You mean smaller plant goals are more of a stretch?"

"Yes. Larger plants meet production targets more easily. They already process at maximum capacity. It's not logical to stretch their production goals further. They couldn't physically produce more unless the plant itself was expanded." Anderson opened his hands in papal fashion. "And, of course, managers have no control over that. It's a head-office decision.

"Bonuses for larger plants relate primarily to efficiency and quality of output. Operating at capacity means lower costs per pound. We tie their bonus to minimizing cost per pound, which, all else being equal, means greater profit."

"Of course," St. James agreed, "more pound throughput means less overhead cost per pound, and labour is more efficient … less downtime. I had a lengthy discussion with Marcel on that very point."

"Overall strategy is to incentivize small plants to become larger in the shortest possible period of time," Anderson said. "To reduce average production cost per pound. Improve margins. Maximize profit. Smaller plants usually have some excess capacity to absorb. More inefficient. When they reach higher production levels, bonus criteria shift from growth to production efficiency. That occurs as they approach the larger plant category.

"Bonuses are generous, but managers earn them, believe me."

St. James nodded. "I'm sure they do. How can smaller plants physically catch up to the volume and productivity of larger ones? You don't measure large plants by growth because they're constrained by size. Isn't it the same for small plants? They have even greater restrictions. And the managers don't control plant size any more than the managers of large plants do."

"When a smaller plant's production hits maximum capacity and remains there for three consecutive years, we pay the manager an extra $20,000 per year and budget the plant for expansion. So, managers are financially motivated to drive production past physical capacity as quickly as possible, and to sustain it for three years. That's how small plants get to join the big boys club. It's a status thing as well as promising a financial reward."

"Why three years? Why not one or two?"

"One year at capacity could be an extraordinary catch year, an aberration. Two might be a coincidence. Three years provides greater confidence in sustainability. We must have confidence that the greater volumes will continue. Plant expansions are very expensive: if we decide to expand too soon, volumes may revert back to their lower, historical levels. Then we have even greater excess capacity, an expanded plant with no additional product to pay for it."

St. James nodded. "I see."

He wanted to understand the motives at every level. "What about larger plants? Aren't they encouraged to grow too?"

"Of course. It's just when plants reach a certain size, they also reach catch limitations within acceptable distances from the plant."

"You mean so the timespan between landing and processing catch doesn't erode its quality?" St. James interpreted.

"Close," Anderson conceded. "Trawlers have freezing capacity, so fish can be preserved for some time. But time and handling erode quality even with freezing, albeit at a slower pace, so there's a maximum time between fish coming out of the water and fillets coming off the production line beyond which quality wanes. If that wasn't so, we could have the world's largest processing plant in one location and trawlers travelling months to catch fish."

"Makes sense." St. James continued. "Which plants are smaller?"

"Lagos, Portugal is the smallest. It's a canning plant. Processes about three million pounds annually. Next is Tampa with about five to nine million. Then it jumps to Boston with about fifty million pounds."

"How well do you know the lifestyles of plant managers?" St. James said.

"Not very well. Don't know anything about their personal lives. But someone in Karen's group visits each plant quarterly. They would have a better idea."

"Which is the largest plant?"

"Plymouth processes ninety-five million pounds a year. Portsmouth, eighty-seven million."

"US plants? Massachusetts and New Hampshire?"

"Great Britain."

"Oh. Those centres are relatively close together, are they not?"

"About 170 miles. Three-and-a-half-hour drive."

"Is that close enough for the plants to help each other with production?"

"Not by road. Fish loses freshness quickly, as I said earlier, and road travel causes more bruising."

"By sea?"

"142 miles. When trawlers are close to the plants they radio for instructions on where to land."

"Wouldn't the bonus plan discourage that kind of cooperation? They'd be shifting profit away from their own plant by diverting catch to another."

"True for everywhere but Great Britain: the managers of Plymouth and Portsmouth are brothers."

St. James felt his brow furrow.

# Chapter 32

"Interesting. They actually help each other?" St. James said incredulously.

"Most unusual," Anderson said, shaking his head. "But I have to admit I like it. The team spirit, I mean. Wish we had more of it."

St. James nodded. "I take it from the website that Henry Jenkins is the chief operating officer?"

"That's correct."

St. James made some notes. "I'll want to meet him at some point."

"Absolutely. Just let me know and I'll arrange it."

"I think that should do it for now, Anderson. Could I trouble you to introduce me to Karen?"

"My pleasure. We'll go down to her office." Anderson's face clouded over. "A word of caution."

St. James pulled back. "What?"

"She's quite stressed these days. Her husband's company is struggling financially. Think he's about to lose it. And they just bought a house a few months ago, a couple of blocks from Nelson."

St. James considered this for a moment. "Thanks for the tip. I'll tread lightly."

Karen Van Hoyt was tall, about six feet, St. James guessed, her red hair worn in a tight bun like a schoolmarm's. Attractive, but in an odd sort of way; maybe the high cheekbones accounted for that.

Anderson introduced them and left them immediately.

They shook hands, and St. James sat in one of the two guest chairs.

Unlike Anderson's, Karen's office was filled with modern furniture and a number of family pictures hanging from light-blue walls.

"Delighted to finally meet you, Hamilton," she offered, her smile less pronounced than Anderson's. "Heard great things about you from Al Dunlop."

"Al and I go back a ways. He's a good man."

"He is indeed. Now, how can I be of help?"

St. James leaned back in the chair looking serious.

Van Hoyt wore a dark-blue blouse and matching skirt. A long gold necklace dangled from her neck, and matching earrings completed the look of a highly professional lady.

"I am just getting into things so for now just a couple of questions. No doubt there'll be more later on." He pulled the pad from his attaché case once again.

"Curious about the inventory adjustment last fiscal year-end."

Van Hoyt nodded. "The $95 million?"

"Yes."

"It's important to know how the adjustment breaks down. That is, where the $95 million originated. Then, if you like, we can chat about reasons for each location," she explained.

St. James nodded but said nothing.

Van Hoyt pulled a brown manila folder from the top right-hand drawer of her desk and flipped it open.

"In round numbers the inventory adjustment was the sum of $49 million for England; $11 million for Rio; $20 million for Boston; and various smaller amounts from the remaining 16 plants, all totaling $95 million. Pounds of course are not proportional to dollar value because more expensive species such as shrimp, lobster, and crab are landed in some locations and not in others."

"Understand." St. James purposely threw a curveball. "I'm more interested in why trawler inventory was not counted in the first place."

"What makes you think it wasn't counted?" she asked with a surprised look.

"Size of the adjustment."

Van Hoyt looked puzzled, and her tone became defensive. "The size of the adjustment doesn't mean trawlers weren't counted. It comes from all locations, including trawlers. Those tied at wharfs around the world were inventoried late. Sheets tallied, costed, added, checked, and re-checked at the plant level, then emailed to us a couple of days after year-end, after the plant managers approved the results. Only then did we know the final dollar amount."

"Sorry, I didn't mean to suggest anything negative. My question was ill-formed. May I have copies of the count sheets and calculations leading up to the adjustment?"

Van Hoyt returned to a less defensive demeanour and smiled. "Yes, of course."

St. James's forehead furrowed. "So, the greatest reason for the inventory adjustment was trawler inventory?"

"Mostly, yes."

"Was trawler inventory counted late afternoon at every plant around the world?"

"Yes. Wherever there were trawlers, of course."

"After plant counts were finished in every case?"

"Yes, I believe so."

"Were the auditors present for all counts, start to finish?"

"Not sure they were present for trawlers in the late afternoon."

St. James moved on.

"So, Portsmouth and Plymouth accounted for almost fifty-two per cent of the adjustment?"

"That's correct."

"I see." St. James thought for a moment. "Cameron tells me the managers of those plants are brothers."

Van Hoyt smiled.

"Bizarre isn't it? Wonder what mathematicians would say about that probability."

"Fairly remote, I suspect," St. James conceded without expression.

"They help each other with advice and analysis, that sort of thing."

"Which is the manager of which?"

"Basil Hughes manages Plymouth. William, Portsmouth."

"I'll try to keep them straight," he said with a slight smile. "What do you know about their lifestyles?"

"Fairly modest I'd say. Been to both homes for dinner on more than one occasion. Comfortable, well-kept homes but not over the top for their income levels, if that's what you're getting at."

St. James nodded. "It is. Automobiles?"

"If memory serves me right, they drive Volkswagen sedans. I am not a car person. But I can tell you they don't have the most expensive vehicles."

"Alcohol or drug addictions?"

Van Hoyt was instantly taken back by the question. "Oh my God! We've no indication or reason to suspect that."

"Gambling?"

"Don't believe so."

"Tax or financial problems?"

"None I am aware of."

St. James's rapid-fire questioning was obviously increasing Karen's anxiety.

"If I asked all the same questions about every plant manager would your answers be the same?"

"All except Lagos, Portugal. The manager there is José Miguel. I watch him closely. I believe he's living beyond his means. He and his wife just built a new house and purchased a Mercedes-Benz, a small one, mind you, but nevertheless a Mercedes. He also likes his wines expensive."

"What is he paid?" St. James asked, continuing to take notes.

"A base equivalent to $75,000 US, plus a bonus if the company surpasses $90 million profit and plant goals are met."

"The bonus, I'm guessing from my discussion with Cameron, would be about $30,000. That right?"

Van Hoyt smiled. "Yes. You did your homework."

"Maximum of $105,000 then," he concluded. "Cost of living's cheaper in Portugal for sure but he'd still have to count on his bonus every year for a mortgage and car loan. Does his wife work?"

"Yes. Bank teller."

St. James stroked his chin. "Not much income there. I take it you haven't been surprised by any improprieties?"

"None so far. But I view him as a risk."

"Smart lady."

Karen's cheekbones rose higher when she smiled broadly. "Thanks."

"What do you get from plant managers once counts are completed?"

"Excel spreadsheets listing species and pounds counted by trawler, cooler room and freezer number, and in-process on production lines at the time of the count. Cost per pound is assigned by local plant accountants and multiplied by pounds counted to arrive at inventory value by species. Inventory costs per species are totaled to arrive at total plant inventory. Then, the inventory's approved or altered by the plant manager. Final count summaries are sent to the HQ accountant responsible for that particular plant. Common count policies and guidelines are given to all plants to ensure uniform procedures are carried out across the company."

"Then what happens?"

"HQ checks all calculations and compares the value of actual inventory counted to book value, and, where necessary, make adjustment recommendations to me. I sign off or amend as the case may be."

"So you still do some manual checks?" St. James said.

"Yes. It's an inefficiency we've identified. At the moment we're evaluating software to address the manual work. Only IT and I know this, so please don't mention it to anyone. It will affect five positions, maybe more, so I don't want to spook the whole department before we decide one way or the other."

St. James raised a hand. "Don't worry. I know how delicate these matters can be."

"Thank you."

"Do HQ accountants ever amend what comes from plants?"

"Only calculation errors that happen from time to time. No way of checking pounds of course, other than count sheets themselves. They're not present when counts are actually conducted. We rely on the count teams' division of duties for that. One member of the team counts a section first. Then, a second member counts the same section. If there are differences they count the same section a third time, together, to agree on or change poundage."

"Seems safe enough," he said smiling.

"We've never had a problem with the procedure itself, not that I'm aware of anyway."

"Once your people check everything do you ever make additional adjustments?"

"Not very often. If I've been to a plant recently and know of problems with excess freezer burn, I may question whether additional write-downs should be taken. Or, if a pounds flow-through analysis suggests significant difference in inventory values, I investigate further."

St. James knew what "pound flow-through analysis" meant but played dumb, hoping to learn more.

"Pounds flow-through analysis?"

"Yes. I take opening inventory, add production cost, and subtract product shipped to customers. What's left should approximate closing inventory. Not exactly though. It assumes consistent yields, that every pound is top quality, and that the same species are being processed. It's impossible to achieve, at best only an approximation to compare with the physical count. If a discrepancy is, say, up to fifteen per cent, I assume physical count is accurate. Anything over fifteen per cent is cause for further investigation. There could be a significant shift in species mix or a write-off of poor-quality fish. Whatever the reason, I want an explanation from the plant manager for anything over fifteen per cent."

"Logical and reasonable," St. James offered respectfully.

Van Hoyt looked pleased with the assessment.

"May I have a copy of the analysis and year-end Excel spreadsheets for larger plants?"

"My assistant will give you copies on the way out."

St. James nodded. "What's the discrepancy between pound flow-through analysis and the physical count last year-end?"

"If my memory serves me correctly, it was approximately twelve per cent."

"So it wasn't high enough to warrant further investigation?" he pressed.

"That's right."

"So, cost of trawler inventory was added to the books when year-end financial statements were prepared?"

"That's correct."

"I may want to visit the plants in England. Should I arrange that through you or Cameron?" St. James asked.

Van Hoyt looked surprised.

# Chapter 33

Van Hoyt went silent for a long moment, then said, "Do you really have to physically go? Can you not achieve the same thing by Skype or telephone or email? We'd like to avoid the cost of extra time and travel."

"I'm afraid if I'm to be thorough in my job, it's obligatory," St. James said.

Van Hoyt looked unconvinced, but reluctantly agreed.

They talked about accounting procedures for another half-hour or so; who did what and why, and what, if any, were CISI's system weaknesses.

Satisfied he'd asked the right questions for now, St. James collected copies of inventory calculations from Karen's assistant on the way out.

He strolled down the hall to Juanita Mendoza's workstation to see about an office. She had a spare office one floor below that St. James could use. He walked down a colourless stairwell and through a fire-retardant door into a brightly lit peach hallway. Two doors down he found a small, bare office containing nothing but a well-used veneer desk, a single chair with a wobbly back, and an old phone.

He settled behind the desk, booted his laptop, and logged online using the guest password Juanita had given him.

An email from Detective Jason Williamson summarizing criminal searches St. James had requested popped up in his inbox.

Jason discovered Stan Gyberson, Samuel Franklin, Bertram Cook, Adam Derringer, and Amanda Fletcher were all registered on FBI watch lists in a number of states. Suspects in a number of different confidence schemes throughout the Midwest. No convictions. Nothing proven, at least not to date.

What St. James didn't know was that Gyberson and Fletcher were husband and wife. Samuel Franklin was a disbarred attorney who, for many years, acted for Gyberson's companies until he was caught siphoning trust funds. And Adam Derringer and Bertram Cook were Gyberson's first cousins.

"Cozy family," St. James mumbled. "Louis will have fun with this."

He pulled a vibrating cell from his sports-coat pocket.

"Hamilton, its Dozer."

"What's up?"

"Two things. First, I got a call from the concierge in your building."

St. James tensed. "Oh?"

"Yeah, 'oh.' A stranger walked through the main entrance today and headed straight for the elevator. At first the concierge didn't think much of it: owners have visitors who come and go all the time. But then the man's black wide-brimmed fedora and raincoat made him suspicious."

"What's suspicious about that?"

"It's warm here, Hamilton, and not raining. No one's wearing coats."

"Oh!" St. James said again.

"The elevator stopped on the fifth floor. The concierge called security and a guard high-tailed it up to your floor. The stranger caught sight of him when the elevator opened and booted down the stairwell as fast as he could, making a clean getaway before security could nail him. The hat and coat were a disguise, not protection from the weather. Neither the concierge nor security got a good look at the man's face."

"Did the guy break in to my condo?"

"Concierge says no. No visible damage to the lock, and when he used the master key to check inside, nothing had been disturbed. Guess Raincoat didn't have time to do anything."

"Still, it's disturbing. An attempt to do something, surveillance maybe, checking the make of the lock so it could be picked later."

"Maybe."

"I'm afraid to ask about the second thing."

"The phone alarm went off two hours ago."

St. James tensed yet again. "The traps at Anna's?"

"Yes. I rushed over and found an intruder lying on the floor bleeding heavily. Couldn't get anything out of him without hurting him more. Didn't think that would be right."

"Sometimes I wonder about you, Dozer," St. James said, shaking his head.

Dozer ignored the jab. "I called 911 and eventually spoke to the detective who dealt with your car crash."

"Spencer?"

"That's the one. He followed the ambulance to the Ottawa Hospital."

"Was the guy carrying ID?"

"No, nothing."

"Where is Anna right now?"

"Still at work. Doesn't know about either event yet."

"Good. Keep it that way until I get home."

He disconnected.

St. James's mind skipped over the raincoat guy, focusing instead on the man caught in Dozer's trap.

The intruder wouldn't be the leader, but he might know who or what was behind all this. As Dozer said, they'd have DNA and fingerprints.

*At least someone to question.*

His computer pinged twice with new emails. The first, DuPont. The RCMP said none of the shareholders in the 139 companies had a record. Second, Scotland Yard's David Kingston indicated the same. Not long after, Slate emailed to say he'd already given FBI on Gyberson's gang to Williamson.

St. James dialed the four-digit extension for Van Hoyt and asked to be introduced electronically to Basil and William Hughes in England.

"I'll send an introductory note right now," she said.

His cell vibrated once again.

Smythe.

"Just want to report I have made no further progress with the code since we cracked sections five and six."

St. James spent the next fifteen minutes filling Smythe in on the five shareholders and what Jason's investigation had turned up; Smythe was vigorously typing in the background.

"Okay," he said hurriedly, "I'll see if I can make something of this. By the way, I took the liberty of passing the flight numbers and dates from sections five and six on to Williamson. You were busy. I thought he should have them sooner rather than later."

"Excellent. Thank you, Louis."

St. James paused for a moment and considered the speed at which the two cases were moving. Stevens was now beginning to bear fruit, albeit just the thin edge of the fruit wedge, but still, progress. St. James's adrenalin was beginning to crank up.

His cell vibrated a third time.

"It's Jason."

"Hi Jason, I just read your email on our five shareholders."

"That's not why I am calling," he said in a sombre tone.

"What's up?" St. James asked.

"Thomas Stevens was found dead in a downtown Fargo hotel room. Shot in the back of the head. Execution-style."

# Chapter 34

Even though St. James had known all along there was a good chance Stevens was dead, he had still hoped for a chance to question him. Now, that would never be. In a way it saddened him. Part of the story would go untold. Generally he knew the man's state of mind from interviews with others, but now he would never experience it firsthand.

St. James had intended to spend the night at the Royal York, down the street from CISI. But with Stevens murdered and her apartment broken into, Anna would be a mess. Maybe it would trigger another flashback, at the very least an anxiety attack. He was confident Dozer could keep her safe physically, but only he could protect her emotionally. So he cancelled the reservation at the Royal York and caught the 6 p.m. flight back to Ottawa.

*** 

A young maid had unlocked the hotel room around 11 a.m. and found Stevens lying face down at the foot of the bed in a pool of his own blood. It didn't take long for Fargo police to conclude it was an execution: the bullet to the back of the head was very compelling evidence.

There was no sign of a struggle, so it was probably someone Stevens knew, someone he felt comfortable letting in the room. The angle of the bullet entry made suicide unlikely. Not a robbery gone wrong either, since nothing seemed to be missing, his laptop, credit cards, and money all present and intact.

It looked as if Stevens had just checked in. Except for the brain matter splattered all over the bureau, mirror, and walls, the room was fairly tidy. Clothes were neatly folded in an open suitcase. The bed wasn't slept in.

Had Stevens threatened to blow the whistle on someone? Or had fellow thieves thought him no longer useful? Either way, he was dead.

***

When St. James opened the condo door at eight that evening, Anna came running from the living room and threw her arms around him.

"What a wonderful surprise, Hamilton," she said, eyes dancing with excitement. "I was just waiting for your call. Never dreamt you'd come home."

"Got homesick" was the only answer he could muster.

Anna was anxious to hear about the investigation. St. James told her about the interviews at CISI: Anderson's better behaviour, and his concern something might be wrong with inventory, a total turnaround from last week.

Anna said, "I found information on The Carstairs Group."

"Fabulous. What did you learn?" St. James's voice was less than enthusiastic, anticipating the bad news he was about to deliver.

"There are a number of newspaper stories about an abandoned property in Chicago. The company ran out of money before it could finish building a retirement home; five liens filed by unpaid suppliers. I think I know what a lien is, although I'd like your take."

"It's a legal remedy available to those unpaid for work done on real property. Triggers the sale of the property so suppliers and trades can be paid from the proceeds," St. James explained.

"That's what I thought."

"Would you like a glass of wine?" he asked, changing the subject.

"That would be lovely," she said, smiling.

St. James draped his sports coat over a dining chair, rolled up his shirt sleeves, then selected a bottle of Primitivo, poured two glasses, and handed one to Anna.

"Let's go in the living room," he suggested.

They sat side by side on the black leather chesterfield.

"Anything more on Gyberson or Nells?" he asked, working up to the bad news.

"Nothing on Nells but quite a bit on Gyberson. He was in all the newspapers as a guy who stiffed creditors then disappeared."

"Any financial information on The Carstairs Group?"

"Some reporter was digging for financial stuff but couldn't find much of anything because it's a private company."

"How was work today?" he asked.

"Same old, same old."

"How are you getting along with Dozer?"

She smiled. "Great. He's very sweet and considerate. Took me by the apartment today to enter the front and go out the back, as we planned. No sign of anything. Then to the pub for my shift." Her brown eyes lit up. "You should have seen the look on Sid's face. Totally spooked by a huge biker-looking dude drinking milk."

St. James laughed. "Oh, Dozer can put away the pints, I assure you, just not when he's on duty."

St. James thought the timing was as good as it was ever going to be.

"Anna, there are a couple of things I want to report."

Her face clouded over as it always did when St. James became serious.

Expecting the worst was how St. James thought she managed disappointment. Think the worst, be relieved when it's something less.

"They found Thomas Stevens in a downtown hotel room in Fargo, North Dakota. Murdered."

St. James waited for a response. But it was him, not Anna, who was surprised.

She sat up straight. "Fargo! That's one of the code destinations."

*Didn't freak.*

"That has to mean something … the location, I mean."

She looked at him. "You said a couple of things."

"Dozer's cell went off this afternoon, after he escorted you to work. Someone broke the sitting room window, smashed the sill just as Dozer predicted when he assessed the risk. When the guy sat on the broken window ledge and swung his legs inside, the trap snapped on his right leg. Dozer found the man on the floor in severe pain, bleeding heavily. The guy wouldn't talk. Dozer called 911. The perp's in the Ottawa Hospital under police watch. Our friend Mark Spencer's the detective on the case."

Anna stared at the floor, looking glum. This news was different than Stevens's murder. Closer to home. It *was* home. Suddenly she felt the invasion of her privacy. St. James pulled her close, brushing strands of long blond hair away from her face. Much to his surprise, she didn't cry. Her expression was more about 'what do I do now' than fear.

St. James's cell vibrated.

"It's Louis, Hamilton. Those five names you mentioned from Jason's email?"

St. James first thought was that Smythe's timing couldn't have been worse.

"What about them?"

"Pull out your paper with the code."

St. James went to the dining area and retrieved his copy of the code from a sports-coat pocket.

"Who is it? "Anna asked.

"It's Louis, honey," he said to her. "Okay, Louis, I have it."

"Look at section four. Anything jump out at you?" he said in an elevated tone.

St. James looked at the code for a few seconds: "*(G, F, D, C, F)*". Suddenly he slapped his forehead and said, "How could I have been so stupid? I've been so focused on the trees I missed the forest! Gyberson, Franklin, Derringer, Cook, and Fletcher!"

"You got it," Smythe said, his voice filled with excitement. "Now we have most of the code!"

St. James turned to Anna, also with excitement.

"Dear, Louis has broken section four!"

Anna said, "But what does it all mean?"

St. James stared at her in silence for a beat.

"Hamilton, you still there?" Smythe said loudly.

"Louis, hang up and call back on the landline so I can put you on speaker."

Seconds later the house phone rang, and St. James pressed the speaker button to reconnect Smythe.

"It's just Anna and me in the room. You can speak freely."

Anna said, "What does the code mean now that that section is broken?"

"Excellent question Anna," said Smythe. "Here's what I think: money was transferred to the main branch of the Cayman National Bank *('g,cnbtkyk1,j')* with the transaction code ABA#021000089 through clearing account number 36148883 to account number 012-67141    *('ABA#021000089-36148883-012-67141-co-na-csprite1')*    on August 23 *('Virgo23')*. Seven days later *('Virgo23+7')* Stan Gyberson *('G')* flew on United Flight 3743 from Atlanta to Chicago *('U3743-5847')* where he connected to Fargo on United 5847. The flight to Chicago left Atlanta at 11:04 a.m. and the flight to Fargo left at 4:19 p.m. *('1104-419')*.

"Franklin or Fletcher, don't know which since we only have the first letter of the last name *('F')*, caught American Flight 3570 from Pittsburgh to JFK, then British Airways flight 0112 *('A3570-B0112')* to Heathrow on September 7 *('Virgo23+7+8')*. The flight to JFK left at 11:30 a.m. and the one to Heathrow was an overnight flight leaving at 7:30 p.m. *('1130-1930')*.

"Derringer *('D')* took Delta Flight 4883 from Columbia, South Carolina to Atlanta, and then Delta Flight 1916 to Denver *('D4883-1916')* on September 11 *('Virgo23+7+8+4')*. The flight to Atlanta left at 7:00 a.m. and the one to Denver left at 11:06 a.m. *('700-1106')*.

"Cook ('C') took American Flight 194 ('A194') from Miami to Baltimore on September 17 ('Virgo23+7+8+4+6') at 1:45 ('145').

"Franklin or Fletcher ('F'), whoever's left, ended up in Toronto from JFK on American Airlines Flight 3657 ('A3657'), which left at 9:05 a.m. ('905') on September 20 ('Virgo23+7+8+4+6+3')."

St. James imagined Smythe looking quite pleased with himself.

"But what does 'co-na-csprite1' in the second section mean?" St. James said. "And what does 'g' before and 'j' after the SWIFT code translate into?"

"I am not exactly sure, but the probability software suggests 'co-na' to be short for 'code name' and 'csprite1' to be the code name for the transaction itself. But I'm not sure. Still have no idea about the 'g' and 'j'."

"Makes sense. Excellent work, Louis!"

"Thank you, kind sir," Smythe said in formal tone.

Anna decided to challenge him. "Both you guys have always said the money was transferred on August 30. Now you're saying August 23."

"August 30 is when the money was discovered missing, not when it was transferred. That was August 23," St. James clarified.

"Louis, I understand the money transfer part, but what do the flights and times represent?" asked Anna.

"I believe the departure cities are where they were when money was transferred to Cayman; they were in those cities for trumped-up business reasons the week before August 30. Arrival cities were where they went after money was transferred to look like they were taking care of personal business separately."

St. James's face clouded.

"But Louis, electronic transfers can be made from any place on the planet! They could have just as easily been made from Fargo, or London, or Toronto."

"Quite true, Hamilton, but if they're apart, in meetings with other people, in different locations from the transfer, it adds a layer of smoke over the trail, proving they weren't with each other at the time money was stolen."

"Okay. For the moment I'll buy that," St. James conceded. "But we don't know if money actually was transferred to Cayman, or from where, or by whom, or for whose benefit. The theory has more holes than a colander."

Smythe went silent.

Anna showed frustration. "Why was the stupid code even on Stevens's computer in the first place?"

"That we'll have to get from Stevens when the police find him," Smythe said.

Anna and St. James glanced at one another. St. James hadn't told Smythe about Stevens's murder.

"Louis, they found Stevens dead in a Fargo hotel room. Shot in the back of the head."

The speakerphone went silent.

"How terribly inconvenient," Smythe said finally, as if he had just missed an appointment. "How do we put the pieces together without him?"

"We'll find a way," St. James said confidently. "We've come too far to fail."

"What about section seven of the code, '(A21+11)'?" Anna asked.

"I don't know," said Smythe. "Like the other sections, it's enclosed by parentheses. No comma between it and section six though. All the other sections are separated by commas. Sits out there all alone, by itself. And it's only one set of letters and numbers, not five. Breaks the rhythm of the code."

"How do you know Stevens wasn't sloppy, left out a comma?" Anna suggested.

"Don't think so. His files are immaculate. A very precise man, not the type to leave anything out. Louis, did you describe the code to Jason exactly as you did for us just now?" St. James asked.

"The email went out late this afternoon."

St. James repeated the question. "But did you describe it exactly the way you did just now?"

"Exactly."

"Excellent. That's probably all we can do tonight. Thanks, Louis. Great work," St. James said again.

They clicked off.

St. James smiled at Anna. "I'm hungry. Murder and mayhem always works up my appetite."

Anna laughed. "You're sick."

"One has to be sick to do what I do."

"Then you're overqualified!"

# Chapter 35

St. James turned on the television. "What would you like to do, go out or order something in?"

"Hmm. It's late. Let's just order a pizza."

"What would you like on it?"

"Pepperoni, bacon, peppers, hamburger, and extra cheese."

St. James grinned, "Oh, the heart-attack special."

"Go big or go home."

St. James dialed the number for Pizza Pizza and placed the order, then refilled their wine glasses and returned to the chesterfield.

Anna, still thinking about the break-in, said, "So, what do we do now?"

"Well, tomorrow's Friday. Janice is already committed to doing the class because I'm supposed to be in Toronto. She can carry on. I'll see if Spencer found anything on the intruder. Might visit the poor fellow in hospital, see how he's coping, pray for his recovery so Dozer can put him back in."

Anna cringed. "That's a horrible thing to say, even jokingly."

He laughed.

"I'll also check if Jason has anything more on our five suspects in the Stevens case. Then there's work to do on CISI."

"Full day," Anna concluded. "Do you expect we'll be going somewhere soon?"

"How do you feel about England?"

"England!" she blurted. "Where did that come from?"

"CISI's two largest plants are there."

"What happened to Washington and Grand Cayman?"

"Could still happen. Everything's quite fluid at the moment."

"Meaning?"

St. James went into detail about the things he'd learned at CISI. When the pizza arrived they moved to the kitchen island, took a sliver each and continued the discussion.

"Do you suspect the brothers inflated inventory?" she asked, taking a second piece of pizza for herself.

"Too early to suspect anyone of anything. However, their plants together account for more than fifty per cent of the inventory write-up."

"Hard to ignore that," she mumbled, mouth full of pizza.

"That's why we're going to England."

First thing Friday morning St. James phoned Spencer. Spencer had fingerprinted the intruder the night before and the guy turned up in police records as Frank Long, a small-time Toronto hoodlum.

Long wasn't cooperating, even though Spencer reminded him of his eight prior convictions. Breaking into Anna's would make nine. That would be good for three years minimum, maybe as much as five.

Open-and-shut case: Dozer caught him in the act and took pictures on his cell. Then there was the blood match. No question about it in St. James's mind: Long qualified for three to five.

"Can you meet me at the Ottawa Hospital, Mark?" St. James asked.

"I have a meeting with the chief in a few minutes but 9:30 would work"

St. James's watch said 8:45.

"Okay," he said, "what room?"

"352."

"See you there."

St. James went into the study, fired up the computer and discovered an email from Nathan Strong. He and his partners were saddened by the loss of their partner, especially by such a horrible demise, and naturally Beth Stevens was beyond distraught.

Nathan had passed the shareholder list around the office and discovered that two partners had completed accounting assignments for Adam Derringer and Amanda Fletcher some ten years prior but had terminated the relationship when the couple cheated on their tax returns. No one had heard of Gyberson, Cook, or Franklin.

St. James's cell vibrated; it was the BMW dealer saying they'd received all the necessary parts from the manufacturer to repair the 750. The shop manager estimated five days for restoration.

So far St. James hadn't driven the Enterprise rental. Long now afforded him that opportunity. He told Anna where he was going, kissed her goodbye, grabbed the rental keys from the fridge-top, then made his way to the underground parking.

The rental was a red Cadillac, still with the new-car smell, with only 150 kilometres on it. St. James fired up the engine and rolled the Caddy up the ramp onto Sussex, turned right onto Wellington and drifted past the Parliament buildings en route to meet Spencer at the hospital.

St. James stumbled on the only available parking spot in front of the Ottawa Hospital's Civic Campus, locked the rental, found the elevator, and pushed the third-floor button. Spencer must have described him to the uniform guarding Long's room, because he stood aside without a word when St. James approached.

Spencer was seated in a visitor chair by the window.

Long was lying in bed in the fetal position, his mangled foot heavily bandaged up to the knee. He was awake, facing away from Spencer.

The room was typical for a hospital. Pale-green walls. Bare, except for a single bed, a plain white three-drawer dresser, and an adjustable mobile table for food trays. Smells of industrial cleaner and medical supplies were a sharp reminder of the room's purpose.

Spencer greeted St. James with a smile but said nothing as he nodded in Long's direction, a signal for St. James to take charge.

Long's eyes held no expression as they rolled toward St. James. He knew who St. James was, that was for sure. He'd have to know his mark.

Long was a small man with close-cropped black hair, plain-featured except for a flat nose and a missing index finger, on his right hand. St. James thought him quite forgettable to look at.

There wasn't a second visitor chair in the room, so Spencer pulled open the door and mumbled something to the policeman standing guard. A moment later the uniform placed a chair close to Long's bed. St. James unbuttoned his coat, and without a word sat for a few moments just staring at Long.

"So, Mr. Long, you know who I am?" he said finally, voice strong and stern.

Long said nothing. No movement. No expression.

"This will go a lot easier if you cooperate. Tell us who hired you to kill me and why."

Long stared straight at St. James, his expression coma-like. That told St. James that Long planned to wait him out.

For a moment St. James considered running a line on Long. Risky. He wouldn't know what answers he might get, if any. Could be something he didn't want to hear. Although, at the moment, he couldn't think what that could be. The worst outcome, Long would remain silent. The best, Long could say something or display body language St. James could draw something from.

When St. James had weighed everything, he decided to go for it.

"I talked to Nells today," he said, shaking his head. "Told him you botched the job."

Spencer flinched as if to say, What the hell are you doing?

St. James ignored him.

Long didn't move an inch or say a word.

"Nells threw you under the bus, Long. Said you acted alone. He's telling the syndicate you can't be trusted. You're washed up, Frank. Smart money says you cut a deal. Give us the evidence we need against

Nells. Maybe Detective Spencer here can help. United States authorities might join in too: they've been watching Nells for years.

"Do you really want to do three to five for a lousy $5K job? For a guy like Nells? That's somewhere between $700 and $1,000 a year. Lousy pay, Frank.

"No! Wait a minute. I'm wrong. You probably just got $2,500 upfront. That's the way it's done nowadays, isn't it? Half down before, the other half when the job's finished. Now you'll never even see the other half. You're going to prison for a lousy $2,500? Think about it, Frank. It's not worth it."

St. James waited for some kind of response.

Long shifted in his bed. His eyes were stressed, face strained, like he was trying to make up his mind which way to go. He opened his mouth, about to say something, then changed his mind.

"C'mon, Frank. No one is going to trust you anymore. You have nothing to lose."

Long's face said he was reconsidering. Then he looked straight at St. James.

"Who the hell is Nells?"

# Chapter 36

St. James was determined not to give up. He looked at Spencer, shrugged, and turned back to Long, "Maybe Nells got to you through one of his gang members, maybe Stan Gyberson?"

Long shook his head.

*Shake, better than nothing.*

"Who hired you then?" St. James persisted.

Long remained still and silent.

"Jeremy Stern?"

Still and silent.

"Arthur Spance?"

Still and silent.

"Clifford Dunning?"

Still and silent.

St. James had hoped one of the names would trigger body language of some sort. But it didn't. Long was either a very good actor or he really didn't know Nells's gang.

Spencer cleared his throat to get St. James's attention and motioned him outside, where he said, "You're not going to get anything out of this guy, Hamilton. He's too scared, far more of whoever hired him than us."

St. James shrugged and said, "Let me try one more thing."

Spencer looked skeptical but nodded in agreement.

Back in Long's room St. James sat in the same chair and paused for a long moment, just staring at Long once again. Long stared back.

St. James sounded sincere.

"Okay, Frank. We know you're scared of this guy, whoever he is, and he'll kill you if you rat him out. So we'll make a deal with you. You tell us the city he lives in and we won't rat you out. I'm not asking for a name or an address, Frank. Just the city where he lives. You won't be squealing if all you give us is the city. What harm can that be?"

Long's eyebrows rose, his expression slowly changing from depressed to hopeful.

Behind Long, Spencer looked at St. James and mouthed the words "'What good is that going to do?"

St. James ignored the detective and waited.

Long opened his mouth.

"Toronto," he mumbled in a weak voice.

"Thank you, Frank."

With that, St. James motioned Spencer out of the room.

Outside, Spencer turned to St. James. "What the hell is the name of a city going to give you? There must be five million people or more in Greater Toronto. Narrowing that down a bit would have been helpful, don't you think?"

"Mark, I know the cities where my enemies live. None of them live in Toronto."

Spencer showed his frustration. "You know that doesn't mean a damn thing, Hamilton. Anyone can fly into Toronto, hire a thug, and then fly out. They don't have to live there, enemy or not."

"Only one suspect has flown into Toronto within the last couple of months."

"And who might that be?" Spencer asked.

"Either Amanda Fletcher or Samuel Franklin, suspects in the Stevens case. And since ninety-nine per cent of hits are ordered by males, Franklin is the best bet for your fly in–fly out theory. How do you feel about asking Toronto police to bring him in for questioning?"

Spencer struggled to bring his frustration under control. "I can do that, I suppose. What do you know about him?"

"Not much. Sketchy background. Disbarred US attorney who practiced in Chicago. I have reason to believe he flew to Toronto from JFK on September 20, on American Airlines flight 3657, at 9:05 a.m."

"Do you know where he's staying?"

"No."

"Not much to go on," Spencer said, scratching his head.

St. James smiled. "It's more than we had an hour ago."

Spencer headed to police headquarters to prepare criminal charges against Long, and St. James headed home to tackle other matters.

When he entered the condo, he found a note from Anna saying Dozer had arrived to escort her to the apartment and then to the Dirty Duck for an 11 a.m. shift.

10:45.

He went into the study and discovered an email from Jason Williamson asking him to please call.

So he did.

"What's cooking, Jason?"

"Good news: I got the manifests for the first flights Louis sent to us. Those from Atlanta to Chicago and on to Fargo for August 30 show Gyberson and Stevens as passengers, seated next to one another. I requested permission from airline officials to speak to flight attendants for those flights."

"Fabulous. Why do you want to talk to the flight attendants?"

"I sent pictures of Stevens and Gyberson to see if they remembered them, if anything odd happened during the flights."

"Like what?"

"Like whether Stevens was seen to be somehow under Gyberson's control. Remember, we still haven't proven Stevens was or was not part of the crime."

"Good point."

Jason continued. "I was allowed to speak with pursers but not junior flight attendants. Too young and inexperienced. It would create unnecessary fear, airline officials said. The purser on the flight from Atlanta to Chicago didn't remember the two men at all. The purser on the flight from Chicago to Fargo remembered Gyberson very well. He flirted with her the entire flight, and she was just about to ask the captain to speak to him when the plane began its descent."

"Not very smart," St. James said, "drawing attention when you're on the run."

Jason interjected. "Or, it's *very* smart. Maybe he wanted to be noticed, so someone totally independent could vouch for his whereabouts."

"I don't know, Jason. Pretty thin."

"Could be right."

"Anything else?"

"She remembered Gyberson laughing and joking with the man in the next seat. Made her feel self-conscious, like she was the butt of their jokes."

"Interesting on two fronts," St. James mused.

"How so?"

"Well, it validates our interpretation of the code, or at least part of it. But, more importantly, it tips the scales in favour of Stevens being part of something. I like it."

"Part of something I got: I was looking for that. But I didn't think about the code. You're right. It gives us more confidence in Louis's work. Not that I doubted it, mind you. I'll know for sure this afternoon when the remaining flight manifests come in."

"Great! Thanks, Jason."

While Jason and St. James were speaking, an email from Basil and William Hughes was forwarded to St. James by Van Hoyt. They pledged their full cooperation when St. James came to England. Van Hoyt left it to the three of them to organize the visit.

St. James now had too much on the go and was becoming increasingly concerned something might slip through the cracks. Everything had to be followed up in an organized manner for the investigations to turn out well. He decided to hold a team meeting to allocate responsibilities.

He booked a private dining area in the Westin Beach Club for six that evening and invited everyone to dinner. All accepted. Smythe would bring his laptop and case files.

It was 12:30 and St. James felt hungry, so he worked his way into the kitchen, made a smoked-meat sandwich, pulled a can of club soda from the refrigerator, and then returned to the study.

Eating lunch with one hand and one-finger typing with the other, St. James managed to get a coherent email off to the Hughes brothers advising that he and Anna would be in England the following Wednesday. He listed a number of documents he'd like to be available when they arrived: original inventory count sheets, summaries, and supporting documentation sent to HQ after year-end counts. He thought advance notice was not only courteous but would give the brothers time to prepare.

Then he booked an Air Canada flight to Toronto for himself and Anna next Tuesday, with an overnight connection to Heathrow.

Just as the printer pumped out travel confirmations, the phone rang.

Jason.

No pleasantries, only uncontrollable excitement.

"I can't believe it. I just can't believe it!"

"Calm down, Jason. Can't believe what?"

"Every flight number, every time, and every date matched every destination travelled by every suspect named in Louis's email," he said in disbelief.

"Wow, that's a mouthful! I take it you received the other manifests?" St. James said with a grin.

"You bet. We're making progress, Hamilton, thanks to you."

"We make a good team, Jason," St. James said.

Jason's news increased St. James's confidence in Smythe and Anna's decoding work exponentially.

"Jason, I know I am overstepping boundaries between us, but I think you need to bring the American Ambassador to Cayman and the Cayman Ambassador to the United States into the picture."

St. James heard Jason clear his throat.

"Let's be clear, Hamilton. I need all the help I can get. My only interest is in solving the case. I'm not worried about my ego. I leave political crap to those who are full of it."

St. James smiled broadly. "I knew there was a reason I liked you, Jason."

"What do we want from the ambassadors?"

St. James laid out the plan.

# Chapter 37

A man named Sterling settled into a booth in the Queen Elizabeth Hotel restaurant in downtown Montreal to wait for a man he'd never met, a man described in detail in an anonymous email.

The man would approach a booth next to the window facing the old Sun Life head office. There Sterling would be sitting, alone. The man would make eye contact with Sterling and then sit opposite him.

They would confirm each other by code. Sterling was told the man would say, "I think the Maple Leafs will make the playoffs this year." In response Sterling would say, "I believe you are right, friend, but will they take the cup?" That was confirmation they could speak freely.

Sterling waited a good twenty minutes while a number of people came and went, none of whom looked anything like the man described in the email.

He eyed the dining room. Only a few tables were occupied, one with ten or so ladies from the Red Hat Society loudly arguing Quebec politics. Large crystal chandeliers dotted the white-and-gold ceiling. Waiters dressed in tight-fitting black suits and matching bowties scurried among the tables.

Finally Sterling spotted a man vaguely fitting the description he'd been given entering the restaurant.

The man paused and looked around the room, seemingly uncomfortable. He spotted a man sitting where he had instructed Sterling to be in the anonymous email. A moment later he walked slowly toward the booth. Sterling studied him carefully as the man approached.

But the man walked past the booth Sterling occupied. Perhaps not the man Sterling was to meet after all. A few steps past him, the man abruptly turned and eyed him.

*Eye contact, good sign,* Sterling thought.

The man sat opposite, waited a beat while studying Sterling, then spewed the words Sterling expected to hear. Sterling responded as instructed.

"We don't seem to be doing very well here," the man mumbled. "First Clayton and Wagner are burned up. Now Long's arrested. Cost me three grand to have an expert dismantle those airbags and seatbelts."

Sterling nodded but said nothing.

"Do you have anyone who is competent?" the man said angrily.

Sterling tensed, concerned about how the meeting was going.

"I have a contract man. A shooter," he said hesitantly.

"Is he any good, or is he just going to disappoint like the others?" the man said harshly.

"He's very good, I guarantee it," Sterling said cautiously, demeanour approaching one of fear.

"You guaranteed the others. I'm afraid your guarantee isn't worth much anymore. Not what it used to be. They all failed. Incompetence," the man barked in a low voice so as not to be heard by those having lunch nearby.

"They were wrong for the job, I admit," Sterling said, anxiously fiddling with his silverware. "Shooter has never let me down."

"Let's hope he doesn't this time."

"I know my pay depends on it."

The stranger's forehead furrowed, and he leaned closer to Sterling. "Maybe more than your pay."

Without another word the man stood and wandered slowly out of the restaurant.

Sterling remained behind, seated for several minutes, overcome by an emotional cauldron of fear, uncertainty, and lack of confidence.

# Chapter 38

St. James's watch said 1:45.

For the next thirty minutes or so he prepared an outline for the team meeting later that afternoon. He made notes. Lists. Questions to be asked by each team member when carrying out their assigned responsibilities.

By 2:30 he was feeling cooped up and anxious enough to take his usual walk up Colonel By. Time to think, put pieces of case puzzles together, at least as much as he could with what he knew.

He arrived back home around five and immediately jumped in the shower. Then he shaved and dressed in a light-grey Nordstrom slim-fit blazer, a dark-blue dress shirt open at the neck, black slacks, and black wingtip shoes. At 5:30 he poured a glass of Primitivo and moved to the study, where he photocopied notes on Franklin and Gyberson and scribbled a few extra key questions he had thought of during his walk.

Anna had left a voicemail saying Dozer was escorting her to her apartment to dress properly for dinner. She would meet him at the restaurant.

He strolled over to the Westin around five after six, through the Beach Club's glass doors to a place rich in décor with suede walls and dark wood paneling. He made his way into the private dining area and found the team already into beer and wine.

Smythe was wearing a red-and-black tartan shirt with pink plaid pants; Anna, a black pantsuit. Both stunning, but for very different reasons. Dozer was in his best black leather Calvin Klein suit, his head freshly shaved and shinier than usual.

Anna was smiling broadly, and St. James knew why. Smythe and Dozer were standing side by side, an indescribable contrast that could only be appreciated in person.

The table was covered with white linen, with blue cloth napkins at each setting together with a full set of silver for four. The spaces between settings were wide enough to allow for files, note-taking, and Smythe's computer. All just as St. James had requested.

On the wall behind them hung a larger-than-life oil painting of a huge ship in rough seas. The lighting was dim, and the smell of exquisitely prepared food swirled about the richly decorated room.

The server was a beautiful girl named Cathy. Dozer was clearly already in love.

St. James said to Cathy, "Forty Creek on the rocks, please."

Cathy nodded. "Anyone like a refill?"

"I'll have another Molson," Dozer said with a huge smile meant only for her.

St. James grinned and pointed to the bottle in Dozer's hand, protesting lightheartedly. "You still have half the first one."

Dozer looked at the bottle as if he didn't know what it was, and then smiled a second time. "A man can plan ahead, can't he?"

Smythe and Anna laughed.

"Put your tongue back in your mouth, Dozer," St. James said. "We've got business to attend to. Let's all sit down."

Anna sat next to St. James, Dozer and Smythe sat opposite. Anna smiled again.

"Anna," Smythe said, "why are you smiling all the time?"

Anna shrugged, "Just seeing you and Dozer together ... well ... it's entertaining."

"What?" Dozer said, sounding slightly annoyed. "What's so funny about Louis and me?"

"Do you really have to ask?" St. James said with a chuckle.

Dozer looked at Smythe, and then at himself. Smythe looked at Dozer, and then at himself.

"I suppose not," Dozer slowly began to laugh along with the others. Smythe, not finding any of this funny, remained stone-faced.

"Let's get down to business, shall we?" St. James said, focusing everyone to the purpose of the evening.

He recounted Jason's findings with the flight manifests in the Stevens case. Smythe and Anna congratulated each other once again for breaking that part of the code.

Everyone was surprised to learn Gyberson and Stevens had travelled to Fargo together.

"If they were in it together why wouldn't they have travelled separately, on different airplanes? Seems a bit cocky to travel together," Anna said.

"That would make Gyberson the number one suspect in Stevens's murder," Dozer offered.

"That's right," Smythe agreed.

Cathy arrived with the Forty Creek for St. James and a second beer for Dozer.

Cathy stared at Smythe's outfit, looking bewildered. Smythe paid no attention.

St. James continued.

"I'd like us to agree on what each of us will be doing over the next two weeks. This is what I propose.

"On Stevens, we still haven't confirmed that $23 million was actually transferred to the Cayman National Bank. Supposedly there's a transfer or transfers with the ID ABA#021000089 to account number 012-67141, a transaction we believe has the code name *csprite1*, but we don't know the amount, whose account it is, or who made the transfer, that is if it actually was made. As we get closer the thieves will become nervous, perhaps trying to move the money before we get to it. So we'll ask the US and Cayman ambassadors to lobby the Cayman government and the bank to block any cash movement. Jason is on that now.

"I spoke with a partner in the Cayman law firm Higgins Johnson. She said legal action would have to be commenced in the United States before a bank account can be frozen in Cayman. Once an order is obtained it must be accepted by Cayman's Grand Court to be enforceable on the island. If and when that happens, the bank has to comply. All this takes time; time we don't have. That's why I asked Jason to go the ambassador route at the same time. Problem is, ambassadors are political people, loathe to get involved in commercial matters unless ordered to do so by their own government.

"Because you're already involved, Louis, I want you to stay close to Williamson, and keep me up to date."

Smythe nodded, typing vigorously.

"Tomorrow I'd like you to phone the woman at the Cayman bank. Tell her our plan. Ask her to unofficially flag the account. That means the bank's senior management will be notified if attempts are made to move money. Meanwhile Jason will work the Cayman government angle and ask his Island counterparts for help. If all else fails, they'll find some technical reason to prevent money leaving the country.

"And ask Nathan to instruct his attorneys to seek the appropriate US court order. Once that's in hand, ask Higgins Johnson to apply for its acceptance by the Cayman Grand Court. Then the bank can be served."

"Will do," Smythe said enthusiastically.

Dozer was scratching his bald head, looking perplexed.

"So, let me get this straight, Hamilton. You're unofficially asking the bank to flag the account, which sounds suspiciously like voluntary freezing to me. Then you're asking ambassadors to lobby for a freeze order from the Cayman government. Then, you're applying for a US court order to have the money legally frozen."

"That's right," St. James said without hesitation.

"Isn't that overkill?"

"I don't think so, Dozer. Look at it this way. Louis notifies the bank that the funds were stolen. The bank talks to its lawyers, who remind them that their fiduciary duty is to the money's *rightful* owner. The bank's lawyers call ours, who'll say an application is being made for a US court order to freeze the account and that the Grand Court will be asked to recognize it. While this is happening, the Cayman government is contemplating using the political process to freeze the account. A remote chance of that happening, but still, they would contemplate it."

All eyes were on St. James. "Now … here is the pivotal point," he said, gesturing with a forefinger. "The bank will not give money to anyone without the blessing of the Grand Court, knowing all this is in play. No banker in his right mind would let money go in that environment."

Anna leaned forward to face St. James. "What happens if the account signatories claim the money before the courts and government can act? What will the bank do then?"

"It has a duty to see that the money falls into the right hands. And the legal process has to unfold to determine whose those rightful hands are."

"That could take months," Smythe said with a pained expression.

"That's right," St. James said, grinning. "Meanwhile the signatories will put heat on the bank, argue the money was accepted by the bank on the strength of their signature and therefore should be released on the strength of their signature. They'll launch lawsuits against the bank for some trumped-up reason. Something like: if monies aren't released right away to consummate a business deal, both money and opportunity will be lost. Or some other such nonsense."

"Then what?" Dozer chimed in.

"We don't expect the bank to give the money to us; nor should they. They'll pay it to the Grand Court on the grounds that there are competing claims. The court holds the funds until the rightful owner can be determined. The money can't disappear, which is all we want out of the whole process anyway. Our problem's solved, the bank's problem's solved, possibly even without a US or Cayman court order, or action from the Cayman government. Sometimes people knowing what's in play, and knowing what's going to happen, behave as if it's already happened."

"Clever," Dozer said thoughtfully.

"How can you be so sure of all this Cayman political court stuff?" Louis asked.

"Cayman laws are derived from British law, just like Canada's. Both countries have parliamentary democracies and develop laws in a similar manner."

St. James let a few moments go by.

Then said, "Any questions?"

Everyone shook their heads.

Cathy returned to drop menus in front of them. Everyone took a moment to study their options.

"May I have another Pinot Grigio?" Anna asked, holding her wine glass high as if proposing a toast.

"And another Cabernet for me too," Smythe chimed in.

"Certainly," Cathy responded, smiling.

That prompted a smile in turn from Dozer.

And that prompted another giggle from Anna, who was quite enjoying the flirtation between the two.

Cathy turned to Anna.

"Would you like an appetizer?"

"Please. Dungeness crab would be great," Anna replied, pointing to a line on the menu.

Cathy turned to St. James.

"And for you, Mr. St. James?"

"I'll try your Bigeye tuna."

Smythe didn't wait to be asked.

"Clams casino."

"Glad you saved me for last," Dozer said, grin so wide that St. James thought his face would crack.

"Always save the best for last," Cathy said in a seductive voice, ignoring Smythe's fake gag.

"Would you like an appetizer?" she said to Dozer.

"Beef tenderloin, please."

"How would you like it done?" Cathy asked.

"Medium rare." Dozer said in a trance-like tone.

"Very well," she said, "thank you. Shouldn't be too long."

With that she walked away slowly, for Dozer's benefit, St. James was sure; and Dozer took full advantage of the view. His eyes didn't return to the table until Cathy was well out of sight.

St. James grinned.

"If I can persuade Dozer to rejoin the meeting, we'll proceed."

"Yeah. Yeah. I'm here," he said as if St. James was nagging.

"Then there's Malachi Jensen. He'll have to be interviewed a second time. I'll do that when we return from England.

"Gyberson and The Carstairs Group need to be chased down. Fargo police put an APB and BOLO on Gyberson as suspect one for Stevens's murder. He's also on an FBI wanted list. We'll be there when he's picked up. Dozer, you're the best man for this job. I'm told he's a smaller man. You'll intimidate the hell out of him."

Smythe squinted, "I know APB stands for All Points Bulletin from  cop shows. What's a BOLO?"

"BOLO stands for Be On the Lookout," St. James said as he handed Gyberson's duplicate file to Dozer. "There's a list of questions to ask inside."

Dozer's huge hand flipped open the cover. "Gotcha," he said, as he ran a finger down each page.

"Dozer, Anna will be with me in England, so I'll be her guard. I have a friend at Scotland Yard I've worked with many times, Inspector David Kingston. He'll provide whatever protection he can spare while we're there. That frees you for the Gyberson job and one other I'll mention in a minute."

St. James stopped there. The team had a number of questions, mostly around logistics and communication while he and Anna were in England.

Dozer was worried about the traps and electronic surveillance equipment at Anna's apartment while he was doing other things. Someone had to monitor all this.

"There will be other Frank Longs," he said. "We have to plan for that."

"I agree. What about your brother? Can he handle that while you do other things?" St. James asked.

"You mean Denzel?"

"Well, how many brothers do you have?" St. James asked lightheartedly.

"One," he said calmly, as if St. James's question was serious.

"Is he between jobs?"

"You could say that."

"Can he do the surveillance job?" St. James persisted.

"With a little training, maybe."

"How much training?"

Dozer looked somewhat distant. "About a day."

"Can he be trained before next Tuesday?"

Anna interrupted.

"I don't mean to be disrespectful, Dozer, but why am I feeling uncomfortable with your brother watching my apartment?"

Dozer turned to Anna. "Well, Anna, it's like this ... you're not feeling uncomfortable with Denzel. You're sensing that *I'm* feeling uncomfortable with Denzel. And that's making you uncomfortable. You see, Denzel is all right when I'm right there, working alongside him, constantly giving direction."

"Dozer," St. James said abruptly.

"What?"

"What's wrong with Denzel?"

Dozer hesitated. "It's ... hard to describe."

"Dozer," St. James said firmly, "we don't have all night."

"Denzel's slow," Dozer finally blurted. "I'm embarrassed by it. I shouldn't be, I know. But I am."

Dozer looked down at his place setting like a child about to be scolded.

St. James momentarily looked at the ceiling, debating how to get out of this without ruining the evening. Anna looked about to tear up. Smythe didn't know what to say or where to look, so he stared at the painting on the far wall.

"Look, Dozer, I'm sorry. I had no idea."

"No way you could have known, man" he said softly. "I never talked about it. I was ashamed of him all through childhood. We were teenagers before I fully understood his disability. Then I found myself protecting him from bullies. Kids made fun of him and pushed him around. Now I'm ashamed of myself for being ashamed of him."

St. James considered this as he stared at the artwork along with Smythe.

"Then you owe him a great debt," St. James said finally.

Dozer shot St. James a sharp look. "What do you mean I owe him a great debt?" he said, as if St. James meant to insult.

"One of your greatest gifts is you don't tolerate bullies; it's burned into your DNA from protecting Denzel. His younger years made you a better person.

"Lack of tolerance for bullies and never giving up on a case is why you are a superb detective, what makes you an exceptional person, and why you have my most prized possession."

"What's that?" Dozer said, now sounding more confused than annoyed.

"My everlasting respect! Your brother has a job with me on this case. Train him. You're the best at what you do. Teach him. Give him a chance. We all have limitations. Some more than others."

Anna smiled, seemingly proud of St. James's handling of the situation. Dozer's face was strained.

Cathy arrived with appetizers, the second Pinot Grigio for Anna and Cabernet for Smythe, but stopped suddenly when she saw everyone's faces. Her smile faded.

"What's wrong?" she asked. "When I left everyone was so happy, poking fun at one another."

Suddenly realizing she'd crossed the server–customer line, she said, "I'm sorry. That's none of my business. I misspoke."

St. James raised his hand in Cathy's direction.

"Don't worry, Cathy. This is a team-building night. You've done nothing wrong," he consoled.

Cathy's eyes moved rapidly from face to face as if to ask what kind of team building exercise could make people this sad.

Cathy struggled to refocus.

"Would you like wine with your meal?" she said finally.

St. James's eyes surveyed the table.

"Red or white?" he asked.

Everyone's lack of composure left St. James's question floating out there, unanswered.

St. James turned to Cathy.

"Give me a second if you would, Cathy."

"Of course."

St. James opened the wine list.

"We'll have a bottle of each to start. Then we'll see where the evening takes us."

"Wise approach, Mr. St. James," Cathy said with a forced smile.

"For the white, we'll have a bottle of Ronco del Gelso Pinot Grigio 2007. For red, the Talenti Rosso di Montalcino 2008."

"Both excellent choices, sir. When I return with the wine, I'll take orders for the main course."

"Thank you, Cathy," St. James said soberly.

With that, she whisked herself away toward the bar.

Dozer's eyes didn't follow her this time. He was pensive, reflecting on what had just happened.

When everyone had more or less restored themselves, they nibbled away at their appetizers. The room was quiet, and St. James decided to leave it that way, let someone else break the silence. Surprisingly, it was Dozer who took the plunge.

"What you said about me owing Denzel: you're right, Hamilton. I have to appreciate Denzel for who he is, and for what he's capable of being, not dwell on what he can't do. I'm afraid I've been looking at this through childhood eyes. Immature ones. I have skills to grow him, more than I have wanted to up to now."

"That's the spirit, Dozer!" St. James said with a fist pump. "Think of it this way: there are jobs demanding consistent and reliable behaviour that are mind-numbingly boring, because they're repetitive. Denzel might be very good at them. Once he learns what to do, he can just repeat the steps, over and over. Same routine every day. Repetition brings familiarity. Familiarity brings comfort. He's not likely to drop the ball. You and I would, because we're used to greater challenges. Our minds would wander all over the place just to keep entertained. We'd lose focus on what we're supposed to do, maybe miss something important."

"Thanks for opening my eyes, Hamilton. I'm grateful to have you as both a client and a friend. I'm also grateful for you giving Denzel a chance."

St. James straightened in his chair and lightheartedly wagged a finger in Dozer's direction.

"Let's be clear. I'll pay a fair wage for a fair day's work. He'll earn his keep, albeit with your training. His confidence will grow, hopefully allowing him to do more jobs down the road."

"I believe that too, Hamilton."

The appetizers were finished in silence.

Cathy returned with two bottles of wine and poured each goblet according to preferences.

"Now, what would everyone like for the main course?"

Dozer said, "I'll have the New York striploin, medium rare, sautéed mushrooms and onions, with a baked potato."

Cathy scribbled the choice.

Cathy and Dozer were back to smiling at one another.

Anna followed. "Maple-glazed salmon, pink in the centre, please."

"Very well."

Cathy stared at Smythe.

"I'll try the macadamia-crusted halibut."

"And for you, Mr. St. James?"

"King crab, thanks Cathy."

Cathy finished scribbling the selections and hurried off.

St. James sipped wine and returned to the agenda.

"As you know, Samuel Franklin flew to Toronto from JFK on September 20. When Spencer and I questioned Long, I specifically asked what city his employer lived in. He said Toronto. Spencer said anyone could fly in, make an arrangement with Long, and then fly out. Long might have just assumed he lived in Toronto. Either way I have never been threatened by anyone from Toronto, and Samuel Franklin doesn't have a motive, at least not yet.

"Dozer, this is the second assignment I have for you. Spencer asked Toronto police to find Franklin and bring him in for questioning to see what can be learned about Stevens, the money, and his relationship with Gyberson. I'd like you to work with them. When they find Franklin, you'll have a crack at him too. Here are some notes and questions."

St. James handed Dozer a file, and Dozer took a few moments to scan its contents.

"Easy enough. I have no questions," he said conclusively.

"Good. That's all I have on Stevens," St. James said. "Now, if there are no questions, we'll turn to CISI."

No one spoke.

"As you know, I started the investigation this week. Anna and I leave for England this Tuesday to investigate their two largest fish plants. There was a huge inventory write-up last fiscal year, and these two plants account for more than 50% of the adjustment. No one on the board really understands the write-up. That's the crux of the case: to find out what happened with inventory and if wrongdoing was involved."

Smythe interrupted. "Didn't this all begin with the board not trusting the CEO?"

"Yes. But when I met Anderson one-on-one he had inventory concerns too. And he was more civil with me than he had been earlier. I may have misjudged him at first. I believe his initial behaviour was driven by frustration with the board showing no appreciation for the company's financial success. Most likely he saw me as a vote of non-confidence by the board, a threat to his position."

"Well maybe he'll become an ally for you, Hamilton," Dozer said.

"Good point, Dozer," said Anna.

Smythe nodded in agreement.

St. James looked reflective. "Possible, I guess. We'll see what happens."

The conversation drifted from business to chatter about hockey teams and politics until Cathy returned with the main courses.

St. James ordered more wine.

St. James could see Dozer wasn't quite over outing Denzel's handicap. But surely Dozer would feel better in the long run. Keeping it to himself for all this time must have been stressful. Conflicting feelings of embarrassment and guilt isn't healthy for anyone, even if they are tough as nails.

They said goodnight around 8:30 and went their separate ways. St. James and Anna strolled back to 700 Sussex, poured a glass of Bailey's Irish Cream on the rocks each, and sat quietly on the living room chesterfield.

"That was a helluva meeting, Hamilton," Anna said as she popped off her shoes and put her feet down on the large glass coffee table. "One minute we're laughing, the next we're close to tears. Can't imagine what's going through Cathy's mind."

St. James said, "I feel sorry for Dozer, keeping Denzel's condition to himself all this time. Must have been difficult."

"Would eat him up inside. I was proud of how you handled the situation, though, linking Dozer's hatred of bullies to defending

Denzel. If you hadn't done that, I'm not sure what would have happened."

He nodded.

"You didn't have to give Denzel a job either. Very generous."

"It's the least I could do for a man who's saved my life on more than one occasion."

Anna leaned over and kissed him.

"You're wonderful, Hamilton," she said softly.

He returned the kiss. "So are you. I'm lucky to have you in my life."

Suddenly Anna pulled back, and St. James sensed a bout of panic coming.

"Hamilton, we're going to England in a couple of days!"

He chuckled.

"I know, Anna. I'm the one who invited you, remember?"

"I don't mean it like that, silly. I mean I don't have much time to get ready!"

"We won't be visiting the Queen. You don't need much."

Anna's panic turned to excitement, her words gathering speed as she spoke. "I have to get clothes from the apartment tomorrow, and my suitcase, and cosmetics. Do I have enough of everything? There's so much to think about!"

# Chapter 39

Saturday morning St. James woke to the sound of blaring car horns and yelling rising from the street. Anna was asleep. He hauled on clothes, shuffled over to the window, and discovered a three-car pileup on Sussex; a black limousine, a red sedan, and a blue half-ton pickup. The pickup's driver was doing most of the yelling. From what St. James could make out he was blaming the limo driver for hitting the sedan and driving it into his tailgate. The tailgate was sprung, and cabbage and turnips were rolling around the street. Most likely the pickup was headed for a market stall to sell vegetables. Losing time and inventory more or less accounted for his irritable state. The sight of two uniformed policemen chasing turnips rolling down Sussex made St. James laugh.

He went into the kitchen and fumbled with the Keurig, managing to fill it with water and pop in a Colombian ground pod, then fetched the morning paper.

When the coffee had fully percolated he settled on an island stool to read the newspaper.

The phone rang. Call display said Dozer.

"Hamilton, thank you again for last night, for making me see more clearly."

"Only too happy to help," St. James said nonchalantly.

"I've worked it out."

"Worked what out?"

"Denzel's training."

"That's wonderful, Dozer. How will you do it?"

"I was up at six this morning thinking it through, writing down every step in detail. Times to check Anna's apartment, the number and locations of traps, what to do if someone's caught, your telephone numbers, plus Detective Spencer's and the hospital's. I laid out every step from start to finish with little boxes to check after he completes each one."

"You mean like airport washrooms?"

Dozer was silent for a beat. "Huh?"

"You know. Charts on the back of washroom doors showing when they were serviced last, little boxes ticked for each action completed, and the attendant's initials proving he was there."

Again silence.

"Whatever, man … Whatever. I don't go in there to read doors."

St. James shrugged at the phone.

"Next team meeting, you bring Denzel. All team members are equal."

"I'll have to think about that. I have to grow into this, Hamilton. I can't be pushed, man."

"Fair enough," St. James conceded. "I'll take Anna to her apartment this morning to gather things for England. After that I thought we'd drive to Wakefield, let her wander through some shops. Maybe grab lunch at the Wakefield Mill. I know Anna would feel better if you were with us. Can you rent a car?"

"No problem. What time?"

"Hmm. We'll need two hours or so to get ready. How about 10:15?"

"Yeah, that gives me enough time," he said confidently. "I'll call you from the rental at 10:15."

"Good enough," St. James said and disconnected.

Anna yelled from the bedroom. "Any coffee?"

"Make one for you in a jiffy."

"Would you be a dear and bring it to me before I shower?"

"Right there, honey," he yelled.

St. James repeated the Keurig procedure, placed Anna's coffee on the dresser, and kissed her good morning.

"What was that racket I heard earlier?" she said with a yawn.

"Fender-bender on Sussex. A farmer's half-ton hit from behind; he lost cabbage and turnip all over the street."

"Oh? And who was on the phone?"

"Dozer. He called to tell me how he was going to train Denzel before we go to England."

Anna sat up to drink her coffee. "How'd he sound?"

"Like a man who knows he has to change."

"Hmm." Anna nodded. "Hope he and Denzel will be okay."

"If I know Dozer, he'll figure it out. He always does the right thing, in the end."

"In the end? What do you mean?" Anna asked.

St. James shrugged. "Sometimes he needs time to process things. Just the way he is."

Anna nodded.

St. James said, "I asked him to rent a car to shadow us today. I told him we'd be ready by 10:15. Hope that's okay with you."

"Oh! What are we doing?" she asked with a surprised look.

"First, we'll go to your place to gather things for England. Then I thought we'd do something fun."

Anna's face lit up.

"Fun? What kind of fun?"

"I thought we'd drive to Wakefield, look in some shops, and maybe have lunch at the Mill."

"What a great idea, Hamilton," she said enthusiastically. "I heard it's a lovely little village, but I've never been. How far?"

"About a half-hour."

"I'll hurry. We'll need something to eat before we go."

St. James mimicked a well-known western movie actor. "I'll go out to the chuck wagon, ma'am, to see what I can rustle up while you're fixin' to get pretty for me."

"Okay, cowboy." Anna jumped from the bed and headed toward the shower, coffee in hand.

St. James turned on Newsworld while he scrambled eggs and made fruit cocktail and dry whole-wheat toast.

About fifteen minutes later Anna emerged, ready to go. They wolfed down breakfast and cleaned up the kitchen. Then it was St. James's turn to shower. When he resurfaced he found Anna sitting at the table reading the newspaper.

"Dozer called while you were in the shower. He's sitting in a rental car on Mackenzie Avenue waiting for us."

"Excellent. Have everything you need?"

"Everything but the apartment keys, which Dozer has."

Anna folded the newspaper and placed it on the kitchen counter.

They grabbed jackets from the hall closet, locked the condo, and hit the parking-level button.

Dozer had rented a lime-green Chrysler, which he thought would be easier to spot if they got separated in traffic. St. James pulled the red Cadillac up from the underground onto Sussex and waited for Dozer to turn the corner before heading to Anna's apartment.

When they turned into Anna's laneway, Dozer pulled in behind. Another man St. James assumed to be Denzel was sitting in the passenger seat.

Denzel was a bit taller than Dozer, a lot thinner, and, unlike his brother, had a full head of curly black hair. Dozer introduced them, but Denzel said nothing. He just swayed back and forth with a faint smile. St. James and Anna studied Dozer's interaction with his brother, mostly to learn how they should communicate respectfully. It was easy. Dozer just talked to him like anyone else. Anna liked that.

"You wait here," Dozer said. "I'll go up first to check the apartment."

The three waited by the cars until Dozer reported everything was okay. Then they all went up. Dozer pointed to the trap under the window in the sitting room.

"Don't go close to this one. It's the most sensitive, triggered by the slightest motion."

Anna looked disgusted. St. James thanked God Dozer had cleaned up Long's blood before they got there.

St. James sat in the big orange rocker while Anna pulled a suitcase from her closet's top shelf and began filling it with things she thought she'd need in England. Meanwhile Dozer took Denzel through every step he'd listed earlier that morning, methodically covering each room three times. In addition to the sitting room trap was one under the narrow kitchen window, and another under Anna's bedroom window. Dozer carefully explained how each worked, how to release someone from their clutches, and the people and numbers to call if it actually happened. Then Dozer snapped one of the traps so Denzel could practice resetting it. Dozer wanted to be sure he could handle it on his own. To be certain Denzel mastered everything, he had him repeat every step three times. Denzel gained a little more confidence each time.

Denzel stopped swaying whenever Dozer spoke and began again when his brother went quiet. St. James was impressed he asked for steps to be repeated. It showed he was either getting it or trying to. It wasn't only Denzel who had to gain confidence: Anna and St. James had to be sure they were leaving her apartment in capable hands.

Anna emerged from the bedroom fifteen minutes later, dragging a Pullman suitcase. St. James looked at the size of it, and then at her, then at the case once again.

"We're only going for a week. You realize that, right?"

Anna smiled. "A girl's got to be ready for any occasion, you know."

He pointed to the case. "Hope I don't get a hernia lugging that thing downstairs."

"Don't be so silly," she said as she entered the kitchen.

Dozer and Denzel reappeared in the sitting room.

"We're finished, Hamilton. All set to go," Dozer said with a smile, giving his brother a loving pat on the shoulder. "Right, Denzel?"

"Right, Erasmus," Denzel said.

Dozer turned to St. James.

"Denzel doesn't like the nickname Bulldozer."

St. James nodded and turned to Denzel.

"Welcome to the case, Denzel. Glad to have you on board."

"Thank you, sir," Denzel said slowly. "I like to be with my brother."

"I'm going to drive Denzel home, Hamilton. You and Anna stay here. I won't be long; he lives just four blocks away."

When he returned ten minutes later Dozer said reassuringly, "Denzel will be fine. He's excited to be working."

"Does he live alone?" St. James asked cautiously.

"In a group home. He has a room with twin beds so there's a spot for me when I visit. The people managing the place are wonderful. They love Denzel, probably because he's always pleasant and no bother."

"He's lucky to have you, Dozer," Anna said smiling.

"Are we ready for Wakefield?" St. James said with an enthusiastic clap of his hands.

"I am," Anna replied cheerfully.

"Have one quick stop to make first," said Dozer. "It will just take a minute."

St. James nodded.

"We'll follow you."

And they did, to a condo building on York Street. St. James pulled in behind Dozer's green rental and left the motor running while Dozer entered the main door, emerging minutes later with a lady on his arm.

"Is that who I think it is?" Anna said in an astonished voice.

"If you're thinking Cathy, you'd be right," St. James said with a chuckle.

Anna giggled. "He works fast, I'll give him that."

"It appears we are four for lunch," St. James quipped.

St. James pulled the Cadillac onto Sussex and rolled toward the Macdonald-Cartier Bridge, maintaining a distance of one car length ahead of Dozer and Cathy.

When he thought about taking Anna to Wakefield, flashbacks hadn't entered his mind. Anna hadn't been on this part of Sussex since they were almost killed just days ago. A feeling of thoughtlessness crept over him. He pulled the Cadillac to the curb, bringing it to a halt in front of the Global Affairs building.

Dozer pulled in behind, shrugged, his hands raised as if to say, What's wrong man? St. James waved everything okay.

"What's wrong, Hamilton?" Anna said, looking surprised.

"I'm sorry, Anna. I've been thoughtless and inconsiderate."

She turned to him, looking amused.

"Whatever are you talking about?"

"We're on the same route as the night the two thugs tried to kill us. Your flashbacks … I never thought what today might do to you."

Anna broke into a gentle smile as she leaned into him.

"Considerate of you, Hamilton, but I can't avoid fun the rest of my life because of one unpleasant experience. What kind of life would I have? Especially hanging around you. Why, in a few months I wouldn't be able to leave home at all." Her smile grew wider.

St. James laughed. "Suppose that's true." He shifted the Cadillac into drive and continued on toward Wakefield.

Halfway to Wakefield Anna said, "Do you mind if I ask you a personal question?"

He looked over at her, wondering what was coming next.

"Go ahead."

"How do you pay for your lifestyle? You don't have a steady paycheque, other than the university, and that wouldn't even begin to cover what you spend. Cost of travel and restaurants means nothing to you. You live in a beautiful building, drive an expensive car, and gamble as if you don't have a care in the world."

St. James smiled.

"It's more difficult to explain than it is to show, which I will gladly do. Do you mind giving me a couple of weeks to do that?"

Anna felt awkward. "Yeah ... Sure. Of course. None of my business anyway. Just wondering, that's all. Only now got up the courage to ask."

St. James reached over and took her hand in his.

"All in good time, my dear. All in good time."

St. James felt Anna's eyes on him for most of the remaining drive.

It was 11:20 when they arrived on Main Street in Wakefield, Dozer and Cathy close behind. A shop called Boutique Jamboree caught Anna's eye.

She said, pointing, "I'd love to explore that shop, Hamilton."

"Absolutely. It's a fun day, let's do it."

St. James pulled into the parking area next to the building, and Dozer brought the green Chrysler to a halt next to the Cadillac. When they all climbed out Anna latched onto Cathy, and the two went inside while Dozer and St. James sat on a bench on the front porch.

"Hey man, why'd you stop on Sussex?" Dozer said quizzically.

St. James explained the flashback thing with Anna. Dozer just nodded.

"Did you see anything unusual on the way up?" St. James asked, eyes surveying the street.

Dozer pointed to a maroon late-model Accord parked in front of a grey building across the street. "You see that Honda Accord?"

"Yep."

"Two guys are sitting in the front. They kept tight behind us all the way up. I'd speed up, they'd speed up. I'd slow down, they'd slow down. They're running surveillance for someone."

Dozer paused, rubbing his head and trying to decide how to handle the situation.

"You sit here," he said finally. "I'll go into Boutique Jamboree and out the back, work my way around a couple of buildings, then cross the street and have a little chat with the boys. See what I can find out."

St. James nodded. "Be careful. We don't know what we're dealing with here."

Dozer nodded and went into the store, passing Anna and Cathy without a word, and out the back. The women paused long enough to watch him pass through, looked at one another, shrugged, and went back to inspecting what the store had to offer.

St. James watched Dozer work his way down Boutique Jamboree's side of the street and cross over toward a bank building two doors to the right of the Accord. The Accord guys never took their eyes off St. James. St. James figured that's why Dozer told him to stay put. He was the decoy so Dozer could sneak up unnoticed.

Dozer worked his way behind the building and along the southern wall. When he got to the front corner of the building, he noticed that the Accord's driver-side window was all the way down. He crouched behind the vehicle, then quietly duck-walked toward the open window, low enough to not alert the driver. He quickly rose and drew back his huge fist and punched the driver's nose so hard the man cried out like a child, partly in pain, partly out of surprise. Blood spewed over the Accord's dash as the driver doubled over the steering wheel, rapidly rocking back and forth as if motion would ease the pain.

The passenger leapt from the vehicle and bolted around a red-brick church toward the bank. St. James catapulted from the porch and ran to head off the passenger before he escaped completely.

St. James stood a good six inches taller than the passenger, with enough stride to overtake the man as he rounded the church. Tackling him from behind, St. James shoved his face into gravel and wrenched both arms behind as if to cuff him. The passenger yelled in pain.

"Okay, buddy, on your feet."

"Ease up," the passenger yelled. "You're hurting my arm."

"It'll hurt more than that if you don't cooperate," St. James growled through gritted teeth. "Come on."

He pulled the man to his feet and pushed him to the side of the building where the Accord was parked. Dozer was already there holding the bloodied driver. They shoved both men behind the building so as not to draw any more attention than they already had. Simultaneously, they slammed the two up against the back wall.

"Who hired you?" Dozer demanded.

"Nobody hired us," the driver yelled. "Just out for a drive. You'll be charged for this."

"I doubt it," Dozer barked.

He slammed the driver against the wall a second time.

"Who hired you?" he repeated.

"No one," yelled the passenger.

"Then we'll hold you until the police arrive. Maybe you'll tell them," St. James said angrily.

The driver's nose, obviously broken, continued to spew blood. He appeared to be rethinking his position.

"Look, we weren't sent to hurt you," he said finally.

Dozer released his grip slightly, enough for the man to wipe blood from his face.

"Why were you following us?" Dozer said forcefully, an inch from the driver's face. With all his force he slammed the man a third time.

The driver winced with pain but said nothing.

"Why did you follow us?" Dozer yelled again, pinning the man against the building, his huge, meaty hands tight around the driver's throat.

"To see where you were going," the man said, wincing again.

"By whom?"

The driver tried to catch his breath. "Some guy named Sterling," he squeaked, voice rattly from a blood-filled throat.

"First name?"

"Never gave it. Just Sterling," the passenger cried.

Not to be outdone by Dozer, St. James slammed the passenger up against the wall again too.

"How much did he pay you?" Dozer said in a harsh tone.

"$500 up front, $1,500 when we delivered information."

"How were you to deliver information?" St. James asked.

"Email."

"Give me your phone," Dozer demanded, tightening his grip around the man's throat.

The driver pulled a cell from his pocket and Dozer snatched it from his hands. He scrolled through a conversation back and forth with a man located in the Montreal area code.

"Montreal," Dozer mumbled as he turned to St. James. "A running commentary on tailing us."

Dozer grunted as he read the total exchange, then hit reply.

*We have your stool pigeons and they are singing. We're coming to get you!*

*Regards, Hamilton St. James and Dozer White.*

"I thought the regards thing was a nice touch," St. James said, smiling.

With that, they let the pigeons fly.

# Chapter 40

Bulldozer and St. James were in agreement: if they couldn't identify Sterling they may as well make him paranoid.

"Reverse intimidation," St. James called it when Dozer showed him the email he had sent to Sterling. "That'll have him looking over his shoulder for a time."

Dozer nodded and smiled.

No point holding the men, even less turning them over to police. They were engaged by email, probably a public email address like a library's, no face-to-face with Sterling. A dead end.

Dozer pocketed the cell thinking Spencer might make something of it. He probably had contacts in the Quebec Sûreté who could help track this Sterling fellow down.

They made their way back across the street to Boutique Jamboree where the women had found a number of treasures, each grabbing two bags from the counter when the guys walked in.

"What happened to you two?" Anna asked suspiciously.

"Ran into a couple of old friends," Dozer lied.

Anna gave St. James a look but decided to let it go.

"Anyone hungry?" he asked, to force Anna off the scent.

"Starving," Dozer said enthusiastically.

Cathy chimed in. "I could use a bite too."

"Great," St. James said. "Let's go up to the Mill."

The Wakefield Mill was situated in a park-like setting next to a waterfall with enough strength to turn a grist mill wheel in the 1800s. The restaurant had wonderful food choices and a well-stocked wine cellar. Fireplaces, exposed stone walls, and rough-cut wooden beams made for a warm atmosphere.

The restaurant overlooked the falls: delightful eye candy for diners.

The maître d' escorted them to a table by the window with a full view of the river. St. James ordered pasta, everyone else the roast beef.

An hour later everyone had finished lunch and was anxious to get back to Ottawa.

The drive back was uneventful. No sign of a tail. And no attempt to run them off the road, for which St. James was grateful.

When they arrived on Wellington, Dozer tooted the horn and waved goodbye as the rental veered left into the Market, to Cathy's condo, Anna assumed. St. James pointed the Cadillac down 700's parking ramp to his usual space.

Sunday morning turned out to be foggy. Many flights in and out of Ottawa were cancelled, others delayed for hours.

Anna busied herself getting ready for England, laying out clothes and checking lists to make sure she wasn't forgetting anything. By 11:00 what she owned was spread over the chesterfield and everything else.

"Jesus, Anna, there's no place for me to sit," St. James complained.

"Nothing wrong with the kitchen island," she said lightheartedly.

Feeling violated in his own space St. James grabbed a coffee and headed for the study where he emailed Williamson to ask about progress with the ambassadors and the Cayman authorities. He hoped political heat would persuade the bank to freeze the accounts and release information that might be relevant to the case.

St. James copied Nathan and Slate on the email to Williamson to keep them in the loop. Then he prepared an email update for Mary DeSilva, outlining in detail the political strategy he and Williamson had in play. She would have it first thing Monday morning when she got into the office.

Satisfied everything was under control, he decided to walk his usual route.

Anna objected.

"Do you really think that wise? After all, someone clearly wants you dead. Walking the canal makes you an easy target."

"I can't become a recluse every time someone threatens me. It's part of what I do."

"Well, at least take Bulldozer with you."

"Naw, I want to be alone. I need time to think. Dozer would babble the whole walk. I wouldn't be able to hear myself think."

Anna frowned.

St. James laced up his Nikes, grabbed a windbreaker from the closet, and headed out the door.

Some but not all of the early-morning fog had lifted, and the sidewalks were damp from a light overnight mist. The air was fresh and clean. Church bells rang in the distance, a reminder it was Sunday.

He walked slower than usual, enjoying the fresh air, his mind awash with a rampant stream of consciousness.

The men he and Dozer had rousted in Wakefield.

*Who is Sterling? Where does he fit in all this? Who is he working for? What's next?*

Somehow it didn't feel like Nells's gang. Nells wasn't sophisticated enough to engage others to do his dirty work. His gang consisted of hands-on crooks, scam artists, and thieves, but not murderers.

He thought about Anna. Where was the relationship going? How did he really feel about her?

What was next with the Stevens case? He had to tie it off soon, if for no other reason than to pump life into his winded cashflow.

He second guessed himself again for taking on the CISI case. Anderson was not the spin doctor Graves had made him out to be.

*Am I just a pawn in some internal political game?*

When he was almost to the Pretoria Bridge St. James felt a presence. At first he didn't know from where, then he realized it was from behind. Not a runner or a cyclist, they would have passed already. It felt more like a lingering presence, as if someone or something wanted to maintain a consistent distance.

When he reached the Pretoria Bridge he turned right over the canal onto Elgin instead of straight down Colonel By as he usually did. The presence made the same turn, keeping pace. St. James was reluctant to confront whatever it was: it could be something he wasn't prepared for. But, that wouldn't work for long. Nor would it solve anything. The ostrich strategy never worked.

Police headquarters was located on the next block, after the Queensway–Elgin Street overpass. That gave him some comfort, but not much. It was Sunday morning. Very little traffic. Police officers would already be assigned and cruising different parts of the city. There wouldn't be many at headquarters itself, maybe a skeleton staff; some off for the weekend, but most on patrol.

The presence had to be confronted one way or another, police or no police. Under the overpass at the corner of Elgin and Catherine, St. James in one swift move snapped an about-face.

There, twenty feet behind, startled by St. James's move, was a man wearing a long black coat and a white toque. He seemed familiar, but at first St. James couldn't place him. Then he could. The guy's nose was bandaged. It was the Accord driver from Wakefield.

A small black SUV crept alongside the man. Maybe a Honda CR-V, tinted windows, St. James couldn't be sure.

Then bandaged nose pulled something from his overcoat, something St. James couldn't see. Then he could. It was a gun. A sharp, excruciating pain ripping through his left shoulder was the last thing he remembered.

# Chapter 41

At first St. James couldn't see. Then he couldn't focus. Everything was murky like the early morning fog. Yet it seemed more eerie than fog. Then he winced. His left shoulder throbbed with all the intensity of a badly decayed tooth, times ten.

Vision recovery was a long slow process. He saw white, a white mass. Then the white mass spoke.

"I am Dr. Lee. You're a very lucky man, Mr. St. James," said the white mass. "Nothing vital was hit. Two inches lower and you wouldn't have a worry ever again."

"Where am I?" he mumbled.

"Ottawa Civic."

"What day is it?"

"Sunday. Take it easy. You're just out of surgery. A lot of anxious people are waiting to see you, but I can't let them in all at once. You've had enough excitement for one day. I'll just let your girlfriend in for now."

Feeling terrible, St. James was content with Doctor Lee's gatekeeping.

Dr. Lee opened the door and signalled Anna into the room. She brushed past him and ran straight to St. James's bedside, tightly holding his hand.

"I have rounds to make," Dr. Lee said. "I will look in on you later."

Anna sobbed.

"I was never so scared in all my life. So afraid, I could have lost you," she cried frantically.

St. James tried to reassure her.

"Anna, it's not that serious."

But that wasn't her point. It most certainly could have been serious.

"Who else is out there?" he asked groggily.

"Everyone. Nothing could keep them away. Spencer's here too, although he may be here more out of duty than love," she babbled.

"Oh, I don't know. Mark and I get along pretty well." A feeble attempt at humour. "Ask them all to come in. Easier on me to tell the story once and not four times."

"Are you sure?"

"I'm sure."

Anna beckoned in the herd. Smythe, Dozer, and Detective Spencer traipsed in, all wanting to talk at once. St. James held up his hand. The room went quiet.

"Where's Denzel?" he asked looking at Dozer.

Dozer said, "Waiting in the hall."

St. James frowned. Dozer got the message. Without another word he opened the door and waved Denzel into the room.

"Hi Denzel," St. James said with as much warmth as he could muster.

"Wanted to be here because you gave me a job," Denzel said, staring at the floor.

"Glad you came, Denzel."

Denzel smiled.

Spencer had his notepad out ready to take notes.

"What happened, Hamilton?" he said anxiously.

St. James began with the start of his walk, giving as much detail as he could given his physical and mental state. He described the presence, the same feeling as someone standing in a pitch-black room with you. Nothing you can point to. No sound. No touch. No smell. Nothing but the feeling someone had entered your space. That was the presence.

"Had you seen or heard anybody or anything up to this point?" Spencer said, scribbling in his notebook.

"Nothing. I hadn't turned around at that point. I wanted to assess the risk before making a move."

"Then what happened?" Dozer said.

"I walked under the Queensway overpass and out the other side on Elgin, then made an abrupt about-face."

Smythe was anxious too. "And?"

"I saw someone vaguely familiar, someone I couldn't place at first, but I knew I'd seen him before. Then it hit me: his nose was bandaged."

Dozer stiffened with anger.

"Sonofabitch I hit in Wakefield?"

St. James nodded.

Anna frowned, first at Dozer and then at St. James. "Was he the old friend you ran into while Cathy and I were in the shop?" she said tersely, obviously annoyed at being lied to.

St. James nodded again. Any pity Anna had for him just went out the window.

"You provoked the guy!" she said accusingly.

St. James shook his head. "You're upset, Anna, not thinking straight. Someone's ordered a hit on me, plain and simple. Nothing to do with Dozer hitting the guy."

Spencer said, "Anna, a guy doesn't shoot another person because of a busted nose. If St. James had taken him to dinner, he still would've shot him. He was paid to do it, no matter what."

Anna relaxed some but was clearly finding it difficult to forgive the two for lying.

Dozer looked at St. James and shook his head. "I should have done him in while I had the chance, man. But why were you so stupid to walk the streets alone, without me?"

Spencer lightly scratched his facial scar, bristling at Dozer's choice of words.

St. James's dazed mind chose to throw twisted logic at Dozer. "Oh, quit stewing, Dozer. Even if you'd been with me and taken the guy out before he shot, they'd just send someone else. Look on the bright side. Mark has a bullet for ballistics: first step to finding a smoking gun."

Spencer tried to refocus the conversation. "Did you notice anything else?"

"Only other thing I can remember is a small black SUV, with dark tinted windows I think, creeping alongside the shooter as he walked."

"Make?"

"Can't say for certain. Think it was a Honda. Late model CR-V, I believe."

"Did you get the plate?"

"Couldn't see. It happened so fast."

"Hmm. Okay."

"How stupid is it for a guy to shoot someone so close to police headquarters?" Smythe said, shaking his head.

"Actually, not as stupid as you may think," said Spencer. "It's Sunday. Light traffic. Squad cars would be already assigned patrols across the city. There'd only be a skeleton staff at headquarters, it being the weekend and all. All the shooter would have to do is jump in the SUV and have the vehicle turn left up the Queensway ramp. These guys could have been parked in a garage anywhere in the west end watching television within thirty minutes."

Spencer turned to Dozer.

"I'll need you to come down to headquarters to help with a sketch of the nose guy. Meanwhile I'll process the bullet and see what we have on criminals with small black SUVs. That'll be a needle in a haystack for sure, I'm afraid. It's a popular model. Hundreds in the city. If nothing else, ballistics and a sketch will provide Toronto police with something to ask Franklin about when they finally pick him up."

"Sure thing, Detective. How's first thing in the morning?" Dozer said.

"Good enough," Spencer said.

Suddenly Dozer remembered the cell he'd taken from Broken Nose in Wakefield. He pulled it from a pocket and handed it to Spencer.

"This is the cell we took off Broken Nose on Saturday. There's an email exchange between him and a guy named Sterling in Montreal. Last name unknown. I figured you or the Sûreté could make something out of it, maybe find this Sterling guy and wring something out of him."

Even though Spencer was becoming used to Dozer's vocabulary, he still found himself frowning at his choice of words.

He cleared his throat. "I'll see what I can do," he said sternly.

Spencer turned to St. James.

"I'll need coordinates for the Washington detective on the Stevens case to pass on information."

"Anna, can you get that to Mark?" St. James asked, words slurred. She nodded. "Of course."

Dr. Lee pushed his way back into the room.

"Okay, troops, that's enough. The patient needs rest."

Suddenly a loud smash came from the hallway, a full kitchen tray hitting the floor, cutlery flying, dishes breaking. Then, a woman yelling,

St. James closed his eyes. "Oh no. Just when I thought things couldn't get any worse."

Anna and Dozer threw bewildered looks at St. James at the same time.

Shaking his head, St. James read the look.

"You'll see," he whispered.

Anna and Dozer both shrugged.

Dr. Lee stuck his head out the door, then quickly pulled it back to avoid a flying dish.

"You weren't by any chance expecting someone else, were you, Mr. St. James?" Dr. Lee said cautiously.

Everyone turned to St. James. His eyes opened.

"It was just a matter of time," he said with a heavy sigh.

Anna looked puzzled. "A matter of time till what?"

St. James resigned himself to what would happen next. "Let her in, Doctor."

Dr. Lee pulled open the door, and in walked a plain-looking woman in her mid-sixties with greying hair touched by blue rinse. She was plump, less than five feet tall.

"Ladies and gentlemen, meet my sister, Betty Sparks," St. James said, closing his eyes once again.

Betty ignored the introduction, and everyone else in the room.

"What the hell happened?" she said bluntly, giving St. James no time to answer one question before firing off another. "Why do I have to hear this on the television like a total stranger? Your only sister, left out. Christ, I haven't heard from you in weeks."

Betty's demeanour was not enhanced by her baggy, faded patterned dress and unkempt hair.

She looked at the others.

"Who is this motley crew?"

St. James felt tired all over, and not from the gunshot wound.

Dozer struggled to keep himself from laughing.

"These are my *friends*," St. James said slowly, trying to maintain his patience.

"Will some of you please leave now," Dr. Lee pleaded.

"Okay," said Anna. She leaned over and kissed St. James.

"I'll be back later to see how you are doing," she said softly.

Dozer grabbed St. James's hand and leaned over so Spencer couldn't hear.

"I'll get the sonofabitch, Hamilton. Don't worry."

St. James said nothing.

Smythe said goodbye and Denzel offered an abrupt wave.

Spencer said to St. James, "I've ordered an officer to stand guard outside your door, in case the guy tries again."

"Thanks, Mark. I appreciate the protection."

St. James was left alone with Betty, and his own misery. Great combination.

When everyone had left, he turned to Betty.

"Why do you have to be so rude? These are people I work with and care about."

"What am I, chopped liver?"

"You are my only sister and I care about you deeply, but you make it very difficult for anyone to like you. You have no patience for anybody or anything."

"You'd have no patience either if you'd lost a spouse in their prime, before you had time to enjoy life."

"While we are all sorry you lost George, it's no one's fault. Driving everyone away with anger doesn't solve anything. It won't bring George back. You're only isolating yourself."

"Bullshit!"

"Have it your own way. I'm happy, and I'm staying that way. There's no incentive for me to connect with someone who uses negativity as a crutch. I would like to have you in my life, but only in a positive way. When you're ready for that, I'll be there for you."

"Who tried to kill you?" she said, ignoring his admonishment.

"Don't know."

"Who were those people here?"

"They help me with cases."

"Are they any good?"

"The best."

"You're lucky."

"Yes, I'm lucky to have them. And I work hard to keep their friendship and loyalty. You should learn something from that."

Betty gave him a disbelieving look.

"Hmm. The woman, she your girl?"

"She's the only one in my life at the moment."

"She nice?"

"Very."

"You serious?"

"Don't know."

"Hmm. If you are, don't lose her. They're hard to find."

"I know."

"You look exhausted."

"I am."

"You mind if I sit a while?"

"I can't guarantee I'll be good company."

"Shit, Hamilton, you were never good company," she said, shaking her head.

He smiled.

It wasn't long before he fell asleep.

Anna sent Spencer the coordinates for Jason Williamson as soon as she landed back in the condo.

Dozer hung around the lobby of 700 Sussex for a while, worried that with St. James incapacitated someone might try to get to Anna again. He told the concierge about St. James and asked for a closer watch over the building. The concierge agreed to be even more vigilant. Dozer gave him another $500, then went over to Anna's to check on Denzel.

Sometime after the gang and Betty left, Dr. Lee woke St. James to check his vitals. That's when St. James told him he was going to England on Tuesday. Dr. Lee couldn't believe it.

"You underestimate the impact of a gunshot wound," he said in an alarmed tone.

"You said it was a clean wound, not near vital organs," St. James argued.

Lee was incredulous. "There's been a tremendous shock to your body, your nervous system. Travel is stressful at the best of times. It's not going to be any better with a bullet wound. Besides, the dressing has to be changed frequently; you can't risk infection."

"Anna can change the dressing and apply anything you prescribe."

"She's a nurse?"

"Waitress."

Lee rolled his eyes.

"There's no way I'll sign your release until you are ready," he said authoritatively, over-emphasizing each word as if scolding a child. "You have the right to sign yourself out, but the hospital will not be responsible for whatever happens to you. If you insist on going against my advice, you should have the Victorian Order of Nurses teach your girlfriend the dos and don'ts of preventing infection."

"You have nurses here. Why can't they teach Anna?" St. James protested.

"There's no way me or my staff will take responsibility for your stupidity."

With that, Dr. Lee left the room.

"Well, that's plain enough," St. James muttered.

The next time St. James's eyes opened it was Monday morning and Anna was standing over him.

"How are you feeling?" she asked in a soft and caring voice.

His normal sarcasm kicked back in. "Like I've been shot."

He told Anna what Dr. Lee said about travelling to England.

"I have to agree with him," she said. "I can't believe you're that stupid either."

"Does that mean you won't book the VON for instruction?"

She wagged a finger in his face. "You're ten times more stubborn than me. What's even more maddening is that you know, and I know, that you've already made up your mind to go, so if I don't get instructions and something happens to you in England, I'll be the one having to deal with the fallout."

He bit his lip. Not because he was upset: he was trying hard not to laugh. Then he grinned. "You know you're even more attractive when you're angry?"

"I'm going now," she said, ignoring the tease.

"Where are you going?" he asked in his best pitiful voice.

"Where do you think?"

Anna walked out of the room.

# Chapter 42

St. James knew Anna well. She had left to call the VON. She was mad, that was for sure, but in a good way. She didn't want him having a setback in another country. And the best way to prevent that was not to go in the first place.

St. James was feeling a little stronger. He sat up in bed, paused long enough for the dizziness to pass, then swung his feet over the side and held onto the mobile table to steady himself.

The door swung open and a nurse trotted in, scolding him for getting out of bed as she took his temperature and blood pressure and made notes on a handheld computer. All very efficient and procedural, even the scolding.

St. James slowly shuffled around the room, trying to regain his balance. Kitchen staff opened the door and slid a breakfast tray onto the mobile table and left without a word.

*Friendly place.*

After ten minutes of movement he was exhausted and beginning to think the doctor and Anna were right. It was stupid to even think about England.

Then, as if a switch went off in his head, he suddenly became more determined to go.

*Damn the pain.*

If he didn't go, someone, somewhere, would think they'd won. He wouldn't contemplate that. He sat on the edge of the bed and ate cold runny eggs and burnt hospital toast. Awful, but he was hungry enough not to care.

He lay down and slept for a while longer until Dr. Lee woke him at 9:30 to check his vitals once again. Satisfied everything was normal, Lee pulled the stethoscope from his neck.

"You still planning to check yourself out?" he asked, resigned to logic being no match for St. James's determination.

"That's the plan."

"Thought so," he said with a long sigh. "I brought you a prescription for pain, a week's supply. They're strong, so use them sparingly, when you can't stand it anymore. Here's my card. I hate to say this to someone who ignores my advice, but call me if you get into trouble."

"Thanks, Doctor ... for everything."

He handed St. James his card, wished him well, and continued on with his rounds.

Anna arrived shortly after, carrying a small case containing fresh clothes.

"Are you still determined to do this?" she said, hoping he'd changed his mind.

"Yes, I am."

"Thought so."

"You sound like the doctor."

Anna remained silent as she opened a locker, pulled soiled clothes from a shelf and shoved them into an empty compartment in the case, then laid fresh clothes out on the bed. Holding the blood-stained jacket with the bullet hole up to the light, she said, "I suppose you want to keep this for your memories."

"Absolutely. Battle trophy."

Anna rolled her eyes. "Some battle."

St. James struggled to his feet and slowly changed into the fresh clothes Anna had brought while she went to the nurses' station to inform them he'd be signing himself out

St. James signed the necessary release papers, and a nurse in scrubs wheeled him onto the elevator with Anna by his side. He sat by the front door until Anna pulled the Cadillac up to the entrance. Then Anna and the nurse guided St. James from the wheelchair into the front seat.

When Anna pulled the rental up to 700 Sussex she asked the concierge to fetch the same wheelchair she had occupied just days before.

"I've been working here five years. You're the first couple to use this wheelchair," the concierge said, smiling, eyeing them one at a time. "Nice that you take turns."

"Smartass," Anna said, smiling.

A wide, boyish grin suggested he liked the label.

Anna wheeled St. James onto the elevator and pushed the fifth-floor button. He struggled to the bedroom, gingerly slipped out of his clothes, and fell into bed.

Their flight was at 3 p.m. Tuesday afternoon. It was now 11:00 Monday morning, giving him just one more day to recover before travel; not nearly enough, but it would have to do.

At 12:30 Anna woke him to introduce Sally, an attractive young VON nurse who showed Anna every step of the necessary care, from removing old bandages to cleaning the wound, applying antiseptic ointment, and securely re-bandaging St. James's shoulder.

"It's to be done twice a day," Sally said, "more often if it gets wet or soiled."

When Sally finished, she gave Anna a list of supplies to buy.

"I'll be gone a half-hour or so," Anna said to St. James. "I'll probably have to wait for the prescription to be filled. Is there anything you need before I go?"

"I'm fine."

"Oh, I almost forgot. Dozer called to ask how you were doing. He'd already been to police headquarters to give Spencer a description of the shooter."

St. James just nodded.

St. James went back to sleep only to wake a short time later to sounds of Anna packing.

"Have you been to the drug store already?" he mumbled.

"Yes. You've been sleeping. I was gone for forty-five minutes."

"Oh."

"I'm just guessing what you need for a week away," she said. "Never packed for a man before."

"Glad to hear that."

St. James slept most of Monday afternoon and evening. It was clearly too soon to be out of hospital, but he was too stubborn to admit it, even to himself.

On Tuesday morning he stayed in bed while Anna scrambled a couple of eggs and made toast for him.

At 11:00 she said, "You have to dress now, we haven't much time." She stuffed a few last-minute items in each bag. "We need to allow extra time. It'll take longer in your condition. Do you want a painkiller?"

St. James winced, then said, "No, I'm okay for the moment."

It took ten minutes for him to dress. Then he shuffled to the kitchen where he hauled the bottle of Macallan single malt from the cupboard and poured a double shot of scotch into a crystal glass. He had survived another attempt. Almost the last one, too. Closest he'd ever come. The rate attempts were happening, he'd need a new bottle before the end of the two cases.

Anna emerged from the bedroom struggling with two suitcases.

"Drinking? You're drinking now, when we're rushing to catch a flight?" she exclaimed in disbelief.

"Not really." St. James explained the ritual.

Anna just looked at him with a weird expression and her head cocked sideways.

"You're a strange man, Hamilton St. James."

"Man has to have traditions."

Dozer arrived to carry suitcases and escort them to the taxi stand next door. St. James and Anna shuffled arm in arm ahead of him.

When the plane took off, St. James's pain reached an unbearable threshold, so he asked the flight attendant for water to take a painkiller. He wished he'd had enough foresight to book a direct flight to Heathrow to avoid changing planes in Toronto.

The connecting flight to Heathrow was on time, and St. James was glad to finally lie in a business-class reclining bed. Anna adjusted it for him and moved the TV screen closer so he could watch. But he immediately pushed it away.

"Don't feel like watching anything," he said.

The last thing he remembered before falling asleep was the sound of the landing gear folding into the belly of the plane. He slept the entire seven-hour flight to Heathrow.

# Chapter 43

Half hour before landing, Anna woke St. James to change his dressing.

A curious flight attendant stopped to look on.

"What happened?" she asked.

Looking for shock value, St. James replied, "Gunfight." He got the response he was looking for. She gasped, covered her face with both hands, and hurried down the aisle.

St. James looked at his shoulder and said to Anna, "How does it look?"

"It's clean. No sign of infection."

She carefully applied ointment and re-bandaged the shoulder tightly so it wouldn't slip out of place, just as Sally had shown her.

"Not bad nursing for a waitress," he said smiling.

Anna grinned. "I wonder if this ointment heals smart mouths."

She kissed him and went back to her seat.

"Thank you," he said, loud enough to be heard across the aisle.

She just waved and picked a magazine from the seat pocket in front.

When they finally entered a room in the Copthorne Hotel on Plymouth's Armada Way it was 3:45. Walking through airports, standing in lines, and climbing in and out of limousines strained the muscle tissue, causing St. James significant discomfort. He gave in and took a second painkiller, feeling fortunate to have gotten by with only two so far. He laid down while Anna unpacked their suitcases.

At 6:00 on Thursday morning St. James's eyes met the face of an alarm clock on the night table. For a moment he had no idea where he was. The smell of french fries threw him off. Anna must have ordered room service.

Anna was still sleeping. St. James noticed the bruise on her forehead had faded some. And his pain of yesterday was now merely a tormenting ache.

*Both on the mend.*

He swung his legs over the side and slowly forced himself upright, then shuffled to the window and quietly pulled back the beige curtains.

The room overlooked a small park-like area separating the hotel from what looked like a four-story red-brick office building across the way. Concrete walkways neatly crisscrossed a well-manicured lawn. Several countries' flags flapped in the wind atop twenty-five-foot poles.

"How are you feeling?" Anna mumbled.

"I was trying not to wake you."

"It's all right. Jet lag messes up my sleep pattern. You must be hungry. I can't remember when you ate last."

"Neither can I. I'm starving."

"Do you feel strong enough to go to the dining room?"

"Think so."

Anna hopped out of bed and into the shower while St. James watched the BBC news. In ten minutes she was dressed and ready, and it was St. James's turn. Once he had toweled himself down, Anna removed the wet bandage and cleaned and redressed his shoulder.

She held St. James's good arm as they made their way down to the dining room. Anna ordered toast and jam. St. James, more ravenous, went for the full English breakfast.

"That should hold you for a while," Anna said when he had finished the big meal.

At 9:00 St. James phoned Basil Hughes at CISI's Plymouth plant. Basil, of course, was expecting him and suggested they begin with a plant tour at ten. He would send a car around to collect them at 9:40.

"Would you prefer I stay here?" Anna asked. "I did bring a book."

"Absolutely not! Wouldn't hear of it. You are part of the team. Besides, I'm not fit to go alone."

Anna smiled. She would have been devastated if he had said yes.

At 9:40 sharp a chap named Henry asked for them at the front desk. Twenty minutes later they were shaking hands with Basil Hughes at the plant on SW Coast Path.

Tall and lanky, Basil Hughes was in his mid-forties with a thin face and a full head of black hair, greying at the temples. Bushy eyebrows matched an equally thick draping moustache, and the largest Adam's apple St. James had ever seen moved up and down like a piston whenever the man spoke. Basil's accent marked him as neither upper nor working class.

Basil turned out to be quite pretentious. St. James guessed being General Manager of CISI's largest plant made him upper class, at least in his mind.

Basil delivered an excellent tour of the spotless plant. As they moved through the building St. James asked for a detailed explanation of last year's inventory count, the location of inventory at the time, and how trawler catch was treated. Basil was thorough and forthcoming. St. James didn't get the sense he was withholding anything.

Production lines were humming at full tilt, one processing cod, another haddock. Fifty or so line workers were milling about, some cleaning fish, some deboning, and some running filleting machines. Others wrapped and packed. One fellow ran a forklift carrying pallets of ready-for-market product into one of the eight freezers lining a wall. A modern plant in every way with its new stainless-steel processing lines.

Freezers were numbered, containers of fish separated by species, in neat rows. Appropriately well-organized for proper inventory counts, St. James concluded. Packaging inventory was just as neat. Workers swept loading bays. Outside, company trucks were lined up evenly in parallel formation. Neatness, orderly inventory, and sanitation was the backbone of plant culture. St. James was impressed.

St. James asked Basil to explain why trawler inventory was not counted at the same time as freezers.

"Three trawlers were originally destined for this plant. Later, Toronto switched them to Portsmouth, for catch to be counted and processed there. Then, Toronto reversed that decision, so the trawlers didn't arrive here until late in the day. That was when the catch was finally counted and included in Plymouth's inventory numbers."

"Did Toronto give any reason for the switch?" St. James probed.

"Not really … not a clear one anyway. They said it was some sort of mistake."

St. James nodded and made a note.

When they returned to Basil's office he pulled a file bearing St. James's name from the top drawer and handed it to him.

"Here is the information you requested in your email. I think you will find everything's there … count sheets, summaries, analysis completed by my accountant, as well as correspondence with head office."

"Thanks so much. I appreciate the work you put into this, Basil. During the count did you receive any special instructions from Toronto?"

Basil twisted the end of his moustache. "Special instructions?"

"Procedures or steps out of the ordinary, compared to prior years, that is."

Basil considered this for a moment, staring down at the desk.

"No. Nothing that I recall, except what I already told you about the trawler inventory."

"Has there been confusion in the past concerning which plant should process catch-in-transit?"

"Not since I've been here." Basil paused and looked at St. James. "Are you all right? You look very pale."

"Jet lag. Not used to travel," St. James lied. "Think we'll go back to the hotel to work on the file."

Anna gave St. James a look.

"Very well. Penelope and I were hoping you could join us for dinner; perhaps tomorrow night when you are time-adjusted?"

"That would be wonderful," Anna said enthusiastically.

"No doubt I will need some time with you tomorrow morning. Will that be okay?" St. James said respectfully, taking into account Basil's exaggerated self-importance.

"Absolutely. I and the plant accountant will be here. Call and I'll send Henry around for you."

They shook hands and Basil summoned Henry to take them back to the Copthorne. As soon as they entered the room St. James went to bed. While he slept, Anna changed the bandage once again.

# Chapter 44

When St. James awoke mid-afternoon Anna was nowhere to be seen. A sticky note on the bureau mirror said, "Gone shopping, love Anna."

He ordered a chicken sandwich and coke from room service, then settled in at the room's small table with Plymouth's inventory file from CISI HQ and the one Basil had given him that morning.

*Time for the tedious work.*

He created two piles of documents, one for each file, and then sorted sheets in each pile by date prepared. He followed all species counts from count sheets themselves through to Basil's inventory summaries, then to copies given to him by Karen's assistant. Partway through the exercise, room service knocked on the door to deliver the sandwich and coke. He took five minutes to wolf down both, then went straight back to work.

He had been at it for two hours when a key turned in the lock. Anna walked in carrying an armload of parcels that she tossed on a chair and gently threw her arms around St. James's neck.

He pushed aside his work and turned to her. "Where did you go?" he asked with genuine interest.

With her usual enthusiasm Anna said, "Hamilton, I had such a wonderful time! The concierge recommended the Drake Circus Shopping Centre. I found the most delightful shops and stumbled on a few things I couldn't resist. How are you feeling?"

"Bit better."

Anna pointed at the two piles of documents. "What are you doing?"

He thought quickly.

"Organizing things for you."

She smiled. "Liar."

"I hate that word," he said disingenuously.

"What do you call someone who doesn't tell the truth, just to take advantage of another?"

St. James grinned. "I would say they were economical with the truth."

"Great line." Anna resigned herself to helping. "Okay. What do you want me to do?"

He laid out detailed steps for her to follow and explained what to look for and make notes of.

"I need to get some air. Do you mind if I leave you for a bit? A stroll around the park would do me good, I think."

"No, go. But don't overdo it."

He leaned over to kiss her. "I won't. I appreciate your help, as always."

The day was damp, overcast with a gentle breeze. It looked like rain, but then again England always looked like rain.

He strolled through the small park, sat for a while on a bench, and took in several deep breaths; breathing exercises to manage what now was a constant dull shoulder ache. Sounds of heavy traffic spilled over from the A374, spoiling the quiet of the hotel grounds.

A man sitting on a bench opposite St. James reading a paper periodically looked his way.

# Chapter 45

St. James had always been active. He played basketball as a kid, hockey as a teenager, and ran track at university, moving fast in one sport or another most of his life. Now he was content with just lengthy walks and the odd golf game. Being forced to be completely sedentary was making him feel like a caged animal. Mind raring to go, body saying no.

His mind drifted over the two cases, what the next steps should be.

He would ask the Higgins law firm to search Cayman records for the names of everyone associated with the Stevens case, property titles, and commercial registries; hopefully uncovering information that would bring him closer to uncovering what had become of Jensen's $23 million.

For the CISI case there were a couple of Toronto people Dozer's men should investigate. And this week he would see what could be learned from Basil and William Hughes. That could change everything yet again.

He strolled around the grounds for another fifteen minutes or so, then wandered back to the room.

Anna had moved the two piles of documents from the small table to the bed: more room to spread everything out, easier to cross-reference.

Sprawled across the bed with her back to St. James, Anna said, "Everything checks out as far as I can tell. Every pound of every species in Basil's files ties into the sheets in the Toronto file: no differences whatsoever."

"Hmm. What you just did was a very important first step, but only the first."

Anna sat up to face St. James. "Oh, what's next then?"

"Electronic versions of the same thing."

Anna watched St. James pull his laptop from its case, fire up Outlook, and send separate emails to Van Hoyt and Basil Hughes, asking each for electronic versions of the paper files Anna had just cross-checked. He also asked Basil for the name of the head office accountant assigned to his plant.

While at it he emailed Higgins Johnson to request that they conduct the Cayman registry searches. Then, an email to Dozer asking him to run surveillance on Van Hoyt, Graves, and Blakie.

Realizing he hadn't notified David Kingston at Scotland Yard that he was in the UK, he emailed him to outline all that had happened and why he was on British soil.

Ten minutes later his laptop pinged with electronic files from Basil. The head office accountant for Plymouth was a lady named Jennifer Quigley. He emailed her straight away and asked for electronic copies of Plymouth's year-end inventory records, the very same documents he had requested from Basil and Karen.

"Do you feel up to going out to dinner tonight, Hamilton?" Anna asked.

"That could be the best medicine right now. I'm feeling cooped up; not a very good patient, I'm afraid."

"I'll ask the concierge for recommendations. He was excellent with shopping advice, no reason that wouldn't extend to restaurants," she said cheerfully.

Anna pushed the concierge call button and discussed dinner venues with a man at the front desk.

St. James's computer pinged again. This time, a trail of emails. An email to David Kingston from DuPont dated the previous day, outlining attempts on St. James's life and requesting protection for him and Anna while in England. Next, an email from Kingston to

268    Double Shot of Scotch

Plymouth's Chief Sergeant Dempsey and Portsmouth's Chief Sergeant Collingwood requesting protection the days they'd be in each city.

"God bless them! Looking out for us," St. James mumbled.

"What's that?" Anna asked, waiting for the concierge to check dining establishments.

"Nothing, dear."

She let it go when the concierge came back on the line.

"If you are looking for a true taste of traditional British dining," he said, "Kitley House in Yealmpton is your best bet. It's about eight miles outside Plymouth. You'll love it."

Anna thanked him, disconnected, and relayed the choice to St. James.

"Sounds like fun. Let's do it."

Anna made the reservation for seven, then arranged a car to collect them at 6:30.

They continued working files until six, then took turns in the shower.

En route to Kitley House St. James noticed the driver frequently checking his rearview mirror.

"Something wrong?" St. James said.

"Police are following us, sir. Not sure why, I'm well within the limit," he said in a rough British accent.

St. James smiled but said nothing.

*Chief Sergeant Dempsey on the job.*

It was 7:05 when the limo pulled up to Kitley House's grand entrance.

"My God," Anna said as they approached the Inn. "It's a mini Downton Abbey!"

"Amazing," St. James said, gazing over the vast, immaculately kept estate.

The view on the drive up to Kitley's entrance accented the beautiful silvery marble-granite manor. Situated on six hundred acres of beautiful English countryside, Kitley sat at the head of the Yealm estuary, which had been dammed to create the property's freshwater lake. The gardens were extensive, the grounds perfectly manicured.

Seconds later a police car pulled in behind, and a young, slightly built constable Anna thought could be no older than sixteen got out and introduced himself as Sandy Anderson. St. James recognized him immediately as the man on the park bench behind the hotel pretending to read the paper.

"Chief Sergeant Dempsey asked me to provide you with security," the constable said, smiling as they shook hands.

St. James said, "We appreciate the help, Constable. Please thank the chief sergeant for us.

"I will. I'll shadow you for the next couple of days. How long are you planning to stay in Plymouth?"

"Just until Saturday, then we're off to Portsmouth," St. James said.

"Travel safe," he said as he climbed back into his vehicle to stand watch.

Inside they found themselves back in time a good five hundred years, and were instantly spellbound by a grand, sweeping oak staircase, antique hand-carved chests, solid wood panelling, and a wall of heraldic shields. They were captivated by a vast collection of rich art, all original paintings, each worth a fortune, each impossible to replace.

The house manager met them in the foyer and introduced himself as Alec Simms, who took an immediate shine to Anna. Anna wasn't shy about soaking up the attention, peppering him with questions about the property's history and accepting Alec's every word as gospel.

Alec, who spoke with an upper-class English accent, was a dapper gentleman who reminded St. James of David Niven. He was immaculately dressed in a black custom-made Clements & Church suit and designer Gucci shoes, the shiniest St. James had ever seen.

"It was built during the reign of Henry VIII," Simms explained, "many famous artists and authors stayed here. Samuel Johnson, Sir Joshua Reynolds, and Sarah Catherine Martin, to name a few."

St. James was hungry and didn't care to dive this deeply into Kitley history. When the timing was right he politely pulled Anna away to the dining room where they enjoyed a bottle of Barolo, roast beef, and Yorkshire pudding.

But Simms was not giving Anna up that easily. He came into the dining room while they were still eating and insisted on a personal tour when they were finished. Once they had enjoyed the last bite and turned down dessert, St. James paid and they strolled back to the foyer where Simms latched onto Anna's arm to guide her around, totally ignoring St. James.

St. James had to admit the tour was interesting, but after an hour or so he was tired, and it was time to change the dressing. Eventually he persuaded Simms to arrange a car back to the hotel. As they left they waved to the young constable.

Back in the hotel room, Anna tended St. James's shoulder.

"It's looking much better, Hamilton," she said as she redressed the wound. "Did you take a painkiller today?"

"No. It wasn't that bad. I think I'm over the worst."

When she had finished bandaging, Anna sat on the bed and paused for a long moment.

"I was thinking about Betty. She's probably feeling very lonely without her husband. Does she have many friends to console her?"

"I doubt it. She drives people away with her attitude."

"Maybe when we get back I can spend time with her. Woman-to-woman time might help."

"You're welcome to try. Hope for all of our sakes, especially hers, you're successful."

With that, they kissed, wished each other pleasant dreams, and turned out the light.

Next morning St. James felt more energetic. He rose and made coffee in the small percolator provided in the room while Anna slept. He opened emails from Van Hoyt and Jennifer Quigley with the attachments he'd requested. No mention of Van Hoyt speaking to Jennifer or vice versa. He had hoped that would be the case. He wanted files from Jennifer's computer independent of Karen's. If they had talked they would have assumed the two requests a duplication, an error on his part, and he would've received just one set from one or the other. But he wanted the two files separately to see if Jennifer's electronic files were identical to Karen's. Without the two, he'd never know, and that would leave a significant hole in the investigation.

So, he began comparing every pound of every species from the electronic versions to those on the hard copies. They all tied in exactly, as did costing and totals for the plant.

Next he opened all electronic documents in different windows, beginning with Basil's Excel inventory spreadsheet, and ran a finger down each column on the screen. Then he did the same with Jennifer Quigley's, and finally, Karen's. Just like hard copy to hard copy and electronic copy to hard copy, all species-pounds and dollars matched perfectly between all three electronic files.

Satisfied with the comparison he set aside the hard copies and concentrated only on the electronic versions. Clicking back and forth he compared Basil's spreadsheets to Jennifer's, Jennifer's to Karen's, and Karen's to Basil's. Then he went around the circle again, repeating the process several times.

Something was gnawing at him, but he couldn't quite pinpoint what. With three files from three different computers matching perfectly in every detail, that should have been the end of it, the dead end he dreaded. But for some reason he couldn't let go; an obsession that something he wasn't seeing was actually there, hiding in plain sight, but at the same time feeling it was all hopeless.

He continued studying each window for some time. Again he clicked back and forth, back and forth. He wasn't sure, but something seemed slightly different. He moved the cursor across Basil's inventory summary and clicked on a single cell. Book Antiqua was the typeface and 12 the font size displayed in the dropdown window on the screen. He highlighted the whole worksheet. Typeface and font size were the same, Book Antiqua 12.

He did the same with Jennifer's. Once again the typeface and font size was Book Antiqua 12. Frustrated, he was about to give up, shut down the laptop, and go for a walk. But for some reason he stopped himself and moved the cursor to Karen's file and clicked on a single cell. It wasn't Book Antiqua that appeared in the dropdown window. It was Century 12.

A huge smile washed over St. James's face.

# Chapter 46

Anna stirred.

"How are you feeling?" she asked, rubbing her eyes and yawning as she swung her feet from under the blanket.

"Much stronger, thanks to excellent nursing," St. James replied cheerfully.

"What time is it?"

"8:30."

"You plan to go back to the plant?"

"Yes. When you're ready I'll call Basil."

It was ten when Henry dropped them off at the plant, and they walked to the back of the plant and into Basil Hughes's small, sparsely decorated office.

"Would it be possible to meet your plant accountant?" St. James said after pleasantries were exchanged.

"Absolutely," Basil said. "Follow me."

In an office two doors down they were introduced to a short round freckled-faced kid named Eli who might have been twenty-five.

"Eli, these people are from head office doing some consulting work for Cameron," Basil explained. "Please be completely open with them and provide anything they ask for."

"Right, Mr. Hughes," Eli said obediently.

"I have some work to do, I am afraid. I leave you in good hands," Basil said.

Anna and St. James nodded simultaneously, then turned to Eli.

"Eli, how long have you been working here?" Anna said.

"About two years," he said, seeming somewhat hesitant.

"What's your background?" St. James said.

"Two years college. Bookkeeping diploma."

"Is this your first job?"

Eli smiled. "Yes. And I like working here very much."

"How much interaction do you have with Jennifer Quigley?"

"Almost daily. There's always procedural changes, things to check, clarify, analysis to do, that sort of thing."

"Generally, what are procedures for inventory counts?" St. James said.

"We get email instructions about a week before the count, then daily updates up to and sometimes after counts, whenever they think of something new or remember something left out of the first instructions."

"Hmm. Were you here during last year-end's count?" St. James asked.

"Sure was. It was my job to organize it," he said proudly.

St. James continued. "Tell us about inventory on trawlers then, how the process worked around that."

Eli pointed to a window laden with grime and dead flies facing the waterfront.

"Well, sir … There were three trawlers tied up out there. One was a shrimp boat, very high-value product."

"What were the other two carrying?"

"One was haddock, the other cod. First set of instructions from HQ said the trawlers were coming here. Then, a short time later, Jennifer said the trawlers were going to Portsmouth to be processed and included in their inventory."

St. James interrupted, "What time was that?"

Eli's face clouded, trying to remember.

Finally he said, "I can't remember the exact time, but it was late morning, maybe noonish."

"Then what happened?"

"Then I got another email saying the trawlers were now coming here. By this time I was starting to panic. I didn't know whether to call in night shifts. Line workers need time to plan, to make arrangements at home. Some are single parents and have to find someone to look after kids. On top of all that I was getting vulgar messages from the three captains who were receiving the same confusing messages I was. They wanted to know what the hell was going on."

"What time did the trawlers actually tie up?" St. James asked.

"Somewhere around 3:30 or 4:00."

"Were the auditors still here?"

"They finished observing plant counts somewhere around three, I think. That's when they returned to their office."

"So the auditors didn't see the trawlers?"

"No. Long gone by then."

St. James made a note.

"Are you sure about that, Eli?" he asked politely, wanting Eli's answer confirmed without sounding doubtful of him.

"Quite sure."

"That was a number of months ago. How can you be so sure?" Anna said.

"Because count teams were mad because they had to stay late. They were yelling at me. Auditors didn't have to stay, why should we, is what they said. It was memorable. Captains yelling at me. Count teams yelling at me. And when I called in two shifts with very little notice, they yelled at me too. There's no forgetting the worst day of my life."

St. James smiled. "Good enough, Eli. Thank you."

"Did Jennifer say the reason for the change?" Anna asked.

"No ... and I didn't ask. HQ doesn't like to be questioned."

"Didn't you think it odd that there were conflicting instructions?" St. James said.

"Very odd. It made no sense at all. If catch was to go to Portsmouth, it should have been sent there in the first place. At the time I received the first instruction, trawlers were almost equidistant from both plants. So why tell them to set sail here first and then Portsmouth a short time later? And sometime after that, reverse the instructions again? That's why they were so late arriving here.

St. James took another moment to make notes.

"What did the captains say about all this when they docked?" St. James asked.

"They were very upset, yelling at Basil and me as if we gave the instructions. Said we wasted their time and fuel, that they wouldn't be accepting any price reduction per pound for catch that was hours older than it needed to be."

St. James paused a few seconds, peered out the window and pointed to a vessel tied up at the wharf.

"Was that one of the trawlers here on count day?"

Eli squinted, looking through the grimy window.

"Yes, that's Captain Thorne's trawler."

"Would he be around now?"

"Most likely. He's never far from *The Mistress*."

St. James hesitated a moment, then said, "I'll see if Captain Thorne is willing to chat. Excuse me. Anna will have more questions for you if you don't mind, Eli."

"Not at all, Mr. St. James. Happy to help any way I can."

Anna gave St. James an evil eye that could only mean, "What the hell am I supposed to ask this kid?"

He smiled.

"Oh, before I go … most companies use Times New Roman or Calibri typefaces for electronic documents. I notice here you use Book Antiqua. Curious about the choice."

Eli looked at St. James in an odd way, as if to ask what that had to do with inventory counts.

"It's Mr. Hughes's preference. He insists everyone use that font." Eli shrugged. "Just likes it, I guess. Don't know any other reason."

St. James thanked him and left in search of Captain Thorne.

It was only a two-minute walk to the wharf. St. James maneuvered around several heavy cables and a number of containers lined up in a neat row, perhaps containing dried fish or supplies.

The day was damp and chilly, a strong salt smell in the air. Seagulls squawked loudly as they circled *The Mistress* looking for easy pickings.

A few feet past the containers St. James came across a scruffy-looking young deckhand.

"Looking for Captain Thorne," he said to the boy.

The deck hand said nothing, just pointed to a stocky middle-aged bearded man standing on the bow of the trawler peering through binoculars, seemingly scanning the horizon. St. James thanked him and made his way up the gangway.

He introduced himself to Captain Thorne. They shook hands and he told the captain why he was in Plymouth.

Thorne's fingers and teeth were yellowish-brown, most likely nicotine stains from years of smoking. His eyes were grey and sunken, his face as weather-beaten as forty-year-old barn board. His hands were rough, dirty, and scarred, maybe from years pulling lines bare-handed.

At first Thorne was reluctant to talk. Trawler captains, St. James guessed, were not on Anderson's email list, so he wouldn't have received the request for cooperation. When St. James sensed the man's reluctance, he suggested Thorne check with Basil.

"You must be telling the truth. If you weren't, you wouldn't suggest I ask Basil."

St. James nodded and smiled. "I didn't come all the way from Canada just to lie to you, Captain."

Thorne spit tobacco juice over the side. Particles of something or other fell when he ran fingers through his long white beard.

"Remember the day well," he said when St. James asked about the last year-end catch.

"What instructions did you receive before docking?"

"Keep a log of that stuff. C'mon up to the wheelhouse and we'll see."

St. James followed Thorne up a rusty steel ladder and into a wheelhouse that hadn't been cleaned since World War II. In one corner was a pile of rusty chains, a small broken anchor, a tarp full of holes, and a filthy fishnet. The stench was indescribable. The wheel console was covered in dust and grease. In the opposite corner was a weather-beaten handmade chest of drawers that screeched when Thorne pulled on the drawers. From the third drawer he pulled a logbook the same colour as his fingers, its pages dog-eared and crumpled. The book had to be twenty years old.

"Let's see," he said, stroking his beard as he flipped through pages.

"Yes, here it is ... here's the day," he said, tapping the musty page.

He recited entries as his finger moved down the page.

"8:30 a.m. we pulled the last net. Good haul, couple of tons. We were seventy-eight miles offshore, maybe more, maybe less; just a guess."

"Closer to Plymouth or Portsmouth?" St. James asked.

"About the same distance from each plant, I think. I don't record that but given the shelf we were fishing that day I would have to say slightly closer to Portsmouth, ten, maybe twenty miles closer."

"What was your catch?" St. James asked.

"Cod. I only fish cod."

"What about the shrimp boat and the one with haddock? They must have been in different areas."

Staring out over the bay Thorne scratched at his beard once again. "Shrimp are mostly warm-water catch off Indonesia, Florida, Australia, places like that."

"If that's the case, where would a ship have been coming from for it to make sense to land in southern England?"

"Norway. Good shrimp fishing up there. Where they can survive cold water, the shrimp are larger. Jumbos," Thorne said.

"Must have been sailing for a couple of days then?"

Thorne thought for a moment. "It's about 1,100 nautical miles from Oslo to here. Not sure how long it would take in that vessel. Don't rightly know its knot capacity, never sailed her. All I know is it arrived in Plymouth about the same time as I did."

"Okay."

Thorne continued down the logbook page.

"9 a.m. we received instructions to bring the catch to Plymouth."

"Instruction from Basil or William?"

"No. Toronto."

"Hmm. Who in Toronto?"

"According to my notes, the accounting lady that deals with Eli. She was the only one to send messages that day."

"She has authority to direct inventory?"

"Think she's just a messenger."

St. James pressed.

"On instructions from the CFO?"

"Don't know."

"CEO?"

Thorne shook his head. "Don't know."

St. James made a note and moved on. "Okay. Then what happened?"

"We set course for Plymouth as instructed. Next transmission was from Basil, about 9:20, wanting to know if we were coming to his plant or William's. I remember this now. Thought it very odd at the time. Toronto and Plymouth were out of sync. That never happens."

Once again St. James made a note.

"At the same time, we received another transmission from the accounting lady sending us to Portsmouth, written like the first transmission never existed."

"Then what?"

"We shifted course from Plymouth to Portsmouth."

Captain Thorne continued.

"At 10:45 I received a message from William. He wanted to know if I was bringing the catch to his plant or Basil's. I remember thinking the company must be handing out free dope. No one was making sense."

"Then what?"

"At 11:15 we received the final transmission from Toronto to switch back to Plymouth. By this time I was really mad."

"Don't blame you," St. James consoled.

"All this stupid confusion made us very late landing to count catch. Not to mention the extra fuel *The Mistress* burned."

"What time was that?"

Thorne consulted his log.

"Just before 4 p.m."

"Then what?"

"I sent a transmission to the Toronto lady, Basil, and William that I wasn't moving until I was paid for my catch in full. Wasn't risking non-payment or a big discount for deteriorated catch just because they couldn't make up their minds where to process it. That was that," Thorne said, snapping his head to emphasize the point.

"Would the stock deteriorate that much more in a few hours?" St. James asked.

Thorne's face broke into a devilish smile. "Not really; catch is kept on ice. But I thought if they're this screwed up with instructions, I couldn't trust them to pay the full amount, fresh or not. Companies put a lot of pressure on the little fishermen to force prices down. They control the market. Not a lot of trust between us. They could drum up any reason for paying less."

"And were you paid?"

"Damn right I was paid. Eli had the catch counted and weighed and had a manual cheque issued to me inside of three hours."

"Manual cheque?"

"Yeah. Usually we're paid by direct deposit, but Eli wanted to process the catch right away. Head office cash transfer would take another day. By then there could be real catch deterioration. He wrote the cheque by hand, so that I'd release the catch on the spot."

"That would be early evening at that point, would it not?"

"Given the time we tied up it, would have been around seven-thirty or eight when I got the cheque."

"There wouldn't be anyone in the plant to process at that hour, would there?"

"Oh yes. Eli had called in two crews for eight, and they processed until around five the next morning."

"So with a couple of crews already at the plant Eli had no choice but to pay you. Otherwise he would have to pay labour for an entire shift with no production to show for it. That plays hell with labour cost per pound," St. James reasoned.

Thorne smiled. "That's right. Had him by the you-know-whats," he said, clearly proud of his negotiating skills.

"Just one more question," St. James said, raising a finger.

"What's that?"

"Were you the only captain to receive conflicting instructions that day?"

"No," Thorne said quickly, "spoke to Captain Jamison and Captain Earl. Both received the same instructions at the same times I did."

"Thank you, Captain. You've been most helpful."

They shook hands. St. James disembarked and walked back to the plant, where he collected Anna from Eli's office to revisit Basil.

"Are you still available for dinner with Penelope and me tonight?" Basil said.

"We'd be delighted to join you," St. James said with sincerity.

"We're early diners, if that's okay. Can Henry pick you up at 5:30?"

"Perfect," said Anna. "What would be appropriate dress?"

"Very casual."

Back in the hotel room Anna picked up a book and lay on the bed to read. St. James opted for a short walk, nodding to the faithful constable following a few paces behind.

He thought about the conversation with Captain Thorne. Conflicting transmissions had never happened before, he had said. And why were instructions coming from Toronto accounting instead of the plants? That was most unusual. Instructions should come from Basil and William or the chief operating officer if there was a dispute over where catch should go. That would make more sense. Instructions from accounting made no sense at all. He made a note to check with CISI's competitors to determine standard industry practices.

# Chapter 47

St. James and Anna were sitting in the Copthorne lobby at 5:30 when Henry pulled up to the entrance.

Basil and Penelope Hughes lived in a modest grey clapboard and stucco building, vintage 1800s, located in a well-kept area of Plymouth. It had an "Estate Sale" sign on the front lawn, which St. James knew to be the British term for "Property for Sale."

When they knocked, the door opened immediately, and they were warmly greeted by Basil and Penelope. Penelope, a tall woman with short black hair, was plain featured with white, almost chalky skin. Anna guessed her to be about forty-five. Basil was wearing a traditional brown English smoking jacket that had seen better days.

Penelope and Basil escorted them into a sitting room where Basil fixed drinks.

"I see you're selling your house," St. James said when they were settled in the sitting room.

"Yes. I'm so excited," said Penelope. "We're building a larger home on the outskirts of the city. Should be finished by spring. I'm having such a great time picking things to decorate."

"That would be so much fun," Anna said enthusiastically.

Basil stroked his mustache. "Do you have real estate experience, Hamilton?"

"Not much, I'm afraid."

"William and I are looking to invest in a rental property. We thought the wives could manage it. Add to our retirement. I'm not comfortable relying entirely on the stock market, you know."

"Wise man," St. James said, pausing to sip the Bloody Mary Basil had just handed him. "Real estate has been an excellent investment in Canada, for sure. Don't know anything about your market here."

"Steady price increases in recent years."

When they had finished their drinks, Basil ushered them into the dining room, where Penelope served dinner and Basil poured wine.

"Are you getting everything you need for your investigation?" Basil asked when they had begun to eat.

"Yes. Very pleased with the cooperation. Very professional. Thank you so much for making it easy."

"You're most welcome. I am a big fan of Cameron's. He treats me well. Anything he asks gets priority."

St. James recounted his conversation with Captain Thorne and Basil confirmed the accuracy of Thorne's story.

"Never found out what was going on in Toronto," he said, shaking his head. "Whatever it was damned near cost us three boatloads, very expensive boatloads, I might add, when you consider one was shrimp."

St. James nodded.

By this time Anna and Penelope were knee-deep in decorating talk, paying no attention to Basil and St. James.

"I am fascinated by the cooperation between you and your brother. Since plant managers are bonused based on individual performance, there doesn't seem to be an incentive for one plant manager to help another."

"Quite true," said Basil, smiling. "But for William and me it makes sense because of our proximity to one another. We have actually improved individual performance by making sure each other's plant has a steady supply of fish to process. When Plymouth is at capacity we direct catch to Portsmouth, and vice versa. And because our two plants are close we attract more independent trawlers than one plant would. There's always room for more fish in one plant or the other. Captains are content to supply us rather than single-plant competitors ninety miles up the coast. Less fuel used, and catch doesn't have to travel as far. Fish is fresher when it goes into production. The fresher the fish, the more captains are paid per pound. Win–win all the way around."

St. James considered this for a moment. "Makes sense. Other CISI plants are too far apart to cooperate with one another. They stand alone. So managers can only be bonused on individual performance. Can't help one another even if there was motivation to do so. If the North and South American plants were closer together, they'd benefit from cooperation too."

"Exactly," Basil said, pointing his fork in St. James's direction.

"If you and William make sure each other's plant has a steady supply, you must normally be the ones to give instructions for where catch should go, not Toronto."

Basil sipped on his wine. "That's correct. For some reason or another accounting hijacked that role at year-end."

"Did you ever find out why?"

"No, not really, at least not to my satisfaction."

St. James's forehead furrowed. "I don't understand."

Basil sat his wine glass next to the cutlery.

"I asked Cameron for the reason. He simply said Karen wanted to make sure as much product as possible was processed, to maximize profit, to make sure everyone got their bonus."

St. James looked puzzled. "Wouldn't that be Henry Jenkins's responsibility as COO?"

Basil nodded, obviously still perplexed.

"It was every other year. He's really quite good at maximizing production at year-end. A trained logistics man, exceptional at his job. There was no reason that I could see to change from him to Karen. But I felt it unwise to press further. It would probably come back to haunt me."

St. James made a mental note to follow up on that.

The rest of the evening was occupied with casual discussion around political affairs around the world and travel, always a favourite for St. James and Anna.

Basil called Henry shortly after 9:00, and St. James and Anna were back in the hotel bar by 9:30.

"They're spending like they just won the lotto," Anna said, sipping a liqueur.

"Could be stringing themselves out a bit. Or maybe they've been frugal all their lives. The English are noted for that, you know."

"What's up for tomorrow?" she asked.

"When we go upstairs I'll email William Hughes. Tomorrow we'll travel to Portsmouth. Hopefully he can meet us on the weekend."

"How far is it?"

"About 170 miles, all A roads. Three and a half hours by car, I believe."

Nightcaps finished, they went to the front desk to see about Portsmouth accommodations. The Clarence Boutique Hotel came highly recommended by the night manager, who was gracious enough to book two nights for them and arrange a car for nine the next morning. Back in the room St. James emailed William about his availability, and William replied saying he would make himself available any time.

Next morning they woke at about seven, packed their things, ate breakfast in the dining room, then checked out. The limo driver showed shortly after nine, driving a new black Citroën. He was neatly dressed in a white shirt, black tie, and chauffeur's cap.

It was late afternoon when the Citroën pulled in front of the Clarence Boutique Hotel in Portsmouth. St. James paid the driver and they climbed out.

The Clarence Boutique Hotel was a charming red-brick place on Clarence Road not far from Portsmouth's waterfront. They checked in, unpacked, and settled into a very colourful, newly decorated room.

St. James checked his email and found one from William saying he could meet them at the plant Sunday morning. He'd gladly pick them up if he knew where they were staying. St. James replied with the hotel address and said nine on Sunday morning would be quite convenient.

It had now been seven days since St. James had been shot, and when she examined the wound, Anna concluded it could be left open to the air.

St. James's computer pinged. Two messages. The first was Smythe saying he'd spoken with Antoinette at the Cayman National Bank. Their lawyers had confirmed St. James's legal and political strategy with Higgins Johnson. The bank would now flag the account voluntarily. Smythe had communicated the plan to Nathan Strong, and Nathan had approved the use of firm attorneys to obtain the US court order for the Cayman law firm.

"Love it when a plan comes together. It's such a turn on," St. James muttered.

"What did you say?" Anna said.

He showed her Smythe's email.

"Aren't you clever? Dozer isn't going to think your approach overkill now," she said, smiling.

The second email was from Dozer. Toronto police had found Samuel Franklin holed up in a small apartment on Finch and had brought him in for questioning. Dozer would interview Franklin tomorrow. And he had passed the information on to Jason in Washington.

"Everything seems to be progressing, Anna," St. James said, happily.

She smiled. "Were you expecting it wouldn't?"

St. James just smiled.

A second email from Dozer said Denzel was continuing to watch Anna's apartment, and there had been no break-ins.

"Saturday night, you feel like doing something?" St. James asked, buoyed by the progress.

"Wouldn't mind some kind of entertainment."

"What do you feel like? Music? Comedy? A play?"

"Play might be nice, depending what's on."

St. James googled entertainment in Portsmouth.

"*Pride and Prejudice* is playing at the Kings Theatre."

"Bit too heavy for me," Anna said quickly.

"There's a double comedy at the New Theatre Royal."

"I like the sound of that. Who's performing?"

"Two British comedians I've never heard of."

"Let's do that," she said enthusiastically.

St. James went online and booked two tickets for the 7:30 performance.

Online restaurant suggestions included a number of venues, and they settled on Las Iguanas at Gunwharf Quays.

Las Iguanas was wonderful, and the comedians made St. James laugh so hard he thought his wound might break open. They were back at the hotel by 10:30 and went straight to the Florence Arms pub next door for a nightcap.

St. James waved the bartender over. "Dry vodka martini for me, Baileys on ice for the lady."

Anna said, "Wonderful evening, St. James."

"I laughed so hard you may have to dress my shoulder again!"

The next morning William was waiting in the lobby when they came down at nine. They shook hands and jumped into his red Volkswagen Passat.

As William pulled away, St. James noticed a police car across the street from the hotel. He smiled.

*Chief Sergeant Collingwood.*

Although much shorter than his brother, William was slightly heavier with red hair. Quieter than Basil. Social but not outgoing, and certainly not as pretentious.

As soon as they arrived at the plant, William produced a file of documents, just as Basil had.

"I'll spend some time reviewing this at the hotel," St. James said as he took the file. "Would you be good enough to show us around?"

"Delighted to," William replied. "Won't be as interesting as a workday when everything's running full tilt, but I'll do my best."

"If there's something we need to see in action we'll come back tomorrow morning," St. James said cheerfully.

William's plant tour was every bit as thorough and efficient as Basil's. The building was smaller than Plymouth but just as orderly, neat, and clean.

They went through all the same questions St. James had asked Basil and Eli.

"I may want to speak to the plant accountant as well, depending on what I find reviewing the file."

"Not a problem. We'll make sure you have everything you need."

William confirmed Basil and Captain Thorne's descriptions of count-day events to be his understanding as well. St. James now felt he had as true a picture of what went on that day as he was ever going to have.

He asked William to send electronic versions of the file, just as he had with his brother, which William did while St. James and Anna were sitting in his office.

William's office was larger than Basil's, and better decorated too, with several floor plants, modern art, and much newer furniture.

"Did you have trawlers tied up on count day?" St. James asked, knowing the answer but wanting everyone's confirmation independent of each other.

"No. We waited for the three that eventually ended up in Plymouth. We didn't have catch to process that day. Shift workers were angry we brought them in for trawlers that never appeared."

"What is the name of the accountant in Toronto assigned to your plant?" St. James asked.

"Same as Basil's, Jennifer Quigley."

"And your plant accountant here?"

"Kathy Holmes."

For a half-hour or so St. James asked several questions about plant procedures and authorization policies, then thanked William for taking time out of his weekend to meet. He drove them back to the hotel, and St. James and Anna spread the files over the bed, just as they had done in Plymouth. Anna compared all count sheets, dollars, and summaries with those in the file given to St. James by Karen.

St. James sent a second set of emails to Van Hoyt and Jennifer asking for electronic Portsmouth inventory files. It being Sunday, he didn't expect a response until Monday morning, so he was surprised to see the documents in his inbox Sunday afternoon.

While Anna traced inventory on the hard copies St. James did the same electronically. William and Jennifer's typeface and font size were Times New Roman 12; Karen's was Century 12.

At 4:30 the phone rang. It was William inviting them to Sunday dinner.

"I apologize for not mentioning it this morning. I was so focused on your getting everything you need it slipped my mind."

St. James accepted the invitation enthusiastically. William would be around to pick them up at 6:00.

William Hughes's home was not far from the hotel. His wife, Camilla, a large jolly person, greeted them at the door with a huge smile. Drinks were served before they sat down to their second roast beef and Yorkshire pudding dinner since arriving in England.

Partway through the dinner St. James said, "William what do you *really* make of this inventory situation?"

"Puzzled the hell out of me," he replied casually, wine in hand. "I stopped trying to understand head office a long time ago. Now I just keep my head down and do my job as best I can."

St. James smiled. "Smart. Did the auditors ever talk to you about it?"

"With no trawlers here there really wasn't much point in them raising the issue. They were only concerned with count procedures and accuracy for the plant. You know, freezers and packaging. We didn't even have catch in progress on the production line, which bothered me immensely since it affected the plant's financial performance, which means *my* performance."

"And Basil was powerless to help because Toronto was calling the shots," St. James offered sympathetically.

"That's the sum total of it all. Not Basil's fault."

St. James ate the last of the Yorkshire pudding apportioned to him. "Did you and Basil talk about it at the time?"

William nodded. "I never saw Basil so upset with Toronto. The three trawlers didn't arrive at his plant until around four that day. The auditors had already left, so his teams were forced to count trawler catch alone. The three captains were wild with anger, worried quality would deteriorate and they'd receive less on settlement when the delay wasn't their fault."

St. James nodded.

"Would you like some more, Hamilton?" Camilla asked.

"It was wonderful, Camilla, but I'm too full."

"You're a fabulous cook, Camilla," Anna said graciously. "I could learn a thing or two from you."

"Thank you, Anna. You're very kind."

Table discussion drifted to the possible real-estate investment William and Basil were contemplating.

"Have the two of you been planning this for a while?" St. James asked as Camilla placed crème caramel in front of him.

"We've put away a couple thousand pounds each year now for some time to have a smaller mortgage. We're very conservative people. Not big risk-takers."

"Good planning," St. James said on the last bite of dessert.

They chatted over coffee for a while, then thanked the hosts for their wonderful hospitality. William arranged a cab to drop them back at the hotel at 8:30, and as usual they stopped for a nightcap.

"So, do you think the brothers were in cahoots on this inventory thing?" Anna asked when drinks were served.

"No. They don't have enough control over the system. They live modestly, save to make investments rather than borrow. Not the profile of a crook."

"What *is* the profile of a crook?" Anna said quizzically.

"They are usually high-livers. Spend beyond their means, make a big show of everything: expensive cars, houses, that sort of thing. Overconfident. Cocky."

They finished their drinks, signed the bill to the room, and headed off to bed.

Monday was a beautiful day with a warm, gentle breeze. Noisy seagulls greeted them when they emerged from the hotel.

St. James concluded he didn't need anything further from William and could think of nothing the plant accountant could provide he didn't already have, so they decided to spend the day touring Portsmouth.

The lady at the front desk suggested a hop-on, hop-off bus tour of the city. Tickets were available a couple of blocks away, and fifteen minutes later they hopped off one bus to tour the HMS *Warrior*, the fastest warship of Queen Victoria's time. They were back on the bus an hour later and off again at Fort Nelson and the Royal Garrison Church, finally landing at Azzurro's in Gunwharf Quays for drinks and an early pasta dinner at four-thirty.

"I think I might change my travel arrangements, Anna. Go straight to Washington," St. James said out of the blue.

Anna was surprised. "Why?"

"For the Stevens case: Jensen needs a second go-around from me. The case is moving along nicely now, but I do have to clear up some details, see if I can turn theory into proof."

"That means you know what happened."

St. James smiled. "No, not for sure. For the moment it's just a theory to prove or disprove. Loose ends. Still need to examine Jensen's investments, grill him on dealings with certain shareholders, perhaps go to Cayman to trace money."

"Care to share the theory, at least?"

"Not yet."

# Chapter 48

Tuesday afternoon St. James hired a car and driver to take them to Heathrow where they checked into the Airport Hilton for the night, convenient for travelling to North America on early Wednesday morning flights. Then he went online and changed Wednesday's flight destination from Ottawa to Washington and made hotel arrangements there. Anna elected to stick with her Ottawa flight.

Exhausted, they chose room service over the restaurant downstairs.

Anna fell asleep shortly after dinner. But St. James was restless and went to the lobby bar and climbed onto the first available stool.

The bar was crowded, and it took a while to be served. Eventually St. James ordered a double Forty Creek on the rocks.

Halfway through his drink a bald man, about forty-five, climbed on the stool next to him. Wearing a cheap grey suit and a white shirt bulging at the waist, the man looked as if he'd fallen on hard times. He introduced himself as Harry Jameson.

Harry turned out to be a talker, and a loud one at that, with little discretion when it came to his own personal affairs. He bragged about the money he made, his net worth, and several big names he knew in Washington.

The president of his own business, Harry imported everything from booze to women's apparel into the United States. He was in London on a buying trip and on his way home next morning; as it turned out, on the same flight as St. James.

It wasn't long before Harry got around to asking St. James what he did for a living. St. James simply said he was a CPA. Any more information than that St. James was convinced would be all over Washington by next Tuesday.

"Well, well, a CPA?"

"That's right."

"Are you with a firm in Washington?"

"No. I'm kind of on my own." St. James said cautiously.

"Are you taking on new clients?" he asked enthusiastically.

St. James didn't like where this was going.

"Afraid I'm at capacity at the moment."

"Too bad," he said, staring down at his glass. "My accountant disappeared."

St. James looked at Harry.

"On holiday?"

"Nope. Just disappeared … some time ago. Gone. Nobody knows where. Something about missing money."

Harry waved at the bartender for another drink. St. James did the same.

"Did you know him well?" St. James asked casually.

"Not really. The wife and I had dinner at his house a couple of times. Very uncomfortable. He and his wife were obviously unhappy together and tried to hide it. Not well, I might add."

"Don't recall hearing about this," St. James said. "Which firm would this be?"

"Stevens, Gables & Strong."

"Never heard of them," St. James lied.

"Good firm. But as a client you have to wonder. If there's one bad apple there could be more. Can I trust them to do my work, is what I'm thinking."

"What did he do?"

"Took a client's money … a lot of money … millions, I believe, and flew the coop."

"You think it's true?"

"Why would he run if it wasn't?" Harry insisted.

"Don't know. Maybe he has a girlfriend."

They chatted a few more minutes until St. James exhausted what little bit of substance there was to Harry. On the way up to the room he wondered if Jameson and his wife were the couple Beth Stevens had talked about, the drunken husband who had embarrassed his wife. Harry certainly fit the bill.

On Wednesday morning St. James and Anna went through airport security together as far as they could, kissed, then went their separate ways to different departure lounges.

The flight to Washington was smooth and on time. Harry Jameson sat four rows ahead but made no attempt to connect. Just to be sure, St. James kept his nose well and truly buried in a murder mystery he had bought in the airport bookstore, a signal to Harry he wasn't looking for company.

It was 4:30 Washington time when St. James checked into the InterContinental The Willard Hotel on Pennsylvania Avenue. He unpacked and opened his laptop to find emails from both Dozer and Smythe.

Dozer reported that Samuel Franklin had admitted to being a crony of Gyberson's, but denied knowing  Jensen, or Stevens, or anything about $23 million disappearing. Not surprising. Dozer pushed him hard to learn if he knew Long, Martin Clayton, and Clint Wagner, but Franklin was steadfast in his denial. Nor did he know anyone from Montreal named Sterling.

He had admitted to doing business with Adam Derringer, Amanda Fletcher, and Bertram Cook though, but refused to say what sort of business. Dozer grilled the man for over two hours only to conclude he most likely had nothing to do with the attempts to kill St. James. Franklin's story appeared bulletproof to Dozer, which to St. James meant it was. If Franklin had something to hide, sooner or later he'd crack under Dozer's methods.

According to Smythe, Nathan Strong's lawyers had successfully obtained the court order to freeze the Cayman bank account and Higgins Johnson would be applying to Cayman's Grand Court to enforce it this coming Friday.

When St. James finished reading emails, he wrote Mary DeSilva to bring her up to date. He would interview Jensen again tomorrow, or the day after, depending on Jensen's availability.

Last but not least he called Anna. She had arrived home safely and was about to have a sandwich before heading off to bed.

"You should stay up as late as possible to adjust to Ottawa time," St. James suggested.

"No, I'm going to bed right now. To hell with adjusting," she said. "I'm too tired."

"That's my girl."

When they disconnected St. James went to the bar and spent a very comfortable scotch evening talking about various models of automobiles with a bartender named Mack. Next stool over was a fellow named Cyril, an Iowa farmer, in Washington to lobby about something or other to do with pigs. Mack and Cyril didn't follow hockey and St. James didn't follow baseball. Cars were their only common interest.

# Chapter 49

Next morning St. James got on the phone with Jensen. The large man was amenable to meet at eleven, provided St. James came to his office. Most likely he assumed a meeting would speed up a cheque from Global.

At 10:50 St. James hailed a cab that dropped him in front of Jensen's four-story grey brick office building on K Street, where Jensen Holdings occupied the top two floors. It was the first meeting to be held at Jensen's office, the previous one had occurred in hotel board rooms.

The morning was cold and damp, a reminder that winter wasn't far off, and having come from England, St. James wasn't properly dressed. Cold, he wasted no time getting inside.

The building directory said Jensen's reception was on the fourth floor.

When the elevator opened St. James was greeted by a plain-looking young lady who immediately escorted him down a long, narrow, pictureless hallway to dark-brown double doors that opened into Jensen's private office.

She announced St. James's arrival and returned to her post.

St. James eyed the room for a long moment, stunned by its size. Statues of naked women were scattered unevenly among the six granite columns that guarded either side of the rectangular room. An overabundance of abstract art crowded the walls. The floor was white marble. The drapes, made of a heavy maroon fabric, were accented by elaborately painted ceiling murals. Stuffed African animals stood here and there. It was a confusing mess of Roman and African culture all wrapped up to look more like a French brothel than an executive office. St. James's eye saw only god-awful-ugly.

Then there was Jensen's desk, the largest St. James had ever seen. It had to be fifteen feet wide. Most likely custom-built proportional to Jensen's size. Hand-carved gargoyles were embedded in the solid oak; a reflection of Jensen's exaggerated self-importance.

A sickening cloud of stale cigar smoke filled the air.

Jensen made no effort to come from behind the grotesque desk to shake St. James's hand.

Jensen was as red-faced as the day they had met, and was wearing the same three-piece blue pinstriped suit, white shirt, and red tie he wore to every meeting. St. James had come to think of it as the man's uniform.

Jensen sat there, larger than life, chomping on an unlit cigar, looking disgusted.

"When do I get my cheque?" he barked before St. James could even take a seat.

St. James sunk down in a huge grey leather wingback that rested well below Jensen's desk, most likely designed for him to feel above everyone else.

*Insecure.*

St. James crossed his long legs, folded his arms, and smiled. "All in good time, Malachi, all in good time. We have a few loose ends to tie off first."

"Okay, shoot. Ask whatever," he said, waving a hand dismissively.

St. James pulled the shareholder list for the 139 companies from his black leather case, placed it on the mammoth desk, and slid the paper in front of Jensen.

"Tell me about people you know on this list."

Jensen stared at the paper. Placing the unlit cigar in an overflowing ashtray, he grabbed reading glasses from an open desk drawer and slowly mouthed each name as his chubby finger crept down the list.

"Well, I've met them all at one time or another," he said finally.

St. James pressed. "Who do you know best?"

Jensen studied the list once again, then rhymed off six or seven names, none of whom were Gyberson's people.

"Samuel Franklin — didn't he do legal work for you on a property investment in Chicago?"

"Long time ago. Haven't kept in touch."

"Wasn't he recommended to you by Gyberson?"

"Can't remember exactly who recommended him."

"When did you first meet Gyberson?"

Jensen snorted. "Couple years ago. He was looking for financing for a company."

"Which company?"

Jensen pursed his lips and stared at a large angel mural on the ceiling. "Can't rightly remember. Think it was named after a nut or something."

"Macadamia Investments?" St. James offered.

Jensen brightened. "That's it, that's the one. Macadamia owns shares in a company that builds retirement homes. It was short of cash. Macadamia wanted someone to invest so it could inject more cash into the construction company, complete projects it had on the go."

St. James nodded. "You mean The Carstairs Group, the construction company Macadamia Investments owned?"

Jensen raised a finger. "That's the one."

"Who introduced Gyberson to you?"

"You asked me that the first time. Answer's still the same: Stevens."

St. James continued pointing to the list. "You see the names Adam Derringer, Bertram Cook, and Amanda Fletcher?"

"What about 'em?" Jensen said impatiently.

"You have investments in them I take it?"

"Yeah."

"How often do you interact with them?"

"Talk once a year at shareholder meetings."

"Nothing in between?"

"Nothing! Is this leading anywhere St. James or are you just fishing?" Jensen snarled.

St. James ignored the question. "How many companies have you invested in with any of those three shareholders together with Franklin and Gyberson?"

Once again Jensen stared at the ornate ceiling as if pondering a more difficult question than the one being asked. "One each, I believe."

"How well do you know Gyberson?" St. James said forcefully.

"As well as I want to know anyone I do business with. Never get too close: never know when you might have to make a tough decision. Emotion's a liability in my business."

Suddenly Jensen began to cough, lightly at first, but it quickly became more violent. He took three quick gulps from a glass of water sitting on the desk, and, struggling to regain his breath, he wiped away tears with a sleeve. "Got to give these damn things up," he managed to squeak out, pointing to the overburdened ashtray.

St. James wondered what Jensen meant by "tough decisions."

Jensen recovered as much as he could, and St. James continued.

"So, you, or rather Jensen Holdings, invested in Macadamia to help Gyberson?"

"That's correct," Jensen said after drinking more water.

"What did Jensen Holdings get in return?"

"What do you think it got?" he snapped. "Shares in Macadamia. Nothing else *to* get."

"Was it a condition of Jensen's investment in Macadamia that all money flow into Carstairs to finish the retirement home in Chicago?"

"Yes. Macadamia was to loan money it got from Jensen Holdings to The Carstairs Group in return for a promissory note, secured by a mortgage, repayable over ten years at ten per cent interest. Once the home's completed and operating, Carstairs repays the note to Macadamia from its profits. Macadamia uses that cash to purchase its shares back from Jensen Holdings."

"And that's when your money disappeared?"

Jensen wiped sweat from his brow with a handkerchief.

"The only shareholder of Macadamia was Gyberson, and he signed cheques made payable to Carstairs in return for a promissory note payable back to Macadamia, as contemplated by the agreement. But money never made it into Carstairs's bank account. Sonofabitch never intended to finish the building. Stole my money and left town."

St. James pressed once again. "Then Gyberson must have had signing authority in Carstairs too, otherwise he wouldn't have been able to cash Macadamia's cheques made in Carstairs's name."

A sheepish-looking Jensen said, "Yes, he did."

St. James frowned at the stupidity. Jensen should have known Gyberson had signing authority for both companies, that his investment was at risk with no division of duties or financial controls between the two companies. Or, maybe he did know.

St. James decided to have a little fun. "Sounds to me a lot like contributory negligence, Malachi. Maybe you caused your own loss. Maybe you have a claim against yourself, not the Stevens firm or Global."

Jensen jumped from his chair and shouted, "Stevens should have known the guy was a crook! He was supposed to check Gyberson out. I don't believe he even looked at the financials, let alone investigate Gyberson's character."

"Did you?"

"Did I what?" he barked.

"Look at the financials and check out Gyberson's character."

"Hell no! That's what I was paying Stevens for."

St. James pulled a paper bearing the Stevens code from a pocket and placed it in front of Jensen.

Jensen calmed slightly, looking puzzled as he scanned the code.

"What the hell's this mumbo-jumbo?"

"It's a code we found on Stevens's computer. Ever see it before?"

His eyes squinted. "No. What's it supposed to mean?"

St. James's grin was superficial. "Was hoping you could tell me."

"Haven't a goddamned clue," Jensen said dismissively as he shoved the paper across the desk back to St. James.

St. James's forehead furrowed at the man's arrogance.

"Do you have a bank account in Cayman?"

"No, I don't."

"Have you ever had trouble with tax authorities anywhere in the world?"

"No, I haven't," Jensen said without hesitation.

"Tell me, Malachi, were any investment recommendations from Stevens winners for you?"

Jensen considered this for a moment, concluding it to be a trick question.

"Yes. Why do you ask?" he said aggressively.

"Just curious."

"All of them paid some return except Macadamia and its investment in Carstairs."

"So Stevens wasn't a complete dud?"

"If you're trying to defuse the Macadamia–Carstairs mess with successes, it won't work. I lost $23 million, plain and simple. Nothing to do with other successes. You're trying to create a diversion, St. James, dilute my claim."

Jensen was now even more red, and St. James was worried the man might stroke out.

St. James changed his line of questioning once again, spending the next hour or so moving through every other name on the shareholder list. After three or four names Jensen began to calm, claiming he had met each shareholder only a couple of times before investing, and after that only at quarterly board or annual shareholder meetings.

"Were you ever invited to dinner at the Stevens home?"

Jensen looked at St. James as if he was somehow being set up. "Couple of times, I guess," he said cautiously.

"What was the relationship like between Beth and Thomas?"

Jensen almost came out of his chair a second time. "What the hell does that have to do with my claim?" he shouted.

"Everything," St. James replied without batting an eye, "everything to do with Thomas's health, happiness, and state of mind when dealing with you."

Jensen didn't seem to grasp this.

"Uh…?"

"Never mind," St. James said with an air of disgust. "I have other names I want to run by you."

"But we've gone through all the names on the list," he said.

"These are additional ones." One by one St. James rhymed off the names of the two burned in the Mercedes, Long, and Sterling from Montreal, then listed the four ex-cons he had helped put in prison. After grilling Jensen a number of ways, St. James was satisfied he had nothing to do with any of them.

Jensen looked at his watch. "How much longer is this going to take? I have a luncheon appointment."

"Just one last question," St. James said.

"What's that?"

"Where did you go to university?"

"Florida State. Why do you want to know that?"

St. James ignored the question.

"What years?"

"'72 to '75. Why do you want to know that?" he repeated.

"Just curious."

"Don't see what that has to do with my claim either. Matter of fact, you asked a lot of questions that have nothing to do with my claim. You're curious about some strange things."

St. James ignored the comment. "Now, Malachi, before I go, I have to review your investment records for a few companies on the list."

Jensen was stunned. He hadn't seen this coming, which gave St. James a certain amount of pleasure.

"Absolutely not," he barked.

"Too bad," St. James said shaking his head, feigning the closing of his file.

"What do you mean, too bad?"

"Well, you don't get a cheque unless I sign off. And if I can't complete my investigation, I can't sign off," St. James said with glee he barely managed to conceal.

Jensen jumped to his feet. "Look here, St. James, nobody said anything about you messing with my records. You can't just waltz in here like you own the place!"

"All I'm asking is to see records related to relevant investments. If you won't do that, I'll close the file and advise Global the claim cannot be verified. Your choice."

# Chapter 50

Jensen fell into the large chair behind his huge desk, staring blankly at the ostentatious ceiling. St. James could see he was considering the risk of him roaming through Jensen Holdings files.

*Trying to remember what's damning.*

Jensen knew he could kiss the insurance money goodbye if he didn't cooperate. St. James wasn't going any further if he couldn't verify what had transpired between Gyberson and Jensen.

After several seconds Jensen let out a long sigh. "Okay."

"Wise decision, Malachi," said St. James. "I'll need a place to work and someone to bring me files."

Resigned to the corner he was forced into, Jensen buzzed his executive assistant. A moment later an underweight, sickly-looking woman in her late 60s wearing a baggy, flowered dress, and a well-worn grey sweater entered the room.

"Yes, Mr. Jensen?" she said in a low voice.

Jensen pointed rudely to St. James. "This here's St. James. Put him in the spare office and bring him the files."

Jensen's disposition certainly didn't improve in the presence of ladies. It was his nature no matter what. St. James doubted there'd be any difference if the president of the United States walked in.

"Very well, Mr. Jensen," she said, looking at St. James. "Please follow me."

Down the hall she said, "Is St. James your first name?"

"Actually it's my last name. First is Hamilton."

"Thought so. Mr. Jensen calls everyone by their last name. My name is Eleanor."

"Pleased to meet you, Eleanor. That's quite a guy you work for."

Eleanor rolled her eyes. "Just three months till retirement. Nerves couldn't take much more."

St. James said nothing.

Eleanor showed him into a medium-sized bright and airy office bearing absolutely no resemblance to Jensen's tomb down the hall.

"Now," she said, "what can I get for you?"

St. James rhymed off the list of companies he wanted to see, emphasizing that he'd like every file related to each one and that nothing should be left out or considered irrelevant.

"It will take some time to gather them all at once. Do you mind if I bring one company at a time?"

"Not at all, Eleanor."

"Which would you like first?"

"Macadamia and then Carstairs, please."

"Very well, I'll be back in a few minutes. Help yourself to coffee. Servery's next door."

St. James went into the next room, popped a pod of Colombian dark roast into a Keurig, and waited for the machine to fill his mug. Then he returned to find Macadamia's files neatly stacked in the centre of the desk. Eleanor was efficient if nothing else.

He took a couple of sips of coffee and then flipped open Macadamia's correspondence file, which consisted mostly of emails between Gyberson and Jensen with occasional CCs to Stevens. There were also copies of wire transfers to Macadamia's bank account from Jensen Holdings's.

He whipped out a calculator from his attaché case and, running a finger down each internal document, began tapping in amounts transferred to Macadamia. When every amount had been entered,

$23,122,699 flashed up on the calculator screen. Not exactly $23 million, but close enough for his purposes.

Emails CCed to Stevens were confirmations that legal and other documents had been executed by Macadamia. St. James could see that Stevens was orchestrating everything from the exchanges. Yet, he seemed privy only to some, but not all, emails. Odd. Why wouldn't all correspondence be shared with him? He was, after all, quarterbacking the work. It would be normal to be copied on all correspondence; if not, actions could be missed or could go off the rails and Stevens wouldn't know.

St. James made several notes before moving on.

Just as he finished examining Macadamia, Eleanor arrived with Carstairs's files. St. James went through the very same procedures with Carstairs that he had with Macadamia.

Documentation confirmed that $23 million was transferred from Jensen Holdings to Macadamia to Carstairs, which was internal evidence that funds had made it through to the contractor.

But internal evidence didn't prove that money had actually moved from one bank account to another: only external evidence could verify that. It was one thing to record transfers in company records; it was quite another for a bank to acknowledge that transfers had actually taken place.

St. James asked Eleanor for Jensen Holdings's bank statements, which she promptly delivered.

"Even though they are not his companies, would Malachi happen to have copies of bank statements for Macadamia and Carstairs?"

"Well, Jensen Holdings owns shares in Macadamia, and Macadamia owns Carstairs. Under the shareholder agreements, he has the right to all bank statements. I'll get them."

"Thank you, Eleanor."

Eleanor returned a few minutes later with stacks of bank statements.

St. James opened bank statement files for Jensen Holdings, Macadamia, and Carstairs and ran a finger down each page, following deposits, cheques, and transfers in and out of all three bank accounts, comparing each date and amount recorded by the bank to those recorded in the internal records.

The bank statements confirmed that Jensen Holdings had transferred $23 million to Macadamia, just as Jensen had said. That corroborated the internal records. The statements also confirmed $23 million coming out of Macadamia's account. However, no $23 million had been deposited into Carstairs's.

St. James considered this. Why did internal documentation show money being transferred into Carstairs when it wasn't? If money was taken when leaving Macadamia's bank account, why would Carstairs's internal records confirm it being received? Internal and external didn't match. Puzzling.

St. James made a note.

The last piece of correspondence from Gyberson to Jensen caught St. James's eye. It simply said, *Good to go. Can do anytime.* Two short, intriguing sentences. But there was nothing to indicate what they meant. St. James made a note anyway. He did notice that Stevens wasn't copied in on this one.

The remaining Carstairs files held nothing of interest until he got to an unlabelled one containing a single piece of paper: a note in Jensen's handwriting describing dissatisfaction with Stevens's investigation into Gyberson, Macadamia, and Carstairs.

"Probably when he first contemplated suing SG&S," St. James mumbled. "He's manufacturing evidence for the lawsuit."

Jensen had said that he communicated with shareholders only once or twice a year, at shareholder and director meetings. Yet communication with Gyberson amounted to considerably more.

Eleanor arrived with another stack of files and left with Carstairs's. St. James made another coffee and then selected another company's files.

The stack was held together by three large elastic bands, which St. James removed to separate the pile into individual files. As he pulled files from the stack, a leather-bound document fell onto the desk.

St. James was surprised to see it labelled *Jensen Holdings Inc. Financial Statements*. It had to be misfiled; no other logical reason for Jensen Holdings's financial records to be among investment files. It should have been filed in Accounting.

If Jensen knew that Jensen Holdings financial information had fallen into the hands of St. James, he'd have a coronary and fire Eleanor on the spot, even with her being only three months from retirement. He was a nasty piece of work. In Eleanor's fragile state, St. James didn't think it likely she would survive his rage. St. James decided to place the financial statements back where they came from before Eleanor re-boxed the files.

But not before reading them. It was a wonderful opportunity to gain insight into Jensen's true financial state. Right or wrong, he couldn't pass it up.

St. James flipped open the leather-bound document to the Balance Sheet page and was immediately shocked by what he saw. All the money Jensen had invested was borrowed from third parties. And not from banks at reasonable interest rates, but from syndicates at higher rates. The company was losing money fast. Shareholder equity had been completely wiped out the previous year. The company was a house of cards, ready to fall.

"No wonder he's pushing so hard for an insurance cheque. He can't survive without it," St. James mumbled.

He spent the next twenty minutes or so reading cashflow and income statements, as well as the notes on the statements themselves. He was stunned; he just couldn't believe the disaster. Unless the company received a major equity injection soon, it would be bankrupt.

For a moment he thought about keeping the statements, to make sure they were never found. But that was wrong, and he was in the business of detecting wrongdoing, not committing it. If he took the document, he'd lose all respect for himself, as well as that of those who might one day find out.

He carefully placed the document between two files, then positioned them in the middle of the stack and re-applied the three elastic bands just as he had found the stack an hour earlier. Satisfied the document was secure and concealed he delivered the stack to Eleanor's workstation, thanked her for the help, and wished her a long and happy retirement.

All told, the review had taken a little over two and a half hours, long enough for Jensen to make it through his luncheon meeting. St. James stopped by his office and found Jensen reading a legal document.

St. James knocked lightly on the doorjamb. "Malachi, I've finished the investigation."

Jensen just grunted. He didn't look up, nor ask St. James what he'd found, if anything, or if he would now sign off so Global would issue a cheque.

"Make sure you speed up that cheque," was all he said as St. James left the office. "I've obligations, you know!" he yelled as St. James closed the door behind him. St. James said nothing; he just kept walking.

On the way back to the InterContinental, St. James wondered how such an arrogant, deranged, angry malcontent like Jensen had survived in business as long as he had.

St. James's cell vibrated.

Jason Williamson.

"Just got word from Fargo. Police picked up Gyberson this morning on suspicion of murder. He's being questioned as we speak."

"Excellent. Can you ask the chief there if Dozer can question him when they're finished?"

"Already have. No problem, after they have first crack."

Back in the hotel room, St. James discovered an email from Higgins Johnson with legal searches attached and another from Dozer saying his best men were tailing the CISI people.

St. James replied, asking Dozer to fly to Fargo to question Gyberson. Dozer confirmed his next-day Fargo flight a half-hour later.

St. James's cell vibrated a second time.

Anna.

"Sorry I was cranky with you last night," she said apologetically. "I really don't do jet lag well."

"Don't worry about it. I need you to do more searches."

"What for?"

"To satisfy a hunch."

# Chapter 51

St. James called Anderson from his Washington hotel room to report on the UK trip. He described his investigation into CISI's two largest plants, their inventory records, the excellent cooperation he had enjoyed from Basil and William Hughes, and his discussions with Captain Thorne. Anderson was pleased with the thoroughness.

St. James then asked Anderson if it would be possible to review a list of internal shareholders. Anderson said he would arrange it.

"Would you know if any director or employee pledged shares with a broker on margin?" St. James asked.

"Well, we'd know if shares were pledged for a loan, but not whether it was on margin. I believe most institutions ask for a letter before lending against employee shares."

"To ensure the bank is repaid loans if shares are redeemed before money reaches the borrower's hands?"

"That's right. Security thing I guess."

"I'll be back in Toronto on Monday. Could shareholder files be available then?"

"I don't see why not. I'll have my assistant pull the files and book a room for you on this floor."

"Excellent."

St. James was beginning to like Anderson. Odd, considering their rocky beginning. Anderson's strong focus on company performance and doing what he said he would when he said he would were two qualities St. James admired. Not many executives had both. To some, a commitment to deliver by a certain date was merely a suggestion.

St. James's flight to Ottawa was not until eight the next morning. He had time for himself. At 4:00 he felt the need to walk; exercise was always his best head-clearer.

The air had turned damp, even colder than when he met with Jensen that morning. The wind had picked up substantially. The hotel concierge directed him to a men's shop four blocks from the hotel where he found a suitably warm jacket. Now more comfortable, he walked up Pennsylvania Avenue, as close to the White House as Secret Service would allow.

The usual army of media personnel dominated the White House lawn: vans covered with advertising, each sprouting multiple antennas and dishes pointed in every direction.

St. James wondered what all the fuss was about. Maybe a major policy speech from the President, or a natural disaster somewhere in the world?

He stood watching the activity for some time, thinking of all the times he'd seen this very picture on television. It felt surreal to be standing there in person.

He walked a number of other streets before returning to the hotel. He grabbed the Stevens file and went down to the bar, where he ordered a double Forty Creek. Mack was off duty and there was no sign of Cyril the pig guy.

Slowly and methodically he began to put the Stevens story together, separating fact from supposition, and isolating holes that needed to be filled to close the case. He had the theory of the case. For a moment, he wished DuPont was there to help with details, to challenge him on specifics. That was Pierre's strength, not his.

One loose end was whether a deep clean actually could completely sanitize, leaving no prints. St. James wasn't sure how he would prove that, one way or another. So he called Nathan Strong who, by chance, was still in his office.

"Thought you would have already left for home," St. James said lightheartedly.

"Used to leave earlier when I was young but found sitting in traffic to be a waste of time. I am afraid the older I get the more impatient I become. I can't tolerate bad, indecisive drivers like I used to. A weakness, I'm afraid. Besides, I get a lot done during the hour and a half everyone else sits in traffic."

"A much more productive use of time," St. James offered. "Nathan, I need a favour."

"Name it."

"I need to talk to your cleaning company. But they won't talk to me unless you authorize it."

"What would you like?"

"I'd like to tag along with them when they do a sanitation clean, see how it's done, that sort of thing."

"I'll call the owner right now and get back to you."

St. James went back to his notes and scotch.

Anna didn't know it, but she was researching the second major hole in the case. And, depending upon what she found, he could be going to Cayman sooner rather than later.

He waved the bartender over for another scotch and when it arrived he closed the file and carefully considered what he'd summarized.

His cell vibrated.

Nathan.

He had spoken with the owner of the cleaning company, a man named Mohammed, who was anxious to please him. It so happened that Mohammed was starting a clean in an investment house the next morning and was happy to have St. James tag along. Nathan gave St. James Mohammed's coordinates.

Meeting Mohammed in the morning meant St. James had to change flight plans from Friday morning to evening and let Anna know, both of which he did as soon as he returned to the room.

Mohammed was an early riser and wanted to meet at 7 a.m. at an address on L Street. An ungodly hour, but he had to start then because the client's employees couldn't work with cleaners milling about, and certain offices on the executive floor had to be done before nine.

The next morning, St. James made his way to the address Mohammed had provided, arriving promptly at seven after gulping down a blueberry muffin and a large coffee.

Mohammed was a short man with dark skin and sunken eyes who walked with a limp. Greeting St. James as he stepped off the elevator, Mohammed introduced himself as a hard-working Palestinian Christian who had arrived from Ramallah seven years ago. He had grown the cleaning business from two to forty people, mostly with Middle Eastern workers who couldn't find work at American companies.

They entered a large executive office that St. James assumed belonged to the president of the investment house. There, Mohammed began to explain the details of a sanitation clean. Fortunately, his people were just about to begin, so St. James was able to witness each step firsthand.

"First we wash everything down with soap and water. Then we apply various types of cleaning products based on surface material to be sanitized, being careful not to cause a damaging chemical reaction. The most common cleaners are Lysol, Virox, and Fantastik, all with different dilution ratios to minimize corrosion and still achieve the job. Whatever the product, it should contain sodium hypochlorite, quaternary ammonium, or hydrogen peroxide in sufficient quantities to kill 99.99% of bacteria."

St. James wasn't looking for this much detail, but Mohammed was so enthusiastic he didn't have the heart to suggest more brevity. In the end, he was glad he didn't. It was Mohammed's detail that ultimately gave him the confidence he had in his own conclusions.

"Do you do every surface? Walls, furniture, doors, finish work, that sort of thing?" St. James inquired.

"Everything within six feet of the floor. Above that nobody touches. Even there we take no chances. We damp mop above six feet with a solution of vinegar and water."

St. James nodded. "How do you know you've covered all surfaces?"

Mohammed smiled as he produced a checklist that went on for pages and covered everything from doorknobs to toilet handles, and all points in between.

"My people use this for every room," he said, pointing to the checklist. "Each room has a supervisor who also cleans as they go. The cleaner checks off boxes as each step is completed. The supervisor checks the work and signs off. A cleaner has to be with me more than eighteen months and earn my trust before I make them a supervisor. Can't afford to lose a client. It's a cutthroat business, and once you lose a client they're gone forever."

St. James nodded again. "What are the chances of a fingerprint anywhere in this room surviving?"

Without hesitation Mohammed said, "Less than one per cent."

"You answered that very quickly, Mohammed," St. James said with a smile.

"That's because I get asked that question a lot by police whenever there's a homicide and no prints."

"How did you arrive at the 'less than one per cent' figure?"

"I hired a marketing company several months ago to help grow my revenue. They suggested that a test could be an effective way to market our services. If we could prove more than ninety-nine per cent success sanitizing a room, it would give us a competitive advantage. Good branding, they said. We had already perfected training and quality control programs ahead of our competitors. We just weren't telling anyone.

"So, I picked a client to film a commercial in exchange for five free cleanings. We made sure the office was laden with prints. I asked police if they would join in, which cost me a hefty donation to their charity foundation, but it was worth it to have the independent verification reinforcing a client endorsement. Plus it helped the police understand why there were no fingerprints at certain crime scenes."

St. James nodded.

"Police lifted fingerprints before and after we sanitized. Lots of prints before, but only a single partial unclear thumbprint was found after. What soap and water didn't get, cleaning products did. The commercial plus police verification boosted revenue forty per cent over eighteen months. Best money I ever spent," Mohammed said jubilantly.

St. James laughed. "Your enthusiasm is admirable, Mohammed. You're your own best salesman."

"Thank you, Mr. St. James, for those kind words."

St. James watched for almost an hour until he had the evidence he needed. He thanked Mohammed for his help.

Back at the hotel, St. James went online to find two more cleaning companies. With very little variation he got the same answers to the questions he had put to Mohammed.

St. James looked at his watch. 10:15. He was thinking about an earlier flight back to Ottawa when his cell vibrated again.

"I'm in Fargo," said Dozer. "Got in last night about ten. Colder than hell here, man."

"Thought hell was supposed to be hot."

"Okay, it's colder than Ottawa. Same thing."

St. James smirked at the phone. "That's what I've heard. That's why you're there and I'm here."

"Thanks, man," Dozer said disingenuously.

"What's your plan?" St. James said.

"I'm on my way to police headquarters right now to meet Detective Hanlon, the guy heading up the murder investigation. We talked first thing this morning and he's okay to team with us. He's interested in what we're doing, if it could somehow help them nail Gyberson."

"Let me know how it goes." St. James clicked off.

St. James was able to catch a 2:30 flight to Ottawa, and was home by 5:30. The first thing he did was call Anna at the pub.

"How late do you have to work?" he asked.

"I'm here till nine, I'm afraid."

"Take a cab when you're off. In the meantime I'll open a bottle of wine, read my mail, pay some bills, and do laundry. So probably best I don't pick you up. I'll either be too cranky because of bills or have had too much wine."

"Or both," she said, laughing.

"See you when I see you," he said.

Bills were mounting, and St. James was feeling pressure to tie up the Stevens case. His bank account was anemic, and that was without invoices from Dozer and Smythe. He kept the two so busy they didn't have time to bill.

*Good cashflow strategy.*

While the wash wound its way through the dry cycle, he paid creditors, opened a bottle of Conquista Mendoza, and poured it through the aerator. He sat on the living room couch, flipped on the news, and saw the very same view of the White House he had seen in person the previous day.

Anna had been home from England for more than a day now and had found time to replenish the fridge with a cooked chicken, fresh vegetables, cheese, and a variety of juices.

After grilled chicken and mixed vegetables, he poured more wine and headed for the shower. Five minutes under hot, steamy water was wonderful. He examined his wound, which was now just a reddish scar. He could finally forget about it, as much as anyone could forget being shot.

Showered and shaved, he dressed and wandered down the hall at precisely the same time that Anna came through the front door.

"You're a half-hour early," he said, looking at his watch.

"What? We've been apart for a couple of days and that's how you greet me?" she said, mock-hurt in her voice.

"Sorry. Let's start over."

He walked closer, held her in his arms, and they kissed.

"Now that's more like it," she said, smiling. "My feet are killing me. I'm going to run a bath. Would you be a doll and pour me a glass of wine?"

"It would be my pleasure."

St. James headed to the kitchen, Anna to the bathroom. A few minutes later he handed her a glass of Pinot Grigio in the tub.

"Did you eat?" he asked.

"Had a sandwich at the pub. By the way, I forgot to mention that the owners fired Sid yesterday."

"About time! What brought it to a head?"

"A group of Jim's friends wrote a complaint letter saying if Sid wasn't gone by today, they'd drive business away from the Duck. Everyone signed it. That was all it took. No more Sid."

"Pity someone didn't think of that before. Put us all out of our misery. Who's in charge now?"

"Katie Cameron. She's great. Everyone loves her. We felt the tension lift the minute Sid left the building."

"Not a job you were interested in?"

"No. I've been thinking of our conversations, about my capabilities, that is. You're right. It's time I made a move."

"What do you have in mind?"

"Don't know. Still thinking."

St. James left it at that.

When Anna finished bathing, she dressed in a comfortable grey track suit and joined St. James in the living room, where he refilled their glasses.

"I managed to dredge up the university list you asked for," she said when they had settled together on the chesterfield.

St. James smiled. "Great. Let's see?"

She handed him a paper she took from her purse, and he looked down the list of names.

"What did you want it for, anyway?"

"You'll see."

"Thought that's what you'd say. You sure do have a funny way of team playing. Sometimes we're in, sometimes we're not."

He smiled.

"This is your first case. When all the facts are gathered, I go through a fermentation phase, when pieces in my head coagulate into a total picture. It's a one-person job. Soon all will be made clear."

Anna gave him a look that more or less said "bullshit."

# Chapter 52

Arthur Spance, Jeremy Stern, Clifford Dunning, and a tall, thin man crowded into a booth in Earle's Bar & Grill in downtown Boston. Spance's huge frame wouldn't fit in the booth. Wheezing and looking pale, he was forced to sit on a chair at the end of the cracked Arborite table.

Stern, a man of average build, bearded, blond, mid-forties, commented, "How are we going to do this?"

"If we do Slate and St. James together, it will draw police attention. Not smart," said Dunning, in his strong British accent.

The tall man looked at Dunning. "If we do them separately, we're still suspects, stupid."

Dunning's fists clenched. "I told you before never to call me that."

The tall man finished his beer. "Relax, Dunning. I don't mean anything by it."

His teeth gritted, Dunning said, "Don't care. I don't like it."

"What does your man in Ottawa say?" Spance said, turning to the tall man.

"St. James has been travelling back and forth between Washington and England. A few days ago he was shot, but unfortunately it wasn't fatal. Still going strong, my associate tells me." The tall man signalled the server for another beer.

Stern stared off into the distance. "Pity he wasn't finished off. Wasn't a day gone by in prison I didn't think about him and Slate.

Every rotten meal. Every lousy sleep with one eye open in case my cellmate got sexually weird. Every fight for cigarettes. Every fight over the TV remote. All a constant reminder of how much I hate those bastards."

The others nodded, each staring blankly into their beers.

"It would've been nice if he was done in by someone else," said Dunning thoughtfully.

"Doesn't matter. We've got what we've got," the tall man said sharply, gulping the beer the waiter had just plunked in front of him. "Can't be traceable to us."

"That goes without saying, doofus," Dunning said in a condescending tone.

Stern and Spance nodded. Spance scratched his three-day-old stubble and said, "What about a hit and run with a truck, not a big one, maybe just a half-ton."

Dunning gave Spance an impatient look. "Too risky. Someone might see you. Besides, damage to the truck is hard to cover up. Body shops are snitches for police. And what if the targets don't die? Too many things can go wrong."

"What, then?" Stern barked.

"Car accident," said Dunning.

"Together, in one car?" Spance said, his unhealthy lungs causing him to wheeze.

"Too difficult. They aren't together very often. Could wait a long time for that, and that means it would have to be spontaneous, with no time to plan. Wouldn't work," the tall man concluded.

"I agree. Has to be separate. Have to study them individually. Movements, daily habits, that sort of thing," said Dunning, wiping froth from an unshaven face.

"Do we all agree?" said the tall man, looking at everyone around the table one by one.

Everyone nodded.

"Good," said the tall man.

"Next thing is to agree on how we do it," Spance suggested.

"To make it look unrelated, there must be two different … shall we say … accidents," said the tall man with a wink. "Here's what I propose…"

# Chapter 53

When Dozer arrived in Fargo one night earlier, he checked into the Radisson Hotel on Fifth Street. Up at seven the next morning, he shaved, showered, and ate a huge breakfast before making his way to the police station.

When Dozer entered the grey two-story building at 222 Fourth Street, the duty officer was expecting him. He was quickly escorted down a pale-green hall to a room where he met Detective Hanlon standing in front of a one-way mirror, looking into the room where Gyberson was being questioned.

Hanlon was of medium height, with thinning salt-and-pepper hair, determined green eyes and wearing a dark-grey Brooks Brothers pinstripe suit.

He briefed Dozer as two detectives pressed Gyberson for answers on the other side of the glass.

Gyberson was seated on a chair, handcuffed to a metal table in a windowless, green cinder block room about three times the size of a prison cell. His head was drooping with exhaustion from hours of intense questioning. His grey denim shirt was drenched with sweat, his jeans faded and well-worn. Dozer could tell he'd been worked over for some time.

The detectives were grilling him very hard. One was in his late forties, portly and bald, face heavily scarred like it had gotten in the way of a few fists. The second detective was younger, maybe in his late thirties, with sandy hair and better clothes, and was in much better physical shape.

*Could be a potential recruit for White Investigations*, Dozer thought.

The detectives took turns machine-gunning questions in different ways, rotating every five minutes. The portly one was clearly the bad cop. His face was stuck in Gyberson's the whole time, yelling questions instead of asking them, an intimidation tactic familiar to Dozer's. The younger cop was appealing to Gyberson to end the interrogation quickly, to answer truthfully, to get it over with so he could sleep, recover, and have a hot meal. The good cop.

They were determined to break him, hoping his increasing exhaustion would make him crack. A mistake by Gyberson could help push him to confess.

Gyberson was a small, thin man, looking more like an aged bicycle courier than a murderer. Long, stringy brown hair, a patchy beard, and large ears made him cartoon-like, causing Dozer to smile.

The older officer emerged from the interrogation room to take a break. Hanlon introduced him to Dozer as Gerry.

"Getting anywhere in there, Gerry?" Hanlon asked anxiously.

"Tough one to crack," Gerry said, wearily rubbing an aching neck. "You can tell he's been through this many times before. He knows when to give useless answers and when to clam up. We're throwing everything at him. He looks weak, but he has more stamina than the two of us put together." He shook his head.

Hanlon gave a long sigh. "Well, keep at it. We'll see if something breaks before the day is out."

Gerry nodded as he headed off to a washroom.

Detective Hanlon excused himself to return to his office.

Dozer continued staring through the one-way glass for a long while, turning up the audio to better hear the exchange inside. He studied Gyberson's way of answering, his tone, and body language, paying particular attention to his breathing and facial expressions.

Gyberson's breathing was rhythmic. Long, slow intake when being asked a question, and long, slow exhale when answering. Dozer thought he might actually be meditating to tune out the detectives, managing interrogation stress through a mild hypnotic state.

His breathing was also tied to lowering his eyelids and relaxing his face muscles, giving him a tired look. He wasn't using meditation just to survive: he was using it to project exhaustion, a begging-for-sleep look. An act. The two detectives were being had. Dozer thought the technique brilliant.

Despite Gyberson's technique, the detectives were doing their job well, using modern interrogation techniques. Right questions, right timing. They were certainly skilled at their jobs. They were so focused on breaking the man that they didn't see that Gyberson was clearly controlling the show. On some level, Dozer admired his skill.

Hanlon came back down the hall and invited Dozer to his office, where Dozer explained the commercial case: the $23 million, the code, Jensen, the Cayman bank accounts. Hanlon was intrigued and wanted as much detail as Dozer could provide. Leads were often identified by merging murder and commercial cases together. Information from one could reinforce a theory in the other.

"I take it you have officially charged him and he's lawyered up?" Dozer said, eyebrows raised.

"Arrested him yesterday morning and read him his rights, and of course he invoked the right to an attorney," Hanlon replied with a wave of a hand. "An attorney named Jackson showed up a half-hour later, talked to his client alone first and then came out to make all the litigation threats. Usual theatrical nonsense."

Dozer nodded. "Do you feel confident the charge will stick?"

Hanlon stroked his chin like he was weighing the evidence against Gyberson for the first time. "Well, we did find a handgun hidden in the trunk of Gyberson's rental, under the spare tire. Ballistics matched it with the bullet taken from Stevens's body. And Gyberson's prints were on the weapon."

"Pretty good start," Dozer said with a grin.

Hanlon looked concerned. "Problem is, Gyberson's prints could not be found anywhere at the scene. Nothing on the door or anywhere else in the room. And no one saw him come or go. We interviewed hotel maids, guests on the same floor, and personnel who could possibly have seen something. Nothing came of it. That makes it less than an open-and-shut case. Someone could have set him up, planted the gun."

"Alibi?"

"Hooker."

Dozer winced. "Great. Not always the most reliable witnesses."

"They are if you pay them enough," Hanlon said solemnly. "Unfortunately, buying alibis is all too common here."

Dozer nodded. "When do you think I can have a crack at him?"

"This afternoon. My boys need a break, so you're a welcome diversion," Hanlon said, offering a faint smile.

"Excellent," Dozer said, rising to shake Hanlon's hand. "Appreciate the cooperation."

Dozer left to grab a sandwich from a small café down the street, taking time to consider Gyberson's breathing technique and how he would handle him that afternoon.

At 2:15 Dozer entered the small interrogation room where Gyberson was sitting.

He slammed his massive foot down on the top rung of Gyberson's chair. "So, you're close friends with Jensen, that right?"

Gyberson stared at the floor. No response.

Dozer waited a few minutes. "We know you sold shares in Macadamia to Jensen Holdings for $23 million so it could fund Carstairs to complete a construction project in Chicago."

"Yeah, he invested some money," Gyberson mumbled, feigning exhaustion.

"What'd you do with it?"

"Just like you said, finished the home."

"But the home isn't finished," Dozer insisted.

"Well, I paid to have it finished," Gyberson lied.

"Who did you pay?"

"Contractors. Macadamia."

"Macadamia is not the contractor. It's your holding company. Carstairs is the contractor. Don't play games with me, Stan. I know the facts and all the players. Besides, one-word answers aren't going to help you. You'll have to do better than that."

Gyberson said nothing.

Dozer continued. "We know you flew out here sitting next to Thomas Stevens, the man you murdered."

No response.

"Have you no interest in helping yourself?" Dozer said aggressively.

Gyberson looked up at Dozer. "Who the hell are you, anyway?" he sneered.

"I'm a man who doesn't give up," Dozer barked, inches away from Gyberson's face.

Gyberson suddenly lunged forward, which could have resulted in a serious head-butt if not for the handcuffs restraining Gyberson. "You're also a man with bad breath. Get out of my face!" he yelled.

*This is gonna be tough*, Dozer thought.

"I work for a man who's investigating the theft of Jensen's $23 million for Global Insurance, the insurers for Stevens, Gables & Strong. But, then again, you know all that. Stevens was your buddy … up until you killed him, that is. He told you everything. He helped you steal $23 million from Jensen. You were down and out."

"Tell me how you stole the money."

"Don't know what you're talking about," Gyberson said disingenuously.

Dozer didn't want a police record of what he was about to say, so he leaned down close to Gyberson's ear and whispered, "I know the game you're playing. The breathing. The fake exhaustion. The meditation. Actually, I admire it. But here's the thing: I'm not a cop. I'm a private citizen, not bound by the rules around this place. Haven't taken the oath, nor a pledge to follow humane interrogation techniques. I'm free to do what I want, when I want."

Anyone watching through the one-way mirror would assume Dozer was pleading with Gyberson to tell the truth. So Dozer held his own hands in papal position and whispered, "So if you get out of here because you won't talk, I'll find you. And I guarantee your mother won't recognize you when I'm done."

Gyberson's eyes showed greater concern as they rolled toward Dozer.

Dozer eyed Gyberson's change in body language. "If I leave here with nothing, one of two things will happen. Either you will be convicted of murder and never see the light of day again, or you'll go free and be fed through a tube the rest of your life. Some things are worse than dying, Stanny-boy."

Gyberson's eyes opened wider.

Dozer waited.

Gyberson's look of feigned exhaustion suddenly turned to fear. His forehead furrowed and his lips went dry, moving without forming words.

Then he said, "Not as they appear."

"What do you mean, 'not as they appear'?" Dozer barked.

"Just what I said."

Dozer pressed. "Tell me more."

"Can't."

Dozer verbally worked Gyberson over for another two hours, only to quit after the man fell asleep at a quarter past five.

# Chapter 54

Saturday night, Dozer called St. James to report on the interrogation of Gyberson and on his meeting with Detective Hanlon. He told St. James about Gyberson's breathing, the timing and pace.

"That's brilliant!" St. James exclaimed. "If you're consistent, with enough stamina you could wait out anything but physical torture with that method. Wonder how many times he was interrogated before catching on to the technique."

"Don't know, man," Dozer said.

"Dozer, could you do that if the roles were reversed?"

"Wouldn't get caught," Dozer replied smugly.

St. James rolled his eyes at the phone. Dozer gave St. James all the details leading to Gyberson's only intriguing response.

"Not as they appear," St. James repeated slowly, trying to make something of Gyberson's words. "What could it mean? That it looks like he murdered Stevens but didn't? Hard to believe with a positive ballistics report and fingerprints on a gun."

"I agree, St. James. But I was questioning him on the theft, not the murder, so I assumed it had something to do with that."

"Would make more sense," St. James mumbled. "But what?"

"I pumped him for most of this morning too before I left. Nothing more," Dozer said, obviously frustrated by his lack of success.

"Maybe he means it only looks like he took money. That something else happened," St. James mused.

"Maybe some other person was involved," Dozer countered.

"But Stevens transferred money into Macadamia from Jensen Holdings and took back shares in return, just as Jensen directed. Sure looks like Gyberson was the only one in a position to snatch the money as it left Macadamia's bank account, before it could be deposited into Carstairs's. He had signing authority in both companies. In a position to siphon cash from either one, depending on where it sat. All he had to do was endorse Macadamia's cheques over to himself or another company he controlled. But then again, his signature would be on the back of cheques. An evidence trail," St. James reasoned.

"Didn't you look at paid cheques for Macadamia and Carstairs when you examined Jensen's records?" Dozer queried. "Those stamped and returned by the bank, I mean. See if Gyberson's signature *was* on the back."

"Cheques weren't there. Only the bank statements were in the files."

"We can get copies directly from the bank," Dozer pressed.

"We'll do that if there's a civil trial. Then we'll have to lay out an uninterrupted evidence trail. No need to do it right now. Remember, all we have to do is prove that the Stevens firm wasn't responsible for a $23 million loss, and Global's not liable. Everything else is up to police. Jensen says Gyberson stole the money. We'll go with that for the moment."

"That's what it appears to be," Dozer said. "That has to be what Gyberson meant. Looks like he's the only one who could have taken money, but things aren't as they appear. Crazy part about all this is that Stevens was sued by Jensen for taking money he couldn't possibly have taken; money that had already left Jensen Holdings and gone to Macadamia, a company under Gyberson's control. There's no credible evidence against Stevens, that we know of, anyway."

St. James cleared his throat. "Jensen may be a blowhard maniac but he's not stupid. He lost $23 million and someone has to pay. His very words. He argues that Stevens was to vet investments and credibility of people who ran them before he invested. But even if Stevens knew Gyberson was a crook, he still recommended that Jensen invest in Macadamia."

Dozer was quiet for a long moment, then said, "What if it was the other way around?"

"What do you mean?"

"What if Stevens advised against the investment in Macadamia and Jensen overruled him? Did it anyway?"

St. James considered this for a moment. "It's a thought. But why would he do that?"

"There'd have to be an angle, something in it for Jensen. An upside of some sort," Dozer offered.

"But both Macadamia and Carstairs were insolvent. That's why they needed Jensen's investment in the first place," St. James reasoned. "Macadamia can't even afford to pay Jensen a return on his investment. No cash to pay dividends. So, if we consider that Stevens advised Jensen not to invest but he did anyway, I can't see how he'd have an upside. Doesn't make sense. Unless something else is at play. Something we don't know about."

"What could Jensen be up to? Certainly the firm and Global are better payoff bets than Macadamia," Dozer said conclusively.

St. James told Dozer about Jensen's financial statements, how they came into his hands in Jensen's office.

"Holy shit," Dozer said under his breath. "Insolvent! If Jensen Holdings is insolvent, how could it have invested $23 million in Macadamia in the first place?"

"Maybe the same way it invested in other companies: syndicate money at high interest rates. Every investment would have to pay big-time to generate a decent profit after operating expenses and interest. And not every investment pays off. When Jensen can't pay the syndicate, they'll squeeze him until he does, force him to take from other investments or family. Threaten him and anyone he might care about. Syndicates never lose. If they do, someone dies."

"You say Jensen isn't stupid. But all this sounds stupid to me," Dozer concluded.

St. James shrugged at the phone.

"If Stevens didn't steal the money, why are we still messing around with this? Why don't you just tell Global the claim isn't valid?" Dozer said, his voice pained.

"Consider this, Dozer: Jensen's back is against the wall. Jensen Holdings desperately needs cash. But it has no legitimate source. No one throws cash into an insolvent company financed by the syndicate. So he trumps up the theft story to create a lawsuit against Stevens's firm. But he's too emotional and stressed to think it all through before suing. It doesn't occur to him until after that cash can easily be traced from Holdings to Macadamia. And once it's in Macadamia's bank account, Stevens can't touch it because he doesn't have signing authority. De facto proof Stevens couldn't have stolen it.

"With the lawsuit issued and no real evidence for theft against Stevens, Jensen has no choice but to switch the claim to negligence. Stevens didn't do proper due diligence before advising him to invest. Without that, Jensen would have no claim at all. He needed the money badly and had to manufacture something to justify a claim."

"Wow!" Dozer said with more than a little surprise in his voice. "When you put it like that, it's the only thing that makes sense." He paused a beat, then said, "But why would the syndicate invest in Jensen Holdings in the first place if it was losing money? They'd demand to see financial statements, the same as any other investor, statements that you say aren't pretty."

"If I was a betting man…"

Dozer chuckled as he cut St. James off. "You are a betting man, Hamilton."

"Smartass! What I was about to say was, I would bet anything Jensen has another set of financials. More rosy, showing enough profit to justify the syndicate lending."

Dozer whistled. "One helluva dangerous game! Syndicate catches on, old Jensen's dead. No ifs, ands, or buts."

"Not to mention his family. But maybe Jensen has a larger plan, an escape of some sort."

"What the hell could that possibly be?" Dozer said slowly.

"Be damned if I know."

They talked of other possibilities for a few more minutes before clicking off.

St. James and Anna dedicated Sunday to shopping, replenishing wine, and topping up the groceries she had purchased while he was in Washington.

To help him shadow them, St. James told Dozer they'd be walking through the ByWard Market.

The Market was surprisingly quiet for a weekend. A few couples were strolling hand in hand, window shopping, perhaps searching for a place to have lunch. The sky was grey, looking like snow could be on the way even though temperatures didn't seem to support the white stuff. Produce vendors had long since folded their stalls and retreated for the winter.

They met Denzel on Dalhousie, on his way back from checking Anna's apartment.

"Any sign of a break-in, Denzel?" St. James asked.

"No sir. I go three times a day, just like Erasmus said. No sign of anything, Mr. St. James."

"You can call me Hamilton, Denzel."

"Yes, Mr. St. James."

St. James smiled.

"You're a good man, Denzel," Anna said in a comforting voice. "I feel my apartment's in good hands with you."

"Thank you," he said and walked off without another word.

When they returned home, the message light was flashing. Janice McPherson had called to say that the dean and students were wondering how his recovery was coming and were asking if he would be returning to the classroom anytime soon. St. James heard anxiety in her voice, no doubt from covering for him for such a long period.

St. James knew he had to re-engage soon. He didn't want the university thinking he didn't care. The problem was that he was at a very critical stage in both the Stevens and CISI cases. Not easy to put aside a case and pick up the pieces later. Momentum is always lost. Leads dry up and trails go cold. But still, he had a responsibility to the university and to the students. That had to be fulfilled too. So he decided he would teach Friday and phoned a greatly relieved Janice to tell her so.

# Chapter 55

Monday morning St. James walked into Cameron Anderson's office and was handed a dozen or so files by Anderson's executive assistant.

"I'm putting you in a locked office two doors down," she said authoritatively. "Here's the key. If you leave for coffee, washroom, or anything else, lock it. What's in those files is highly confidential and this place has wandering eyes."

"Absolutely," he said, feeling slightly like he was being scolded before he had done anything wrong.

With the files under his arm he made his way down the hall to the designated office, where he connected his laptop to the internet and opened the first shareholder file: Anderson's.

Anderson had 400,000 CISI common shares and had been granted options to purchase an additional 600,000 at $18 per share. A quick internet check showed CISI shares trading at $54.

"Hmm. Anderson would make a tidy profit. Buy shares from the company at $18 and sell them immediately for $54. A $36 profit per share. Not bad," he mumbled.

The rest of the file consisted mostly of correspondence between Anderson and Andre Fox outlining details of his remuneration and the dos and don'ts of selling stock as an insider. No correspondence with financial institutions. Anderson had not borrowed money pledging CISI shares as collateral.

The next file was Van Hoyt's. She had purchased CISI shares and then immediately borrowed $300,000 from the Bank of Montreal, pledging the shares as collateral. St. James guessed it was for remodeling the new house. Correspondence said the pledge was collateral for a term loan, no margin against the shares.

The remaining files held documentation that revealed that twenty insiders had borrowed money in one way or another using CISI shares as collateral. What St. James couldn't tell was whether the shares were held on margin or just straight collateral for term loans like Karen's.

St. James's cell vibrated. Anna's number flashed on the call display.

"How's it going?" she asked.

"Plodding along," he said with little enthusiasm.

"Cheer up. You'll get there. What is it you're actually doing?"

St. James took a few moments to explain.

"What's a margin account?" she asked.

"The simplest way to explain it is to use an example. Say you invest $100 in shares and the bank is willing to lend you $60 for your investment. It expects you to contribute the remaining $40, which in this case is 40% of the original purchase, the bank's exposure being the other 60%. In a margin account the bank's exposure can never rise above the 60% of current market value. If it does, you are obligated to pay the loan down until the bank's exposure is reduced to 60% of market value. Your 40% represents an ongoing security margin, a cushion to absorb losses should the bank be forced to sell your shares for less than your loan. That's why the 40% cushion must be maintained at all times. It's your skin in the game, so to speak."

"I don't understand," Anna said slowly.

"Well, if the $100 in shares drops to say $90, the bank applies its 60% formula and concludes the share value will only support a $54 loan. That means you must now put up $6 to reduce the loan from

$60 to $54 in order to maintain the 40% margin between the shares' market value and the amount of your loan.

"If you don't put up, the bank sells your shares until the loan equals 60% of market value or all the shares are sold, whichever comes first. And if the loan isn't completely paid off after all the shares are sold, the bank comes after you personally for the difference."

"So you have to be sure the market price will go up to even consider buying on margin?" she said quizzically.

"Yes, but you can't know everything going on in a company; not even the people who run it know everything. So you can never be sure that the share price will actually rise. At best it's a crapshoot."

"Then why do people buy on margin?"

"Beats the hell out of me," St. James said with a chuckle.

# Chapter 56

St. James pulled up CISI's website and recorded the average daily share prices and trading volumes for the six weeks prior to and following the publication of last year's financial results, looking for the impact on public trading. Did share prices go up or down? Did trading volumes go up or down? What would share prices do with or without the $95-million inventory adjustment? Somehow or other he had to determine who would have the motivation to drive up the share price.

Before the release of the financial reports, shareholders expected the company to exceed profit expectations, as it did every year. There was no indication to the contrary, either from within the company or from analysts.

With a $95-million adjustment, the company easily exceeded shareholder expectations; without, it would be significantly below expectations, greatly disappointing shareholders. They'd punish the company for sure, sell shares, flood the market, drive share prices down.

He closed his eyes for a beat, considering who would benefit from an inflated inventory adjustment, and concluded that there were two very distinct groups.

The first included shareholders who had purchased shares below current market prices. They were motivated by the opportunity for gain if profit expectations were exceeded; a group inclined to purchase additional shares, driving market price up. Greed motivation.

The second included shareholders who had purchased shares above current market price. They were motivated to avoid losses if profit expectations fell short; a group inclined to sell shares, driving market price down. Fear motivation.

Greed and fear. St. James believed every buy–sell decision boiled down to one or the other. Greed to make money, fear of losing it.

Either group could be motivated to include the $95-million adjustment. The first question was which group would have the greatest motivation. The second question was who within that group had enough at stake to risk wrongdoing. The third question was who would be in a position to effect wrongdoing, if indeed it had happened. Who had the most to gain? Who had the most to lose?

Gains, in military terms, are like taking a hill from the enemy. Once you take it, you want to keep it. It's a badge of honour. Gains are a shareholder's badge of honour. Losing realized gains while chasing additional ones amounts to a setback.

In St. James's mind, the answer to the first question was the group motivated by fear. The negative psychological impact that comes with the potential for loss seemed to far outweigh the potential for gain. The investor loses a hill.

Additional gains is pursuing something you don't have. Sure, you're disappointed if you don't succeed, but you've lost nothing other than opportunity. Real loss hurts, a lot, and can mean financial disaster. Opportunity loss means you live to win another day.

All that led St. James to consider who'd be at risk of losing the most if the $95-million profit didn't exist. Those who purchased shares on margin were the obvious conclusion. Who'd have to cough up the most if shares plummeted below margin thresholds? That was money that those shareholders might not have had. That would be strong motivation to influence share price, if you had the power to do so.

The problem was that St. James didn't know who, if anyone, had bought shares on margin. Somehow, he'd have to determine that. It wouldn't be easy. It was information brokerage houses would never divulge, an ethical choice that St. James respected.

An easy way to begin eliminating suspects might be to assume every share purchase was margined, whether they were or not. Those who wouldn't be out-of-margin, even without the $95 million in extra profit, could be eliminated right away. There'd be no margin call to avoid, no motivation to manipulate inventory just to stay in margin.

To estimate how much the share price might decline without the $95 million, he looked at ten public companies of similar size and share volume to CISI that had disappointed shareholders without advanced warning. What was the reaction? Did shareholders sell shares immediately? If so, by what percentage did volumes increase and prices decline?

From volume increases and price declines experienced by the ten companies, he developed what he called a Punishment Index, which measured the average percentage that share prices declined in response to bad news from the company. When he applied the Punishment Index to all ten public companies, he was amazed at how little the results varied. Not perfect, but a reasonable indicator, accurate enough for his purpose.

He applied the Punishment Index to CISI's market price immediately prior to year-end to estimate how much prices might have declined without the $95 million in extra profit. Then he compared the price decline to each shareholder's holdings, assuming every loan was margined at 60%.

When all was said and done, the original twenty suspects suddenly became five. Five shareholders who would be out-of-margin if last year's profit had been $95 million less.

He sat back for the first time in three hours, satisfied with the reasonableness of his assumptions and the results he had generated. The problem with all this was that if no one's shares were margined, there'd be no margin call to avoid. It would be another dead end.

# Chapter 57

St. James still hadn't received Dozer's surveillance reports on Karen Van Hoyt, Blakie, and Graves. The information from those reports could define next steps with the CISI case. So he emailed Dozer and invited him to dinner at the Royal York for six that evening.

St. James had to check that the plants' inventory totals equalled head office records. There was no reason to believe they wouldn't. But it was critical to prove that it was the same total on the audited financial statements blessed by Marcel. That meant meeting Jennifer Quigley, the lady in accounting responsible for Plymouth and Portsmouth.

The internal phone directory said Jennifer Quigley's extension was 2567, and she answered right away. St. James introduced himself and asked if she could spare a few minutes. Five minutes later, she was standing in the doorway of St. James's temporary office.

Jennifer was slim and petite, maybe five-three, with short black hair, large blue eyes, and a huge, warm smile.

"Please sit down," he said as they shook hands.

"I was wondering if we would meet," Jennifer offered, obviously pleased to be included in the investigation.

St. James smiled.

He stated the obvious to break the ice. "As you know from our emails I was in England last week with the Hughes brothers."

She nodded. "Yes."

"Regarding inventory count documentation, has there ever been a case when you've had to make changes?"

Jennifer thought for a moment.

"Only twice that I recall."

"Hmm. And what gave rise to those changes?"

"In both cases Basil meant to make corrections before sending stuff but was too quick to press send."

"I see. I take it you made the changes?"

"Yes, exactly as he requested."

"Did either case occur during last fall's inventory?"

"No sir. This was two or three years ago."

"Okay. Would you ever make changes without authorization from a plant manager?"

Jennifer looked surprised by the question. "Oh, never. Ownership of schedules and documentation rests with the plants. If I notice something odd, I email to see if it's right or wrong. If it's wrong, they authorize me to make changes. Then I email the amended documents back for final approval. If right, it's left the same."

"Has anyone else ever asked you to make changes to inventory documentation?"

"No. No one."

"Not even Karen?"

"No."

"Are you aware of Karen or anyone else making changes to documentation after you've finished your work?"

"I wouldn't know. If someone made changes, it wouldn't necessarily come back to me. I don't know what happens when everything gets consolidated."

"I see. When you're finished your work do you send the results to Karen directly?"

"Yes, of course," she said.

"Jennifer, can you think of any reason why anyone would change the typeface from the original author's?"

She paused for a moment. "No, not really; not a practical one, anyway. We all have our preferred font. But it would be extra work just to please the eye. And chances are you would never see the thing again anyway."

St. James smiled.

"Tell me a little about the instruction confusion with trawlers last count day."

"On count day, Portsmouth had no fish to process while Plymouth was receiving too much. Karen wanted all fish processed at year-end. Processed fish has greater value than whole fish. And higher value means higher profit."

St. James nodded.

Jennifer continued. "So, she asked me to divert trawlers to Portsmouth so all fish could be processed before closing year-end. Not long after, she came back to my office and reversed the decision. When I asked why, she said everyone felt there'd be too much spoilage before it got there. That made sense to me. So that was the end of it."

"Makes sense to me too. But who did she mean when she said 'everyone'? Who would have a say over spoilage management and catch allocations to plants?"

"I didn't ask at the time, but I assumed Mr. Jenkins and the plant managers ... Possibly trawler captains too, especially regarding spoilage."

"How many trawlers were involved?" Of course, he knew the answer, but he wanted everyone's recollections independently.

"That day, three."

Jennifer had brought with her a binder of all year-end inventories around the world, even though she was only responsible for Britain and Portugal. She had worked the other plants in the past and was thoroughly familiar with the processes and procedures at each one.

For the next hour or so, Jennifer took St. James through inventory records for all plants, inventory adjustments, and the typefaces used for documentation sent to head office. There was no variation between Plymouth's and Portsmouth's procedures.

She forwarded emails between head office, plants, and trawlers from her iPad while they talked, as St. James requested.

"Thanks, Jennifer. You've been a great help. I may need to call on you again."

"Pleasure," she said as she stood to leave.

When she was almost through the door St. James said, "Oh, just one more thing."

She turned to him. "What's that?"

"Are you authorized to give inventory instructions directly to plants and trawlers without approval?"

"That's how you get fired around here," she said, smiling.

"Who tells you what to say?"

"Karen."

"Anyone else?"

"Karen is very protective of her staff. She demands the utmost loyalty. She would never allow anyone else to give me instructions. If someone tries, I'm to go to her immediately."

"Thanks again, Jennifer."

St. James rang Karen.

"Any chance you could see me for a few moments?" he asked.

"Absolutely. Come on down, as the game show host says."

So he did.

"How was England?" she asked when he appeared in her doorway.

"Excellent. I was very well received. Everyone was cooperative and forthcoming. I'm very impressed with the efficiency and cleanliness of the plants."

"Our best managers," she said proudly.

St. James nodded. "I met Captain Thorne while I was there."

Van Hoyt suddenly looked concerned. "Oh? How'd that go? He can be a crusty old codger sometimes."

"He was great. Could use a bath though." St. James grinned.

Van Hoyt laughed. "Guess there aren't many ladies to impress at sea. Other than the state of his hygiene, what did you learn?"

"He took me through his logbook for the day of the count. He was upset with the instructional flip-flop on where to take catch."

Van Hoyt shrugged as if to say, "these things happen."

"Can you explain the confusion?" St. James asked in a nonthreatening tone.

"Thorne was approximately halfway between the two plants," Van Hoyt said. "Plymouth was operating at capacity on the last day, and Portsmouth had no fish to process. We were trying to balance the flow between the two. We debated which location to send the trawlers to but in the end decided Plymouth was best to minimize spoilage. Unfortunately, Jennifer jumped the gun and sent instructions before the matter was finalized. If she'd waited, there would have been a lot less confusion. Only one instruction would've been sent."

St. James's forehead furrowed.

"I see. How many trawlers were in play that day?"

"Three."

"That clears up the loose ends. Thanks, Karen."

When he returned to unlock the temporary office, he found a note on the desk from Juanita Mendoza. Nelson would like to see him. St. James strolled down the hall to Graves's office, and Juanita beckoned him in.

"Go right in, Mr. St. James. He's expecting you."

St. James nodded and walked straight into Graves's inner office.

They shook hands and exchanged pleasantries.

Graves was uncharacteristically relaxed, leaning back in a large brown leather chair behind a matching desk. "I just wanted to see how everything was going, Hamilton."

For ten minutes or so St. James recounted the steps he had taken on the case, from the head office to England and back. Graves looked surprised to learn that he had been through shareholder files.

"What does that have to do with inventory?" he asked.

"Nothing really. Standard procedure for an overall management review. It's important to know who invests in the company."

Graves chuckled. "You mean who has skin in the game, as they say."

"Something like that," St. James said without expression.

"Thank you for the update, Hamilton. I appreciate you stopping by."

St. James wasn't ready to be dismissed just yet. "I have a couple of questions for you if you don't mind, Nelson."

Graves looked surprised again. "Sure."

"What involvement did you have around the inventory adjustment?"

Graves's wider eyebrow twitched. "Not much really. Karen briefed me on it a couple of times and I spoke with Cameron about the issue. That was about it. Mostly we relied on the auditors to provide comfort around the amount of the adjustment."

"Of course, as chairman, you'd be concerned."

"Very much so. But Karen explained it all in great detail, and I trust her judgment. She's very thorough."

"And Cameron? What was his explanation?"

"The same as Karen's. Except Cameron was a bit defensive. That caused the board to be concerned, which of course led us to engage you."

"Thanks, Nelson. That's great."

St. James had one more interview to do before calling it a day.

He went down to the next office and tapped lightly on the dark wooden door to the chief operating officer's office.

Henry Jenkins was a short, thin, rather sickly-looking man with thick black glasses that were too large for his face.

St. James introduced himself, and Jenkins promptly invited him to sit in a well-worn green fabric chair just as pale as Jenkins himself.

The office was almost bare; no family pictures or mementos, no indication of who occupied it. If Jenkins hadn't been sitting there, St. James would have guessed it a spare office.

"Henry, I just have a couple of questions today. Are you okay to chat for a few minutes?"

"Absolutely. Take as much time as you need," Jenkins said in a mild voice. His glasses slipped and he pushed them back up the bridge of his nose.

"Last year-end there were three trawlers that unloaded at Plymouth, but not before confusing instructions were given to captains about whether to take catch to Plymouth or Portsmouth," St. James said.

Jenkins nodded. "That's right."

"Were you involved in those decisions?"

"No, but I was kept informed by Karen. She told me Portsmouth had nothing to process that day and she wanted everything processed for year-end financials."

"Then what happened?"

"She switched the trawlers back to Plymouth to preserve quality of catch."

"Why was she managing this instead of you? The COOs of your competitors make those calls, not the CFOs. Seems most peculiar."

"Normally I do. But in this case she asked Cameron if she could manage year-end processing to maximize value. Profit is Cameron's number one focus, and Karen's the numbers lady."

"How did you feel about that?"

"At first I was a little put out, quite frankly. Then Cameron talked to me about it. Only a year-end thing, he said. And I would be back in charge after that. It was no reflection on me, and I should not interpret it that way, he said." Jenkins shrugged. "So I let it go."

"Hmm. Still seems peculiar. You could have easily done the same thing as Karen. As COO it's your responsibility to maximize profit too. You would've loaded up capacity just as she did," St. James pressed, scratching his head.

Jenkins shrugged once again. "That's what they decided to do, and I chose not to make a fuss."

St. James checked his watch. 4:10.

Concluding that he'd accomplished what he could for the day, he returned the shareholder files to Anderson's executive assistant, then made his way over to the Royal York and checked in. By the time he had showered and dressed it was 5:30, and the bar was calling.

The Royal York made the best vodka martinis in Toronto, so St. James's choice was a no-brainer. Three-quarters of the way through the martini, Dozer climbed onto the stool next to him.

"I'll have what he's having," Dozer said to the bartender, pointing to St. James's glass.

"Hey, man. How's the shoulder?" Dozer said.

"Coming along. Worst is over. So, no luck squeezing Gyberson?"

"Just what I told you on the phone. Man's a human clam. 'Not as they appear' is the only thing he said that could possibly be useful. That is, if we knew what it actually meant. I could have gotten more, but I didn't think it wise to beat the hell out of him in a US police station," Dozer explained.

St. James smiled. "Might not have gone well for you."

The bartender deposited a cocktail napkin and a full martini in front of Dozer. Dozer raised the glass, first to salute the bartender, and then to touch St. James's for a toast.

"What did your guys find following our three CISI people around?" St. James said, anxious to get business out of the way for the evening.

"I have a couple of things to share about Karen and her husband," Dozer said, pulling a notepad from an inside coat pocket.

"Oh?"

"Yeah, they just bought a new house. It's in her name alone, not joint, and it's a good thing it is."

"Why is that?"

"Greg, her husband, owns a company called Van Hoyt Construction. It's drowning in debt. Owes the bank $5.3 million, fully guaranteed by him personally. Trade creditors haven't been paid for over ninety days. They've already filed liens on the only two projects he has on the go, both of which have cost overruns and are still not finished. No construction draws left to finish either one. No money to pay trades or to repay the bank. Way I see it, Hamilton, he has maybe a couple of days before the bank pulls the plug. And then he'll face bankruptcy because of the personal guarantee."

St. James was incredulous. "How the hell do you find this stuff out, Dozer?"

Dozer gave St. James one of his huge smiles. "If I told you that, then you wouldn't need me, and that would make me sad."

St. James laughed. "Okay, what else you got?"

Dozer went back to his notes. "Karen took out a mortgage to purchase the house, again in her name only, for $500,000. She paid $1 million for the property. That still leaves quite a bit of equity."

"What about movements?"

"Everything the woman does is about the house. We followed her to tile, paint, plumbing stores, you name it. No interaction with Blakie or Graves since we started surveillance."

"Hmm. Blakie?"

"He and Graves had lunch together a couple of times."

"Lunch?" St. James said in a startled voice. "Graves and Blakie?"

"That's what I said."

"They hate each other. Why would they be having lunch?"

"People do eat you know, Hamilton."

St. James shook his head. "Not these two, not together."

Dozer looked pained and his voice rose. "Hey, man, I'm just reporting what we saw, I'm not justifying it."

"Okay! Okay! Don't get your knickers in a twist. It's a surprise, that's all. I'll have to think about it," St. James said in a much quieter tone.

Dozer went back to his notes. "I almost forgot one interesting thing we found."

"What's that?"

"Van Hoyt worked with Graves at IBM for a couple of years."

"I didn't know that," St. James said, once again sounding surprised. "Food for thought."

"Speaking of food, I'm starving," said Dozer. "Let's go to the dining room."

# Chapter 58

It was 9:45 p.m. when Dunning pulled himself up from the garage floor, dusted himself off, and quickly picked up the tools he had used to partially sever the brake lines on Hamilton St. James's newly repaired BMW.

Dunning smiled, proud of his work. Small cuts meant slower leaks, only about a half-hour of driving before the brakes would fail.

*No one will know when or where the lines were cut.*

Dunning would be long gone. His surgical gloves meant leaving no prints, no way to trace it back to him.

At that moment the elevator doors opened, and a tall woman dressed in black emerged into the parking area. Dunning quickly ducked behind the BMW, accidentally dropping the cutting tool as he went down. The woman froze, startled by the sound of metal on concrete.

"Who's there?" she shouted in a frightened voice.

Dunning remained silent. Motionless.

Again she asked who was there. No response.

Dunning suddenly darted from the far side of the BMW, head down so not to be recognized, up the down ramp, and climbed into a white 1987 Cadillac idling at the mouth of the parking garage.

# Chapter 59

Stern wore a black hood covering most of his face and a green knapsack slung over his right shoulder. Slowly, he crept around the perimeter of the middle-class Washington home, eyes scanning every direction like a lighthouse beacon, ensuring no one was watching.

10 p.m.

The house was dark except for a flickering television screen visible through a side window. There were loud voices inside: two men arguing over something, Stern couldn't make out what. Thinking he was about to be discovered, he dropped to his knees. Crouching, he slowly moved toward the flickering light, and realized the loud voices were coming from the television; it was playing a police show he himself had watched a number of times.

Shifting his position to the left of the window, he saw a man slouched over in a large black rocking chair, sleeping. Even though the man's face was turned away, Stern could tell he was middle-aged and had the build of Slate.

Satisfied he wasn't being watched and was under no immediate threat, Stern duck-walked back to the end of the driveway, dropped down behind Slate's white Lexus, and pulled a small white metal canister from the green knapsack. With a gloved hand, he wiped dried mud from the car frame next to the gas tank, making sure the magnetic canister attached firmly, metal to metal, with no debris impeding the magnet's work. He placed the canister and jiggled it to make sure it stayed in place, then pushed a green button on its face, immediately powering a flashing dim red light. Satisfied everything was secure as planned, he stood, looked around once again, and walked quickly down the street and around the block to the nearest bus stop.

# Chapter 60

At 8:00 Inspector DuPont answered the telephone to the sound of Miss Barnes's voice.

"Chief of intelligence here to see you, sir," she announced pretentiously.

"Didn't know I had a meeting with him."

"You don't, he just arrived. Says it's urgent and he must speak with you right away."

"Send him in."

Seconds later, an average-height man in his early forties dressed in full RCMP uniform entered Pierre's office and stood at attention.

"Good morning, Chief. Please, be seated." DuPont motioned to a guest chair. "What's this about?"

"You asked me to keep tabs on the four criminals recently discharged from prison."

"Go on," Pierre said.

"We picked up social media chatter from a couple of them, sir. It became clear after a number of exchanges that they're planning to kill Hamilton St. James and Bill Slate."

Pierre's face grew grave. He was quiet for a moment, playing with the end of his moustache.

"Where are Slate and St. James now?" DuPont asked finally.

"Can't say for certain, sir, but as near as we can tell Slate is home in Washington and St. James is in Toronto."

"Did the chatter describe how they might do it?"

"Sabotaging cars in some way, but the exchange wasn't specific on timing or method."

"You said a couple of them. Which ones?"

The chief referred to his notes.

"Arthur Spance, Jeremy Stern, and Clifford Dunning. There was also a fourth man."

Pierre interrupted. "That would be Nells."

"No, that's not the name."

DuPont straightened.

"Then who?"

"Man named Calvin Vinner."

"Sounds familiar."

"Should, sir. You put him away ten years ago. In our records as a hit man, and a cheap one at that. Does anyone for ten grand."

"Yes, yes, now I remember. Tall, skinny guy."

"That's right, sir."

"Don't remember any connection with the other three, though," DuPont mused.

"There isn't."

"Then what do they have in common?"

"As far as we can tell they all hate Slate and St. James."

"Hmm. Do we know where Nells is?"

"Sources say he works construction in Chicago."

DuPont nodded. "Get ahold of Slate right away. Tell him what we know. He'll have Bureau people go over his car with a fine-toothed comb — and before he starts it!"

"Yes, sir, immediately."

The chief left quickly.

DuPont buzzed Miss Barnes. "Find Hamilton St. James, now!" he barked.

# Chapter 61

Slate pulled himself out of the large black leather rocking chair around 2 a.m., stiff from sleeping slumped over. He turned off the television and climbed the stairs to bed.

The next morning he rose at the usual time, showered, shaved, and made his way to the kitchen where he brewed coffee, pausing long enough to drink a cup before making scrambled eggs, bacon, and toast. While bacon sizzled in the frying pan, he prepared the same lunch he had every day, and placed the turkey sandwich, fruit cup, and bottled water in the blue canvas lunch bag his wife had given him a year before she died. He hated the damn bag, but it carried so many fond memories of her he couldn't bring himself to part with it.

When he finished, he placed the dirty dishes in the sink and wiped the table clean. The wall clock registered a few minutes before eight.

*On time.*

Slate grabbed the keys to his new white Lexus and headed out the door, stopping in the driveway for long enough to assess the day's weather. Taking a deep breath of crisp air, he looked up at a clear blue sky.

*Can tell it's fall.*

Slate lived in a middle-class subdivision about ten miles from downtown Washington. The drive to work usually took forty-five minutes, placing him at his desk by nine.

He backed the Lexus out of the red brick drive onto a cul-de-sac and slowly rolled out of the neighbourhood toward the freeway that would take him to central Washington.

Morning traffic was unusually heavy, chewing up an extra five minutes just to reach the freeway. As he approached the ramp, he had the feeling he'd forgotten something. He scanned the car, eyes coming to rest on the empty passenger seat. No lunch.

"Damn. Stupid."

Making a quick illegal U-turn, he headed back toward home.

*Another ten minutes wasted,* he thought as he wheeled into the drive.

He climbed out of the car, rushed into the house, grabbed the lunch bag from the counter and was almost back out the door when the phone rang. He stopped to answer.

"An RCMP officer in Ottawa wishes to speak with you urgently," a lady said.

Seconds later the security chief came on the line. "Inspector Slate?"

"Yes, this is Slate."

"I just met with Inspector DuPont concerning intelligence we picked up. He asked me to call you straight away."

"Well, what is it?" Slate said sharply, impatient from losing valuable time.

"There are a few ex-cons who are planning to kill you and St. James."

"Who?" Slate demanded gruffly.

"Arthur Spance, Jeremy Stern, Clifford Dunning, and another fellow named Calvin Vinner," the officer said.

"Vinner?"

"Hit man."

"Yeah. I have a faint recollection of him," Slate said, not completely sure. "Where's Roger Nells in all this?"

"That's what Inspector DuPont asked."

Suddenly, Slate was shaken by a loud explosion that rocked the house, shattering a kitchen window not five feet from where he stood. Glass flew in every direction. The largest piece landed on Slate's right foot, and many smaller pieces were spread around the floor .

Slate immediately dropped the phone and ran to the front door and down the driveway where he found very little left of his new Lexus. Flames spewed several feet into the air. Bits of metal peppered the lawn, and one rear tire had landed in the middle of the street.

"Jesus Christ," Slate mumbled slowly. A wave of fear washed over him, and a lump rose in his throat.

Neighbours rushed from their homes. Someone yelled, "Call 911!"

Slate stared at the wreckage, unable to move. His new Lexus, less than three months old, totally destroyed.

*Would've been me if I hadn't forgotten lunch.*

Suddenly he remembered the RCMP officer. He rushed into the kitchen and grabbed the dangling receiver, still swaying from the sudden drop minutes ago.

"Are you all right?" the officer asked, voice panicked. "I heard an explosion."

"Yeah, someone just blew up my car. I'm all right, thanks to you. Please express my gratitude to Inspector DuPont and to your intelligence people. 911 will have police and firemen on the way by now. I'll have a shitload of explaining to do."

When Slate disconnected, the doorbell rang. It was the police, wanting to question him. Firemen were already hosing down the burning wreckage and a smoldering lawn. One fireman wheeled the rogue tire in from the street.

Slate was explaining everything to the authorities for over an hour before a flatbed truck removed the remains of the Lexus. Police took down details of the four ex-cons as well as the RCMP contacts in Ottawa.

When he had finished with the police, and both the car and the neighbours had disappeared, Slate went into the garage and found cardboard and a roll of masking tape to cover the shattered kitchen window. Then he made two phone calls: the first to the Bureau saying he wouldn't be in today, the second to give the bad news to his insurance company. Afterward, he cleaned up the broken glass and drank five beers.

# Chapter 62

After dinner with Dozer, St. James retired to his room at the Royal York.

He flew home first thing the next morning, and when his taxi arrived at the condo he spotted four police cars with their emergency lights flashing, all parked on sidewalks around the building. Traffic cones blocked the street. St. James paid the driver and grabbed his duffle as the driver pulled it from the trunk. He eyed Spencer talking to a uniform at the entrance to the underground. When St. James approached, Spencer turned to him.

"You are now officially my best customer," he said with a wide grin.

"What do you mean?"

Spencer explained the RCMP intelligence report and Inspector DuPont's involvement, Slate's near-death experience, and his team in the underground checking his car.

"Is Slate all right?" St. James asked anxiously.

"A little shaken perhaps, but all right, thanks to his lunch."

"His lunch?" St. James said quizzically.

Spencer explained. St. James shook his head in disbelief just as two members of the bomb squad, dressed in protective gear, walked up the ramp.

They all walked down the ramp together to find two more squad guys lying on their backs partway under St. James's BMW.

Spencer bent over and said, "Find anything?"

"Nothing by way of explosive material," one man said, his voice somewhat muffled from being under the car. "But the brake line's been cut, quite cleverly I might add. Hard to see. It's a professional job for sure. The brake fluid would drip slowly. Mr. St. James might have made it to the 417 before being in trouble, but certainly no further."

"Hmm," Spencer said, stroking his chin.

St. James said to Spencer, "Let me know when you're through, and I'll call the dealer and make arrangements for the car."

Spencer didn't respond immediately.

St. James sensed Spencer's distance. "What's troubling you?"

"Just thinking about the intelligence chatter and how we should get these guys off the street, fast, before they get lucky."

"Amen to that," St. James said, nodding his head. "Why don't we talk to Pierre?"

"Good idea," Spencer said.

St. James pointed up toward the fifth floor as he turned to Spencer. "We'll call from my condo."

"Yeah, okay. I can leave now. They can finish up on their own," Spencer said, pointing to the two under the car.

They entered the condo, and St. James called the BMW dealer first to arrange repairs.

"You're getting to be a regular, Mr. St. James," said the collision manager.

St. James frowned. "Funny, that's what everyone's saying."

He disconnected, then placed the phone on speaker and punched in Pierre's number.

"I'm here with Detective Mark Spencer of the Ottawa Police department, we have you on speaker," St. James said to DuPont when he answered. "Thank you for acting on the intelligence so quickly."

"That's what friends are for, *mon ami*. Just glad you and Slate are all right. I wouldn't want to lose you. Maybe we're up to three golf games now," DuPont said with his usual chuckle.

For the next five minutes or so, Spencer and St. James filled DuPont in on the crime scene.

"Did your people get the intelligence from cell phones?" St. James asked.

"Let's see. Have the report in front me now. Just a second. Says cell calls and text messages. Five-way conversations. Details on how they planned to kill you. Times. Methods. Which one would do what. That sort of thing."

"Don't they realize the world is listening?" Spencer said, shaking his head.

"These fellows are not very smart, Detective Spencer," DuPont said. "We caught them the first time because they did something stupid. Not likely they've gotten any smarter."

"Are these cell phones traceable?" St. James asked.

"Yes. We've already traced most of the cells. They're coming from the Boston area," DuPont added conclusively.

Spencer looked surprised. "Boston? I thought they were here, in Ottawa."

"Can you trace the exact location, Pierre?" St. James asked.

"I am emailing intelligence as we speak, asking them to provide the information."

"Thank you," St. James said.

"Purely selfish. I had a hand in those thugs going to jail too. I could be next."

Disconnected.

Spencer said, "Speaking of cell phones, the one Dozer took from the thug in Wakefield traced through to a guy named Rodney Sterling, an underground character, well known to Montreal police. They brought him in for questioning yesterday."

"Learn anything?"

"Just that Sterling was engaged by email from a man who wanted 'unique work' done, as he put it. He doesn't have a name. Names are never given, so they can't snitch on each other."

"First time I've ever heard it called 'unique work,'" St. James said, smiling. "Did he give a description?"

"Don't think so. But you should talk to the interviewing officer yourself." Spencer gave St. James a number for the Montreal detective.

# Chapter 63

It was 4:15 on a very wet Wednesday afternoon when Boston police stormed Earle's Bar & Grill and arrested Stern, Spance, and Dunning for the attempted murder of Slate and St. James. Police anticipated they might run for it through a side door, so an officer was posted just outside before the pub was swarmed.

When Stern spotted the police, he jumped from a booth and bolted for the side door, only to be grabbed immediately by the waiting officer. He struggled to break free, but the officer managed to cuff him when Stern's energy expired.

Spance went into full cardiac arrest and fell to the floor, gasping for air. Police yelled for the bartender to call 911. Fifteen minutes later, medics were administering oxygen and taking Spance's blood pressure. When he stabilized, they carted him off to Boston General with a policeman riding in the ambulance to guard him.

Dunning remained in the booth, calmly drinking beer as if nothing was happening. But when an officer approached him, Dunning's calmness quickly disappeared, and he swung hard at the policeman. Two other uniforms rushed to pull Dunning from the booth, throwing him to the floor face down and holding him there until a third policeman slapped on cuffs.

The entire operation took less than seven minutes.

# Chapter 64

St. James was seated at his desk in the study working on the CISI case when Spencer called.

"Just talked to Boston police. They arrested three of our guys in a Boston bar yesterday afternoon."

"Which three?" St. James asked calmly.

"Spance, Stern, and Dunning."

"When Pierre's people traced the phones, three were traced to this bar, where they apparently used to spend almost every afternoon."

"I see," St. James said thoughtfully. "One of the other phones belongs to this Vinner fellow, whom I remember, but not as a member of this particular gang. Who's the fifth?" St. James asked.

"They say they don't know. The guy is Vinner's contact only. Never shared a name with them. All they knew was Vinner had a guy in Ottawa watching you."

"Watching me?"

"Yes. You."

St. James was silent for a long moment, then said, "Can't we trace the phone for the fifth guy somehow?"

"Yes. We're working on it right now."

"Great," St. James said, and clicked off.

St. James went back to his CISI research, but it wasn't ten minutes before he was interrupted by the phone again. It was Detective Luc St.

Jacques of the Montreal Police returning St. James's call from the previous day.

"Officer St. Jacques," he announced in a strong French accent.

"Thank you for returning my call, Officer. I understand you questioned Sterling."

"Yes."

"Was he cooperative?"

"As cooperative as an underworld thug would be with police, yes."

St. Jacques spent the next fifteen minutes reading excerpts from his interview with Sterling and answering St. James's questions. After considerable pressure, Sterling had admitted to hiring Martin Clayton and Clint Wagner to run St. James off the road, and then Long to break into Anna's apartment to kidnap her and lure St. James into a trap, and after further probing, the two clowns who had followed St. James and Dozer to Wakefield.

# Chapter 65

St. James had most of what he needed to wrap up the Stevens case, but the Cayman bank end of things was gnawing at him. Smythe had done a great job working with Antoinette, but St. James had to have more solid ground for his conclusions to be credible. He had to see for himself. He had to go to Cayman.

He telephoned Anna at the pub.

"Would you like a little holiday in the sun?"

She laughed. "Is that a trick question?"

"Absolutely not."

"Where?"

"Cayman."

"Sounds wonderful," she said enthusiastically. "When do we go?"

"Sometime within the next day, if I can get meetings lined up and travel arrangements made. It's only three days, so you won't need a trunk."

"Very funny. I won't get too excited until you tell me for sure."

They clicked off.

St. James tapped Smythe's number on his cell. "What are you doing, Louis?"

"Ironing my favourite plaid kilt. Why?"

St. James let it go. "Do you think Antoinette could get me a meeting with an officer of the bank?"

"So you decided to go after all," Smythe said, ignoring St. James's question. "Want me to come with you?"

"Nah, I can handle it myself."

"How come I always get left out?" he said in a pouty voice.

St. James had little sympathy. "Bad luck I guess."

Smythe made a snorting sound. "Well, the least you can do is bring me a picture of Antoinette. I checked the bank website: there isn't one of her there. I was disappointed because she sounds wonderful on the phone. Love her accent. Wish I could see what she looks like."

"What if she wants a picture of you?" St. James said, biting his lip.

"I'll email you one right now."

"Great. She'll be delighted to see what a snappy dresser you are."

"Up yours." Smythe hung up without another word.

While waiting for Smythe to confirm a bank meeting, St. James called Higgins Johnson to see if they could meet early the following week. They were available Tuesday morning at nine, which St. James thought would work provided it didn't conflict with a potential bank meeting.

An hour passed before Smythe called back. "Antoinette says Vice-President Alvin Bodden can see you at two on Tuesday."

"Fantastic, Louis. Thank you. By the way, does Antoinette have a last name?"

"Ebanks. Antoinette Ebanks. Say hi to her for me."

"I will."

Now satisfied that a Cayman trip could be productive, he confirmed with Anna and went online to book flights and accommodations.

A wrinkle: cheapest return flight to Grand Cayman was Saturday to Saturday. A week, not three days.

"A sacrifice I have to make for Global," he mumbled, smiling to himself.

He broke down and booked a week in the Ritz-Carlton on West Bay Road. But, a week in the Ritz-Carlton cost more than the Saturday-to-Saturday flight. A lot more. He rationalized it as part business, part vacation.

If her yelp was any indication, Anna took the news that they'd be staying a full week quite well.

"Maybe I'll need a trunk after all, smartass," she said. "I'll be home to pack in a half-hour."

Reservations went off without a hitch, except that some turbulence between Toronto and Cayman upset Anna's stomach. They landed at Owen Roberts Airport forty-five minutes late due to bad weather, cleared customs in record time, and walked into the hotel at two fifteen.

The Ritz-Carlton was a wonderful resort, equipped with recreation for every enthusiast. The building itself was roughly the shape of a lobster. Two wings of residential suites extended outward toward the beach like lobster claws; regular rooms were bunched in the middle like the body.

The beachfront was peppered with two long rows of neatly aligned lounge chairs, matching wooden cabanas perched directly behind.

Their suite was a little less than 1,200 square feet of luxury, facing Seven Mile Beach.

"My God, Hamilton! I can't imagine what this costs."

He smiled. "You don't want to know."

When she recovered from eye-candy shock, Anna lay down, hoping to settle her stomach.

While Anna rested, St. James strolled Seven Mile Beach. It was eighty-two degrees and not a cloud in the sky. The Caribbean waters were a pristine blue-green, not a piece of litter to be seen in any direction. The cleanliness itself was a tourist attraction.

A warm, gentle breeze drifted from the west, renewing St. James's energy after the long flight. Whiffs of sizzling sunblock rose from sunbathers lining the beach, and the sand was white and hot.

A half-hour later, St. James returned to discover the Ritz-Carlton's Bar Jack. He climbed onto a stool and signalled to the bartender for a double Forty Creek.

Just as the bartender delivered a second Forty Creek, Anna positioned herself on the stool next to him.

"Feeling better?" he asked.

"Much better, thank you."

She took a moment to take a deep breath and eye the scenery.

"Isn't it gorgeous, Hamilton?" she said enthusiastically.

"Beautiful, absolutely beautiful."

"When you experience a wonderful place like this, you wonder why we live in such a cold climate," she said wistfully.

"Having four distinct seasons offers many more activities than a place like this. Can't skate here in January. Canada's huge. Cayman's only thirty-five kilometres long and thirteen wide. Just sixty thousand people. Two months here and you'd be out of your mind with island fever," St. James remarked.

Anna gave him a pained look. "It was just a casual comment, Hamilton."

He smiled. "What would you like to drink, my dear?"

"Pinot Grigio."

They talked about how they'd spend the week. St. James had meetings on Tuesday. The rest of the time they would tour the island and learn the culture and history of Cayman.

When they finished their drinks, St. James signed the bill to the room and they headed down the beach arm in arm, laughing about this and that — but mostly about whether Smythe owned a multi-plaid bathing suit.

Anna pointed to the sky. "Look, parasailers."

St. James shaded his eyes. "Looks like they're racing."

Further down, they spotted fishing boats a short distance offshore.

"Probably charters fishing for snapper, yellowtail, or bar jack," St. James suggested.

"Ah, bar jack! That's where the bar's name comes from."

St. James nodded. "That's it."

When they reached Kirk Market they brushed sand from their feet, re-shoed, and headed back to the Ritz-Carlton along West Bay Road.

Both exhausted from a long day of travel, they opted for an early dinner at the Andiamo restaurant and were in bed by nine.

Sunday morning they rose with more energy. St. James didn't feel like working, so he asked Wendell, the concierge, for day tour recommendations. Neither he nor Anna had ever been to Cayman and were keen to see as much of the island as possible. Wendell said he wouldn't recommend posted tours for a one-day Cayman experience. They'd disappoint.

"Most tours focus on single activities like scuba diving, sailing, snorkeling, or fishing," he said in a well-pronounced island accent. "Since you're only here for a few days, you should have a customized tour that combines many things at the same time."

"Sounds good to me," St. James said. "Where do we get one of these custom tours, as you call them?"

"Just happen to know someone," Wendell said with a glint in his eye.

St. James smiled. "Thought you might."

Anna laughed.

"Tell me, Wendell, would this someone happen to be related to you?" St. James asked with a grin.

"Not really, he's married to my sister. He owes me money, man. If you pay me to arrange the tour, he won't owe me money anymore. What banks call an offset. I get money from you for his services and use it to offset what he owes me."

St. James rolled his eyes. "Got it."

Anna just shrugged.

"Okay, Wendell. What's your brother-in-law's name?" St. James said.

"Wendell."

"You're kidding," Anna said, laughing.

"No, when we have family get-togethers everyone calls me Wendell One and him Wendell Two. No confusion." Wendell's huge smile showed perfectly white teeth.

"You're the oldest Wendell?" Anna said.

"No. He's the oldest. I have a job. He doesn't. A job is seniority in my family."

Anna laughed again. St. James just shook his head.

"We'll be in our room, Wendell. Call us when Wendell Two arrives," St. James said as they walked toward the elevator.

Fifteen minutes went by before Wendell called to say Wendell Two was waiting for them in the lobby. They gathered bathing suits and towels, in case a swim would be in order, and headed down to the lobby.

Wendell Two was a Bob Marley lookalike, complete with scraggy beard, dreads, hole-laden jeans, and a ratty orange t-shirt. For the first five minutes his entire vocabulary consisted of a lazy "Ya, mon."

When everything was arranged, they climbed into the backseat of Wendell Two's dark green 1999 manual Toyota Camry, which spewed black smoke when the engine turned over and jerked violently when it pulled away from the hotel parking.

Since they were down to one Wendell, St. James figured he could drop the Two. "Where are we going first, Wendell?"

"Hell," he said casually.

Anna's face scrunched up, fairly certain she had misheard. "Huh?"

"Hell," Wendell repeated without expression. "A place up the road in West Bay. Popular with tourists because of its name. Only a couple of buildings, mon. Small area, formation of grey-black dolostone called phytokarst. A combination of acid rain and carbonate-loving organisms turned the rock into a scary-looking pile of black rubble about the size of a soccer field. There's even a Devil's souvenir shop."

"Dare I ask how it got its name?" Anna asked innocently.

"You'll see, ma'am," was all Wendell would say.

A few minutes later they came upon a red building bearing a painted sign saying "Welcome to Hell." Wendell pulled the ailing Toyota in front, and they climbed out to look around. The field of burnt black rock was eerie looking, with a carving of the devil carefully centred in the middle.

Wendell explained. "Some years ago a lady came here to tour around. Since everything looked burnt, she said 'this is what hell must be like!' The name stuck."

They had their passports stamped in the souvenir shop to show their friends that they'd gone to Hell. Anna couldn't resist sending a postcard to Sid, saying "Wish you were here!" St. James was pretty sure she meant the other hell.

The rest of the day was captivating. First, a tour of the National Museum, Cayman's living connection with its past, then a refreshing swim in Smith Barcadere off South Church Street, its beautiful lagoon well known to snorkelers the world over. Later, Wendell drove them to Savannah, where they enjoyed wine and fresh broiled fish for lunch. Afterward, they paid a visit to the restored Pedro St. James National Historic Site, an 18th century, three-story mansion that locals called "the Castle." It had been built by slaves from Jamaica. Then they moved on to Bodden Town, where they checked out the underground Pirate Caves and the Queen Elizabeth II Botanic Park with all its beautiful gardens and exotic floral displays.

Seven Mile Beach was on Anna's mind. "Seven Mile is the most beautiful beach I have ever seen, Wendell."

"Big tourist attraction, ma'am. Severely damaged by Hurricane Ivan in 2004. Took a lot of time and money to clean it up."

A superb guide, Wendell knew the history of every site they visited, in great detail. And not the embellished stories to dazzle tourists — he spoke of true Caymanian history. His knowledge greatly enriched their day's experience.

Wendell turned back into Wendell Two at 5:00 when he dropped St. James and Anna back at the Ritz-Carlton.

Happy hour.

Because Wendell One kept the money for the tour, Wendell Two wasn't being compensated. Receiving nothing for the day when Wendell Two worked so hard to please wasn't sitting well with St. James, so the tip was more than generous.

They bid Wendell Two farewell and seated themselves at the bar.

"What a wonderful day, Hamilton. We saw so much in such a short time," Anna said enthusiastically.

St. James was just as mesmerized. "The gardens were spectacular."

They sipped drinks for an hour or so and discussed what they'd do with the next couple of days.

On Monday morning, St. James's work ethic kicked back in. He booted up the computer to read whatever emails had arrived over the weekend while Anna went to spend time at the pool.

A large email had arrived from Higgins Johnson with numerous title and registry attachments in anticipation of tomorrow's meeting. Corporate, vehicle, land, and court registries had been searched for several names associated with the Stevens case. Most searches had turned up nothing, but St. James made note of one item in the land registry.

Considering what he'd learned, he picked up the phone and pushed the concierge button. "Good morning, Wendell One."

"Mr. St. James, you don't have to call me that when my brother-in-law isn't around."

St. James "I know, I just like saying it."

"How was your tour yesterday?" he asked, ignoring St. James's remark.

"Wonderful. Wendell Two was very accommodating and very well informed of island history. We were educated beyond our expectations."

"Excellent, glad to hear it. Now, what can I do for you today?"

"I'd like you to arrange a hire-car, just for the day."

"Do you want a driver or a rental?"

"Rental, please."

"Are you okay driving on the left?" he asked politely.

Jokingly, St. James said, "As a left-handed person, I'm a natural."

"There's a bit more to it than that, Mr. St. James," he said seriously.

"I know, Wendell, I was just pulling your leg. I've driven through England, Ireland, and Jamaica. Very comfortable driving on the left."

"Very well, sir. You'll need a provisional driver's license, which can be arranged through the rental company. I'll ring you when arrangements have been made."

Just as St. James disconnected, Anna walked through the door. Her long blond hair was wet and stringy from swimming, and she was wrapped in an oversized red beach towel.

"I couldn't stand the noise down there any longer," she said impatiently. "The pool was full of screeching children. Couldn't concentrate on my book for a moment. Why is it that children playing in pools raise their voices five octaves higher than normal?"

"It's the same at any resort pool, Anna. Combination of excitement and wanting to be heard above everyone else," he said without really paying attention. "I've arranged a hire-car for the day."

Anna looked surprised, "Oh, I didn't know we were doing something like that."

"Momentary whim."

She stared at him with a grin. "You don't do anything on a whim."

He pecked her on the cheek and said nothing.

They spent a few minutes putting clothes away and organizing the room until Wendell called to say the rental was waiting. They went downstairs and met a short, jolly lady named Sue, who checked their Canadian driver's licenses and issued provisional ones for Cayman.

When all was organized, they pulled away from the hotel and drove through George Town, getting acquainted with the capital. It was nerve-racking for St. James, maneuvering through a sea of scooters and bicycles swerving back and forth without the slightest concern for safety.

They drifted up Esterly Tibbetts Highway and found the Cayman Islands Yacht Club on Governors Creek. They enjoyed a lobster roll and a glass of Chardonnay at the club restaurant, and then rounded the northwestern tip of the island, admiring beautiful mansions along the way.

St. James stopped for a few minutes to look at a stunning property on Orchid Drive, a huge pastel blue-green home situated on an expensive lot with an immaculately manicured lawn and well-tended gardens.

"How would you like to live in that?" he asked with a smile, pointing to the estate.

Anna glanced over the property.

"Naw, too big. Too much to keep up."

"If you could afford that you could probably afford a maid, cook, and gardener. No upkeep for you."

"Then we wouldn't be alone. We couldn't walk around naked."

"That's my girl. Always thinking."

Further along they came upon the Cracked Conch, an upscale restaurant nicely situated on the water. St. James pulled into the parking area, and they climbed out to look inside. Both thought it would be a wonderful place to have dinner for their last night on the island.

At 4:30 they turned the car in and, as usual, headed for the bar. St. James ordered a double Glenfiddich on the rocks and Anna the usual Pinot Grigio.

"What's up for tomorrow?" she asked.

"Busy workday for me I'm afraid. Calls to make, a meeting with lawyers at nine and the Cayman National Bank at two. The day after, I hope to be finalizing the case. That is, if tomorrow's meetings go well."

"Do you want me in the meetings?" she asked, glaring questionably into his eyes.

St. James knew this wasn't going to make her happy. "You would find them too boring, I'm afraid. You would have a better time looking at island shops. Perhaps Wendell Two could escort you around."

"Sounds like a very polite way of saying you don't want me there," Anna said sharply.

"Pouting is your least becoming feature."

"Secrecy is yours," she retaliated.

"Anna, let's call a truce," he said with a sigh. "I've been investigating for a long time. I have my methods. They work, and I have to conduct them in my own way."

She knew pressing harder would be crossing the line, so Anna cleverly diverted the conversation.

She smiled. "Well, okay ... how much can Wendell Two and I spend?"

He began to laugh. "The equivalent of one night's tips at the Dirty Duck."

Anna was outraged. "That's not fair! One night of tips won't buy a hamburger on this island."

He kissed her. "I'm sure you'll figure something out, darling. You always do."

# Chapter 66

Higgins Johnson was located in First Caribbean House on Main Street in George Town. St. James entered a well-appointed teak-and-glass reception area at exactly 9:00 on Tuesday morning, and was immediately ushered into a small meeting room by an attractive lady offering coffee.

"Cream or sugar?" said the receptionist.

"Just black, thank you."

Minutes later she handed St. James a fresh cup.

Not long after, two gentlemen working the Stevens file along with St. James entered the room and introduced themselves as Paul Statham and Garth Winchell, both of whom had exchanged emails with St. James on numerous occasions since the case had begun.

Paul was tall and thin, about forty-five, with thinning light-brown hair and a wide mouth. He looked tired, possibly a by-product of too many billable hours. By the way the two interacted, St. James thought him the senior of the two.

Garth was a shorter, heavier man wearing thick black-rimmed glasses. His hair was salt and pepper, his hands large.

Both men were immaculately dressed in dark-blue Armani suits.

Paul and Garth spread a number of documents out over a square teak meeting table to facilitate an orderly explanation of the work they had completed. For the next two and a half hours they tediously walked St. James through every legal search in the order they had been conducted, explaining Cayman's legal and banking systems as they moved through each transaction.

"Paul, how confident are you with what you've found here?" St. James said evenly, pointing to the documents.

"Confident enough to give a written opinion, if you wanted one," Paul replied without hesitation.

"Not necessary. Your word is good enough," St. James said respectfully. "Had to ask because the nature, order, and timing of these transactions are fundamental to the case. I need to be comfortable sticking my neck out."

"I understand completely," Paul acknowledged dryly.

Satisfied he had what he needed, St. James thanked them for their excellent work and left in search of a suitable place for lunch.

He turned off Main down Cardinal Avenue past the post office, Scotiabank, and a number of stores, eventually stumbling on Breezes Bistro, where he ordered jerk chicken and a beer.

At 1:50 he entered the four-story white stucco-and-glass building on Elgin Avenue housing the Cayman National Bank and asked for Bodden. Five minutes later Bodden appeared in reception.

"Welcome to Grand Cayman, Mr. St. James," Bodden said with a warm smile.

St. James was gracious. "Pleasure to be here, Mr. Bodden. You have a beautiful island."

"First time?"

"It is. My girlfriend and I love it. Wonderful, friendly people. Very accommodating to us cold-blooded northern folks."

Bodden grinned. "That's because we depend on cold-blooded northern folks to come here and spend cold-blooded northern dollars to keep our warm-blooded economy prospering."

St. James laughed.

Bodden escorted St. James into a spacious pastel-green office with a decorating theme that merged Caribbean and British into one. There were antique wood carvings from previous Caribbean generations, countryside pictures from the Isle of Man, pictures of London at night, and photos of Bodden's family waterskiing and fishing.

Bodden was a medium-build, handsome black man with a charming personality, conservatively dressed in a three-piece blue suit with a gold pocket watch wedged in a small vest pocket.

Right away St. James sensed the man was guarded, most likely coached by the bank's legal counsel. If the meeting was to be successful at all, St. James had to somehow put Bodden at ease: a guarded Bodden probably wouldn't offer the evidence St. James needed to solve the case.

"I can assure you, Mr. Bodden, the bank has nothing to worry about from this investigation," he said as they sat down. "You're only holding monies for its rightful owners; only the custodian. There is no suspicion of bank wrongdoing whatsoever."

"Thank you, Mr. St. James," Bodden said, his accent distinctively upper-class British. St. James wondered if he had been educated at Oxford or Cambridge.

Bodden looked slightly more at ease, but not completely. He wasn't about to let a Canadian detective take advantage on his turf, no matter what comforting words he offered.

St. James smiled, "Please, call me Hamilton."

Bodden reciprocated.

"So how can we help, Hamilton?"

St. James handed him a paper bearing account numbers, the one found on Stevens's computer and others St. James had gathered from different sources.

"I'd like to see transactions in and out of these accounts over the last several months. Account signatures and correspondence, emails or otherwise, bearing instructions to the bank."

"Not a problem," Bodden said. "I anticipated some of what you're asking from discussions Antoinette had with your Mr. Louis."

"Actually, Louis is his first name: Louis Smythe."

Bodden nodded and continued. "Legal counsel also anticipated what you would need based on their conversations with Higgins Johnson."

"Excellent."

"I'll ask Antoinette to join us, if you don't mind. She is the brains behind all the backup. I wouldn't know where to begin," Bodden said, smiling.

A moment later Antoinette entered, laden with files and a laptop. *Louis would be pleased.*

Antoinette Ebanks was a gorgeous, well-proportioned black lady of about thirty-five with a beautiful smile and a jovial personality. She was dressed in a smart business suit the colour of the bank's emblem.

*Yes, Louis would be very pleased indeed.*

"Antoinette, I would like to personally thank you for the wonderful help you have given us on this case," St. James said before getting down to business.

"You are most welcome," she replied, looking quite happy with the compliment. "Louis is wonderful to work with."

Bodden suggested they move to the larger meeting table so Antoinette would have room to spread documents.

For the next hour and a half Antoinette led Hamilton through bank files related to the accounts and transactions he was interested in. Bodden quietly watched, like a chaperone at a junior-high dance: there to make sure nothing untoward happened.

Antoinette reviewed all account-open documents, transaction instructions, and cash movements with Hamilton. Then she opened the laptop and logged onto the bank's internal system to show him actual cash ins and outs for each account he was investigating. Finally, St. James flipped through copies of paid cheques, paying particular attention to signatures and endorsements.

As Antoinette explained each transaction, St. James vigorously took notes.

St. James said to Antoinette, "When you and Louis first spoke, he asked about the transaction ID ABA#021000089. It was before the account was flagged, so you couldn't discuss details. What transaction did it refer to?"

She looked at the computer screen. "It was attached to a transaction for this account." She pointed to an account number on the screen. St. James made a note of the number and the account holder's name.

"You look surprised, Hamilton," Bodden observed.

"I am, very!"

St. James dug into his sport coat's pocket and once again pulled out the paper bearing the code taken from Stevens's computer. He showed it to Antoinette and Bodden.

"There is the transaction ID you just showed me," he said, pointing to the second section.

Bodden and Antoinette looked at the paper and nodded at the same time.

St. James moved his finger to the next set of numbers.

"I believe you confirmed with Louis that this is an account number. Is that correct?"

"Yes, it's the right format and number of digits to be an account number. Let's see who it belongs to."

Antoinette keyed in the digits as they appeared in the code.

"Yes," she confirmed seconds later, "it is an account number, but not the one tied to the transaction ID ABA#021000089. It's an account belonging to another person."

"Who?" St. James asked anxiously.

Antoinette swung the laptop around for St. James to view the screen.

St. James smiled as he made notes.

He moved his finger to the word 'csprite1' appearing after the account number.

"Any idea what that word means?"

Antoinette typed the word into the bank's internal search engine and waited a moment for results.

A second later she said, "It's the password for the account number appearing before it, the one in your code."

St. James's mind drifted off, considering what he had just learned, unaware seconds had passed.

"Are you all right, Hamilton?" Bodden said cautiously.

"I am sorry, folks, I was just thinking about how all this ties into what I have already learned."

Having no clue what St. James meant, Bodden and Antoinette remained quiet.

Suddenly St. James's face brightened.

"I can tell you think this may be relevant," Antoinette said with a grin.

"You bet it is!" St. James said, beaming. "Thank you both so much. You have been more helpful than you could ever possibly imagine."

Bodden and Antoinette smiled with amusement at St. James's electrified reaction.

St. James looked at his watch. Twenty to four.

"I'm so sorry to have taken up so much of your time," he said as they stood to shake hands.

"Only too glad to help, Hamilton," Bodden said, still smiling.

On that note, St. James left for the hotel, where he found Anna back at the pool.

"More quiet today?" he asked.

"Much better. How did your meetings go?"

"Very well, thank you."

"Did you get what you need?"

"Yes, I did."

"Care to share?"

"Not yet."

# Chapter 67

It was 9:00 on Wednesday morning when St. James called Jason Williamson in Washington.

"How much trouble is it to get information from the IRS, Jason?"

"Can be a lot of trouble, quite frankly. What is it you're looking for?"

"Income tax paid by each person of interest for the past five years."

"They'd never give that information to a private investigator."

"Would they give it to a public one?"

"Smartass," Williamson said with a chuckle.

"Not you too. Anna calls me that all the time."

"Smart lady. I may be able to get you something. I have a contact. We have a good working relationship, sometimes. She's moody. Can't guarantee anything. Never know which one of her will show up."

"Somehow I knew you'd know someone. How long do you think it will take?"

"Maybe by end of day."

"That fast?" St. James said in disbelief.

"If she's there and if she's in a good mood."

"Do your best. That's all I can ask."

Next, St. James phoned Nathan Strong.

"Can we use your boardroom Monday morning?"

"Sure. I'll book it," said Strong.

"Can you attend a meeting then?"

"Afraid I'm fully booked Monday, Hamilton."

"It's important, Nathan. I'll be revealing what happened."

"For that, Hamilton, I'll cancel anything, even my own funeral."

Closest thing to humour St. James had heard from the man.

"Great, Nathan. See you Monday morning."

"Care to share anything now?" he asked.

"Not yet."

Next call was to Mary DeSilva at Global.

"Mary, is there any chance you could make a meeting on Monday at 9 a.m. in Washington?"

"Have a staff meeting then, Hamilton. Sorry."

"You may not want to miss this one, Mary."

"Is it good news for Global?"

"You'll have to come to the meeting to find out."

"Okay, smartass, I'll see you Monday morning," she said. "Where is the meeting?"

*Jesus, it's an epidemic.*

"Stevens, Gables & Strong."

St. James's final call was to Jensen.

"Where's my cheque?" Jensen said gruffly.

"We've finalized everything for you, Jensen. Can you come to a meeting at Stevens, Gables & Strong on Monday at nine?"

"If that's the end of it, yes."

"Yes, Malachi, that will be the end of it."

St. James emailed Slate, Dozer, and Smythe inviting them as well. After juggling commitments, each confirmed their attendance. Now all he had to do was to wait for whatever Jason learned from the IRS.

For a moment St. James debated calling Nells. The man would probably hang up, or worse, start yelling. Nothing to be gained from that, for sure. Then again, what if he could persuade Nells to talk? Nells had nothing to fear now. He had done his time, paid his debt to society. Best case, what could be learned? There was only one way to find out.

St. James punched in the number he found online for The Carstairs Group in Chicago and a receptionist answered.

"Roger Nells, please."

"Just one moment."

A couple of minutes later, an unsavoury voice St. James remembered all too well came on the line.

"Nells here."

"Roger, it's Hamilton St. James."

"What the hell do you want, asshole?" he said, voice raised and angry.

*That's a touch worse than "smartass."*

"A moment of your time."

"Why the hell should I give you anything? You ruined my life."

"I didn't ruin your life, Roger, your partners did. If they hadn't left a trail a blind man could follow, you would have been home free. You were the smart one."

"That's why I won't have anything more to do with the stupid bastards. They couldn't organize a barn dance. What do you want?" he asked again, tone only slightly milder. "Can't believe I didn't just slam the phone down."

"I just want to clear up a couple of things. Something I don't think you are involved in."

Nells grunted.

"Come on, Roger. It'll only take a few minutes."

He grunted again.

"You work for Gyberson now?"

"Yeah, what's it to ya?"

"Nothing really. Just interested in what kind of a person he is."

"He gave me a job when nobody else would. Helps a lot of us ex-cons. But I don't think I'll be here much longer."

"Why is that?" St. James queried.

"Company can't pay its bills and Stan's nowhere to be found."

"Does he pay a fair wage?"

"Depends what you call fair. Guys like me aren't exactly in high demand. We have to take what we can get. Fair for him, I guess."

"What are your plans?"

"None of your business."

St. James ignored the response.

"Are you working to get back on your feet, or just until another scheme comes along?"

"Done with schemes. Need to make money in a way where I don't have to keep looking over my shoulder to see if some asshole like you is creeping up on me. If I get a little money saved, I'll buy into my brother's locksmith business. I want a normal life. Tired of all this bullshit."

"One last question. What did Vinner have to do with the gang?"

"Hit man. One of the others met him in the joint. I stay away from hit men. Murder's not my thing, you know that about me, St. James."

"Yes, I do. Thanks for speaking with me Roger. I wish you well in your new life."

Nells grunted one last time and ended the call.

St. James looked at his watch. 11:30.

He made his way down to the beach and found Anna lying on a lounge chair in front of the hotel talking to a woman named Jackie from Illinois.

St. James asked, "Do you want to grab some lunch?"

Anna told Jackie she'd see her later, and she and St. James strolled up to the hotel patio to order lunch.

When they had settled into salads and wine St. James said, "Would you like to know what happened in the case?"

Anna looked up from the table.

"You know I would, Hamilton. Why would you even ask me that?" she said, slightly annoyed.

"Then you shall come with me to Washington for a meeting Monday morning at Stevens, Gables & Strong, where all will be revealed," he said with a smile.

"A bit theatrical don't you think?"

"Not really. Everyone will be there. I'll only have to tell the story once."

"It's like you say, Hamilton, you have your methods," Anna said. *Distinct chill in the air.*

After lunch Anna went back to the beach and St. James returned to the room to wait for Jason's call and to handle what emails may have come in since he last checked.

Jason's call didn't come until around 4:00. By then St. James had all but given up on the possibility that the tax information would be available.

"Have pen and paper?" Jason asked without saying hello.

"Okay. Shoot."

It took a half-hour for Jason to take St. James through every piece of income tax information for every party related to the Stevens case for the last five years. Painful. But when St. James boiled everything down, he concluded that the proof he needed was there. He thanked Jason and asked if he could attend the meeting at Stevens, Gables & Strong on Monday morning.

"Since I can see where all this is going, I guess I have to," he said with a laugh. "After all, I'm the *official* detective on the case."

"Smartass," St. James said.

"Doesn't sound as good as when I say it," Jason quipped.

They disconnected.

St. James couldn't resist. It was the little boy in him.

He dialed Louis's cell.

"This is Louis."

"Louis, Antoinette is drop dead gorgeous. You would be over the moon pleased."

"Really, Hamilton?" he said in an almost dreamy voice. "You wouldn't kid a fellow, would you?"

St. James could practically hear him salivating.

"Did she ask about me?"

"She said you were great to work with. But I do have some disappointing news."

"What's that?" Smythe asked anxiously.

"She hates plaid."

"Smartass," Smythe hung up without another word.

*It's official now. I am a smartass.*

In the remaining three days on Cayman, Anna and St. James stuck to fun and didn't discuss the case even once.

On Wednesday evening they treated themselves to a wonderful seafood dinner at Legends on Seven Mile Beach. Thursday and Friday, they rented another car and enjoyed a more detailed tour of the eastern part of the island, back in time to have their last dinner at the Cracked Conch as planned.

Later, seated at the hotel bar, they debated going home Saturday. But then they'd have to fly back to Washington on Sunday for Monday's meeting. No point. So they decided to switch flights from Ottawa to Washington.

They arrived in Washington at 11:00 Saturday night and checked in to the Washington Hilton on Connecticut Avenue Northwest. The only problem with coming straight to Washington from Cayman was not having proper clothes for Monday's meeting. Shorts and brightly coloured shirts wouldn't cut it in a Washington boardroom. Anna was upset over the whole thing until St. James promised they'd shop for business clothes first thing in the morning.

As soon as shops opened on Sunday morning, St. James made sure Anna walked through the front door of an upscale ladies' boutique. He figured if Anna's anxiety disappeared first, his shopping would be a lot easier. He was truly grateful when she found a brown suit she liked with a blouse and shoes to match. Problem solved, anxiety diminished.

In a men's shop not far from the ladies' boutique, St. James found a charcoal-coloured suit. A white shirt, green tie, and black shoes completed the business look he desired.

They were all done by noon.

"See, Anna?" he said, "there's never a need to panic. Money and time take care of just about everything."

Anna rolled her eyes as they looked for a place to have lunch.

On Monday morning St. James was up early reviewing notes and putting papers in order.

After breakfast he said to Anna, "You take a cab to Nathan's office. I have a few more things to check and then I have to speak with Jason."

She kissed him. "Okay. I'll see you there at nine."

St. James called Jason to confirm everything was lined up on his end. Jason assured him it was.

Everything prepared, St. James walked to Nathan's office. It was a beautiful sunny October morning. He could see his breath in the crisp air. Clear skies and no wind to speak of.

Walking to close a case had become just as much a ritual as a double shot of scotch after surviving attempts on his life.

The morning would be interesting.

# Chapter 68

Everyone was present when St. James walked into Stevens, Gables & Strong at 9:10. Jensen, wearing his usual dark-blue pinstriped suit, was seated near the head of the large oak table, staring blankly at the ceiling, face puffy and red.

Nathan, at the opposite end, was looking forlorn, clearly a chairman under stress; Jason was standing, staring out the window.

Anna was on the far side, looking anxious for everything to begin. Next to Anna, Smythe, in a brightly coloured clashing plaid outfit, was busy preparing to take notes. Mary DeSilva was rushing to send a last-minute email; Slate was slouched, looking quite disheveled. Dozer, in his favourite black leather suit, disconnected headphones from his cell at the sound of St. James's voice.

"Thank you all for coming on such short notice," St. James said, bringing the meeting to order. "We have much to cover this morning."

Jason turned from the window and smiled.

St. James sat next to Nathan, who was fidgeting nervously with a pen.

"I asked you here today to share the unraveling of the Stevens case, the $23-million claim against Nathan's firm and Global, and the death of Thomas Stevens."

The room went quiet; the tension was thick enough to cut with a knife.

"On August 30, $23 million was discovered missing by Malachi, and the loss was reported to my friend Jason."

Jason nodded.

"From there the investigation began.

"Jason's theory was that Stevens stole Malachi's $23 million. Bill, on the other hand, believed Stevens had been kidnapped. Bill and Jason worked well together despite their theoretical differences, and in my view are beacons of cooperation among police forces."

Slate and Jason nodded in appreciation.

"Can we get on with this?" Jensen said impatiently. "I've got business to attend to. Just give me my cheque and I'll get the hell out of here."

"Most certainly, Mr. Jensen. But before we do anything, everyone would like to hear the story," St. James said authoritatively.

The red-faced Jensen scowled.

"Going back to August 30, we recall there were no fingerprints in Stevens's office, except his own. At the time I questioned how that could be. Even though cleaners had conducted a deep clean, I found it difficult to believe there'd be absolutely no prints, not even a single smudged one. On this score I was wrong. After speaking with three cleaning companies and personally observing a deep clean, I'm satisfied it *is* possible to have a room completely free of fingerprints.

"Next there was Stevens's computer. Wiped clean. This played hell with the conflicting theories of kidnapping versus theft. On the one hand, a clean computer suggested Stevens covering his tracks: the theft theory. On the other, a computer left behind suggested Stevens may have been taken suddenly, without time to gather what he was never without: the kidnapping theory.

"These conflicting theories, I believe, were intended by Gyberson and Stevens, but for two different purposes.

"Gyberson wanted misdirection, confusion, to throw everyone off his trail. Misdirection created by two possible scenarios: kidnapping or theft. Police would waste time running down each one, allowing more time for Gyberson to disappear.

"Stevens's passport being left in the home safe and no clothes or travel cases missing supported the kidnapping theory. If Stevens left the country, he'd need his passport and couldn't obtain a replacement without it being reported to Bill. So, by all accounts, Stevens was most likely still in the United States.

"If he had known about it at the time, Gyberson would have liked Stevens wiping his computer. It would strongly implicate him as a person of interest: a thief covering his tracks.

"Stevens liked the two theories to keep his options open, to seek a new life elsewhere or to return to the old one if things didn't work out. More on this in a few minutes."

St. James paused, opened a bottle of water, and downed a couple of mouthfuls before continuing.

"Through the genius of Louis Smythe, we discovered that the computer was not wiped completely clean. There was a code buried deep in the hard drive. Not able to be found by the average computer user. Only by someone who knew where to look or more importantly, how to look. An expert. Someone like Louis.

"I don't believe Gyberson ever knew about the code. More about that in a few moments as well."

Smythe beamed from St. James's praise.

"If you were a thief, you wouldn't leave a code about travel plans, a map for police to track you. It would be the first thing you'd erase. A computer wiped clean, but not completely clean, was significant.

"Evidence gathered by Jason's team supported Nathan's belief that no one had access to Stevens's computer but Stevens himself. So whatever was on it, or not on it, as the case may be, was by Stevens's hand alone. Data erased would have been removed by Stevens. The code, found deep behind a number of hard drive partitions, was placed there by Stevens.

"Stevens's purpose for agreeing to misdirection was choice. Kidnapping meant he had the option of returning to the firm as a victim if he had second thoughts about taking on a new life. He would have pitched the kidnapping angle and been pitied for suffering under the hands of kidnappers.

"If everything worked out in Stevens's new life, he would continue to live it. If it didn't, the story would have been that the kidnappers let him go, or his release had been negotiated. He could return to his old life. Kidnapping, not theft, would be a more palatable message for the firm. It would invite pity for being kidnapped rather than blame for stealing, and no one would be any the wiser. Of course, the firm had no knowledge of any of this at the time.

"Choice for Stevens. Confusion for Gyberson."

St. James turned to Jensen.

"At first I thought Stevens might have missed the code. An oversight when he wiped the computer. Then, when I reviewed his files supporting the 139 investments, I knew it wasn't an oversight. Stevens was a very meticulous and deliberate man, not given to overlooking things. Weighing everything, it pointed to him leaving the code for us to find, if he was double-crossed. So that whoever double-crossed him could eventually be outed, punished when the code was broken."

"What was the purpose of the code?" Nathan said, his voice distressed.

"It represented a plan for the thieves to be apart, far from each other when the theft occurred. It was a communication plan among themselves, flights each would take and when, what city they'd be in until things cooled down."

Dozer interrupted, "But you said Gyberson never knew about the code. How can it be a plan for all the thieves if the main thief didn't know about it?"

St. James smiled. "Gyberson was most certainly part of the plan, but he never knew Stevens wrote a code to describe it, to leave a trail behind, a trail to out Gyberson if he double-crossed him. If he returned a kidnapping victim, he'd just erase it. It would no longer have purpose because he could only return if he wasn't double-crossed by Gyberson. To Gyberson, it was just a verbal plan."

"What made him so confident the code would be discovered, and more importantly, broken?" Dozer said with a confused look.

"I imagine he thought a clean computer would raise enough suspicion that investigators would thoroughly search every corner of the hard drive for some sort of clue, or to confirm it actually was *completely* clean. Eventually the code would be found. Jason's technology team would know where and how to look. And when they found it, they'd stop at nothing until it was broken."

"Huge gamble on Stevens's part," Dozer mused.

St. James said, "Yes, it was. I have been speaking as if we knew Stevens and Gyberson were in cahoots. In fact, at this point we didn't know for certain Stevens had anything to do with this. It was only alleged by Malachi."

He turned to Jason.

"When you traced manifests for the flights in the code and found Gyberson travelling to Fargo with Stevens, that made it certain that Stevens at least started out as a member of Gyberson's gang. But the fact that Stevens left the code in the first place meant he didn't trust Gyberson.

"Gyberson flirted with a flight attendant on the plane to Fargo to an extreme. She felt threatened and was about to report him to the captain. A man on the run usually doesn't want attention drawn to himself. Unless, of course, it's his seatmate he wants attention drawn to.

"The attendant would remember two people travelling together: the obnoxious Gyberson and his seatmate. Gyberson joked and laughed with Stevens, so the attendant knew they were together.

"Gyberson didn't care what people thought of him. He was heading for a new life no matter what. He wasn't contemplating the choice like Stevens. What he worried about was Stevens weakening, blowing the whistle on him. If everyone knew Stevens was part of it, he'd have no credibility. So, Stevens could never go back to his old life. Gyberson was making sure Stevens wouldn't have the choice he wanted. He could never leave Gyberson as a kidnap victim because the two looked like friends travelling together, not like kidnapper and victim. The stewardess Gyberson flirted with was meant to be a witness.

"In the end, Stevens had no choice but to continue with the new life, whether he realized it or not. Neither one trusted the other, and each took steps to protect himself should one or the other double-cross him.

"All this makes it certain Stevens wasn't kidnapped."

# Chapter 69

Once again St. James paused to drink water.

"Gyberson's holding company, Macadamia Investments, was the only shareholder in The Carstairs Group, a company seemingly incorporated to build retirement homes. Carstairs needed money. Badly. But Macadamia didn't have money to fund it: it was insolvent too. And Carstairs's poor financial history meant no traditional lender or investor would touch it. Gyberson would have to find less conventional sources to finance his company.

"Malachi would have me believe that Gyberson connected with Stevens because of Stevens's reputation for handling the investments of wealthy people. Wealthy people take higher risks than conventional investors because they can afford to and usually don't have many shareholders to answer to. Of course, they expect higher returns to compensate for additional risks, but Gyberson had nowhere else to turn. Isn't that right, Malachi?"

Jensen shrugged.

St. James continued.

"When I interviewed you, you said Stevens introduced you to Gyberson. But that wasn't so, was it, Malachi?"

Jensen scowled again.

"You weren't introduced to Gyberson by Stevens. It was the other way around. You introduced Gyberson to Stevens as someone who had contacted you looking for financial help. You never told Stevens that Gyberson was an old friend."

Surprise washed over the room.

Jensen remained still and silent.

"Stevens thought Gyberson was just another referral from you, someone you thought he could find money for. But Stevens wasn't able to source funds from traditional sources. Macadamia was too far gone. So you ended up providing cash to help save the company, but not without a scheme.

"Macadamia received financial transfusions from Jensen Holdings, amounting to the $23 million in question here. In exchange, Jensen Holdings received shares in Macadamia.

"Then, Macadamia was to lend Carstairs the same $23 million to finish constructing a retirement home in Chicago."

Nathan interrupted. "Who owns the partially completed retirement home, Carstairs or Macadamia?"

St. James turned to Nathan. "Macadamia owns the property. Carstairs was contracted to build the home. All Carstairs owned was the construction contract. It has no other assets."

"Then Macadamia has another asset besides shares in Carstairs. It owns land and a partially completed building."

"True," St. James said. "Technically."

"Technically?" Nathan said.

"Yes. Technically Macadamia has title to the land and unfinished building. But liens against the property by unpaid trades and a mortgage far exceed the value of the property in its unfinished state. There would be nothing left for Macadamia if Carstairs's world ceased financially before finishing the retirement home."

"So the $23 million would be enough to finish the building? Wouldn't that take care of the problem? Building's worth much more finished, probably enough to settle the mortgage and liens," Nathan pressed.

"It could. If that's what the money was actually used for," St. James said after drinking water.

Everyone looked puzzled.

Jensen grunted in disgust.

St. James turned to Jensen.

"Money *was* transferred to Macadamia all right. And Macadamia's shares were transferred to *your* holding company in return for the $23 million. But that's when everything stopped. The injection into Macadamia never made it through to Carstairs's bank account, did it, Malachi?"

Jensen stared at the boardroom table, motionless.

"Gyberson siphoned the $23 million from Macadamia's bank account before it could make it into Carstairs's. Then the money disappeared, along with Gyberson himself."

Everyone except Jensen gasped.

"How do you know all this?" said a perplexed Nathan Strong.

"When I went through Malachi's investment records, I traced money transferred from Jensen Holdings to Macadamia, confirmed by emails between Jensen and Gyberson, and verified actual transfers on bank statements.

"Stevens never had signing authority for Macadamia. Only Gyberson did. That meant that once money landed in Macadamia's bank account, Stevens couldn't possibly have stolen it. If money *was* stolen, it had to be by Gyberson. Gyberson also had signing authority in Carstairs. He controlled money in both companies. So, with a failing company and signing authority in both Macadamia and Carstairs, Gyberson had both motive and opportunity. The question at this point in the investigation was whether he actually took the money.

"At this juncture, it was certain that Stevens didn't steal the $23 million."

# Chapter 70

"Well, who did steal the money?" Anna asked impatiently.

St. James finished the bottle of water and grabbed a second from the centre of the boardroom table. "All in good time, Anna."

Anna's face clouded from suppressed annoyance.

St. James carried on.

"As our investigation progressed, I learned that over the years Gyberson illegally moved bits of income to an account in the Cayman National Bank, to an account in his name. The bank showed me records proving this last week. Money he couldn't have paid tax on in the United States he took to Cayman by suitcase.

"IRS records show Gyberson never declared more than $50,000 taxable income each year. Jason confirmed that. Certainly not enough income to build a $23 million nest egg, at least not the honest way. The only way to accumulate that amount of money was to not declare income in the United States over many years. It was tax evasion, one suitcase at a time, over many years. With periodic deposits and interest, the account grew to — guess what — $23 million."

Once again the room rumbled with expressions of surprise.

"Because substantial losses were incurred by both Carstairs and Macadamia, liabilities mounted. Now Gyberson needed money in the United States, but he couldn't transfer money back from Cayman without attracting tax and criminal charges. Bringing it back in suitcases, the same way it got there, would take too long. His creditors would soon be taking action. He needed money right away.

"But Gyberson never intended to use Jensen Holdings's $23 million to pay Carstairs's creditors, nor Macadamia's for that matter. If he did, he wouldn't have anything left to live on. He intended to use it to finance his own disappearance. The creditors would be left high and dry. I believe when Fargo police wring out all the facts, they'll discover Gyberson has $23 million stashed somewhere."

"In the Cayman National Bank?" Smythe suggested.

"No, not Cayman," St. James said confidently. "In the United States, where he needed it to be.

"The only way for Gyberson to get $23 million in the United States quickly was to find someone with $23 million already here, someone who had reason to want the same amount in Cayman. That's when Gyberson phoned Jensen and learned he was planning to retire to Cayman."

Jensen continued staring at the table.

"You weren't as smart as your old friend Stan, were you, Malachi? You didn't take money outside the country in suitcases over a number of years. You hid money with friends here in the United States, also to avoid taxes. Now, with reporting rules banks face, you can't move money offshore without declaring it and paying the tax. You were stuck. You couldn't move your $23 million hidden here to support your retirement in Cayman without attracting attention. In effect, you'd be blowing the whistle on yourself."

Jensen remained still.

"When I was in your office I saw the most recent financial statements for Jensen Holdings Inc."

"You what?" Jensen blurted. "You had no right to do that. Those are private statements of a private company. I swear to God I will sue your ass off for this!"

St. James ignored the outburst.

"Up to that point I thought Jensen Holdings was rolling in cash, profitable from many years of operations. But your company was losing money for some time because you expensed the funds you siphoned to hide with friends. Otherwise, Holdings would have been profitable. You purposely created your own losses to fund a $23 million retirement fund. Liabilities mounted in Jensen Holdings; liabilities that couldn't be paid because you siphoned all Jensen Holdings's resources. The company was insolvent, about to collapse under the weight of its own debt, just like Macadamia and Carstairs.

"Holdings's funds to invest came from syndicates, not financial institutions. Syndicates run by the mob. People who don't tolerate losing money. People who will resort to anything to get their money back. Jensen Holdings was in debt to them big-time. And time was running out for you, Malachi. Just a matter of days before they'd show up on your doorstep. You had to escape. You had to get out of the United States to save your own life. To Cayman.

"If you had left money in Holdings you could have repaid loans, if not all of them, then at least enough to keep the wolves away from the door for some time. But then you'd have nothing to retire on. No money to escape with."

St. James drank water.

"And so, there we have it. Gyberson running from the insolvent Macadamia and Carstairs, and Jensen running from the insolvent Jensen Holdings. Each looking to finance an escape: Gyberson from angry creditors, Jensen from angry loan sharks.

"You stole from the mob, Malachi. The sentence for that in the mob world is death."

"How can this possibly be blamed on us?" Nathan exclaimed.

"Excellent question, Nathan," St. James replied sympathetically. "Malachi told me he relied on Stevens to check the legitimacy of companies, and the people who ran them, before investments were ever made. Isn't that right, Malachi?"

Jensen ignored the question.

"It seemed odd to me that a sophisticated investor such as yourself would pick companies you wished to own, give instructions to Stevens to make investments with your money, and then hold him responsible for your decisions. If your lawsuit ever went to court, I believe you'd have difficulty gaining sympathy from a judge for that very reason."

Smythe struggled to keep up, trying to type as fast as St. James was unfolding the story.

Jensen's face became redder.

"Maybe it was a mistake to come here in good faith without my attorney," he said, shifting in his chair.

St. James shrugged.

"So, where's the money?" Mary asked with a look of annoyance.

"The trail will lead us there shortly, Mary."

Jensen scowled, his forehead furrowed. Anna and Smythe looked at one another and shrugged. Nathan Strong remained stone-faced. Slate was expressionless. Jason, who by now had moved from the window to sit next to St. James, was the only one in the room with a smile of anticipation.

"This brings us back to the code itself," St. James said as he handed photocopies of it around the table.

"I call your attention to the first two sections, being *(g,cnbtkyk1,j)* and *(ABA#021000089-36148883-012-67141-co-na-csprite1)*. The first section, *(g,cnbtkyk1,j)*, contains the country and bank code. The first set of characters in the second section is a transaction ID *(ABA#021000089)* for money transferred from Citibank in the United States to Cayman National. Next is the bank's international clearing account number *(36148883)* that accepts all money transfers from Citibank. Transactions coming into the clearing account would also have the recipient's full name and personal account number attached. The transfer is cleared to the bank account number *(012-67141)* you see there."

Smythe interrupted. "We never did solve section eight of the code."

"Louis, I think you'll find that section represented the date they intended to meet up, a date to divvy up the spoils, so to speak. *(A21+11)* is most likely April 21 of next year plus eleven days, which would make it May 2."

"I'll feed it into the program," said Smythe, anxiously typing away.

St. James continued.

"The Cayman bank did a word search in its system for *cspritel*, the last word in section two of the code. It's the password for the account number appearing just before it on the paper before you.

"We couldn't get the signatory's name through normal channels because of Cayman privacy laws. However, when we involved courts and ambassadors in both the United States and Cayman we were able to formally obtain the information."

"Well, whose account is it?" Nathan blurted.

"In a moment, Nathan," St. James replied.

Nathan shot St. James an impatient look.

"I went to Cayman and met with the lawyers I had engaged to search the island's registries for each member of Gyberson's gang and anyone else associated with this case. Then I met with the Cayman National Bank to trace transactions I suspected were there as well as the ones lawyers had found in registries. Of particular interest was the account number found in the code."

"Well, whose account was it?" Nathan asked again in a more impatient tone.

St. James waited a long moment.

"Malachi Jensen's."

# Chapter 71

Jensen remained expressionless.

Nathan was somewhere between incredulous and outraged. "Jensen's?" he shouted.

Anna gasped. Smythe looked stunned. Slate showed absolutely no surprise. Mary just smiled. Whispers erupted around the table.

Nathan turned to Jensen. "You stole the money from yourself?"

Jensen didn't answer. Or move. Or show any kind of body language.

"Not quite, Nathan," St. James said cautiously. "Remember, a transfer involves two accounts."

"He transferred $23 million from his US account?" Nathan said.

"No, he didn't," St. James replied with conviction.

Jensen stood.

"I've heard enough for one day. You'll hear from my attorneys."

With that, Jensen left the boardroom, only to be stopped by two of Jason's uniforms posted outside, placed there after everyone had gathered inside earlier that morning. The taller of the two turned Jensen back into the boardroom.

Jason stood and gestured to the chair Jensen had just left.

"Malachi, you do not have to respond to anything you hear today without an attorney present. But it is important that you hear it," Jason advised.

"Am I under arrest?"

"No, you are not under arrest," Jason confirmed.

Jensen reluctantly sat down.

"Please continue, Hamilton," Jason said waving a hand.

St. James nodded.

"With support from both the US and Cayman ambassadors and the Cayman government, and with cooperation from the Cayman National Bank, we confirmed that $23 million was transferred from a Cayman bank account belonging to Gyberson to the account belonging to Malachi Jensen."

"My God!" Nathan blurted out. "Conspiracy? Gyberson steals money then gives it back?"

"Not quite," St. James interjected. "When Gyberson was arrested in Fargo we arranged for Dozer to question him. Gyberson didn't provide much, but what he did say had me looking at the case quite differently."

"What was that?" Mary asked.

"He told Dozer things were 'not as they appeared.' That got me thinking about what things in the case were not as they appeared. Perhaps others were involved, or different transactions took place that we knew nothing about. One possibility was that Gyberson and Jensen had more of a relationship than just investor–investee. When Anna searched, she discovered that the two were university roommates at Florida State. The two of you go back many years," he said to Jensen. "So the fact that Gyberson turned to you for money when Macadamia and Carstairs were in financial difficulty was no coincidence."

Jensen's began to grit his teeth.

"When you began planning this scheme you realized you couldn't make it look legitimate without Stevens's help. You'd already given him power of attorney and signing authority. To exclude him now in a scheme to transfer money would be a dead giveaway. Stevens was no fool. You'd run the risk of him finding something in the company records, maybe blowing the whistle on you.

"The more you thought about it, the better it looked to have a well-respected CPA as a front man, someone to lend credibility. So you had to include him. You had to make some kind of deal with Stevens. But part of your scheme was to sue Stevens's firm later for $23 million. So how does one have his accountant participate in a scheme where he gets sued by his partners? Why would Stevens agree to that? I don't think he would have if he'd known about it. He was left out of that part, wasn't he, Malachi? It was just between you and Gyberson, a private scheme."

Jensen said nothing.

"The only way for you to be in a position to sue the firm was to maintain distance from Stevens, treat him like the arm's-length professional he was supposed to be in the first place.

"To maintain arm's length you couldn't be seen making a deal with him. It would compromise your ability to sue later. Gyberson would have to make the deal for you. So Stevens would facilitate funneling your $23 million through to Macadamia for Gyberson to siphon, just as the two of you had planned.

"I discovered Stevens knew nothing about your plan to sue when I was reviewing your files. Stevens wasn't copied on all correspondence between you and Gyberson, just the ones related to organizing cash injections into Macadamia. I thought that was strange for a three-way partnership. Something else had to be at play.

"I believe Stevens would have been reluctant at first when Gyberson broached the subject of participating in a scheme. Fundamentally a good man; but in a very unhappy marriage. He was miserable. You knew this and so did Gyberson. Gyberson saw the stressful relationship between Beth and Tom firsthand when he had dinner at their house. Beth remembered a dinner guest, a man who frightened her. She said he had a certain look, like he'd do anything to get what he wanted. She couldn't remember his name other than that it started with 'S.' As the case unfolded, it became clear to me that Gyberson fit her description perfectly.

"The troubled marriage gave Gyberson an opportunity to offer Stevens an escape from an unhappy life. A man with nothing left but work, no pleasure whatsoever, begins to fantasize about something better. But all his assets were in his wife's name. He couldn't have a better life, even without her. He had no means of his own to do so. All Gyberson had to do was offer to finance a new life for him.

"Here's where it gets interesting," St. James said, smiling.

"After thinking about Gyberson's offer, Stevens decided escaping was the way to go. But he'd need capital to generate income, to sustain himself. My guess is about $5 million, maybe more; invested at 6%, that would generate about $300,000 a year. Not what Stevens was used to, but he'd have only himself to support, and a shot at happiness. Am I right, Malachi?"

Jensen was rigid, stone-faced, still working hard to control himself.

"I'll take that as a yes," St. James said with a grin.

"I don't understand any of this," said Smythe. "The money in Cayman was transferred from one of the guys here, wasn't it?"

St. James continued without answering.

"Malachi, when Higgins Johnson searched your name and those of your holding companies in Cayman registries, they found a luxurious five-bedroom, four-bath, 4000-square-foot house on Orchid Drive, not far from the Cayman Yacht Club. Purchased in your name last month for $3.5 million with a cheque drawn on account 012-67141 at the Cayman National Bank: the very same account as in the code Louis cracked. Funded from the $23 million transferred to your account from Gyberson's. Gyberson's money was in the same bank. It was convenient, perfect for both of you. He needed money in the United States to live, and you needed money in Cayman to live.

"All you had to do was switch amounts. Trade bank balance for bank balance, in equal amounts. Gyberson gets the $23 million you siphoned from Jensen Holdings, hidden with friends in the United

States. You had to gather the $23 million back from friends in order to make the investment in Macadamia. Then all Gyberson had to do as the only signing officer at Macadamia was just take it. All part of the scheme between the two of you.

"You get his $23 million in Grand Cayman to escape the insolvent Jensen Holdings in the United States. No money crosses borders. No record for US authorities to trace. Very clever. This was confirmed by an email from Gyberson in Malachi's files saying, 'Good to go. Can switch anytime,' referring to the money switch itself.

"I might have missed it if Stevens hadn't left the code on his computer. Thanks to Louis and Anna we were able to unwind your scheme, Malachi."

Dozer sat up straight with a troubled look. "So let me get this straight, Hamilton. Malachi siphons $23 million from his own company, hides it here in the United States, screwing the mob to finance his retirement. Gyberson hides money in Cayman over the years that eventually grows to $23 million, avoiding US tax in the process.

"Malachi opens a bank account in the Cayman National Bank. Then Gyberson transfers $23 million from his Cayman National Bank account to Malachi's. In exchange, Malachi transfers the $23 million he gathered back from friends in the United States to Gyberson's company, Macadamia, for Gyberson to siphon in order to fund *his* retirement, screwing his company's creditors in the process."

"That's right, Dozer," St. James said with a smile. "Dollar for dollar, bank account for bank account, retirement for retirement."

Anna's face suddenly lit up. "That's the house we looked at in Cayman, the reason you rented the car that morning."

St. James smiled at Anna then turned back to Malachi. "We did take a look at your mansion. Very nice."

Dozer remained confused. "But you said Jensen couldn't transfer money to Cayman without paying tax. What about the transfer made with the transaction ID in the code, the one to his account?"

"The transfer referred to in the code was only $1,000, just enough for Jensen to open an account to facilitate the switch with Gyberson, not enough to attract attention from authorities," St. James explained.

"If all they wanted was to exchange cash, why did Gyberson sign over Macadamia shares to Jensen?" Nathan asked.

"The shares were worthless. Neither party placed any real value on them. It was done to make it look like a share-purchase transaction, to throw off the IRS should they ever decide to look at it. Gyberson couldn't run the risk of authorities finding his money in Cayman. So, he sold a worthless company for $23 million."

"Bizarre," Smythe said.

Anna shook her head.

Nathan interjected. "Tom was an honest man. What would Gyberson and Jensen have said to him to get him to participate in all this?"

"I believe Stevens thought Malachi and Stan were just switching accounts to fund retirements. He probably guessed Gyberson didn't pay tax on the $23 million in Cayman. But Malachi didn't move the money down there. That was Gyberson's crime, not his client's. He probably justified it that way, shrugged it off.

"But money had to be stolen for Malachi to claim a loss against Stevens's firm. When Gyberson got Malachi's $23 million, Malachi reported it stolen, just to manufacture a claim.

"When we discovered Stevens couldn't possibly have stolen it, Malachi had to create another phony angle to substantiate a claim. Then the story became that Stevens was supposed to have thoroughly checked out Gyberson, known he was a crook. So Malachi trumped up a negligence accusation to replace the theft claim."

Slate interjected. "I assume this is only part of the scheme. You still haven't told us where Stevens's $5 million came from."

St. James turned to Bill. "As far as Stevens was concerned, his new life's funding was coming from Malachi. No other source. As I said earlier, Stevens didn't know about the ensuing insurance claim — that

that's where Malachi intended the funding to come from for Stevens's escape. Malachi and Gyberson never intended to fund Stevens personally. They needed the money switch for their own new lives.

"The whole idea of the money switch was not just for Malachi and Gyberson to solve retirement problems: it was to create the lawsuit against Nathan's firm for the purpose of extorting insurance monies from Global. Stevens was to be funded from the proceeds of the insurance claim; after funding him, the balance would be split between Jensen and Gyberson."

Jensen continued his non-responsive state.

St. James paused to clear his throat.

"Stevens did the accounting for Jensen Holdings and would have known it was insolvent. So why would he think his escape money would come from Jensen?" Nathan challenged.

"Malachi would have lied to Stevens; told him he had the money in a separate bank account outside the company. After all, Stevens knew the $23 million to facilitate the switch with Gyberson came from outside the company. He had no reason to believe there wouldn't be another $5 million to fund his escape," St. James replied.

Nathan shrugged.

St. James drank water.

"What got you onto Macadamia and The Carstairs Group in the first place?" Nathan asked.

"There were four holding companies that received multiple funding tranches from Malachi in addition to Macadamia. Five in total. Transaction volume and dollar amounts triggered my initial interest. That interest subsequently grew into suspicion when I learned two facts. First, Jason discovered all five shareholders were on FBI watch lists. Second, background checks showed all five were related to each other in one way or another. Bill confirmed this from the FBI side too. Collectively, they were Gyberson's gang. But Gyberson was the only one involved in this scheme. The others were silent partners. They may or may not have been promised a piece of insurance money. Who knows?" St. James shrugged. "For our purposes here, it doesn't really matter.

"What moved Gyberson to the top of the suspect list was his hiring of Nells in The Carstairs Group. Except for Bill, none of you will have heard of Nells. He's a swindler whom Bill and DuPont put in US prison a few years back, with a little help from me."

Slate nodded.

"That made Gyberson's character complete.

"Losers hang around with losers. Gyberson hired a number of ex-convicts when sentences were up. They needed money and were not in a position to demand top dollar. No one else would hire them. So, Gyberson got cheap labour and ex-cons got a paying job. It turned out Nells had no part in the Stevens affair. He just needed money. He was working to raise enough money to buy into his brother's locksmith business."

"My God. I can't believe Thomas did this to us. I just can't believe it," Nathan said in a defeated tone, staring solemnly out the window.

"My guess, Nathan, is that he was a very desperate, lonely man who did his best to keep you out of it. It was one reason for the kidnapping scenario. The public would feel sorry for the firm's loss of a key partner. Sounds better on the street than stealing from clients."

Anna grimaced. "So what you're saying is no one stole money?"

"Nobody. No money was ever stolen. Never a theft. And never a kidnapping. Only an exchange of equal amounts of cash. Income tax evasion, yes. Attempt to swindle Global, yes. But no theft. There's no valid insurance claim because there was no loss," St. James said triumphantly, smiling at Mary DeSilva, whose smile back was much bigger. St. James had just saved her $23 million.

"What a maze," Anna muttered

"Remember Gyberson's words to Dozer. 'Not as they appear.' It looked like theft, but it wasn't. It was fraud."

Mary interrupted. "We skipped over the rest of the code. What does it all mean?"

"The 'g' in front of section one stands for Gyberson, 'j' at the end for Jensen: money from Gyberson to Jensen. The middle part is Cayman National Bank's SWIFT code, from Gyberson's Cayman account to Jensen's."

St. James looked at Smythe. "Louis, would you mind taking everyone through the rest of the code?"

Smythe explained the remaining sections. Flights, times, initials for the five shareholders, and the cities they landed in.

Nathan had no interest in the rest of the code. "Let's not forget Tom's murder," he said. "He may have done irreparable harm to the firm, but he was still a human being pushed to the limit. Over the years he contributed a lot to this firm and to the community."

St. James nodded.

"Why do you think he was killed?" Smythe asked.

"My guess is that with time, Stevens's mind began to clear. He probably realized what he had given up, what he'd thrown away. The respect of the firm, its clients, and the many charities he'd raised so much money for. He probably started thinking he'd sold out too cheap, that what he'd given up was worth far more than the escape money he'd been promised. He probably asked for more, turning himself into a liability to Gyberson, which cost him his life. Jason and the Fargo police will determine that during criminal proceedings, I'm sure."

Jensen broke his silence. "You can't prove any of this, St. James," he said angrily.

St. James became rigid and glared straight into Jensen's eyes. "When I interviewed you, you said you didn't have a Cayman bank account. And that you didn't have tax problems. Both lies. I don't have to prove anything to you, Jensen. Jason and Bill will work that out. Although I pledge my help whenever they need it. You can be sure of that. In the meantime, I have enough to have your phony lawsuit and claim against my client thrown out. That was my job. It's done, Malachi. And so are you."

# Chapter 72

When the room quieted down Jason went to the door and beckoned the two uniformed policemen into the room, then returned to where Jensen was seated.

"Mr. Jensen, I am placing you under arrest for tax evasion, attempted fraud, and accessory to murder. Please stand."

Jensen looked shocked as Jason read him his rights while one policeman pulled Jensen's hands behind his back and slapped the handcuffs on.

"You said I wasn't under arrest," Jensen cried.

"That was a half-hour ago," Jason said, smiling.

"Sonofabitch! I'll sue your ass off for this."

"Must be your favourite line, Malachi."

Jason barked at the two uniforms, "Get him the hell out of here!"

The officers dragged Jensen off, and Jason turned to St. James. "Nice work, Hamilton."

"It was a team effort. I couldn't have done it without you."

"Great job, Hamilton," Slate said, shaking his hand. "Looks like Jason and I have some paperwork to do. I hate that part."

"What about the rest of Gyberson's gang?" St. James asked.

"Small potatoes," Slate said. "They can wait. We've got the murderer and the fraudster. Good enough for now."

St. James thanked Jason and Slate for their support as they left the room.

Mary gave St. James a big hug. "Thank you, Hamilton. As always, you didn't disappoint. Don't know what we'd do without you. Your cheque, as they say, is in the mail. I'll be in touch," she said as she walked from Stevens, Gables & Strong's boardroom.

Nathan, about to leave for the meetings he had postponed, shook St. James's hand and thanked him.

As Nathan walked toward the boardroom door St. James said, "Would you like some help with the communication?"

"That would be wonderful, Hamilton. I wouldn't know where to begin," he muttered in a glum voice.

"I'll draft something and email it to you in the morning."

Nathan just nodded and slowly walked away.

It was just Smythe, Anna, and Dozer remaining.

"Excellent work, boss. Well done," Smythe said, enthusiastically slapping St. James on the back.

Anna stared at Hamilton. "I guess I owe you an apology for being so curt on Grand Cayman. Your methods are very impressive indeed. And they do serve you well. I see now why you had to do things the way you did. It was far more complicated than I could ever have imagined."

St. James said nothing. He just kissed her and then turned to Dozer.

"You asked some very good questions, my friend, but otherwise you were uncharacteristically quiet. No smart remarks."

Dozer's grin widened. "I learned a long time ago not to interrupt the master when he's unfolding the truth. Too dangerous."

They all laughed.

St. James looked at all three. "Let's go home, team."

The late afternoon flight to Ottawa was almost full. Just four seats left for them to grab. Anna and St. James landed in the condo at eight, dumped the week's laundry in the wash, and cracked open a bottle of Cannonau di Sardegna, which St. James found lingering in the very back of the liquor cabinet.

They sat quietly in the living room for a time, sipping wine, thinking about the day's events and about how the final evidence would shake out.

"What will you do now, Hamilton?" Anna finally asked.

"I have a lot of papers to sort through, bills to pay, and an invoice to prepare for Mary. She usually sends a cheque before she even gets the bill, God love her."

"Not hard to do the math for what they owe you, 10% of $23 million," she mused. "An incredible sum."

St. James looked into her sparkling brown eyes. "Do you remember our drive to Wakefield? When you asked how I live, how I can spend without worry. And I asked you to give me a couple of weeks to show you, and you would see."

"I remember," she said with a smile. "I guess you just did."

# Chapter 73

St. James knew Nathan would be paralyzed by the whole experience. So early Tuesday morning he went into the study and drafted a communication for Nathan to send internally and a second piece for public consumption. He stressed the good that Stevens had done for the firm, its clients, and the community. That Stevens suffered from depression. And that the partners and staff will honor him by establishing a fund in his name for mental health research through the National Institute of Mental Health. Then he emailed everything to Nathan.

Not five minutes went by before Nathan called.

"Hamilton, this is brilliant," he said, voice much stronger than the previous day. "But is it right that we portray him as a victim rather than as part of a conspiracy?"

"He *was* a victim, Nathan. A victim of enormous stress, a horrible marriage, and a feeling of hopelessness. If Gyberson and Jensen hadn't come along, he may have ended the suffering himself. Even if Gyberson hadn't killed him, the fact that there was no legitimate insurance claim meant he wouldn't have money to live anyway. And he couldn't return to the firm, not after what he had done. A sad man with no future, and no way to support himself. It's difficult to imagine how he could have gone on living under such circumstances.

"Beth is a victim also: bad marriage, murdered husband, and mental health issues of her own. The firm honouring Stevens with a fund in his name may bring her some peace."

"I still have angry partners. What about the damage to the firm?"

"The firm suffered only collateral damage. Stevens suffered direct damage first with emotional pain, then with his life. It's better for you to show compassion to your staff and the public, not anger or self-pity. Ask your partners if they would like this catastrophe to go away quickly and in a positive way. Then ask if they think it would go away faster by portraying the firm as the victim of attempted fraud, or the deceased as the victim of mental illness? If you portray Stevens as a fraudster, that's all the public will ever remember. A senior partner labelled dishonest, permanently. What would your clients think? You would almost certainly lose some to competitors. Clients too embarrassed to deal with a firm whose former partner was a co-conspirator. Wouldn't your partners rather the public think of the firm as caring?

"This is a good thing for the community. You're supporting research for mental illness. That lasts much longer than the victim image, especially if you add to the fund every year, a continuous reminder of the good the firm stands for. It will strengthen your brand.

"Although I can't tell you the number of people suffering from depression, I do know it's the greatest untreated disease in the United States. Mostly because everyone's ashamed to talk about it. Make the firm a champion of it being okay to talk about mental illness. And I guarantee you will rise above this catastrophe in a positive way and come out the other end stronger and more profitable than you would ever imagine."

"Very compelling, Hamilton," Nathan said slowly.

"It's not just compelling, Nathan, it's the right thing to do."

"You will bill me of course?" he asked.

"On the house," St. James said lightly. "Call me if you get into trouble."

"I will. And thank you again… For everything you've done."

They disconnected.

St. James didn't know how long it was, but for some time he stared at his study wall, pondering the end of another journey.

# Chapter 74

When St. James's focus crawled back to the present, he remembered Friday's class. He had to prepare. And CISI was crying out for attention.

First things first. He telephoned Janice McPherson to let her know he was still among the living. She was relieved and happy she could now put her own life back in order. Filling in for St. James had taken up most of her spare time for several weeks, and she had overdue papers for her classes.

For twenty minutes or so she recounted everything that had gone on in the class during his absence, how far they had progressed with the course outline, and where he had to pick up the pieces. St. James was pleased. She was right where the course should be for the time of year.

"Excellent work, Janice."

He would see her properly rewarded.

His thoughts turned to CISI.

Before leaving for Cayman, St. James had had the presence of mind to email Anderson that he'd be off the grid for a week's holiday. Anderson didn't need to know he was working another case.

The rest of the day was spent reviewing where he'd left off. He considered notes from phone conversations with Detective St. Jacques. The detective's interview with Sterling. Very relevant.

The phone rang.

Spencer.

"I thought you'd want to know, Hamilton. We arranged with Bell to trace the phone belonging to the fifth guy, Vinner's contact. This one's going to surprise you."

"Nothing surprises me anymore, Mark," he said matter-of-factly.

"We'll see."

"Well, don't keep me in suspense, who is it?"

"Sidney Gunther."

"What!" St. James blurted in a raised voice. "The grumpy bartender from the Dirty Duck?"

"That's right. He was fired a couple of weeks ago for treating customers poorly."

"I knew he'd been fired. He's the last guy I would have suspected capable of murder. Mean-spirited, yes. Willing to organize hits, no."

St. James remembered Anna saying Gunther was acting weird. Secret phone calls. Asking about him. Now it made sense. He was talking to Vinner all along, reporting St. James's every move.

"I told you you'd be surprised," Spencer said with a chuckle. "But when you think about it, his personality fits a thug's far better than a bartender's."

"You're right about that. What's your plan?"

"We'll bring him in for questioning when we track him down. He could lead us to Vinner."

"Thanks, Mark. Let me know if anything comes of it."

They disconnected.

St. James shook his head and went back to work.

"Sidney Gunther," he mumbled. "Who would've guessed?"

Next, he examined Dozer's surveillance notes on Graves, Blakie, and Van Hoyt. Van Hoyt was shopping at plumbing and fixture stores to renovate the new home. Nothing of interest there. Graves was continuously in meetings, but taking time to have lunch with Blakie, a man he didn't like. Interesting.

For a moment St. James thought about having Dozer run surveillance on Anderson. But, then dismissed it. It would be waste of time. Anderson was a straight shooter, focused only on company performance. Not a man for games.

Instead St. James decided to phone him. "Sorry to bother you, Cameron."

"How was your vacation?" Anderson asked.

"Very relaxing. Thank you. I know you and Blakie are close, so I wanted to check something with you."

"Sure thing."

"I had the impression Graves and Blakie weren't exactly drinking buddies."

St. James heard Anderson force a laugh.

"I would say that's a valid assessment, maybe even an understatement."

"They've been having lunches together, and that's odd for two people who don't like each other."

"Oh, that. Nelson had been having a hard time implementing his board agenda. David's been at odds with it, blocking initiatives, that sort of thing. Nelson asked my advice. It was me who suggested he invite David to lunch a couple of times, just the two of them, to see if they could reach some sort of common ground."

"Makes sense," St. James said thoughtfully.

They chatted for another fifteen minutes or so. Company financial results were strong, ahead of budget and last year's actual results. Product poundage up one per cent overall, yields up half a per cent, and staff turnover down one per cent. All in all impressive results. He congratulated Anderson for CISI's success.

# Chapter 75

St. James had gone to Harvard with a guy named Chip Wilson. They were good friends and had made an effort to stay in touch over the years. Chip landed a job with IBM when he graduated and had since worked his way up to vice-president. He was someone St. James trusted. So he picked Chip's number from the database and tapped it on his cell.

"Hey, Chip. How goes it?"

"You called on a good day, Hamilton. I was just handed my profit-sharing cheque, up nicely over last year I might add. So there's nothing you can say that will piss me off," he said, chuckling.

"Not my style to piss people off, you know that, Chip," St. James said disingenuously.

"Right," Chip laughed. "The streets are littered with people pissed off at you."

"Too kind, Chip. Too kind."

They became serious.

"What can I do for you, Hamilton?"

"I'm looking for information on a couple of people who once worked at IBM. A lady by the name of Karen Van Hoyt and a man called Nelson Graves."

"Nelson ran the Canadian operations for a time," Chip said slowly. "Competent, successfully grew the business, bit of a pain in the ass."

St. James interrupted. "In what way?"

"Upper crust English mannerism. Employees felt he looked down on them."

St. James laughed.

"Based on what I've seen so far he probably did. What about Karen?"

"Didn't know her well. She came up through the accounting side. Nelson was her mentor, I think."

"Anything between them?"

Chip paused for a moment.

"Not that I am aware of. Rumours of course. Usual when you have a man mentoring a woman. But I doubt it."

They talked about university days and sports for a while and then disconnected. St. James made notes.

For a long moment he stared out onto Sussex. Three police cars, lights flashing, were parked on a sidewalk on the opposite side of Sussex, next to the bank. Five or six policemen were standing outside.

*Maybe a robbery.*

No one moved an inch during the entire few minutes that St. James watched.

His mind drifted back to CISI.

Van Hoyt had worked with Nelson at IBM. St. James wondered if he provided a reference for her when she applied for CISI's CFO position. He called Anderson a second time.

"Don't know, Hamilton. Before my time. I'll have HR pull Karen's file and email the contents to you."

# Chapter 76

Something was bothering St. James, and it had been for some time. He had spent time with every team member except Dozer's brother, Denzel. St. James didn't think that was right, and something made him decide to do something about it that very moment.

He grabbed a jacket from the hall closet and stepped out to a damp, chilly November day. The kind of day he always associated with England.

He pulled his jacket collar up tightly around his neck as he crossed Sussex and headed toward Guigues Street. Fifteen minutes later he was in front of Anna's apartment, just in time to meet Denzel leaving a routine check.

"Hi, Mr. St. James," Denzel said when he saw St. James.

"You can call me Hamilton," he said for the third or fourth time.

"Okay, Mr. St. James," Denzel said.

"Do you drink coffee, Denzel?"

"Doctor says I can't. Medication."

St. James nodded. "What can you drink?"

"Coke or water," he said, swaying and staring past St. James.

"Come with me, I'll buy you a Coke," St. James said with a smile.

"Okay, Mr. St. James."

They walked toward the centre of the Market and found a quiet coffee shop on York where St. James ordered a Coke for Denzel and black coffee for himself. They settled at a small table close to the entrance.

"How old are you, Denzel?" St. James asked.

"Erasmus says I'm 22."

"How far did you go in school?"

Denzel's eyes squinted, continuing to look past St. James, searching hard for an answer. He grabbed his thick black curly hair tightly with both hands as frustration grew.

"Wasn't there very long," he said finally. His face clouded over with old memories.

"Life must have been difficult," St. James said sympathetically.

"They're really good to me at the home." Denzel's face brightened. "And Erasmus is very good to me too. He says I can learn to do things. He'd send me to a special school, but he doesn't have much money right now."

"Do you find checking Anna's house difficult?"

"No. Erasmus is a good teacher. He knows how to get things into my head."

St. James gave a sympathetic smile.

"Do you get bored doing the same thing every day?"

"No. Makes me feel good. Watching television and playing video games makes me feel bad about myself."

St. James's heart sank. He paused a beat then said, "If you could go to a special school, would you want to?"

"Erasmus says we can't."

"But, what if you could?"

"I like to learn. I like to feel good about myself. I don't like it when I feel bad. I don't like it when people make fun of me."

"I am very proud to have you on my team, Denzel."

# Chapter 77

Two days later, St. James received a cheque from Mary DeSilva for $2.3 million. That made him feel good about himself, like Denzel wanted to feel. He deposited the cheque in the bank across the street and then paid the balance of Higgins Johnson's bill, as well as Dozer's and Smythe's. Finally, he wrote bonus cheques for each member of the team.

His computer pinged with two emails from CISI human resources, a number of documents from Karen's personnel file attached. He read each one carefully, making notes of relevant points as he went.

*Time for celebration.*

Once again he made reservations at the Beach Club and invited the team for 5:30. Cathy was on duty, sporting a huge smile for Dozer, who had no trouble whatsoever reciprocating. By 5:45 they all had a drink in hand, Denzel a Coke, the rest their usual poison.

St. James had everyone line up in front of the ship-at-sea painting while Cathy took several photos with his cell.

"What's this, a graduation picture?" Cathy asked with a grin.

"GQ," Dozer said sarcastically.

Cathy rolled her eyes.

She took four or five shots from different angles before handing the phone back to St. James.

When they sat at the table St. James proposed a toast for a job well done and thanked everyone for their part in a successful end to the Stevens affair.

"But I didn't do anything," Denzel said sheepishly.

"You're part of the team, Denzel," St. James said. "You're providing a valuable service on the remaining case."

When they finished the main course, St. James handed envelopes around the table. Everyone stared at him, not knowing whether to open them then and there or stuff them in a pocket.

Dozer was the first to speak. "What's this, Hamilton?"

"Why don't you open it and find out?"

Anna and Smythe looked at each other. Denzel just swayed.

When envelopes were opened and contents revealed, expressions of shock washed over everyone's faces.

"It takes me four months to earn this much money," Anna said, staring at the cheque in disbelief. "I didn't do enough to justify this, Hamilton."

"I'll be the judge of that," St. James said smiling.

Smythe chimed in. "Very generous, Hamilton, thank you. Now I can buy some new plaids."

"No hurry, Louis. We were just getting use to the old ones," St. James assured, laughing.

"This isn't necessary, man," Dozer blurted. "You pay me for what I do. That's all you have to do."

St. James ignored Dozer.

"I want to explain something," St. James said, raising a hand to garner attention. "Denzel and I met and talked about learning. He's very grateful for your help, Dozer. And he'd like to learn more. I think Denzel could be even more valuable as a team member if his skills were enhanced."

He paused for a moment to gather the appropriate words.

"Denzel's cheque is a little lighter than the rest. Not because I value him less. I did some research. There is a school in Texas called Warbridge. It does excellent work with folks who have learning challenges. Teaches life skills and job training in a very effective way. I spoke with the director yesterday at some length and explained what a great person Denzel was, how he learns, and the success his brother is now having with a certain learning approach. She felt Denzel could make very good progress if he was willing to spend six months at the school.

"What do you think about that, Denzel?"

"I like to learn. Erasmus teaches me."

"You'd learn a lot at this school, Denzel," St. James said. "I checked a number of references. They're stellar. Would you like to try it?"

"Okay," he said, as if St. James was offering a second dessert.

"But Hamilton, the cost would be out of sight," Dozer objected. "I can't afford it right now."

"Denzel's cheque is smaller because, subject to Denzel's willingness to go and your approval, Dozer, I have committed to send him as an investment in the team."

Dozer's mouth opened wide and stayed there. "Man, I'm speechless," he said in disbelief. "That's too much, man. Over the top. We can't accept a gift like that."

Dozer didn't know what else to say, nor how much to object. He looked as if he might tear up, which got Anna going, which got Smythe staring at the large painting in discomfort.

Cathy arrived with dessert menus, looked at everyone, and frowned.

"Another team-building dinner, folks?" she asked cautiously.

Tears of happiness gave way to loud laughter.

# Chapter 78

Between trips to England and Cayman and conducting research for St. James, life had been too busy for Anna to reach out to Betty as she had promised while in Plymouth. True to her word, she finally got around to phoning Betty to invite her shopping. Betty was reluctant at first but eventually said yes, and today was the day they agreed to go.

"You take the BMW, Anna. I won't need it," St. James offered.

Anna checked the refrigerator and cupboards, deciding on provisions for the coming week, and made a list of four or five items. She planned to drop in to the grocery store after she and Betty shopped awhile.

"What have you planned for the day?"

"Plugging holes in CISI."

"Are you sure you won't need the car?"

"No, I'm good. Good luck taming the shrew," he said with a grin.

Anna gave him an admonishing look.

After she left, St. James phoned his old friend Gabe Fieldstone, who worked for one of the large brokerage houses in the market. Gabe said it was a slow day and St. James was welcome to drop by for a coffee.

*Good chance for a walk.*

At 10:30 he hoofed it down to the brokerage office on Dalhousie and asked for Gabe at reception. Out in short order, Gabe escorted St. James into one of the many small rooms used for client consultations.

At university, Gabe had been a chick magnet: a tall, handsome, body-builder type who on a clear day would have no trouble passing for Clark Kent. About forty-two, Gabe was a golfer, a sports fanatic, and, most of all, wealthy. With all that going for him, he still couldn't seem to find the right woman.

They spent time catching up on personal news and then got down to business.

"So what can I do for you, Hamilton?"

"I have this case that sort of hinges on your profession. Trying to find out whether certain people have margin accounts and if they're in good standing."

Gabe's face clouded over. "You know I can't give out client information," he said sternly.

"Yes, I know that. I'm thinking you don't have to divulge personal information for me to know what I need to know."

Gabe rolled his eyes. "Just how do I go about doing that?" he said incredulously.

"I have a list of names here."

St. James pulled a paper from his pocket and handed it to Gabe. Gabe scanned the names without comment or expression.

"Here's what I suggest," St. James began. "You feed the names into your system. If you get hits, all I want to know is: do they have margin accounts, are they interest-only, and are they in good standing?"

"If all names ring up yes to each question, it's easy," Gabe said sardonically. "I can just say that. Borderline unethical but perhaps there's a way. There's a problem if it's only one or two names. I can't tell you which ones. That would be a clear violation."

"I know. Here's my suggestion. I know the debt amounts each person has with your organization in Toronto. I just don't know if they're margined, interest-only, and in good standing. If you just have one or two names, I'll rattle off loan amounts, and you nod yes or no depending on positive or negative answers. No information given out of trust."

Gabe considered this for a moment.

"It's borderline, Hamilton," he said, stroking his chin in thought.

"You're not giving amounts or personal information," St. James argued. "I'm giving it, not the other way around."

"I am, indirectly. I am confirming names you give me. Same thing, only different," he said lightly.

Gabe thought for a long moment.

Finally, he said, "Here's what I can do. If it's less than all the names, you call out the debt numbers one by one. If one of the numbers is close to the amount of a margin account, interest-only, and in good standing, I'll cough."

St. James laughed.

Gabe was not amused. "Why are you laughing?"

"What's the difference between a cough and a nod? Both acknowledge something I'm not supposed to know."

"In court I can say I had a cough when we met. It's a condition, not acknowledgement of information. A nod isn't a condition," he said, grinning.

"Gabe, you're hilarious," St. James said, laughing. "We'll go with the cough. But there are three questions for each person: margin account, interest-only, and good standing. Does that mean three coughs?"

Gabe thought for another second.

Then he said, "You say the individual amount, then ask the three questions slowly after each amount. I'll cough as many times as answers are positive."

St. James laughed again. "Why does this feel like a game at summer camp?"

Gabe ignored the jab.

"Why do you want to know if an account is interest-only?"

"Interest-only means the principal is not being paid down. Loan's most likely the original amount unless shares were sold to pay it down. The higher the loan, the greater the chance it will be out of margin if the stock price tumbles."

"Gotcha. Okay, you disappear for half an hour," he said, "and by the time you return I might have developed a cough."

St. James left for a coffee shop down the street, ordered a double latte, grabbed a newspaper from a rack, and parked himself at a window table.

He covered the paper in ten minutes, nothing of interest.

*Don't know why they call them newspapers. Never anything new.*

He stared out the window, wondering about timing to wrap up CISI. He still had to put it all together to see if additional evidence was needed. Ten to fifteen days would likely be enough.

St. James looked at his watch. By the time he walked back to Gabe's the half-hour would be up. Five minutes later, Gabe and St. James were seated in the same meeting room they had occupied just a short time ago.

St. James said, "Did all the names qualify for my questions?"

"No."

"Okay."

St. James pulled a second piece of paper from a pocket and slowly rimed off loan amounts for each person on the list he had given Gabe. When he got to the second last number Gabe coughed, and then coughed right after St. James asked each of the three questions.

St. James stood and shook Gabe's hand.

"Thanks for your help, Gabe," he said as he was leaving. "Take care of yourself. That cough could turn into bronchitis."

Gabe laughed. "That would be just my luck."

Walking down York Street, St. James felt his cell vibrate.

Anna.

"You have to get here quick," she said in a panic.

"Calm down. Get where?"

"Police station," she managed to blurt out. "Betty and I were attacked in the Rideau Centre parking garage."

St. James felt his heart pound.

"Are you hurt?"

"No, no. We're okay. Just come."

He hailed a passing cab, and ten minutes later walked into police headquarters. The duty officer said, "Yes, Mr. St. James, they're waiting for you in the third room to the right. Officer's name is Brownlow."

He thanked her and made his way to the case room where he opened the door to complete pandemonium. Officer Brownlow was trying hard to restrain Betty and calm her down. Anna was seated at a table with her head buried in her hands.

"Let me at the son of a bitch. I'll finish him off," Betty snapped.

"Please calm down, Mrs. Sparks," Officer Brownlow pleaded. "You'll have a stroke."

"What the hell is going on?" St. James said in a loud voice.

Betty went quiet.

Anna rushed toward St. James and threw her arms around him. "Oh, Hamilton, thank God you're here."

Officer Brownlow introduced himself.

"Everybody please be calm," St. James said authoritatively as he turned to face Brownlow. "Officer, what happened?"

"At about 11:15 we received a call from a shopper in the Rideau Centre parking garage reporting a hysterical lady beating and kicking a man lying on the floor, swearing she was going to kill him. When I got there the man begged me to pull her away from him."

"Where is he now?" St. James asked.

"He's next door with Detective Spencer."

St. James looked first at Betty, and then at Anna. "What triggered this?"

They both started talking at once, Anna in a distressed voice, Betty with hell, fire, and brimstone.

"One at a time," St. James commanded, raising a hand.

"This goddamned son of a bitch tried to kidnap us," Betty blurted, red faced, nostrils flaring. "I wasn't having any of that. I told the little bastard if he didn't get out of my face, I'd beat him into next week. He just stood there and laughed, as if I couldn't do it. I showed him. He isn't laughing now."

Officer Brownlow was biting his lip, trying hard not to laugh.

"You all right?" St. James asked Anna.

"Just rattled."

"I'm going next door to check on this fellow with Mark," he said. "I'll be right back."

St. James left the room, managing to close the door behind him before breaking into quiet laugher. The mental picture of a sixty-five-year-old woman beating the crap out of a thug was too much.

Next door, Spencer was questioning the victim of Betty's rage.

"This is Robert Clarkstone," Spencer said as St. James entered the room.

St. James nodded.

A muscular man of medium build, Clarkstone's forehead scar looked as if it had been there for some time. Not Betty's handiwork. He wore a mangy goatee.

"What's this about?" St. James asked evenly.

Looking at Spencer and pointing to St. James, "Who's this clown?" Clarkstone spoke with a stutter.

"This 'clown,' as you put it, is your employer's mark," Spencer replied with a disgusted look. "You should know that."

Clarkstone went quiet.

"I take it you were hired by Rodney Sterling?" St. James said, eyes studying Clarkstone for signs of acknowledgement.

Clarkstone's eyebrows rose.

"I'll take that as a yes," St. James said.

"What were you told to do with the women?"

Clarkstone didn't answer.

"Answer the man," Spencer said aggressively.

Clarkstone stared first at Spencer and then at St. James, trying to decide his next move. After a minute or two he decided it was best to cooperate.

"I was to take them to Montreal," he said, trying hard not to stutter.

"Then what?" St. James asked impatiently.

"Sterling was to take it from there. Don't know what he was going to do with them."

St. James turned to Spencer.

"That's all I needed to know. I'll leave you to do what you do. I have to calm two hysterical women."

Spencer chuckled. "Good luck with that."

"That old broad should be locked up," Clarkstone stuttered. "She's a raving lunatic."

"Maybe so," St. James said with a grin, "but that raving lunatic is a sixty-five-year-old woman who just whupped your ass. You'll be the laughingstock of the Montreal mafia."

Clarkstone hung his head.

With that, St. James went back to the room where Brownlow had Betty and Anna, thanked the officer, and then took the women to lunch on Elgin.

When the three had ordered food, St. James looked over at Betty.

"Well, Betty, finally some good has come from your anger."

# Chapter 79

Two glasses of wine and a healthy serving of pasta helped calm Betty. Despite being quiet during the drive home, she managed to thank them when they arrived in front of her house on Sunnyside. There were no suspicious vehicles on the street. St. James checked the house before Betty entered, then he and Anna made their way back to 700 Sussex.

Anna let out a long sigh. "What a morning."

St. James laughed.

Anna became annoyed. "Not funny, Hamilton. This was just as hard on me as the night those two jerks tried to run us off the road."

St. James could barely get words out he was laughing so hard. "At least now you can see I wasn't exaggerating. I'm not laughing at you. I can't get that picture of her beating a thug out of my head."

Anna made a weak smile and broke into a forced chuckle. "Was kinda funny, I admit."

Driving into 700's parking garage, they agreed to put the day behind them. Although St. James was pretty sure Anna wouldn't be shopping with Betty again anytime soon.

Back in the condo Anna went to shower and St. James packed files he had compiled for the Stevens case, enough to fill four banker boxes. There was no sense putting them in storage. He'd soon be lugging them to the United States for a criminal trial.

He phoned CISI competitors to ask who decides where trawlers go to process catch. One competitor said the COO, another said plant managers usually worked it out on their own. When St. James asked if the CFO ever made the call, one contact laughed.

"Makes no sense," he said. "Be like a trawler captain making a head office HR decision."

Telephone rang.

Spencer.

"Hamilton, I've been working closely with Detective St. Jacques in Montreal on this whole Sterling thing. Back and forth a number of times trying to plug holes. We know Sterling hired the guys in the Mercedes. We also know he hired Long to kidnap Anna as bait to reel you in. And we know he hired Clarkstone to kidnap Anna and Betty for the same reason. What we don't know is who the two guys were who followed you to Wakefield.

"St. Jacques questioned Sterling about the Wakefield guys on three separate occasions. Sterling insisted he didn't know who they were. He admitted to hiring them, but through a third party here in Ottawa."

"Who?" St. James said.

"St. Jacques couldn't get that from Sterling until this morning, when he agreed to a plea bargain conditional on him providing all his underworld contacts. Basically, if he rats everyone out, his sentence gets reduced."

"Nothing like honour among thieves," St. James said. "Who's his contact here?"

"Sidney Gunther."

"What?" St. James exclaimed in a loud voice. "Again?"

"Jesus, Hamilton, you almost took my ear off," Spencer squealed.

St. James gathered himself. "I'm sorry, Mark, but this guy keeps complicating my life. He's pissing me off."

"We put an APB out on him this morning based on the new information St. Jacques got from Sterling. We'll get him, don't worry."

"I'm not worried. Just anxious to take a swing at him," St. James said.

"Now, now. We can't have you taking the law into your own hands."

"Never," St. James said with a snort. "At least not without you present."

They disconnected.

"Gunther," St. James mumbled aloud. "Sonofabitch."

Just then Anna emerged from the bathroom. He told her about Gunther.

"Sonofabitch," she said.

"That's what I said."

# Chapter 80

Next morning St. James called Graves to ask about his lunches with Blakie.

"Cameron told me you were having difficulties with Blakie. Thought I'd follow up," St. James said quizzically.

Graves was emphatic. "Difficulty is an understatement. Every positive initiative I suggest, he blocks. Cameron suggested we have lunch a couple of times. See if we could heal the rift."

"What did he block?"

Graves explained, "I wanted an independent evaluation of the board's performance. Normal for large public companies. Not like I wanted to gamble the balance sheet, which was how he reacted."

"Hmm. Anything else?"

"I suggested a management retreat. It meant sending top-tier management to Harvard for a five-day strategy session. Blakie said it was a waste of time and money. Cameron runs a great operation. Not necessary, he said."

"A strategy retreat is not an unreasonable thing for a company CISI's size," St. James said thoughtfully. "Especially when you consider that strategy focuses on future challenges, not necessarily past performance."

Graves agreed. "That's what I thought."

"How did he react to the strategic plan when it was brought forward?"

"That, he was all for. It was created by Cameron so there *couldn't* be anything wrong with it, in his mind anyway," Graves said, his tone slightly sarcastic.

"Did the lunches result in anything positive?"

Graves sighed. "Not really. Civil enough, but his attitude hasn't changed much."

"Anything about all this I should know?"

"Spend a little time looking into their relationship, Cameron and David, I mean. It's a little too cozy. I don't know what evil they could get up to, but there's enough bad behaviour coming from David to warrant a closer look."

St. James thanked Graves and disconnected.

Next he punched in Blakie's number.

*May as well get both sides while I'm at it.*

Blakie answered on the third ring.

"I know you are not a fan of me being at CISI to do this review, but I *am* here, and I really need your help."

Blakie was silent for a long moment. "I know I haven't been welcoming to you, but you are here, and we should get the most out of your work. So ask away."

*Attitude change.*

"Thank you, David. If it turns out that I'm right, I believe you'll find it worthwhile.

"You don't like Nelson, I get that. What I don't get is why he thinks you block all his initiatives, good or bad."

"You know I own an HR consulting firm, right?"

"I do."

Blakie explained. "One cannot do what I do without being a reasonably good judge of character. You could try, but success would not be sustainable. Luck is never a good strategy. I have been doing this for many years, so I must have some solid instincts, or I would have failed long ago."

"I couldn't agree more, David. A lot of my investigations are based on character. Goes to the heart of just about everything."

"We agree on that, for sure," Blakie conceded.

"So tell me about you and Nelson."

"I have been watching Nelson now for some time. How he manipulates everyone around him, how he controls meetings, his highbrow manner. His lobbying board members to support his positions in advance of board debates, before we air pros and cons. And I have to tell you, there is a feeling I have that is not positive. His self-interest always seems to outweigh his responsibility to the company. I find myself believing his initiatives have some underlying motive, not necessarily in the best interest of stakeholders. That colours both my thinking and my behaviour toward him."

"I have to say that is the most mature self-analysis I have ever heard, David."

Blakie laughed for the first time since St. James met him. "You can't be a good judge of another's character if you're blind to your own."

"You are so right. Thank you, David. You have been of enormous help."

St. James took time to reflect.

# Chapter 81

Next morning St. James responded to emails while Anna sat in the living room reading a book. When the last email disappeared into cyberspace he shut down the computer and went into the living room to join her.

"What do you want to do today?" he asked.

"Don't know, I feel lazy," she replied with a smile. "I'm out of clean clothes, so I absolutely have to do a wash. And I need to swing by the apartment to pick up a few things, but that's about it on the 'must do' list."

St. James expression suddenly changed. "That reminds me. I haven't heard from Dozer since we wound up the Stevens case."

"No news is good news," Anna said nonchalantly, in her usual soft voice. "You would've heard if something bad happened."

St. James pulled out his cell and punched the single digit he had set up to speed-dial Dozer. Dozer answered right away.

"Hey, man. I'm just leaving Anna's now. No sign of anything. Nothing disturbed. Traps are exactly as I left them."

"Great," St. James said. "Anna has to come over for a few things this afternoon. Any problem with that?"

"You want me there?" Dozer offered.

"Don't think so."

Dozer paused for a long moment.

"You still there?" St. James asked.

"CISI's still an active case, Hamilton . And we don't know who shot you, or why. Killers and kidnappers are still out there. You don't know what's going to happen, or when," Dozer cautioned.

"I know why I was shot, but I don't know who actually pulled the trigger. Not yet anyway."

"Who orchestrated it?" Dozer asked.

"Can't say."

Dozer chuckled. "You're a piece of work, Hamilton. You want everyone to wait for the show."

St. James ignored the jab.

"You and Cathy want to meet for a beer later?"

"Sure. Where?"

"Normally I'd say the Duck, but Anna doesn't like to go there on days off."

"How about the Royal Oak on Bank at 4:00?" Dozer suggested.

"Good enough. See you at four."

St. James spent the rest of the afternoon summarizing CISI. There were only a couple of holes, most of which could be filled by Spencer, if and when he tracked down the guy who shot him.

When the clock struck 3:45 he and Anna headed to the parking garage, fired up the BMW, and motored to Guigues Street, where she climbed the stairs to gather the few items she needed for the week. St. James had Dozer's okay the apartment was safe, so he waited in the car. Back in five minutes, Anna was carrying an overnight bag stuffed with the clothes she needed. Then they made their way to the Royal Oak to meet Dozer and Cathy.

Cathy and Dozer were already seated in front, nursing beers and talking about a movie they'd like to see. St. James and Anna settled in chairs opposite and ordered the same beer Cathy and Dozer were drinking.

The sun was glaring off Dozer's shiny bald head directly into St. James's eyes. Dozer noticed St. James adjusting his position and sported a devilish grin. "You afraid black brains might burn their way into that white head of yours?"

"Nope. I'm afraid there aren't any black brains to burn into anything," St. James retorted, equally sarcastic.

"Will you guys quit dumping on each other," Cathy said like a teacher scolding kids.

"It's a man thing," Dozer said defensively. "It's fun."

"Well we're not all men at this table," Anna added.

"Right," said Cathy, nodding to emphasize her support for Anna.

St. James thought it time to change the subject.

He said to Dozer, "Thought we'd better connect. Haven't seen you since we wrapped up Stevens."

"Been busy, man. I have other clients you know."

"Can't be anyone more important than me."

Dozer rolled his eyes.

"Am I all square with your invoices?"

"Yeah. Office said your cheque came in this morning. Thank you."

"Good," St. James said. "You can pay for the beer."

"Where is two-plaid Louis these days?" Dozer asked.

"Two-plaid Louis?" Cathy said.

Anna explained, "He's the funny-looking little guy who ate at the Beach Club with us. You served him a couple of times. He always wears clashing plaids, hence the two-plaid Louis handle."

Cathy nodded. "Ah yes, I remember. Bizarre little fellow."

"Bizarre but brilliant," Anna emphasized.

"Louis is in Las Vegas for what he calls a computer show, but it's really a geek convention," St. James said with a grin.

Anna noticed St. James fixating on something on the other side of the street.

"What's the matter?" she asked cautiously.

"Look," he said excitedly. "Across the street. It's Gunther."

"What?" Dozer and Anna said at the same time, quickly turning to see a man standing on the opposite corner.

"Who is Gunther?" Cathy asked innocently.

No one answered.

Dozer and St. James jumped and bolted out the pub door across Bank, running full speed toward Gunther. The traffic light turned green and Gunther was about to cross when he spotted St. James and Dozer running toward him.

Instantly, Gunther wheeled around to run east on Maclaren, St. James and Dozer closing the gap. Gunther saw them gaining ground. Portly and out of shape, Gunther laboured hard to maintain the distance between them. A red Passat backed out a driveway ahead, forcing Gunther to veer around, costing precious seconds. The gap narrowed.

On the next block, a dozen teenagers were walking toward Gunther, bunched up, spanning the sidewalk and not paying attention to anything other than themselves. Gunther crossed onto the same block, heading full steam toward them. Now he had a choice. Go around the teenagers, or through them. Going around was certainly preferable, either to the left or the right. To the left was a commercial building abutting the sidewalk, leaving no room to clear both the kids and the building. To the right, six or seven cars were clogging both lanes of the one-way street heading west.

Going around to the right meant colliding with cars, no longer feasible. In spite of his physical condition and laboured breathing, Gunther managed to increase his speed, hoping the teenagers would move before he reached them. St. James and Dozer were now gaining more ground.

A teenager in front looked up and saw Gunther coming straight at them. The kid yelled for the others to jump aside, to let the fat guy through. But it was too late. Gunther ploughed into the front of the pack, yelling, "Get the hell out of my way!" parting the kids like the Red Sea, driving two to the ground on either side.

The kid in the rear was taller, heavier, more solid than his friends in front, and not so easy to knock down. Being in the back gave the boy extra seconds to think. In one motion he braced himself and folded his arms, like a football player waiting to be tackled. And there he stood. When the boy and Gunther collided, Gunther lost his balance and went down. The large kid instantly placed his size-twelve boot on Gunther's chest, preventing him from rising to his feet.

"You'd better quit being so aggressive, mister," the kid said in a calm, deep voice.

"Let me up," Gunther yelled, trying to catch his breath.

"Not until you apologize," the kid said.

St. James and Dozer caught up seconds later. Dozer grabbed Gunther by the neck and pulled him to his feet, and Gunther yelled out in pain.

While Dozer secured Gunther, St. James explained to the kids why they were chasing Gunther and thanked them for helping to apprehend a suspect. Excitedly, they told each other how cool it was to help catch a criminal.

St. James pulled out his cell to let Spencer know they had Gunther. Ten minutes later, Spencer and two uniforms arrived in a squad car, its lights flashing. A crowd of curious onlookers had already gathered. One policeman held back the small group while the second cuffed Gunther and pushed him into the back of the squad car.

When they finished giving their statements to Spencer, St. James and Dozer walked back to the Royal Oak where they found the two women on their second pint and so deeply engrossed in fashion talk that they paid no attention to the men's return.

St. James looked at Dozer and Dozer looked at St. James, both shrugging at the same time.

"Looks like clothes are more important than us," said Dozer with a smirk.

St. James shrugged again. "Right now a beer is more important than anything."

# Chapter 82

St. James and Anna were no sooner back in the condo than the phone rang.

Jason Williamson.

"Hamilton, are you sitting down?"

"Not really. Anna and I just came through the door. What is it?"

"My guys started interviewing Jensen this morning. Or, I should say interrogating. He's a very belligerent man. What my father used to call 'nasty.'"

"Normal state," St. James said matter-of-factly.

"Hmm. Well, as our fellows pushed for answers, Jensen got redder. And more belligerent with every question. The detectives lost patience and pushed harder and threatened him with obstruction if he didn't cooperate. He came out of his chair screaming like a banshee."

"Wow! Your guys had it worse than me."

"Anyway. A few minutes later he doubled over in pain and collapsed on the floor. When paramedics arrived, they weren't sure if it was a stroke or a heart attack. It doesn't matter now, because he died on the way to the hospital."

"Not surprised. Being overweight and a heavy smoker with an uncontrollable temper, I expected this to happen sooner or later. Better you than me to be there when it did."

Jason said earnestly, "I suppose we could look on the bright side. Big savings for the taxpayer. The cost of lawyers and court would have been huge."

"Hard to feel sorry for him. The most unsavoury man I've ever met. And I've met some pretty bad ones."

"Well, we still have Gyberson to prosecute."

With that they ended the call.

# Chapter 83

Nine o'clock the next morning, Spencer called St. James.

"We're about to question Gunther. Would you like to be here?"

"I'll be there in fifteen minutes," St. James said without hesitation.

He went into the kitchen where Anna was preparing scrambled eggs and toast for herself.

"I'm off to interrogate Gunther," he said cheerfully.

"Give him a kick for me," she said. "Glad to have him out of my life."

"Don't think that would go over too well with Mark," he said lightheartedly.

She kissed him. "Have fun."

"Looking forward to it."

At 9:25, St. James walked through the front door of police headquarters. The duty officer buzzed Spencer, who escorted him to a plain, scantly furnished interview room where Gunther sat behind a bare metal table, large hands tightly clutched together, looking both angry and scared at the same time. A tall uniformed policeman leaned against the far wall, arms folded, feet crossed, looking like he was waiting for a bus.

Spencer grabbed one of the two empty chairs, twirled it around one leg, straddled the seat, and leaned forward to face Gunther. St. James pulled a second chair close to the table and stared directly onto Gunther's eyes, one of his favourite intimidation techniques.

"Okay, Sid," Spencer began. "What can you tell us?"

Sid stared past Spencer, focused on the far wall, and said nothing.

"C'mon, Gunther. You know you have to talk. Why prolong the agony?"

Gunther said nothing.

St. James continued the intense stare.

"Tell me about your relationship with Vinner," Spencer continued in a stern voice.

Gunther broke his silence.

"Never heard of him," he said sharply, in a tone St. James had heard all too often at the pub.

"Not what our sources say," Spencer taunted.

"Your sources are wrong," he snapped.

Spencer raised his voice an octave. "The three slimeballs who tried to kill Hamilton and an FBI agent named Slate say otherwise. They say you're Vinner's snitch, that you were watching Hamilton and reporting every move to Vinner, so he and the others could plan the murder. Isn't that true, Gunther?"

"Never heard of any of those guys," Gunther insisted.

Spencer ignored him.

"We have you cold as an accomplice and accessory to the attempted murder of two people, one of whom is an FBI agent. Do you know what Americans do to people who murder FBI agents, Sid? They never get out. Ever. You become someone's permanent girlfriend."

"Don't know what you're talking about," he said disingenuously, staring at the dark tiled floor.

St. James broke his silence.

"Well, perhaps your memory would improve if we transferred you to the FBI. They're not as gentle as Mark."

Gunther looked at St. James.

"Detective, it's bad enough I had to serve this arrogant asshole at the Duck, do I have to listen to him here too?"

St. James smiled.

Spencer said, "I'll do even better. I'll go for a coffee, lock the door behind me, and leave you alone with him. Not sure what he'll do, but whatever it is I guarantee you won't like it."

Gunther shrugged, as if to dare Spencer.

Spencer pulled an official looking paper from his pocket and passed it to Gunther.

"Do you know what this is?" Spencer barked.

Gunther took the document and a few minutes to read it.

"You can't do this. It's against the Charter of Rights," he said confidently.

St. James wondered what Spencer had handed him.

"Oh yes, we can," Spencer said, snatching the paper from Gunther's hands and handing it to St. James.

Spencer turned to St. James, pointing to Gunther at the same time. "You see, Hamilton, our friend here murdered a guy with his bare hands on the back streets of Berlin. In a rage over some woman. Intelligence said he gave Berlin police the slip a couple of hours later, escaped in the back of a van moving a family across Germany, made his way into Belgium and on to Brussels where he caught a plane, first to Heathrow and then to Montreal."

"Well, Sid," St. James said, scratching his head. "You're just full of surprises, aren't you?"

Gunther's confident look suddenly faded. Not so sure of himself now, he stared down at the table.

Spencer continued, still looking at St. James. "The Germans asked our government to extradite him back to Germany, to stand trial for murder, most likely to spend the rest of his life in prison."

Turning back to Gunther, Spencer said, "Here's the deal. You cooperate with us right here, right now, and we won't lobby the government to extradite you. If you don't cooperate, we'll have you sent back to Germany to a life in prison."

Gunther continued to stare down, looking somewhat gloomy and appearing to weigh his options.

"What do I get in return if I cooperate?" he said sheepishly.

"Only our guarantee we won't lobby for extradition. It doesn't mean the government won't extradite you on their own. It just means we won't take part."

"Not much of a deal," Gunther mumbled.

"No, it's not. But it's all you've got or ever will have," Spencer said sternly. "Before you answer, think about this. Germany is a close ally, and we have a strong relationship. Our government is anxious to maintain that relationship. And by extraditing you, we'd save Canadian taxpayers the cost of running you through our justice system, which is no small amount. All that is to say, it wouldn't take much lobbying for you to be on a plane."

"Not much of a deal," Gunther mumbled a second time.

"Think of it this way, Sid," St. James said. "You have the right to a hearing here, and then the right of an appeal if you don't like the outcome. Germany's a much tougher process, pretty well cut and dried, and the penalty is a lot more severe. Your choice."

Gunther lowered his head, once again weighing his options.

Then in a low voice he said, "What do you want to know?"

Spencer wasted no time answering in case Gunther changed his mind.

"Who is Vinner?"

"Small time hit man."

"Where is he?" St. James asked.

"Don't know for sure. I think he's hiding out in Los Angeles."

"He hired you to keep track of Hamilton. What did you tell him?" Spencer asked.

"Just when St. James was travelling in and out of Toronto, Washington, and England."

"How did you know this?" St. James asked sharply.

"Anna."

St. James bristled at the thought of him using Anna to get information.

"What else did Vinner want to know?" St. James asked impatiently.

"Just about Anna, whether she was your girlfriend, where you kept your car. That sort of thing."

Spencer looked at St. James once again, as if to say, "Do you believe him?" St. James didn't react. Instead he turned back to Gunther.

"Who did you hire for Sterling to follow me to Wakefield?"

Gunther paused, trying to decide what to say. Finally, he said, "The guy with the broken nose is Reg Walker, the other one is Jim Thatcher."

"Who are they?" St. James asked.

"Just guys for hire. Incompetent ones at that, otherwise you wouldn't be sitting here," he said sarcastically.

"Where can we find them?" Spencer asked.

"Don't know. We only communicated by cell."

Spencer pulled a phone from an evidence bag sitting on the floor beside him, taken from Gunther when he was arrested. Spencer scrolled through the call history.

"Which numbers belong to the two bozos?" he said.

Gunther leaned forward and pointed to two numbers.

"That one is Reg's and this one is Jim's."

"Okay," Spencer said, turning to the policeman leaning against the wall. "Take this to the boys. I want to know who the numbers belong to and where bills go."

"Yes, sir," the officer said obediently as he took the phone and left the room.

Spencer and St. James spent another thirty minutes or so grilling Gunther on his past discussions with Reg Walker and Jim Thatcher, as well as Vinner and Sterling.

They also asked about his knowledge of Nells's gang. Gunther insisted he never met any of them except Vinner. He knew Vinner was working with them.

When they finished, an officer appeared to take Gunther to a holding cell, leaving Spencer and St. James alone in the interview room.

St. James's mind was far off in the distance, trying to fit whatever pieces Gunther had just given them into the case.

Spencer sighed and looked at him, "Is there any connection between Sterling and Vinner, do you think?"

"Don't think so," St. James said cautiously. "I'm not aware they ever met. As far as I know Gunther was Vinner's man only."

"What about the other three, do they have anything to do with Sterling?"

"No, those three, along with Nells, were old cases I worked years back, nothing to do with Sterling. They hold a grudge against Slate and me for putting them away. It's just a coincidence they tried to kill us the same time as Sterling."

Spencer nodded. "Who is Sterling working for, do you know?

"Yet to be confirmed."

# Chapter 84

It was late the next afternoon before St. James heard from Spencer again.

"My guys traced the numbers on Gunther's cell to a house on Sheahan Crescent in the west end.

"I arranged for a SWAT team to storm the building this morning. They took Walker and Thatcher completely by surprise. They acted very sure of themselves, like they'd gotten away clean with shooting you.

"You were right about the small black SUV. It was a Honda CR-V. We found it in a garage next to the house."

"Get anything out of them?"

"Just started. So far they're cooperating, scared. I think they picked a vocation not well-suited to them, no backbone. Their account of events matches Gunther's to the letter. They only dealt by phone and never met Sterling in person, just by email."

"So, has Reg Walker actually admitted to shooting me?"

"Yes, and more. The bullet taken from you was sent to ballistics right away with a rush put on the report. They said on first pass it looked like a match with the gun we found under Walker's bed. His nose had obviously been broken and had never set properly. Probably too scared to go to a hospital, afraid he'd be reported.

"Do you want to be here for the rest of the questioning?" Spencer asked.

"No, I have the missing piece I need," St. James replied confidently. "Thank you, Mark."

With all they'd been through, St. James and Spencer had become friends. St. James respected Spencer's dedication and methods and thanked him for all his help the past couple of months. He said they'd get together for beers when CISI was finished. Spencer was down for that.

After St. James finished with Spencer he emailed Anderson and Graves to ask for a meeting with the directors, Jenkins, and Van Hoyt as soon as possible. Graves wrote back asking the purpose of the meeting and why St. James needed everyone there. St. James's response was the same as every other time he was ready to unfold a case: "It's a difficult story, important for everyone to hear, and I only want to tell it once."

Graves grumbled about time away from busy schedules and the cost of bringing the board together for a special meeting, but he reluctantly gave in. Anderson thought the meeting was a good idea. Juanita Mendoza would get back to St. James with a date that worked for everyone.

It was Wednesday afternoon. Anna was doing a shift at the Dirty Duck, Dozer was checking her apartment, and Smythe was still in Las Vegas. Now that Walker, Thatcher, Gunther, and Sterling were all neutralized, St. James didn't see a need for Dozer to continue checking Anna's apartment. And, even though he didn't think the Boston thugs had anything to do with Anna's break-in, they were off the streets too, at least for the time being. No immediate threats from any direction. So he called Dozer, said he figured danger had passed, and thanked him for the peace of mind he provided. They'd connect soon.

"No problem," Dozer said. "Anytime you need me just yell. I'll come running."

"When is Denzel off to the Warbridge School?" St. James said.

"Taking him to Austin this Friday. I'm still in shock over this, Hamilton. I'll never forget it."

"Only too glad to do it. Wish Denzel luck for me. Tell him I want a full report in six months."

"Will do." They disconnected.

While St. James was thinking about what to do next, the computer made its familiar pinging sound: a new message.

He opened Outlook to an email from Juanita Mendoza. It was difficult to arrange a meeting time acceptable to everyone, but a number of compromises were made to make this Friday at two possible. Would that work for him? St. James replied that it would.

Now St. James was in an awkward position. The CISI meeting presented a scheduling conflict. He wouldn't be able to take Friday's class after all. Janice would be pissed. A few extra dollars for her would be a legitimate out-of-pocket expense for CISI.

He shut down the computer and moved to the living room, where he opened the French doors and peered down onto Sussex Avenue, contemplating the unfolding of the CISI case.

# Chapter 85

By the time everyone had gathered in CISI's boardroom on Front Street in Toronto, it was 2:15 on Friday afternoon. Graves, Anderson, Jenkins, Van Hoyt, and all the directors were seated around the table.

Anderson looked relaxed. Harold Tewkesbury was googling something on his cell. Van Hoyt rested her elbows on the table. Jenkins was pale, as usual. Blakie was pacing back and forth, impatient for the meeting to begin. Others were staring off at nothing in particular.

When St. James entered the room, Dunlop smiled broadly. He knew St. James well. There'd be a curveball or two before the afternoon was out. He had no idea what that curveball would be, but he was looking forward to it anyway. It was always entertaining.

"Thank you all for coming this afternoon," St. James said, his tone businesslike. "I know you had to make last-minute schedule adjustments, but I think you will find this to be a very intriguing meeting."

Graves's square face displayed a stern look. "Don't see why we have to make such a big production out of this," he objected. "Why didn't you just report cost efficiencies to Cameron and irregularities to the board, as agreed?"

"Because everyone knows the cost efficiency review was a farce, just a reason to get Cameron to go along with the investigation.

"What you really wanted to know was whether Cameron was withholding anything from the board. Cost efficiency was irrelevant. Especially since CISI financially outperforms its competitors. An efficiency review is what competitors should be doing. It deserved to be ignored as far as CISI was concerned. So I did."

"This is outrageous," Graves blurted, his British accent stronger than ever. "I'm not used to being spoken to like this."

"It's going to get even more outrageous before this meeting's over," St. James retorted authoritatively.

Graves was shocked he had lost control of the meeting before it had even begun.

The directors were surprised by such an abrupt beginning to the meeting.

"Let's hear Hamilton out, Nelson," Anderson said calmly.

Others muttered agreement.

St. James continued. "When I accepted this case I spent considerable time researching the fishing industry. As I said, in all cases CISI financially outperformed its competitors. No other company comes close. It didn't matter what measurement I used. Its performance is superb. The company already had excellent cost-reduction processes. David was correct. Cameron is an excellent CEO. Cost efficiencies were a feeble excuse to mask the real reason for my engagement."

Blakie smiled for the first time.

"I like things out in the open. That's why I wanted everyone here today, to bring things out in the open."

St. James turned to Anderson. "At our meeting some weeks ago, you were abrupt with me. Not a good start. Then when we met one-on-one I saw something different. I saw a CEO concerned about inventory accuracy, a man who had delivered on his goals, a man frustrated by the lack of appreciation from his board."

St. James looked at Blakie. "David, your negative approach with me was probably just the mirror image of Cameron's feelings. They couldn't be personal because we had never met. People usually have to know me before they dislike me," he said with a slight smile.

David nodded.

St. James turned back to Anderson. "You didn't conceal any information. You made sure the way was paved for me to obtain everything I needed for a successful investigation. If you were keeping something from the board, it would have come out early in your behaviour with me. You wouldn't have been so forthcoming."

Anderson nodded.

St. James looked at Karen. "When I met with Cameron I learned two important things. First, your husband's company was having financial difficulty. Second, brothers run the two largest CISI plants, which are not significantly far apart, geographically. They help each other despite being given bonuses only on their individual performance.

"Two managers helping each other presented opportunity and potential for collusion. This became even more interesting when I learned that fifty per cent of the year-end inventory write-up resulted from those two plants. They could have double-counted inventory to meet their financial goals, to ensure they received the maximum bonus. I had to visit the plants, if only to rule out the possibility of wrongdoing originating there. When I mentioned this to you, Karen, you tried to convince me not to go."

"Didn't see the need to incur the expense, that's all," said Van Hoyt defensively.

"I understood that. It's a natural reaction for a good CFO to minimize expenses. Commendable, on the surface that is. But it occurred to me that a company with $19 billion in revenue, and people flying around the world every day, would not normally be so concerned with the cost of one consultant's week in England. It would be immaterial, a rounding error in a company the size of CISI."

Van Hoyt shrugged. "Just doing my job."

"So, I went to England armed with inventory files and analysis Karen provided for me, met separately with Basil and William

Hughes, and traced details of count sheets to plant inventory summaries, into head office inventory summaries, to arrive at total inventory worldwide. I found no errors."

"Are we wasting time here?" Cheryl Tomkins said impatiently.

"I can assure you, Miss Tomkins, I am not wasting your time. Nor are we anywhere near finished," he said, slightly annoyed with the interruption.

Dunlop stepped in. "Please continue, Hamilton."

Graves rolled his eyes and his wider eyebrow twitched.

"I toured both plants and found them to be exceptionally clean and orderly. Neither Basil nor William tolerated sloppiness in their plants, or with records. The likelihood of significant inventory errors occurring because of poor procedures or management at the plant level seemed unlikely. Karen confirmed there'd never been a problem with inventory procedures since she'd been working at CISI.

"Jennifer Quigley said there were only ever two changes in inventory counts coming from Britain. In both cases they were quantity adjustments at Plymouth, ones Basil had already corrected himself, without prompting from head office. There was no history of uncorrected errors at the plant level. And Basil and William didn't operate in a way that would suggest collusion.

"I discovered that Basil Hughes was building a new house and his wife was on a spending spree to decorate it. And Basil and William were looking to invest further in real estate, to purchase a rental property. I mention this only because it's behaviour outside their norm. But nothing turns on it. They saved for years to make the investment. The fact that they were looking to make a property investment at the same time the inventory adjustment occurred was only a coincidence, just enough to bring them up on the radar screen.

"There had to be something larger going on.

"I asked for electronic copies of inventory documents from Karen, Jennifer, Basil, and William, independent of one another, so they'd come to me separately from each computer; presumably the same document, just from three different sources for each plant.

"I carefully compared them to one another.

"On the face of it they were all identical. The same counts for the same species. The same dollar amounts for each line item and the same totals for each plant. I repeated the process with hard copies. There were no differences whatsoever. I was about to chalk the exercise up to a dead-end but couldn't seem to let go. I had a feeling something was different. Then, I found something very interesting. Something peculiar."

Everybody felt the tension.

"I moved the cursor to the electronic copy sent by Basil. In the upper left corner of the screen it showed the document typeface and font size as Book Antiqua 12. Basil insists everyone in his plant use Book Antiqua. That was confirmed by the plant accountant and by Jennifer when I returned to HQ.

"When I moved the cursor to a cell on Jennifer's electronic copy it also showed Book Antiqua 12. That meant she did whatever she had to do in the normal course of her duties, and then saved the document in the same format she received from Eli in Plymouth. Book Antiqua 12.

"Portsmouth uses Times New Roman 12. Jennifer's file for Portsmouth was in Times New Roman 12 as well, further evidence that she saves files in the same font she receives from plants. Again, I confirmed this when I returned from England. She said almost every plant uses a different font, but all use a 12-point type. I checked every plant, and she was right.

"I asked Jennifer if there was any logical reason to change the typeface from the originals sent by plants to something else. She said no. 'It would be extra work just to please the eye,' is what she actually said."

"Where is all this going?" Graves demanded, whipping off his horn-rimmed glasses for dramatic effect. "Please God. Let there be a point."

St. James ignored the outburst.

"The difference came when I compared everything to Karen's electronic documents. When I moved the cursor to a cell on her spreadsheet it showed up as the font Century 12. For those unfamiliar with themes and fonts, the difference between Book Antiqua 12 and Century 12 is so small you would have to be looking for it to actually see it. There's a slightly greater difference between Times New Roman 12 and Century 12, but really, who looks that closely."

"Why did you?" Andre Fox asked without thinking.

"Because I am engaged to make sure there is no wrongdoing, and wrongdoing often hides in odd and sometimes very tedious places."

Andre nodded slowly, feeling foolish for asking the obvious.

St. James went on. "No one changes the theme of a document prepared by others unless they work on it themselves. Unless they make changes. Then they tend to save in their own preferred theme. That told me the odds were that Karen made changes."

"I most certainly did not," Van Hoyt blurted out defensively.

St. James continued. "Then there were the conflicting instructions to trawlers on count day.

"I met Captain Thorne, captain of *The Mistress*, one of the three trawlers with catch full to capacity travelling to the UK plants on count day. He recounted the confusion over inventory instructions. First radio communication told him to bring catch to Plymouth, then later to Portsmouth, then after that to Plymouth once again. He wondered what the hell was going on. Never happens, he said.

"None of the contradictory instructions came from Basil or William. Surprisingly enough they came from head office, from here, from accounting, not operations. Both Basil and William, in separate communiqués with Captain Thorne and the other two trawler captains, asked where they were taking catch for processing. All this was subsequently corroborated by Captain Thorne's logbook, Eli, Basil, and William. All gave the exact same account of communications on that day. They would not ask where catch was going if they were in the loop with Toronto. Very unusual to say the least.

"I checked with two of CISI's competitors. Both said plant managers and trawler captains decided where catch would go, the COO participating only if there was doubt or disagreement. When I asked whether there'd be any reason for the decision to fall on head office accounting, they laughed. For accounting to be responsible for directing catch made absolutely no sense. It would be like trawler captains making human resource decisions for head office, one COO said.

"Basil and William had to know where the catch was going in order to arrange after-hours shifts to process. Day shifts had finished. Night shifts would have to be called in. And that takes advance notice. Many employees have young families and need time to make arrangements if called in for the night. They couldn't just jump on a moment's notice."

St. James turned to Jenkins.

"When I met with you, Henry, I asked why Accounting directed trawlers instead of you or the plant managers. You were the chief operating officer, responsible for worldwide operations. That would normally be the COO's responsibility. And according to the organization chart, plant managers report to you."

Henry, pale and gaunt, said, "That's correct."

"Yet instructions to trawlers came from accounting. When I asked you about that, you said Cameron asked Karen to manage year-end processing to maximize production and, hence, inventory value and profit. You normally managed this process and are more than capable of maximizing profit. Having Karen manage it was a departure from the normal chain of command."

"Absolutely right," Jenkins said with more energy, and sounding vindicated.

Anderson gestured to interrupt.

"Actually, Hamilton, that's not entirely correct. I didn't ask Karen. She asked me if she could. She thought, as worldwide financial information came in on the last day of the fiscal year, she should be

466 Double Shot of Scotch

able to make decisions on a dime, to maximize profit. There wouldn't be enough time to discuss this with Henry and then for Henry to negotiate the appropriate decision with plant managers and still have time for trawlers to get to the chosen plant. The day was too volatile. Because my goal was to maximize the year's profit, she had a point, so I smoothed it over with Henry. It was a one-time thing."

"I surmised that," St. James offered empathetically. "Nice that you confirm it. But it was the one and only time Karen assumed the role. I viewed that as a significant event.

"With all this at play, it was clear something was wrong.

"When I returned from England, I asked Karen the cause of confusion concerning the instructions." St. James turned to Karen. "You told me you debated where the catch should go, Plymouth or Portsmouth, and you finally decided on Plymouth. It was Jennifer who jumped the gun and sent conflicting messages to trawlers. That's what you said. That also seemed strange to me. Jennifer does not seem the type to make such a call without being instructed to do so. As a matter of fact, Jennifer told me she only takes instruction on plant communications from you, Karen, and that she's not authorized to send instructions on her own. 'That's how you get fired around here,' is what she said."

Van Hoyt remained still, without expression.

"After hearing Karen's explanation, I contacted the company's auditor, Marcel Lapointe, to review inventory documentation in his files. Because Karen had already authorized his cooperation, he didn't need to ask permission a second time. I was grateful for that because Karen could have retracted permission. So, Marcel and I carried on. He was very cooperative."

The directors were looking at one another, not believing what they were hearing. Mumblings around the table caused St. James to stop.

"Ladies and gentlemen, while I appreciate the shock value of what I am telling you, it requires full attention to follow the case to the end. This is a very serious issue for CISI and there's a lot more to come."

The room went quiet. St. James cleared his throat and continued. "I compared Marcel's hard copy of inventory documents with those provided by Karen, and once again with electronic copies from all parties. The inventory numbers in Marcel's file were substantially different from those in the documents provided by plants and head office accounting. Marcel's files showed much higher levels of inventory.

"I asked Marcel to scan his proof-of-inventory papers onto my computer. When he did, I checked the typeface and font size and found it all to be Century 12. Since head office files were normally saved in the same fonts as received from plants, Marcel's copies could only have come from one person ... and that person was you, Karen.

"To be sure, I went through the same procedure for the other eighteen plants around the world. They were the same. The total $95 million adjustment was laid out in Marcel's files in Century 12."

"This is outrageous, Nelson," Van Hoyt cried. "Are you going to let him accuse me like this?"

"As chairman he has no choice but to hear Hamilton out, Karen," said Anderson in a stern voice.

Graves was stone-faced.

"We are coming closer to the reason for all this," St. James assured.

"My investigator determined Karen's husband's company was in fact insolvent, underwater by millions, too far gone for Karen's $100,000 bonus to be of any help to him. In other words, Karen couldn't have been motivated to manipulate records because of her husband's insolvent state. Her bonus was a drop in the bucket when it came to his obligations. Nowhere near enough to save him or his company.

"Karen and her husband had just bought a house not far from Nelson's. She borrowed $300,000 to renovate it, pledging shares in CISI as collateral for the bank loan. She was smart enough to purchase the house in her name only, on the strength of her salary, not jointly with her husband. She wouldn't lose the house when her husband and his company went bankrupt.

"So I asked myself, why would Karen be motivated to manipulate company records? If it wasn't financial, something else had to be going on. She couldn't have been worried about losing the house. She can afford the mortgage on her own."

"This has gone far enough," said Graves in a harsh tone. "This meeting is adjourned."

"It's not adjourned until we all agree it is adjourned," Dunlop barked.

Everyone mumbled agreement with Dunlop in one way or another, except of course Graves and Van Hoyt.

"Then, I began to look beyond Karen's inventory manipulation for a different motivation.

"I turned my attention to who would benefit from an inventory adjustment of $95 million.

"Cameron provided insider shareholder files for those who pledged CISI shares for personal loans. One loan was significant. $2.5 million borrowed, pledging 500,000 shares as collateral. Isn't that right, Nelson?"

"Nothing wrong with having loans pledging shares," Graves snapped.

"No there is not," St. James agreed.

"Then what are you insinuating?" Graves demanded angrily.

"People around the table probably don't know Karen worked for you at IBM."

Once again directors expressed shock with various degrees of intensity.

"Why was this kept from us?" Blakie asked angrily.

"I don't think it was deliberately kept from you, David," St. James consoled. "She joined under the old board and the previous CEO. By the time you came on board it was irrelevant. She was already here, and you would have no reason to look into her background."

He paused and turned back to Graves.

"You promoted her to senior roles at IBM, helped build her career. She owed you."

"She earned every promotion. Extremely competent," Graves emphasized with gritted teeth.

St. James nodded. "I agree. She is very competent. You helped her get the CFO position here. Provided a reference to Cameron's predecessor. I checked with Human Resources. Your signature's there."

"Where is this going?" asked an impatient Harold Tewkesbury.

"You'll see in a moment.

"I believe, Nelson, your stockbroker will confirm that the money you borrowed was on margin, invested in CISI shares. You had an agreement with the brokerage side of the bank to pay interest only. That means the loan wasn't being paid down on a regular basis. The original amount is still owed. Because you weren't paying the loan down, you had no margin room for the share price to drop. You'd be significantly out of margin if it did. You'd be called upon to put money in to meet margin requirements.

"If you didn't have money to meet a call, the bank would sell your shares at any price; whatever it took to reduce your loan and their exposure to a loss. But significant share sell-offs often drive prices down even further. The market becomes flooded with sell-side transactions, triggering even larger margin calls as prices drop further. Wealth can be wiped out overnight; lives ruined. That's what you were afraid of, Nelson. You didn't have money to bring shares back into margin, should the share price plummet. Your high lifestyle and excess borrowing put you between a rock and a hard place."

Graves remained silent and stone-faced.

St. James paused for a couple of beats before continuing. "I prepared an analysis of each insider's loans, together with prices paid for shares at the date of purchase, and the number of shares pledged as collateral to financial institutions where loans originated. Making certain assumptions about margin arrangements, only one shareholder would be significantly out of margin if the share price was pummeled because CISI did not meet its profit expectations. That shareholder was you, Nelson."

Whispers dominated the room once again. St. James raised his hand and the room returned to quiet.

Graves remained expressionless.

St. James continued. "CISI was not going to meet its numbers last year for the first time in many years. No guidance had been issued to the public. Shareholders would be taken completely by surprise. In all likelihood panic-selling would follow. Share price would be driven down, most certainly below your margin threshold, Nelson. It only had to drop fifteen per cent for you to get the dreaded margin call from your broker. My calculations suggested it would have dropped by at least twenty-five to thirty per cent, maybe more. It would mean financial ruin for you overnight, Nelson. You were afraid, in a desperate state of mind. You had no choice but to confide in Karen, the woman you helped promote at IBM. Karen owed her career to you."

"This is preposterous. Outrageous allegations," Graves huffed.

St. James turned to Karen.

"It's all true, isn't it, Karen? He reminded you of everything he had done for you. Made you feel guilty. Obliged you to help him in return. So you did. You had to.

"The two of you put your heads together. The plan had to involve activity you controlled completely, Karen, without need for collusion. No one else could be involved. No witnesses to worry about. Just you and Nelson. And you trusted each other. That made it easier."

Gasps filled the room, yet again.

"My Jesus," Dunlop mumbled.

St. James continued. "That plan materialized into an inventory adjustment as the only way for the company to meet profit expectations, to avoid shareholder disappointment and panic, and to prevent share price from being punished, plunging enough to trigger

Nelson's margin call. But it couldn't be just an arbitrary adjustment. It had to be supported. After all, it would be audited by Marcel. It had to stand up to scrutiny.

"So you, Karen, created email trails to Plymouth and Portsmouth, instructing trawlers where to land, separate emails ordering trawlers first to Plymouth, and then to Portsmouth, and then back to Plymouth. I read those emails. None of them were replies to *all*, and none of them carried the history of previous emails to trawlers and plant managers.

"Each communication looked like a separate instruction for three trawlers to go to two different plants at the same time. A single instruction to three trawlers to go first to Plymouth. Then, a different instruction to the same trawlers to go to Portsmouth. And the same for the trawlers to Plymouth a second time. Making it look like three trawlers were going to Plymouth and three trawlers were going to Portsmouth. But there were only three trawlers in play. The instructions were made to look like six trawlers, making the trawler inventory double what it actually was.

"The same duplication happened all around the world on count day; journal entries prepared only by Karen. No one else would see them, except Marcel, the auditor. General journal entries were the route Nelson and Karen chose to inflate inventory. That's how the adjustment got so large." St. James looked at Van Hoyt.

"You didn't care what plant personnel thought. You could always claim it was miscommunication, a mistake, blame Jennifer's impulsive emailing, like you did for my benefit.

"Emails were never meant to be instructions for plants or, for that matter, real instructions for trawlers. The real purpose of the confusing emails was to manufacture audit evidence for Marcel. Phony evidence to satisfy auditors, to support inflated species counts in each location.

"On the last day of the fiscal year, auditors expect inventory adjustments for catch landed after counts. It would be proper accounting, not necessarily suspicious. So inventory purchased is included in the current year's financial statements."

The room was quiet, and the room was tense.

St. James paused once again, and then continued. "The spreadsheets you sent to me didn't have the double-counting of inventory on them. You wanted no trail that could lead me to you. Spreadsheets you forwarded matched plant documents perfectly, giving the appearance that everything was proper. Except there was a trail; a careless but simple mistake. The changing of type themes made when you saved your work as Century. That's what gave you away. Your fatal mistake."

Van Hoyt began to sob.

No one moved.

"It wasn't until I reviewed Marcel's files that I saw different numbers, much higher ones, double counting of trawler inventory, all around the world. If you had not changed the themes you may have gotten away with it."

Blakie spoke. "Weren't auditors present to witness counts and procedures?"

"They witnessed plant counts, yes. Plymouth and Portsmouth finished counting mid to late afternoon. Auditors completed their work and left at approximately 3:45. The trawlers conveniently showed up in Plymouth around four.

"The conflicting instructions weren't just to manufacture audit evidence for Marcel. They were also meant to waste time, so trawlers wouldn't show until after the auditors had left. For Nelson and Karen's scheme to work, auditors and trawlers must never meet... Too risky to be caught."

"I don't get how the auditors were fooled. Why verification procedures didn't catch the lack of proof for inflated inventory numbers," Dunlop said, trying to grasp at a greater understanding.

"It is simpler than it first appears," St. James replied. "All procedures were followed correctly as far as the auditors were concerned. Trawler catches were added both to Plymouth's and to Portsmouth's numbers as instructed, both as set out in the independent emails. Karen's spreadsheets saved in Century supported that, emails supported that, internal controls were strong, and as far as Marcel was concerned CISI was a model client. No reason to suspect wrongdoing. Karen was a trusted CFO.

"Karen is very thorough. She made sure all supporting inventory documentation matched from the time trawlers landed all the way through CISI's accounting system, to the financial statements, to provide Marcel with complete support for the inflated inventory she had created."

Dunlop interrupted again, "You mean there were two sets of inventory records? Phony ones Karen gave the auditors and real documentation from the plants?"

"That's right, Al," St. James said.

"So the only inventory information auditors saw was falsely created to support a bogus journal entry?" David said in disbelief.

"'Fraid so," said St. James matter-of-factly.

Harold's face looked strained. "I have been dealing with financial information and statements for my entire career. I can't for the life of me see how you can manufacture false inventory without any holes whatsoever; considering the vast amount of activity that takes place between trawlers and numbers on audited financial statements."

Anderson remained quiet, his faced strained by it all, not believing Graves's and Karen's disloyalty to him and to the company.

St. James continued, "Let me be more specific, Harold. Karen took past landing sheets for each location around the world, scanned them into her computer, then adjusted dates and quantities to reflect the fabricated numbers. It was strong audit evidence because the original sheets were signed by both trawler captains and plant accountants. No forged signatures. No font change. Absolutely no indication of tampering anywhere on the false documentation. Legible signatures were already there, albeit to approve different catches landed sometime previously. Marcel's files looked authentic and would pass the test of fresh eyes, in the absence of knowing the full story."

St. James paused yet again and took a deep breath.

The directors took turns glancing at Graves's and Karen's solemn faces, mumblings ranging from disbelief to anger at what the two had done to the reputation of the company, its board, and its management.

Van Hoyt was crying, head buried in her hands, knowing full well it was over.

St. James said, "Things will go a lot easier if you help, Karen. It will go a long way to reducing whatever punishment comes your way."

Van Hoyt didn't move. "I'll cooperate," she said, her voice almost inaudible.

"What are you saying, Karen? He can't prove anything," Graves barked.

St. James shot an angry look at Graves. "Yes, I can ... and there is more, a lot more."

# Chapter 86

"More?" Anderson said incredulously.

"You all know an attempt was made to run Anna and me off the road in Ottawa. And you also know I was shot while walking along the canal, also in Ottawa."

Everyone nodded.

"The day before I was shot, we were followed to Wakefield. Two ruffians tailed us. We cornered them, and after a little persuasion they confessed that a guy named Sterling hired them. They didn't know his first name. They'd never met. Arrangements were made online, they said. My associate broke one fellow's nose. The very same fellow shot me the following day.

"At this point I couldn't figure out why someone was doing this. All past cases were solved, no one had anything to gain from my death, except maybe revenge, which also occurred to me, but that's another story for another day.

"A few days ago we discovered that Sidney Gunther, an ex-bartender and small time Ottawa hoodlum, was engaged by Sterling to find the two guys who tailed us. Sterling works the Montreal underworld. He didn't know Ottawa's. But Gunther did. When Gunther found the two guys for Sterling, his work was done. Sterling took over from there, giving instructions directly to the thugs.

"A couple of days later, we chased Gunther down the streets of Ottawa and took his cell with stored numbers for a Reg Walker and

Jim Thatcher, supposedly the thugs in question. Ottawa police traced the billing address for the numbers to a house in the west end, and two days ago a SWAT team arrested the two men. They admitted to following us one day and shooting me the next. Ballistics matched Walker's gun with the bullet taken from my shoulder. I positively identified Walker before flying down for this meeting.

"My associate gave the cell he had taken from Walker in Wakefield to Ottawa police. They traced emails and numbers to a Sterling, the Sterling in question, an enforcer and racketeer, well known to Montreal police.

"St. Jacques, a Montreal detective, pulled Sterling in for questioning. It turned out Sterling hadn't met his employer face to face either. Arrangements were made through anonymous email accounts. When attempts to kill me failed, Sterling's client insisted they meet in person.

"I asked St. Jacques if he got a description of the man who hired Rodney. He said yes."

There St. James paused.

The tension in the room was off the charts.

"Well, don't keep us in suspense, man," Harold said anxiously.

"He was a shorter man with a full head of white hair, well dressed in an expensive, blue pinstriped suit and a grey tie, and he spoke with a strong British accent."

"My Jesus," blurted John Coughlin, who had said nothing up to this point.

Nancy and Cheryl went pale. Dunlop, Blakie, and Andre were stunned; Anderson and Harold stone-faced.

When St. James's words finally sunk in, everyone angrily turned to Graves.

"How could you do this to us, Nelson?" Dunlop yelled.

"You son of a bitch," Cheryl barked.

The other directors expressed anger and disgust in their own way.

Graves was expressionless, head down, trying to decide his next move. All arrogance had completely drained from him.

"You hired Sterling to kill me. And Sterling hired the first two men, Martin Clayton and Clint Wagner, to run us off the road. They burned to death when their Mercedes crashed. The first failed attempt.

"Then you arranged for Sterling to hire another thug, Frank Long, with a different strategy, to kidnap my girlfriend as bait to get to me. The second failed attempt. Long walked into a gruesome mantrap breaking into Anna's apartment and was forced to spend the night in the Ottawa hospital, only to be arrested the following day.

"Long told me he was hired by someone from Toronto. I know where all my past enemies live, and none are in Toronto. That meant it was someone new, someone like you, Nelson. Long didn't work for someone in Toronto; he actually worked for Sterling in Montreal. It was Sterling who worked for someone in Toronto: you.

"Finally, Sterling sent one of his own men, this time to kidnap my girlfriend once again *and* my sister. Robert Clarkstone was instructed to take the women back to Montreal, where Sterling would most likely use them to draw me there. Except Clarkstone got the surprise of his life when he tried to put the two women in a van. My sister, who is sixty-five and has significant anger issues and the mouth of a dockworker, beat the bejesus out of him. And it was Clarkstone who had to be rescued by police."

Blakie snickered.

St. James looked at Graves for a few minutes before continuing. "It appears, Nelson," he said with a sigh, "that you could only afford incompetent losers to do your dirty work. Was financial ruin really worth murder?"

Graves sat, grim-faced, and said nothing.

St. James continued. "There's only one thing I don't get, Nelson. Why did you hire me in the first place if you were afraid I'd catch you? Why risk it? You knew Cameron had done nothing wrong, yet you threw him under the bus to mask an investigation."

"I can answer that," Dunlop said. "We, all the external board members that is, put tremendous pressure on Nelson to engage someone to conduct an independent investigation. He could not have opposed it without raising suspicion."

"That ties in. If Nelson had no choice, and felt I'd uncover the truth, he would have no alternative but to have me killed."

St. James looked at Graves. "I told you this would get more outrageous before it was over."

Graves stared at St. James with eyes that could burn holes in steel.

"I hate you," he said dramatically.

"That saddens me greatly, Nelson," St. James said facetiously.

# Chapter 87

"Hamilton," Anderson said solemnly, "I need help dealing with this. The publicity, I mean."

"I anticipated that. I took the liberty of preparing a public relations plan without your approval. I knew after this afternoon there would be no time to react properly."

St. James pulled a file from his black leather case.

"Here are two letters of resignation, one for Nelson and one for Karen."

He handed copies to everyone around the table. Graves and Van Hoyt reluctantly took theirs.

"Here's what I suggest," St. James said, turning first to Graves. "Your letter says you accept your termination and make no claim for severance."

St. James turned to Andre. "Andre, you should review the releases. Advise the board independently of me."

"Of course," Andre said, hands shaking from shock as he tried to focus.

St. James said cautiously, "One thing I suggest we all agree on, folks, is that no one leaves this room until everything is signed, including a confidentiality agreement specifically related to this meeting."

St. James went around the table and asked each person separately for their agreement. Not surprisingly everyone but Graves and Van Hoyt said yes.

"These documents look fine to me," Andre said, still trembling. "I have no objection to signing them."

"Thank you, Andre." St. James turned back to Graves.

"I want my lawyer to look at this," Graves snarled.

"Too late, Nelson. This is settled right now. Not tomorrow. Not the next day. No signature now means a lawsuit from the company. Complete personal ruin."

"Bastard. What about criminal action?" he asked angrily. "Can't we tie that into a settlement?"

"We don't control the law, Nelson. You should have thought of that when you decided to break it. You did it to yourself. You did it alone. You live it alone," St. James said forcefully.

Graves's wide eyebrow twitched as his face reddened with anger.

A number of directors spoke angrily about what Graves had done to the company and to the reputation of the board. There'd be no mercy from the court of CISI directors.

Graves waited a long moment, weighing the decision, then reluctantly signed the document.

St. James turned to Karen. "Your resignation letter is the same as Nelson's."

Van Hoyt was a totally broken woman and made no attempt to object. She signed and returned the document to St. James without a word.

St. James turned to Anderson. "Marcel will no doubt insist on restating last year's financial statements. Here is a suggested press release stating you discovered an overvaluation of inventory subsequent to year-end. CISI shares will take a hit for a time, but revenue and profit for the current year is ahead of both budget and last year's actual performance. The share price will bounce back."

St. James handed out copies of the press release and confidentiality agreement. Everyone signed without question.

"One more formality," he said, looking first at Graves, then at Van Hoyt. "I met with Detective Edwin Ferguson of the Toronto

Police Commercial Crimes Unit just prior to this meeting. I took Ferguson through the whole story, pretty much as I have here, and showed him all the evidence to support these allegations. I suspect you might hear from him."

Graves and Van Hoyt rose at the same time and left the room in silence.

Anderson stood and shook Hamilton's hand. "Hamilton, this is a terrible blow to the company, and it goes without saying I wish it had never happened. But it did, and I am very grateful you were here to manage it. I can't thank you enough," he said solemnly.

As the meeting broke up, the room filled with more angry comments. Everyone was feeling violated, and they were worried about director liability, personal reputation, and the ensuing publicity.

One by one each person shook St. James's hand as they filed out of the room. When all but Anderson had left St. James said, "Al would make a good chairman."

Anderson smiled faintly. "Top of my list." He paused for a moment. "I know this is irrelevant now, but what made you suspect Nelson in the first place?"

St. James smiled. "In the 1970s Nelson got into financial difficulty and was forced into personal bankruptcy. I spoke with his trustee in London, England. He tried to hide a piece of real estate from her, which is an offence under the Bankruptcy Act. When pressed, he declared that he had hidden the property, placing the title in a relative's name before he went bankrupt. He was never charged because he made a deal and gave the property to the trustee in exchange for not involving authorities."

Anderson squinted, "I don't get the relevance."

"The mere fact that he tried to hide an asset from his trustee said a lot about his character. And in business, character is everything."

# Chapter 88

Saturday morning, St. James was sitting in his study pulling together invoices to pay when Dozer called from Austin, Texas.

"Denzel's all settled in at the school, more excited than I've ever seen him, Hamilton," he said enthusiastically.

"That's wonderful. I'm so pleased this is working out."

"He'll be here until sometime mid-June. I met his instructors. They're wonderful, patient people. They gave me a tour of the place; where Denzel would sleep, dining rooms, classrooms. It's all first-class, Hamilton. As I said before, I can't thank you enough. I don't know how we can ever repay you."

"You will repay me when Denzel is able to handle different types of assignments, a little more complicated than monitoring Anna's apartment. That will re-enforce his self-esteem and help the team with more cases. That's my hope," St. James said conclusively.

"We won't let you down. I'll make sure of that."

"Are you heading back to Toronto now?"

"Yes, via Ottawa. I have to disassemble the traps and pick up my gear. The guys are growling about having to do all the office work without me; it's time I got back before there's a mutiny."

"What about Cathy?"

"We've talked. She'll come to Toronto on weekends after classes, or I'll go to Ottawa depending on what my schedule demands."

"You know what they say about long-distance relationships," St. James cautioned.

"Yeah, yeah, I know. We'll see how it goes."

"Safe travels," St. James said.

It was 10:15. Anna had already left for the 11:00 shift at the Dirty Duck and wouldn't be back before five.

Everything was getting back to normal.

It wasn't just Dozer who had relationship challenges. St. James had to figure out what to do with their relationship, where it was or should be going, if anywhere. He knew he loved her and was pretty sure she loved him. But that was as far as he'd gone. Now that she had experienced the excitement of investigating commercial cases, slinging beer would never cut it. She'd leave the Duck for sure, even with Gunther gone.

He wanted to bring her on full-time, work side by side, solve cases together. But it wasn't like bringing on Smythe, Dozer, or Denzel. The personal side complicated everything. Whether she moved in with him or not, a relationship breakdown meant losing both his girlfriend and the best researcher he'd ever had at the same time. He'd have to take it one day at a time. There was no risk-free decision. And at the moment he didn't know where Anna's head was.

The phone rang. St. James answered to Nathan Strong's voice.

"Just wanted to let you know the partners voted yesterday to set up the mental health research fund in Tom's name for one million dollars over five years. You wouldn't believe the number of emails pouring in. Clients, non-clients, politicians, mental health organizations, and many others," Nathan said with more excitement than St. James had ever heard from the man.

"By the sound of your voice I would say they must all be positive," St. James said, a smile in his voice.

"Over-the-top positive," he said jubilantly.

"I am so pleased for you and your partners, Nathan. I'm glad they bought into the approach."

"It's improved morale 1000%, St. James. You were right. Everyone's talking about the firm's generosity. No mention of a crime-committing partner. You're a genius, Hamilton."

"Hardly true, but thank you for saying so," St. James said lightly.

They agreed to stay in touch.

St. James's computer pinged. Smythe had written to say that he had arrived back from the convention the previous night and had learned many new code-breaking techniques. He could hardly wait to try them on St. James's cases.

For a moment St. James looked at the team photographs Cathy had taken on the night of the celebration dinner at the Beach Club. He laughed. Smythe, short and maybe a hundred and forty pounds, dressed in multiple plaids with the world's worst combover; Dozer, a bald, six-foot-five, 275-pound black man; Anna, a tall, slim, beautiful woman; and Denzel.

*Quarter of an inch this side of the Addams Family*, he thought, smiling to himself. But looks were deceiving. They were the best of the best. *Wouldn't trade them for anything.*

The phone rang again. This time it was Anderson.

"Thought you might like an update," he said.

"Absolutely. Glad to hear from you. I was wondering how the chips fell after I left."

"You were right about the press release. It helped enormously. I issued it after you left. I haven't received one call or email from the media, or a shareholder, or an analyst, so far that is. I don't know what the stock price will do when markets open Monday, but I suspect you're right. Institutional investors will punish us for a while."

"If memory serves me right, your quarterly results will be released next week, will they not?" St. James said.

"That's right."

"And it's all good news. All the important key success factors are up dramatically. The institution guys won't stay away long. Not if there's money to be made with CISI shares. You can't keep a good company down, Cameron."

"You're probably right, Hamilton," Anderson said.

"What about Nelson and Karen?"

"The police were worried Nelson might skip town. I don't know why, but they were. Maybe concerned he'd make a dash for England before they could grab him. They picked them both up from their homes last night. Brought them into custody, pending charges next week. You might be busy on the stand in another couple of months, Hamilton," Anderson said with a chuckle.

"Fully expected that," St. James said with a sigh.

Anderson thanked him once again and disconnected.

Next, St. James prepared his bill for CISI, a hefty one. Satisfied that he had included all his time and every little claimable expense he could think of, including a healthy bonus for Janice McPherson, he emailed it to Anderson.

"Best to send a bill like this while his memory is fresh and he's happy," St. James muttered.

He went into the living room and opened the French doors. It was snowing, cold, and damp. Only a couple of weeks before Christmas. And he hadn't done any shopping yet. He would buy a Christmas tree that afternoon. Something to do.

The snow was driven horizontally by a strong wind. Cars moved slowly on a slippery Sussex Drive, new snow making it more so. Ottawa winters weren't easy.

Suddenly an empty feeling crept over him, one he recognized all too well. It was a feeling that happened every time he finished a case, without another to begin. Perhaps it was insecurity, or worry about what to do next, or maybe a bit of both. The sudden change from an intense investigation to nothing created an incredible feeling of withdrawal, almost like a panic attack. An emotional drop from a high one minute to a low the next. Hamilton called it Post-Case Stress Disorder, PCSD. Not a recognized term, but he felt an overwhelming need to call it something.

A faint ping sound resonated from the study. He strolled down the hall and clicked on Outlook. It was a message from Mary DeSilva.

It simply said, "I need you, Hamilton. NOW!"

St. James smiled. No more PCSD.

# Acknowledgements

I would like to thank my wife, Judy, and my good friends Paul Kavanagh, Bill Knight, Brian Brooks, Stephen McGill, Steve Gallagher, Steve Cannon, and Jennie Enman for taking the time to read *Double Shot of Scotch* and offer comments. Your advice was invaluable and definitely made the book stronger.

CPSIA information can be obtained
at www.ICGtesting.com
Printed in the USA
LVHW051353201020
669280LV00002B/346

9 781771 804417